THE WISDOM OF SAND

TANDEMSTAR: THE OUTCAST CYCLE

BOOK IV

GENE DOUCETTE

Contents

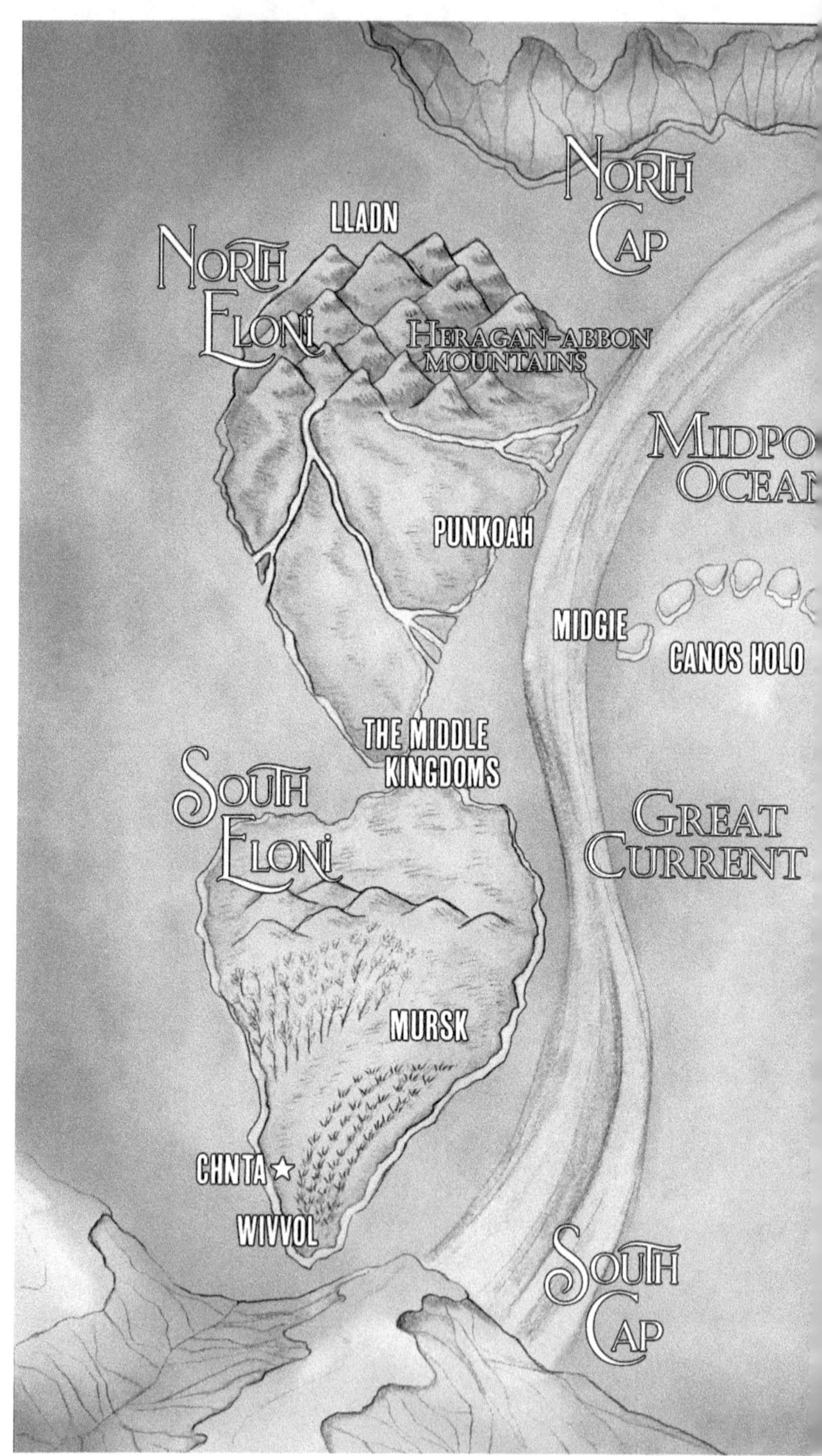

NORTH CAP
LLADN
NORTH ELONI
HERAGAN-ABBON MOUNTAINS
MIDPO OCEA
PUNKOAH
MIDGIE
CANOS HOLO
THE MIDDLE KINGDOMS
SOUTH ELONI
GREAT CURRENT
MURSK
CHNTA
WIVVOL
SOUTH CAP

NORTH CAP
NORTON OCEAN
ANNIBAT
DORABON
GHON-DIK
WRIMMAD
BOTZIS
KINDON
INIMATA
TERRENT MOUNTAINS
VELON
GEO
UNAK
PETHIS
DUNN
SOUTH CAP

Prologue

"Kaketora!" the captain shouted, from the wheelhouse. "Check the nets!"

"Check the nets, check the nets," Kaketora groused. "Yes, yes."

"Hurry, girl!"

Kaketora didn't hurry. She was done with hurrying. She'll check the nets, all right, but she was going to take her gods-damned time with it.

The *Bekohai* had been away from Djuk-Djuk for—if she had been counting the sunrises accurately—nine days now, and Kaketora regretted roughly seven and a half of them. The day they left port, when there was naught to do but appreciate the view of the Botzis shore from the Norton Ocean—rather than (as had been the case for her entire life up to now) the view of the ocean from the shore—had been pretty nice. She liked that day a lot, along with half of the day that followed, up until they reached the spot of their first trawl. That was when Captain Obergango let her know exactly what he thought of his newest fisher.

It had not been the experience she was promised.

Like every city ringing the coast of Botzis, Djuk-Djuk was a fishing village at its core. There were other professions, certainly —her ma was a seamstress and da scraped hulls—but as soon as she was old enough to walk and talk, Kaketora wanted nothing more out of life than to work a fishing boat.

She was at the docks as young as four, listening to the fishers talk, to her or to each other, about their experiences. And maybe, possibly, she had—in her youthful enthusiasm—deliberately forgotten or otherwise ignored some of the stories that made fishing sound unpleasant. But what she recalled...what she'd been *promised*...was glorious days on the open sea, rediscovering magnificent, distant lands, seeing great whales and dolphins and *sharks* (she so wanted to see a shark) and, more than anything, enjoying tremendous *experiences* that could not be had on land, in the dreary village she'd never left.

That was what the fishers claimed was out there.

And perhaps it was, somewhere. Just not where the *Bekohai* happened to be trawling for fish.

"Get a move, you dull cow!" Obergango barked. The first time he called her a dull cow, she was shocked; now, it sounded like a term of affection. There were nine aboard the *Bekohai*, Obergango had a singularly offensive epithet for each of them, and "dull cow" was not the worst.

"I'm *checking* the nets, old man," she said. "You want it done faster, come down here and help!"

"Dry fishers work alone," he said. "Double your time, girl, or get to walking home."

It was just past sunset. Kaketora had been up with the suns, and would not sleep until long after they set, and it had been like this since day two. Since this was her first trip out—a "dry fisher" —she was tasked with all the shit jobs, at all the worst times.

"We've each of us done it," Loban told her, on the fourth day. "If you're still tasked with it by the last pull, you'll know you have your captain's trust."

"And if I want to shove his trust up his ass?" she asked.

"Don't aspire to fail, Kaketora. Them that do don't fish again; some don't make it back to shore at all."

She reached the first net, off the windward side of the boat. They mostly drifted while trawling, so the sails were down and the oars were in; the wind and the waves had been pushing them into a gentle counter-clockwise for well over an hour. It was movement she might not have recognized on the first or second day without the suns to flag east and west.

One of the *many* things it took getting used to was that she had no sense of direction when out of the sight of land. They were southeast of Botzis, that much she was clear on. But the precise coordinates were known only to Obergango, and she wasn't sure *he* knew either.

A quick tug on the first net told her it was light. She braced herself, pulled hard, and brought it aboard.

(The first time Kaketora did this, after ten seconds of instruction from Loban, she very nearly took a header right over the rail. She no doubt would have drowned, not because she couldn't swim, but because the netting would like as not hold her under.)

She was right; it was just a few fish. She dragged the net to the trap and dropped the contents into the hold, which was three quarters full.

If the gods were kind, there'd be enough after this night to lock it down and head back. So far, the gods were not kind.

She stumbled over to the tie-on for the next net, only catching her balance on the railing. The winds had been picking up for the past hour, and now the waves were making so a trip to the rail was a peril.

"Storm's coming!" Obergango shouted.

"I feel it," she said.

Kaketora grabbed hold of the second net and was about to give it a pull when she heard a *howl* come in low, under the wind: a deep bass that rattled all the glass on the *Bekohai*, and turned her blood cold. It was at once the sound of a great beast, and the sound of something that was not in any way a part of the natural world. It was terrifying. She was probably overreacting.

She looked up at Obergango, who surely knew what this was, and that it wasn't something to be concerned with. But he'd gone pale.

"What in the Depths was that?" she shouted.

"Likely a whale," Obergango said.

"I heard me some whales," she said. "That didn't sound like one to me."

"It was a *whale*, now shut it and double-time those nets, cow!"

"Yeah, yeah."

She reached down to check the next net. This one had *no* give to it at all. It was *heavy,* and she knew better than to try a straight pull; she'd pop her shoulders out before it budged. Instead, she guided the main rope into an overhead tackle and pulled as hard as she could, with her whole body, and from a much cleaner angle.

It still wouldn't budge.

"Captain, we got a load in this one!" she shouted.

"Put some muscle into it, damn you! We've a wind to catch."

"If we're to do that before suns rise, I need help, old man," she said. "I know my capacity, and this tops it."

He had a curse or seven at the ready, but one look into her eyes was enough to convince him she wasn't lagging.

"*How* big?" he asked.

"Two more sets of hands," she said. "Maybe three."

He nodded, and stomped his feet. A few seconds later, what crew wasn't already aboveboard and working on the sails came out from below. Loban raced over to the net, while Obergango shouted commands to get the nets on the other side of the boat back in.

"What's the delay, Kaketora?" Loban asked. "You run out of sweat?"

"It's a haul," she said, stepping aside. Loban, much bigger and stronger, gave it a try.

"It is," he agreed. "Pagga! Maffi! Get over here!"

Loban shifted the rope to a second tackle and hooked it onto a mainstay, and then the four of them pulled on the rope until the net rolled up and over the side of the *Bekohai,* and onto the deck. It flapped and undulated with the movement of gasping fish... and another thing, a bigger thing.

She didn't know what it *was,* but it was assuredly not a fish. It was inky black, slick with grease, and full of anger, hissing and clicking and snapping. And it *growled,* which was a noise that things from the ocean were not like to do.

"What *is* that?" she asked. "Loban, what in the name of Honus is that?"

Loban shook his head. "No, no," he gasped. "It can't be."

"What *is* it??" she asked again.

Just then, they heard a second howl, as terrible as the last, but louder; whatever was making that sound was much closer now.

"Something's coming!" Jahamant shouted, from halfway up the mainmast.

Kaketora ran to the railing to have a look. Jahamant was right; something was heading for them, just below the surface. A dark mass, the size of a whale.

It wasn't a whale. Kaketora had *seen* whales, and knew what to expect. This looked more like a school of fish. Very, very large fish.

"Cut the nets!" Obergango shrieked. "Raise the mainsail!"

But it was already too late. The approaching mass split in two, with one massive beast ramming into the side of the *Bekohai,* and the other bursting out of the water and exploding into a swarm of winged, shrieking monsters. They covered the sky, crashed into the deck, and began to tear the ship apart.

The wood beneath Kaketora's feet shattered, and before she even had a chance to scream, she was tumbling into the hold, where she landed in the dark, with all the other dead things.

PART I
UP FROM THE DEPTHS

Chapter One

Makk was born in northern Inimata, in a little town called Hurg, at the base of the Deterrent Mountains along the north coast. But he had no memory of life in Hurg.

Stanto was another matter. That was where the orphanage he called home—until he was old enough to join the army—was located. It was *also* in northern Inimata, about forty kalomaders southeast of Hurg. He remembered Stanto well.

Given this history, when Professor Damid Magly's trail died, leaving Makk and Elicasta on the northern Inimatan coast, he thought *being* there would have felt at least a bit familiar.

It didn't. Either he had too much Velon city in him now, or the north wasn't what it used to be. Or—and this was probably it—he'd spent so much time denying the version of Makk Stidgeon that belonged in this part of the world, that aspect of him died of malnourishment.

I'd probably feel different in Stanto, he thought.

But they had no need to visit Stanto, and since he was trying to stay off the screens of anyone attached to either the House, or the Velon police department, it was probably better that they did not.

Magly interacted with the Stream only once during his brief stay in Inimata, which wasn't a great lead, but it was the best they had. The program that detected him—designed by Ba-Ugna Kev, and now living in Elicasta's rig—was good enough to pinpoint Magly's exact geolocation when he went to the Stream, which led them to a house belonging to a mathematics professor. Somewhat reluctantly, and under threat of arrest and loss of tenure (Makk wasn't actually in a position to arrest her, but she was easy to rattle, and yes, he did feel bad about it,) the mathematician pointed them to Oldhasken, a port city on the northeastern tip.

Oldhasken was where the trail went cold.

Magly and his Middle Kingdoms companion had almost definitely left from the Oldhasken port by boat—to *somewhere*—but after a week of questioning every charter captain, sailor, and anyone else willing to answer questions in exchange for C-Coin, Makk was no closer to knowing *which* boat, to *what* destination.

Which meant they were going to have to wait until Magly went on the Stream again.

Oldhasken wasn't a complete waste of time, though. True, nobody there was willing to give up someone they didn't even know, but the tight lips and pathologically terrible recall of the locals went both ways. Also, there were plenty of seedy dive bars to choose from. All of which made it an excellent place to stage a meeting between people who didn't want to be found.

The bar was called *Nighdemon's Last*, which was just exactly the kind of poetry Makk was looking for in a place he might not leave alive.

Nighdemons were monsters that snatched up any kids foolish enough to get caught outside at nighttime. They lived in all the dark places: the shadows of an unlit hallway; the forest at the edge of town; the alleyways and shadowy nighttime streets of the town itself. In the orphanage, the threat of the nighdemon was what kept them from running away.

Nighdemons were also a kid-accessible (and non-denominational) version of the Outcast. That was the part Makk found poetic. With the possible exception of Elicasta, everyone attending the meeting in the back of the *Nighdemon's Last* was some manner of outcast, provided one hewed to a somewhat broad definition.

That's what we should call this, he thought. *The meeting of the Outcasts. We could get shirts made.*

"They are late," Xto said.

The ex-astronaut was on his second ale, and none too happy about it. Alcohol put him in a sour mood, but being *denied* alcohol resulted in an even worse mood, which was to say that their friend from Wivvol had a drinking problem. He *knew* this, which was why he was only on his second ale and not his fourth or fifth. Also, he had no coin, so he had to rely upon Makk and Elicasta to keep him supplied. Which meant his consumption was regulated by their generosity, and the degree to which he was willing to prostrate himself in the name of coercing them to give him more.

On this day, they needed him lucid, and he wanted to *be* lucid, so everyone was working together to keep him that way. He just really, really hated it.

"Maybe they had trouble finding the place," Makk said. "There are a dozen dive bars to choose from."

He turned to Elicasta, who was set up at the back of the room, working a laptop and her rig simultaneously. With the help of at least one of those instruments, she was piloting a drone to keep an eye on the street. "Anything?" he asked.

"Not since the last time you asked, no," she said.

The *Nighdemon's Last* was empty. This wasn't because the bar lacked for regular patronage, but because Makk and Elicasta had bought out the place for the afternoon, using a (very small) portion of the massive fortune Ba-Ugna Kev handed to them before his untimely demise. The only other person in the place was Tolb, the bartender. Tolb had only one eye, one leg, and one ear. Makk was confident even if Tolb was of a mind to tell someone about who was in the *Nighdemon's Last* on this particular afternoon, he wouldn't be able to see who it was. And if he *did* see who it was, he wouldn't hear what they had to say. And if he was able to do both of those things, he wouldn't be able to run away fast enough to talk.

They had a doorman stationed outside. He'd been turning away people all afternoon, because none of them knew the agreed-upon phrase to gain entry, which was, "the *Cholem* sent me."

"How about our other friend?" Makk asked. "Any luck there?"

"Calcut's still offshore, north of Dorabon," Elicasta said. "He's on something slow-moving, but I can't imagine it's a pleasure cruise."

"Maybe he's on a tour of the North Cap. Or visiting friends in Annibat."

"Nobody lives in Annibat," Elicasta said. "Everybody knows that."

"What of the ice fishers of Annibat?" Xto asked. "Even I have heard of these people."

"Real? They're made up."

"Not real," Xto said, endeavoring to meet her Stream-speak halfway. "We were taught the old trade routes at a young age. The Annibati exchange fish and fresh water for wood and grain alcohol. The lie that they did not truly exist was deliberately promulgated by my people to preserve an exclusive trade arrangement. This they also taught us."

"I have *got* to get you on vid," Elicasta said, laughing. "Are they also five maders tall and covered in fur?"

"I do not know," Xto said. "Perhaps."

"Anyway, whatever Calcut is doing up there," Elicasta said, returning to the point, "I'm hot on keeping half the planet between us."

"Real," Makk said, with a smile.

Makk hadn't told Elicasta this, but there were only two ways the meeting they were about to have could go. One, he arrests Viselle and drops her off at the nearest federal police station, before using the tracking program in Elicasta's rig to hunt down and capture and/or kill Calcut Linus. Two, Viselle convinces him that Ba-Ugna Kev was *not* delusional and something something Outcast something, and he chooses to work *with* her instead.

Makk didn't expect option two to pan out.

"Got someone," Elicasta said.

"Daska?" Makk asked.

"I think it's Dorn. No robes so, it's hard to be sure, but face ident spin says eighty."

"Eighty is good?" Xto asked.

"Out of a hundred," Elicasta said. "Best match we've had so far."

"Hundred is not better?"

"Dorn is a Septal," Makk said. "Or they used to be. We never saw their whole face."

The front door opened for the first time since they arrived at the bar, and in walked Dorn Jimbal. They were in denim slacks and a hooded sweatshirt. The hood was down, giving Makk his first look at the face that definitely would have exonerated Dorn, had they stayed in Velon: the young (possibly ex-) Septal had a scar on the left side of their face, to go with a milky left eyeball that wasn't doing anything for them except take up the socket. They didn't look at all like the spoofed version of Dorn Jimbal shown exiting Orno Linus's home.

Dorn also had an earpiece in their right ear, and a voicer in their hand.

They took note of the empty barroom, shook off Tolb's silent offer of a beverage, and walked to Makk's table, slowly, as if one of the empty chairs might leap up and attack.

"Detective Stidgeon," Dorn said. "It's good to see you again."

"Hello, Dorn," Makk said. "Glad you're not dead."

"I share your sentiment, thank you."

"That's Elicasta Sangristy in the corner," Makk said, pointing over his shoulder. "And this is Xto Djbbit."

Dorn faced Xto first. "The missing astronaut," they said. "A great honor to meet you." They turned their attention to Elicasta then, and less courteously, asked, "is that rig active?"

"It's always on, Other Jimbal," she said, tapping the blue light on the side.

"I would rather my face not make it to the Stream," they said.

"Then why ditch the robes?" Makk asked.

"I would be recognized *far* more easily that way, detective," Dorn said. "Besides, I don't know if you've noticed, but there are no Septals in Oldhasken. I would stand out immediately."

"I'm straight news, no gotcha," Elicasta said.

Dorn looked at Makk, perplexed.

"That means she won't put your face on the Stream without your go-ahead," Makk said. "Where's Viselle?"

Dorn looked uncertain as to whether they wanted to keep talking, as long as Elicasta's blue light was on, but set aside that concern. "Nearby," they said. "I'm here to confirm, as well as I can, that this isn't an ambush."

"Might be an ambush," Makk said. "Might also be, I don't need any help to take her down. But right now, I find *you* more interesting than her."

"You mean to arrest me, detective?" Dorn asked.

"No. Viselle tried to kill me. She tried to kill Elicasta. She *stole* something from Xto."

"My birthright," Xto said.

"His birthright," Makk said. "And she killed my best friend. She framed *you* for murder, kidnapped you, and basically ruined your life. Unless I'm missing something, and you've been in on this from the beginning."

"I was not," Dorn said.

"Why are you working with her?" Makk asked. "You have as much reason not to trust Viselle as any of us, and I assume she doesn't have a gun at your back right now, so why aren't you getting out of here?"

Dorn considered their response carefully. "Detective, I think you know the facts you've laid out lack nuance. Her *father* set in motion the events that led to Ms. Sangristy's life being in danger, and was also responsible for framing me. I was *not* kidnapped. And, I was there when Leemie Witts died; I promise, she was not responsible for it. Moreover, he acted as he did specifically so that we could have this conversation today. But, however we decide to frame the past—whether your version is true or mine—it simply doesn't matter."

Makk leaned forward, and put his handgun on the table.

"I assume she's on the other end of that voicer?" he said.

"She is," Dorn said.

"Good. Tell her to come on in, and we'll see what does and doesn't matter."

"Honestly, Makk," Viselle said, from *behind* him. "You have got to stop whipping that thing out every time you hear my name."

Makk decided not moving was the best option; he assumed Viselle had a gun on him.

"Thought we locked that back door," he said.

Viselle walked slowly around the table, and yes, she did indeed have a blaster trained on him. She held it for a beat—long enough to make the threat abundantly clear—before sliding it back into its holder. "Oh, for Honus's sake," she said, "I've been following you for three days. I could have killed you whenever. Now put that away and let's talk."

Makk reached for his gun, slowly, and holstered it.

Viselle's eyes went to Xto, who had been standing since she

entered the room. She said something to him in Ghshtic. He said something back, louder and angrier.

"What'd you say?" Makk asked.

"I told him I was glad to see he'd recovered from the gravity sickness," she said. "Last time I saw him, he was too weak to stand. Then he said something about my parentage that doesn't have a precise translation."

"You tricked me," Xto hissed.

"Yes, yes," she said, dismissing him by turning to Elicasta. "Turn that off," she said, meaning Elicasta's rig.

"No chance," 'Casta said. "We stay blue for this."

"Makk..." Viselle began.

"If she says we stay blue, we stay blue," Makk said.

"You *can't* put this on the Stream, Elicasta," Viselle said. "The damage it would cause..."

"Yeah, we heard story that already," Elicasta said.

Viselle sighed, and returned her attention to Makk. "You're dressing better," she said.

"And you look tired," he said, which was true. She'd also cut her hair, none of which was relevant. "Now get to the part where you tell us what's so important, so I can arrest you."

"Did you find the professor?" Dorn asked.

"Damid Magly and Battine Alconnot came through this port," Makk said. "A lot of cut-rate charters leave from here; pretty sure they hopped one and took a ride, but nobody's talking, so I couldn't tell you where they were going for sure. We're going to have to wait until he uses the Stream again."

"Why are we looking for him?" Elicasta asked.

"I told you; I think he has a key," Viselle said.

"But you didn't say why I should give a godsdamn about that," Makk said.

"Dorn?" Viselle asked, ceding the floor.

Dorn nodded, and took a seat at the table. "The keys are important because the Outcast is coming," they said. "I know that sounds absurd, but it isn't, because the Outcast—this iteration—isn't a *god*; it's a neutron star, emitting massive quantities of gamma radiation. This star has an orbital period of something in the neighborhood of fifty thousand years, meaning it is technically a member of our planetary system. It's why Professor Linus took particular interest in my thesis: Dibble's irregular orbit will be subtly adjusted when the Outcast makes its next pass between us and the Dancers."

"Uh," Elicasta said. "Okay. Um. When will that be?"

"I haven't been able to complete my observations yet," Dorn admitted. "I need time with a high-powered telescope, and those are not easy to access. My guess is, within the next seven to ten years."

"Sorry," Makk said. "I'm not getting this. So *what* if our orbit is adjusted a little? That's not a world-ending calamity, right?"

"The radiation," Xto said.

"Precisely," Dorn said. "Our planet is bombarded by cosmic radiation every day, but the worst of it is deflected or absorbed by the ozone layer. This *much* radiation, this *close* to us, will be too much. It will kill all life on Dibble."

"All *surface* life," Viselle said. "The House knows, and they're taking precautions. Did you know there are tunnels under Velon?"

"Leemie used to talk about them all the time," Makk said. "I figured it was another one of his... well, you met him."

"The House is storing supplies deep underground," Viselle said. "In a massive bunker, where they mean to ride out however long it will take before the surface is habitable again."

"Is there room for all of us?" Elicasta asked.

"You know the answer to that," Viselle said. "We think all of the older temples have underground shelters, but , yes, *we're* all going to die. Only the House survives."

"There are tunnels under Chnta as well," Xto said. "And a great machine."

"Machine?" Dorn repeated. "What kind of machine? What is it for?"

"I do not know."

"The bad news here is that all life on Dib is going to end, except for everyone lucky enough to get a ticket to one of the House's secret basements," Makk said. "Do I have that right?"

"And the people on Lys," Viselle said. "Archeo Demara knew about this before anyone."

"He didn't *do* anything about it?" Elicasta asked.

"He did do something," Viselle said. "He built a life raft on the dark side of the planet. What else would you have him do?"

"*Tell* people? So there'd be time to *do* something?"

"The *House* has known for thousands of years," Dorn said. "Their solution was to go underground and *not* tell anyone. I assume Archeo was spurred by the futility implicit in that choice. If he even realized they knew."

"Okay," Makk said. "Assuming all of that is true…"

"It's true, Makk," Viselle said.

"It's insane, and *because* it's insane, I'm reserving judgement for now," he said. "Setting that aside, what do you think any of us can *do* about it?"

"Professor Linus's work is your answer," Dorn said. "He believed the House was *wrong* to give up and hide, and that there was evidence in the historical record that the gods provided us with a means to fight back. That the five keys could activate something to *repel* the Outcast somehow. And, that we already succeeded in doing this the last time the Outcast was here."

"Gods," Makk muttered. "The Collapse. You're talking about the Collapse."

"It's *possible*," Dorn said, "that the Outcast's previous traverse coincided with the Collapse. But I'm not sure how *likely* that is. This amount of radiation, I'm not sure. From the calculations I've been able to do, there isn't enough time for the planet to become sufficiently non-radioactive to support life before the Outcast returns to irradiate everything again. But if those figures are correct, life on Dibble should *also* be impossible. Either my calculations are wrong, or there's another factor to be considered."

"Besides," Viselle said, "what we know about the Collapse doesn't line up with what Dorn is talking about."

"We know hardly anything about the Collapse," Elicasta said. "Other than some legit crazy on the Stream."

"Evidence of great conflagrations," Dorn offered. "Mass graves, with bodies showing evidence of violence against themselves and others. Indications of great battles on land and sea against... ourselves, or another. These are the historical catastrophes that all happened at around the same time, resulting in the worldwide collapse of civilization. If there *was* a single cause—and that is very much disputed—radiation poisoning could not have *been* that cause. More directly to our point: if the Outcast was the cause of the Collapse, and we succeeded in stopping the Outcast, then there would have been no Collapse."

"The timing is hard to ignore," Makk said.

"The Outcast's last passage and the Collapse could be centuries apart and *look* proximate from this historical distance," Dorn said. "I promise, detective, we've already gone back and forth on this."

"Moving on," Elicasta said. "Orno Linus thought the House stopped the Outcast before and could do it again. So he stole a key. Yeah?"

"The goal was to collect all *five* of these keys, which Orno thought had been given to us by the gods for this specific purpose," Viselle said. "He believed the five keys, when inserted into the right machine at the right time would activate a weapon to protect us from the Outcast."

"Everything you just said sounds completely insane," Makk said.

"I agree," Dorn said. "And yet, most of it is supported by evidence in the historical record. I admit to have found this surprising as well. Professor Linus had a great deal of that proof, and it was good enough to convince some powerful people that he was correct. Just not all of the *right* people."

"It's still insane," Makk said. "Where is this machine supposed to be?"

"We don't know," Dorn said. "But you understand my interest in citizen Djbbit's underground machine."

"We also don't know where all the keys are," Viselle said. "Orno's plan was to locate all five, and convince the Septal Houses to lend them willingly to his cause. But first, he had to figure out where they were, and he didn't live long enough to even see that much through. Meanwhile, as Dorn said, convincing the right people was a big problem; Duqo Plaint certainly heard a version of this, and wasn't interested in handing over his key. Which was why Orno stole it."

"The second key came from Wivvol," Dorn said. To Xto, they added, "it ended up in the right hands. We're continuing the work begun by Orno Linus, which, if I understand correctly, was the promise you were fulfilling."

"My uncle," Xto said. "The High Hat of Chnta. It was to him that I made this vow. Had I not, I would likely have remained in space."

"How *long* could you have stayed up there?" Dorn asked, their curiosity piqued.

"It's a whole thing," Makk said. "Buy him a bottle and he'll tell you whatever you want to know. But later. That's two keys. You think Magly has the third?"

"Professor Magly left for Extum three weeks before Orno died," Viselle said. "It was Orno's understanding that Magly had a way to get into the great temple on Temple Island, which they were pretty sure had a key."

"Magly's on the list," Elicasta said.

"List," Viselle said levelly. "This came from my father?"

"He fobbed a data dump. Said there were some people on it who were, I guess, part of the same conspiracy."

"I haven't seen this list," Viselle said. "But Orno might have given it directly. He and my father were in communication before I became involved."

"That leaves two keys unaccounted for," Makk said. "And no idea where this machine is supposed to be. Not that I'm buying any of this; I'm just counting."

"What was Professor Linus's search criteria?" Elicasta asked.

"I'm not certain of his methodology," Dorn said. "I had access to most of the professor's notes, but he had a... unique approach to organization, which is to say the information on the keys may *be* there, but I've yet to find it. It may also be unreasonable of us to assume he wrote this down; it's possible that in his mind, the *where to look* element was logical."

"Could be," Elicasta said. "Velon, Chnta and Temple Island are three of the biggest and oldest House temples around, aren't they?"

"They are," Dorn said. "But at least ten other temples are *as* old and *as* large."

"One thing at a time," Viselle said. "We find Magly first. Whether he has a key or not, the more times his name comes up the more I think he knows a lot of what we don't. You said he passed through here, but you don't know where he was headed. Nobody's talking?"

"Nobody so far," Makk said.

"But you know around *when* he left, right? What are his possible destinations?"

"Doesn't matter," Makk said. "It was over a week ago. He could have gotten to wherever the boat took him, and taken another one somewhere else."

"Again, one thing at a time," Viselle said. "Where *could* he have gone?"

"We have their exit stamp down to a two-day window,"

Elicasta said, tapping out something on her computer. "Impossible to say how many private freighters left in that span, but there were five commercial charters. We can bank that they didn't hop a freight, if you want. Chase down the best guess."

"Where did the five go?" Viselle asked.

"One went down the coast to Pethis, one was a middie cruise around Kindon to Canos-Holo. One was...oh, huh, that also went to Canos-Holo. Fourth one went to Wrimmad. Fifth had a stopover in Velon before it rounded the south end and up to Kindon."

"Compare those destinations to the list my father gave you," Viselle said.

"Yeah, but just check Pethis and Wrimmad," Makk said.

"Why?" she asked.

"We tracked your guy across half of Dib already," he said. "Whatever safe havens he had in Kindon and Velon he burned through to get here. And if there *are* any temples on Canos-Holo, they're not old enough."

"I've got hits in both," Elicasta said. "Whoa. Our professor *is* connected. You know Polister Calidon?"

"Doesn't sound familiar," Makk said.

"I do," Viselle said.

"Makk," Elicasta said, "you've gotta flash more shine on the rest of the world sometime. Not everything is about dead bodies in downtown Velon."

"Last time I cared about the rest of the world, I ended up in a war," he said. "Who is Polister Calidon?"

"The Calidons are about as powerful a family as you're going to find in Mursk," Viselle said. "Polister's the youngest son of Dueay and Madda Calidon. Madda's grandfather founded Tandem Insurance."

"Polister's oldest brother's the CEO now," Elicasta said. "And the second oldest brother and the sister both work for Tandem too. Story goes, Polister's gig was to get the whole fam into the Haven."

"He's a Septal," Makk guessed.

"He was in line to be the High Hat of Fendo," Dorn said. "I too have heard this."

"Well shit," Makk said. "Can you all please get to the point now."

"Do not worry, Makk Stidgeon," Xto said. "I too do not know who this man is."

"He renounced," Dorn said.

"Not *just* renounced," Elicasta said. "He went full heretic. He's a Spanner now. He's, like, *the* Spanner now. Heads the whole eastern Unital court from Wrimmad City. If that's who our guy's good with, he's in powerful company."

"Got it," Makk said. "Well-connected. Who's his Pethis contact? The prime minister?"

"I don't know this one," she said. "Don-Ma B'ali. Lemme run the name up against the Stream, see what shakes."

"Don't bother," Viselle said. "He's my uncle."

There was a moment of silence as they let that sink in.

"*Uncles,*" Xto muttered.

"Is he important?" Makk asked.

"Locally, yes," Viselle said. "Probably not outside of Unak."

"Thought Ba-Ugna Kev and his birth home were on the outs," Elicasta said.

"My father vowed to never set foot there again," Viselle said. "This is true. But that was, in part, to avoid being put into an untenable situation; Dunnite politics are horribly convoluted. Which is why his half-brother, my uncle, is in Pethis rather than Dunn. He's in exile."

"*Exile?*" Makk asked.

"Effectively. If he sets foot in Dunn he'll probably be executed. Don't ask me to explain why; I'm not sure I understand it myself. But I *will* say, if there's anyone on the Dunn side of the family that would hold my father's trust, it would be Don-Ma." She turned to Elicasta. "If our logic is sound, and Magly's working from the same list of confederates as Ba-Ugna and Orno, and he *knows* Don-Ma B'ali, that's where he'll be. Pethis and Dunn are actively hostile to international law. Other than Wivvol, Pethis would be the best place to ride out a warrant. Especially if he has a contact who can grease the border crossing."

"If you're wrong?" Elicasta asked.

"I'm not wrong," Viselle said. "But I have what? Between seven and ten years?"

"It's a very rough estimate," Dorn said. "Please keep that in mind."

"Yeah, but there's time."

"I think you're on a tighter clock than that, Viselle," Makk said. "We all are. Let's see: *you've* got a warrant on your head for murder; the international community is still combing the waters of the Midpoint looking for Xto, so I'm pretty sure as soon as his face turns up somewhere that isn't the bottom of the ocean, it's gonna be a big deal; the most powerful criminal boss in Inimata wants me and 'Casta dead, and I'm pretty sure he feels the same about you and Dorn. Meanwhile, the guy you're trying to find is hiding out with a royal from the Middle Kingdoms, and they *both* have international warrants on *them*. Best of all, the godsdamn *House* wants their keys back, so you can bet they're gonna pop up at the worst possible time. Honestly, I can't believe we made it *this* far."

"Fine, it's a risk," Viselle said. "But honestly, it's *my* risk. If you three want out, just hand over your key and I'll take it from here."

Makk laughed. "You're serious."

"Absolutely. You and Elicasta can go back to your lives. Or keep what Ba-Ugna gave you and go on a seven-to-ten year vacation, if you'd rather. Xto, I don't know what you *want*, but it shouldn't be hard to present yourself as a returning hero, if the story is good enough."

"Or, I can keep the key and arrest you," Makk said. "Like I should have done the minute you walked in."

"I had the *drop* on you the minute I walked in," she said. "Let's not forget that part."

"You don't *now*."

It was Viselle's turn to laugh. "You think you can beat me to the draw?" she asked. "Seriously."

"Calm yourselves," Xto said. "Makk Stidgeon, you are not arresting her, nor am I strangling her with my hands." He looked at Viselle. "I have had experiences, of late, that have shaken my faith in the gods. As consequence, I no longer believe much of the Septalism I was taught as a child. I *do* believe those keys open uncanny things in surprising places; I have witnessed this. I will go with you, if you'll have me, if only for the pleasure of discovering what else the keys unlock."

"Dorn," Makk said. "How about you? You're buying into all of this?"

"Detective," Dorn said, "most of what we just told you came from *my* research. I promise, the Outcast *is* coming. It's either continue with this mad quest, or sink into despair."

"We could *tell* somebody," Elicasta said. "Big ball of radiation in the sky, and the only plan in our kit's some crazy idea from a dead professor."

"You don't imagine, if there *were* a better solution, the House would already have it?" Dorn asked.

"All it will take is for a non-House astronomer to detect the Outcast," Viselle said, "and then this isn't a secret any longer. That won't be for a while, unless one of them gets *really* lucky. I say, let's appreciate the relative peace the planet is enjoying, while we can."

"All right," Makk said. "Viselle, I'm not going to arrest you. But you can't have our key, and Elicasta and I aren't going with you to Pethis."

"Makk..." Viselle began.

"We'll go to Wrimmad City," he said. "Go to Wrimmad, look up this Calidon guy, let you know what he has to say. He's on the list, right? Even if Magly's not there, Calidon's worth shaking down."

"You want to *shake down* the Holy Staffer?" Elicasta asked.

"Sure, why not?" Makk said. "Can't be worse than Duqo Plaint."

"We should keep the keys together," Viselle said.

"Yeah well, when you get arrested trying sneak into Pethis, I don't wanna be standing next to you," Makk said. "Don't worry about my key, Viselle. I'll keep it safe. Worry that the smart thing for Damid Magly to do was to slip some coin to a freighter captain, and he doesn't strike me as a stupid guy. He's probably not in Pethis *or* Wrimmad."

Chapter Two

Polister Calidon didn't need to walk through the courtyard to get to the Holy Chamber. His private residence was attached to the center dome on one side, with administrative offices on the other; he could go from place to place without leaving the building.

He took the courtyard anyway, at least on sunny days—which was *most* days on Botzis—because then he got to go past the statue.

Erected nearly a hundred years ago by the great Pethian sculptor Rasimus Cole, the statue was a somewhat modern interpretation of the god Pal, standing legs apart, shoulders squared, arms outstretched, and offering their staff to a penitent believer.

Assumed, but not stated, was that the staff was being offered to Arigo Span, and that this was a visualization of the fifth passage in the first section of the Word of Span.

"And then did the god appear, and I was affrighted..." and so on. (It was one of seventy-two instances in which Arigo used the word "affrighted", which was also memorable.) The genuflecting recipient of the staff actually looked a good deal more like

Rasimus Cole than Arigo Span, but this wasn't common knowledge.

Behind Pal was an ebony wall with pinhole white dots: a constellation-free night sky. And that was it; that was the whole piece.

If one happened upon the statue on most days, one would be, if not underwhelmed, then perplexed by the accolades that accompanied Cole's statue. Yes, the depiction of Pal—twice as tall as an average person, radiant and handsome—was sufficiently impressive that one might say, "I have now seen a god, albeit in granite form." But go no further, and one would miss the true genius embedded in the piece.

For that, one had to look *past* the statue, at the shadows it was casting.

There were five spotlights trained on Pal. One was aimed up at an angle, accentuating Pal's cheekbones and beatific smile. The other four were smaller, and targeted different parts of the torso. These seemed to serve no purpose at all, unless one took the time to walk around the side of the monument, and have a look at that wall of stars.

Rasimus Cole added little cavities—four of them—to the statue. When one aimed a light at these cavities at just the right angle, an additional *four* shadows were cast on the wall, belonging to the other four gods of the Septal Pentatheon: Honus, Javilon, Nita and Ho. Shadow caricatures all, in their own rings of light.

This was what made the piece so extraordinary. Rasimus Cole found a way, simply and effectively, to restate the truth of Unitism, a truth that took Arigo Span eight hundred pages to communicate.

That truth is this: there is only one god, and that god is Pal. The other four are *echoes* (or shadows, or incarnations) of Pal.

It didn't mean Honus, Javilon, Nita and Ho are not *also* gods; only that there's a higher ordination involved.

In fairness to Arigo Span's eight hundred pages, the statue *was* an over-simplification of a complex religious belief system. If pressed, Polister would argue that the only god of Unitism being represented in this installation was the *light* shining on and through Pal. But that was a nuance reserved for conversation among the faithful.

I should incorporate the statue into one of my presentments, he thought, not for the first time. *It's too important to take for granted.*

"Sir," Dwerik said. He was standing a few paces back, patiently waiting for Polister to finish his daily communion with Cole's genius.

Dwerik had been Polister's assistant for six seasons now, and still acted as though he was one false step from a beheading.

(Not that Dwerik had any reason to be concerned, but there *was* a precedent, from the early, ugly days of the faith, of a Holy Staffer ordering the beheading of an underling.)

"I'm sorry; they're waiting," he added.

"I know, I know," Polister said, with a sigh. He kissed the tips of his fingers and touched the fingers to the granite Pal's arm. "Lead on, Dwerik."

In the context of religiously sponsored structures, the Holy Chamber of Wrimmad was new. The eastern Unitist seat of power used to be in Ghon-Dik, in Dorabon, in an overlarge building that formerly belonged to the House. (That location was well over a thousand years old, most of which time it housed more rats than people.)

One of Polister Calidon's prime initiatives, upon taking over as Holy Staffer, was to distance Unitism from Septalism...as much as that was possible, given Unitism began as a "heretical" splinter faction off of the much older House. That meant targeted messaging, more direct community involvement—especially in places where the House's reach was limited—and more modern architecture.

This was the stated impetus behind moving the seat from Dorabon to Botzis. Unstated, Botzis made a good deal more sense, politically. Ghon-Dik was ruled by a merchant collective, which made it perpetually unstable, not to mention insular and xenophobic. It was difficult to get the Word of Pal past its borders, and it wasn't doing so great *inside* the borders either.

Botzis was in many ways *less* organized, politically, but what did exist was built on a parliamentary template, and its representatives at least *tried* cooperating in the interest of the common good, rather than competing in an unwinnable game of, "who can fish the ocean the most profitably."

The democratically elected parliamentary council created the illusion that Botzis wasn't as lawless as it actually was. In truth, the island was little more than a collection of city-states loosely associated with older countries in other places.

Wrimmad—the largest city on the island—was founded by Murskite expatriates. After that, there were the cities Pkwlb (a Wivvol satellite, settled by political exiles,) Dongy (Inimatan profiteers,) and Djuk-Djuk (a Kindonese fishing port.) There were also smaller settlements—not quite at the level of "city" yet—founded by natives from Lladn, Pethis, and Punkoah.

The parliament's cooperative bent was hard-won, ultimately requiring the intervention of a party everyone could agree on as being neutral. Which was how Polister Calidon, Right and Holy Staffer of the eastern Unitist Court, ended up being the de facto prime minister of Botzis.

This role wasn't publicized, but what *was* public was that Staffer Calidon and the Holy Chamber of Wrimmad acted as monthly host to the parliamentary sessions. Given the parliament had no building of its own, that they were meeting in a Unitist hall scarcely raised an eyebrow.

Now, had they met in a House temple *instead*, that would have been another matter. Nobody on Botzis or Dorabon trusted the Septals at all; any official gathering on House grounds would be tainted immediately, regardless of how anodyne the subject. Unitals, in contrast, were largely considered harmless.

There were only two House temples on Botzis anyway. The original—small, and new (for a House temple) it was built by the first settlers—was in Wrimmad City, not far from the Unital Holy Chamber. It was poorly maintained, because despite the sincere efforts of High Hat Porl, it was difficult to amass a sufficient head count to do more than self-sustain. (Polister had spoken to Porl on a number of occasions, in which she expressed that her chief frustration was not the failure of local recruitment, but how hard it was to get relocation commitments from Septals in other parts of the world.) The Wrimmad House campus didn't have a big enough building to host the parliament had they wanted to, never mind the resources to do it well.

The other temple was a self-starter in the Punkoahn settlement that wasn't even worthy of being called a temple, inasmuch as they had no building. Punkoahns practiced a fundamentalist species of Septalism, one that declared anyplace with sufficient adherents to be a temple, and anyone of adequate charisma a High Hat. Even if they *had* a building, nobody—aside from the Punkoahn parliamentary representative—would go near it; the people of Botzis distrusted Septals, but they *despised* fanatics.

In every other part of the world, Septalism ruled, and Unitism was a quirky afterthought. On Botzis, the situation was reversed; everyone was there to get *away* from wherever it was they or their family originally hailed from, and more often than not, one of the aspects of home from which they sought refuge was the House itself.

Unitism was the solution for people who distrusted the House but were still looking for religious fulfillment, which was why it was the majority religion on Botzis. To appeal to the larger masses, Polister was going to have to find a way to attract those who had no quibble with the House, and came to Unitism only because it was the *truth*. But that was a long way away.

~

He found the parliament assembled and, having tired of waiting for Polister, already arguing.

"Piracy!" barked Qotid, the Kindonese representative. It was unclear if she was accusing someone in the room of piracy, or bemoaning its general practice.

"You are always ready with that word," Lm Fyk, the Wivvolian, said mildly. "One day we will have *real* pirates to concern ourselves with, and then you will only look foolish."

"What's the concern?" Polister asked, stepping around the table to reach his chair. They held these meetings in an upper hall of the administrative wing, a space that was intended for banquets. It used to have a large rectangular table, but nobody was happy with that, so Polister had a round one brought in. The room also came with a vaulted ceiling dangling a lovely chandelier made from driftwood, and a picture window overlooking the front grounds.

The Holy Chamber was built on a hill, and so the view from the window also included an exceptional look at the harbor, and the many vessels docked there.

"The honorable Qotid is insistently reclassifying a market imbalance as an extralegal act," Araaaha of Ghon-Dik said. "As is her custom."

"Sinking our *ships* isn't a *trade imbalance*, damn you!" Qotid barked.

"I believe," Polister said, interrupting, "that is a subject for later," He picked up the agenda that was waiting for him at the table. "Yes, there it is. 'Treaties and trade'. Let's table this for after lunch. Yes?"

He got a low grumble back, which was good enough.

"First agenda item is new entreaties. Yock? What news from the rest of the world?"

Yock was one of Polister's three full-time secretaries, and the only one fully committed to parliamentary business. He and a half-dozen other Unitals sat at a smaller table at the back of the room, ready to be called.

He stepped forward with a tablet. "We have two. Admiral Staipa of Asealand is requesting offshore permit off the eastern tip for a period of four months."

"*Admiral* Staipa," Elbring Hain—an Inimatan, and the newest member of the council—said with a laugh. "That's funny."

"Admiral in what navy?" Araaaha asked.

"It doesn't say," Yock said.

"Asealand presumes to be own nation," Polister said. "If Coigo Staipa thinks his one big ship is a *navy* and he's its admiral, who are we to say he's wrong?"

"You are far too generous," Araaaha said.

Asealand was a floating city-state, Coigo Staipa was its owner, and everyone aboard paid a substantial sum for the right to live there. They tended to remain in international waters, but periodically sidled up to a land mass for a short time, so the residents could come ashore and spend their C-Coins locally. Having them drop by was like hosting a cruise ship, except cruise ships went away much sooner.

"Is that the extent of the request, Yock?" Polister asked.

"Yes, Staffer," Yock said. "But if history is our guide, an affirmative from this chamber will be met by a list of follow-up requests."

"Of course," Polister said. He turned to the assembly. "Any objection to having Asealand as our guest?"

"As long as they stay out of the fishing channels," Lm said, "Pkwlb does not object."

"I'm sure our cheap trinket industry will be happy to have them," Myala Dravian—the Mursk representative—said. The longest-standing member of the parliament, she was the one who suggested involving Polister in the first place. She was also the only Unital among the members.

"Sealanders have an affinity for Botzo crafts, if memory serves," Oro Fet, the Lladn representative, said. "And a poor understanding of authenticity."

"As I said," Myala agreed. "Cheap trinkets on markup. If the tribes ever decide to care about C-Coins, they'll be furious to discover how much they could have been making."

"*Primitives*," muttered Orrer Balin, the Punkoahn. He said it in Konnhan, his native tongue, but Polister was sufficiently fluent —at least in the curses—to understand.

Orrer Balin thought everyone in the room was damned to the Depths, but had a specific dislike of the Botzos, as if there was a second, worse Depths to which they might be consigned.

"When it comes to our central neighbors," Polister said, "it would be wise to not confuse a simple existence with a lack of sophistication. Most of you have met Elder Ko; he is no fool." This was directed at the room, but meant for Orrer Balin, whose air of superiority bothered Polister somewhat more than he allowed himself to admit. "We have drifted from the matter on the table. Are there *any* objections to Coigo Staipa's petition?"

"You mean Admiral Staipa," Elbring said, with a laugh.

"I have no objection," Oro said.

"Nor I," Myala added.

Polister looked around the table for any dissent. Seeing none, he said, "Yock, tell the admiral his stay is granted. Four months."

"Yes, Holy Staffer," Yock said. He tapped out a note for himself on the tablet before continuing. "The second is an appeal from the Middle Kingdoms, by way of the League of Countries. There is an international extradition order they're asking us to honor."

"Sorry, did you say the *Kingdoms?*" Oro asked.

"I didn't know they were members in the League of Countries," Pai-Mak Lona said. Pai-Mak represented the Pethis colony. Pathologically taciturn, this would likely be their only utterance in this meeting.

"I believe they are members in absentia," Lm said.

"Do they vote by carrier pigeon?" Myala asked.

"*I* know what this is," Araaaha said. "Our league ambassador forwarded the bulletin. Someone killed one of their sovereigns and made off with a House artifact. They were last seen off the coast of Temple Island. Probably drowned; the Gap is treacherous."

"Continue, please, Yock," Polister said.

"The order is as follows," Yock said. "'The scholar Damid Magly, late of Callim University; and Battine Alconnot, Lady Delphina, late of the Kingdom of Totus, stand accused of the crimes of theft of a holy artifact, and regicide. Both parties were last seen fleeing Temple Island in an unregistered aero-car. We ask that all non-League members honor standing international extradition treaties pertaining to high crimes. Specifically: if found, secure the artifact, detain the accused, and contact the international board of legates immediately. Do not provide safe harbor; do not provide aid. Thank you for your support of international law.'"

"Yock," Polister said, "Did you say *Damid* Magly?"

"And Battine Alconnot, yes sir."

"Alconnot," Elbring said. "That's royalty, isn't it? One of their princesses go a little crazy over there?"

"Am I the only one in thinking they sounded much more interested in recovering their lost artifact than in capturing their king killers?" Qotid asked.

"More fixation on trinkets," Myala said, with a laugh.

"The Kingdoms have more secrets than the Five," Orrer growled. "My family has had dealings with royals from Manalusium. A *king* would be no great loss; a 'trinket', as you say, would be another matter. You're not wrong that they would place a higher value on a lost artifact. The House would behave no differently. Did you say *aero-car*, young man?"

"I did, yes," Yock said.

"Not air*ship*. I wonder how they managed to get one of those to Temple Island."

"Unlikely that they did," Araaaha said. "Which is why I say they drowned."

"You know this Magly, don't you?" Elbring asked Polister.

"I do," Polister admitted. "We all do. You recall, some years back, when High Hat Porl held her fundraiser for the Botsos? Damid was in attendance, as one of my guests."

"I recall an irrigation project the tribes had no interest in," Lm said.

"Indeed," Elbring said. "One wonders what Porl did with all those donations."

This was true, unfortunately. It put to the lie Polister's assertion that Elder Ko was no fool, at least in the eyes of the parliamentary council members. Except he also knew that Porl neglected to *ask* the Botzos if they were interested in an irrigation canal (meant to bring water from one of the island's western river deltas to a proposed artificial lake at the edge of the tribal lands) before arranging the charity event. While it seemed obvious that a people whose harsh existence in a desert territory might like their own lake, it was still generally a good idea to ask them first. And in the case of the Botzo tribes, while they needed water as much as anyone to survive, they had a preternatural fear of large bodies of it. Had Porl asked Polister prior to arranging the fundraiser, he would have told her this.

"I *do* remember him," Myala said. "A Middle Kingdoms expert, yes? I found him quite entertaining."

"What do you think, Staffer Calidon?" Elbring asked. "Is your man a killer?"

"I would say Damid Magly is no more capable of murder than

I am," Polister said. "But international law is international law. What say we to honoring the League's request?"

The affirmations were slightly more reluctant this time around, but the combination of nods and shows of hands passed the resolution.

"That takes care of our first agenda item," Polister said, as Yock took his position at the back table again. "The second item…"

"Petition to move 'treaties and trade' to the top of the agenda," Qotid said. (Like most Kindonese, she had no family name; Qotid was it.)

The petition was met with sighs from the Wivvolian and Ghon-Dik contingent.

"Pirates," Polister said.

"There are acts of piracy to be discussed," Qotid said. "It's an urgent concern."

"I of course agree," Araaaha said. "As I believe is so for every faction at this table, the nation of Ghon-Dik considers fishing the lifeblood of our economy. *Any* high seas skullduggery is taken very seriously. Could the representative from Djuk-Djuk be more specific?"

"You thieving…"

"Qotid," Polister interrupted. "I think we would all benefit from an opportunity to understand the precise issue your city has encountered."

"Ships have gone missing," she said. "Three so far this season. These were fishing trawlers, with good captains. Kindonese, all; they knew what they were doing."

"You believe them seized," he said.

"There's ample precedent."

"*Where* were they fishing?" Lm asked.

"If your question is, did these experienced captains decide to fish the waters of which a certain other nation *claims* ownership…?" Qotid said. "I assume not. But even if I'm wrong, this is not how we handle these kinds of disputes. Not any longer."

"You are correct," Araaaha said. "Piracy *not* how we handle matters. Which is why I can say with confidence that we had nothing to do with your missing ships."

❧

The unpleasantness Qotid kept referencing had to do with one of the reasons the parliament was originally founded, as well as why the nation of Ghon-Dik had a seat on it.

In the lawless early days of the Botzis settlements, Ghon-Dik considered the island, and all the waters surrounding it, theirs by right. It was a preposterous claim, because while Dorabon was indeed the closest land mass *to* Botzis, it wasn't all that close. Also, the Great Current—which in this part of the world brought cold waters from the North Cap down through the Norton Ocean —passed between Dorabon and Botzis. It had long been established that the waters of the Current were international: no nation could lay claim; not even the Wivvolians, whose great shipping vessels practically owned the Current for centuries. It therefore defied logic and reason to argue that the Ghon-Dik fishing collective had a valid claim on territorial waters *beyond* the Current. Yet, that was what they argued.

The problem stemmed from a Ghon-Dik fishing industry that was so competitive, and prone to overfishing because of it, that the solution for many villages was to travel well beyond their own shores. This took them into the shipping lanes of the Current, but when that proved more trouble to fish than it was worth, they kept going until the found the calmer waters off the Botzis coast.

Had they eventually settled *on* the island, perhaps then they would have had a claim. But none of the Ghon-Dik fishers thought to do that. They just kept fishing in the waters offshore. And—because there is no war like a war between rival Ghon-Dik fishing villages—they honored each other's respective territorial claims off Botzis, however informal those might have been.

Then, somewhere in the neighborhood of two hundred and fifty years ago, ships from other countries stopped going *past* Botzis quite so much; some of them stuck around.

The triggering incident for this was an accidental settling. A shipwreck, more precisely, of a vessel from Mursk called the *Herrifay*. It was a passenger ship that was supposed to be taking a small group of Murskite families from the Heragan-Abbon mountain region of Lladn, to Dunn, by way of the Great Current. They were on a diplomatic mission—establishing trade partners— which was the sort of thing at which people from Mursk excelled.

What they did *not* excel at was sailing, navigating, or shipbuilding.

The *Herrifay* began taking on water as it came around the icy northern coast of Dorabon, but managed to stay afloat long enough to beach on the shore of Botzis, at around the same spot as the current Wrimmad City. They *thought* they'd landed on the eastern coast of Inimata, rather than the southern coast of an entirely different land mass. Again: not great at navigating.

They toughed it out for a year, before being discovered by one of the Ghon-Dik fishing boats, by which time the survivors had decided they didn't want to leave. So, when their rescue ship arrived from Mursk—this one being a Wivvolian-made vessel, unlike the *Herrifay*—rather than heading back, they convinced half the sailors to stay, and the other half to tell others about the nice island they'd found.

As the population increased, the fishing in the waters off Botzis increased, and eventually the Ghon-Dikan fishermen decided the only way to deal with this unexpected competition was to start boarding ships and seizing cargo. They argued that it was *their* fish, so this wasn't *piracy*; it was the reclamation of stolen goods.

This went on for about sixty years. For roughly half of that time, the nation of Ghon-Dik denied the whole thing entirely, up until some of the Botzis settlements began fighting back—the Wivvolians of Pkwlb especially—and sinking Ghon-Dikan raiders. Then it was hard to deny.

The practice of piracy in the Norton Ocean finally came to an end after a treaty negotiation between the newly-formed Botzis parliament and the ruling merchant collective of Ghon-Dik. One of the conditions of the treaty was that Ghon-Dik would have a permanent seat at parliament. Which was why Araaaha was there.

Interestingly, there was *no* seat at parliament for the one group of people whose claim to Botzis was better than the Ghon-Dikan fishers: the Botzos, who had been on the island since at least the Collapse.

Polister wondered if, when the parliament was first formed, any effort had been made to include the Botzos. He and Representative Dravian would be making their annual pilgrimage to the midlands shortly. He made a mental note to bring up the question.

"I wonder," Polister said, "if it would be wiser to approach this in a less *adversarial* fashion. Qotid, can you provide last-known coordinates of any of the lost vessels?"

"To what end?" she asked, one eyebrow raised, oozing skepticism.

"To prove they were not where they should be," Myala said. Despite being a Murskan, she was sometimes overly fond of throwing bombs into conversations about which she had no stake.

"No, no, no," Polister said, before Qotid, Araaaha and Lm started chasing each other around the room again. "Listen, please. All of you represent a people who fish the ocean, yes? I would think you *each* have a vested interest in finding out who or what is causing ships to disappear."

"*Kindonese* ships," Lm said.

"We have been fishing the coral shores of Kindon since before..." Qotid began. She was stopped by Araaaha, who put his hand over hers on the table.

"We're missing ships as well," he said. "I am not supposed to say so. My directive was to sound out the room, see which of your little colonies had turned villain."

"We would never!" Orrer said, maximally offended.

"No, not you and your little rowboats and linen nets," spat Araaaha. "But Wivvolians? Kindonese? Even you Inimatans. You could do it."

"Speaking only for Pkwlb," Lm said, "we have done no such thing."

"I'd say he speaks for us all," Elbring said.

"How many?" Polister asked.

"Ships?" Araaaha said. "Five. That have been reported. It may be more; you know how insular the collective can be."

"*Five?*" Lm asked.

"Anyone else?" Polister asked.

"I haven't heard anything," Elbring said. "But I'll check with the harbor minister."

"All right," Polister said. "Back to my original question: what were the last known locations of these ships? And can we establish some sort of timeline? Let's collect what information we have and see where it takes us. Agreed?"

The matter of the missing boats wasn't going to be resolved by further discussion, and so they moved on to other matters, none of which was particularly exciting. Polister spent most of his time musing on the challenge of ships lost at sea in such a chaotic sociopolitical region.

The only boats on the water that were talking to one another were the ones owned by common merchants, and even then, about half didn't have the equipment for it. Fishing boats went out somewhere, and only came back once their hold was full, or when they ran out of food and water, whichever came first. It was exceedingly unusual for anyone ashore to know any boat's intended destination, and even if they *did* know it when the fishers left the dock, it could well change once they were at sea. If a boat went down, for whatever reason—be it bad weather, bad navigating, piracy, or the whimsy of Pal—it could be one or two *months* before anyone even missed them.

The technology that would enable the tracking of vessels, and the communications between them, certainly existed. It wasn't even *new* technology: Wivvolian freight ships had been employing both for centuries. But the Wivvolians were managing a global shipping empire, whereas these people just wanted to catch fish, more than half of which they did from within sight of the shore. (Or at least *a* shore.) Also, for whatever reason, there was a definite Hohite bent among the residents of Botzis; they embraced low-tech solutions whenever possible, as if that made their accomplishments more genuine.

Which was perfectly fine, up until boats started going missing.

It was well past fourteen by the time they broke. Everyone shook hands and chatted quietly for another hour over a light repast, and then all the representatives took their leave, until next month, when they would do it all over again. Hopefully, they would lose no more boats in the interim.

Polister was looking forward to a nice, quiet evening with his thoughts, a decent book, a bottle of wine, and perhaps a soak in a tub—parliamentary meetings were somehow the most stressful part of his life—when Dwerik caught up with him.

"Your guests are waiting, Holy Staffer," he said. "In your office."

"I'm...sorry, Dwerik, was there another meeting on my schedule?" Polister was not in the habit of scheduling Unital Court business on the same day as parliamentary business.

It was Dwerik's turn to be confused. "Not on your official schedule, no," he said. "The two Septals. They carry your family seal. I assumed..."

"My *seal?* Are you sure?"

"Y-yes. I'm sorry, should I have turned them away? My understanding was..."

"No, no," Polister said, interrupting before Dwerik outright fainted. "My mistake. I wasn't expecting them today is all. They're early."

"Yes, Holy Staffer."

"They're in my office, you say?"

"They are."

"Very good. I'll be there presently. Why don't you take the rest of the evening, Dwerik?"

"Most Holy?"

"I can find my own way to my bedchamber," Polister said. "I will see you in the morn." When this didn't satisfy the young man, Polister added, "You're not in *trouble*, Dwerik. I just don't need you again until morning."

"Yes, Holy Staffer," Dwerik said. "Very good."

Dwerik bowed twice, and excused himself. The young man looked terribly conflicted, as if not knowing what to do with himself when not trailing behind Polister.

As soon as Dwerik was out of view, Polister doubled his pace.

The seal Dwerik mentioned was an artifact of an ancient Murskite custom that Polister Calidon—whose family line could be traced back through two thousand years' worth of diplomats— still honored, when it suited him. The object itself was the family crest imprinted on a leather packet containing a flat stone. Someone carrying it could be said to speak *for* that family with absolute and legally binding authority.

Or, they *used* to mean that. In the modern world, when a

contract could be called up instantly on a voicer screen, there was little use for a Murskite seal anymore. Polister—harboring some Hohite tendencies of his own, evidently—still rather liked the concept.

Each member of Polister's immediate family carried seals personal to them. Polister had a dozen, six of which were still in his private chamber. The other six he'd handed over to close friends, who were told that should they require an audience with him, the seal would open whatever doors might otherwise be closed.

Supposedly, somebody had just used one to get into his office. A *Septal*, according to Dwerik. The problem was that only one of the six seal-bearers was a practicing Septal: Orno Linus. But Orno had been dead for weeks, if the news out of Velon was to be believed. It was possible *another* Septal found the seal among Orno's belongings, but the notion that they would know what it *was* and then endeavor to *use* it seemed too great a stretch.

But then, who else could it be?

The trip from the upper hall to Polister's private quarters wasn't long, provided one cut through the center dome to get there.

The center dome was designed not unlike the observatories of old, with a round stage at center, encircled by raked seating. This was where the congregants came for the weekend services. Practically speaking, it was much larger than it had to be; if every Spanner in Wrimmad City came to the same service for worship, the place would only be half-full. But, it was also where the holder of the eastern court seat held services, and thus was sometimes used to handle larger crowds from outside of the city.

Or, it would, someday. In that sense, the size was very much aspirational.

It was not the weekend, so the dome was empty. Polister entered from an upper level door, hurried down the stairs and across the stage, which was lit spectacularly by the spotlights in the ceiling during services, but dark now. Likewise, the frescoes that ringed the back walls—depicting the Unital version of the Tribulations of the Five, among other faith-rooted historical events—were ordinarily illuminated from below by track lights.

From the other side of the stage he climbed halfway up to another door, which got him to a hall, at the end of which was his private office, which was in truth more like a library.

In the beginning—before Arigo Span went in a heretical (by Septal standards) direction—Unitism was just another Septal House variant. The religious texts that belonged to Arigo's House from that time remained in the possession of the eastern court after the Unital split. Back when Polister and the eastern court were seated in Dorabon, the volumes lived below, in the former House vault.

They didn't build a vault below the Wrimmad Holy Chamber. (Although they *did* build a number of tunnels, including a "secret" exit that Polister used from time-to-time, primarily for his personal amusement.) There seemed little reason to, since they'd surrendered most of the House's artifacts when they relocated... all except for the books, which were copies of similar books in other Septal temples. Nobody minded much that Polister kept them.

He pushed through the oak double doors—quite heavy, as they were designed to be impressive—and into the office, where he found two Septals. One was at a table in the corner, poring over one of the pre-Collapse volumes. The other was standing at the window that overlooked the city.

The one at the table *could* have been mistaken for Orno Linus. He was looking at the same volume the late professor had shown such interest in, on his last visit. But it wasn't him.

"Hello, Polister," the man said. "You look winded. Please tell me you didn't run all the way over."

"I'm getting old," Polister admitted. "I took the stairs through the dome because I was afraid of who I would find in here, and I wished to arrive as soon as possible to see if my fears were unfounded."

"And are they?"

"They are not. Take off the hood, Professor Magly; it doesn't suit you."

Chapter Three

It had been over a month since Battine Alconnot last stood on Middle Kingdom soil. She'd spent *all* of that time since, fleeing from location to location, as the avenues Damid insisted were safe quickly became otherwise, forcing them to adjust. Battine was, effectively, a passenger for all of it. Cargo, even.

This was just as well, because Battine was also overwhelmed, to a nearly paralyzing degree.

To begin, there was the small matter of her entire universe collapsing upon itself.

From the night of Kenson's murder, right through to the moment she plunged the tip of her sword through Vilto Alva's chest, Battine had been subsisting on a diet of rage. There was more vengeance to exact, certainly—there were the eight sovereigns who authored Kenson's execution—but one might as well wish violence upon the gods themselves. What she had *not* done, in that entire time, was sit still long enough for a true account of all she had lost. Kenson, yes, and Porra (although, in many ways, she was now *closer* to her sister than before,) but also her land, and titles, and the only *life* she'd ever known.

That she had to cope with all of that, while also traveling outside of the Middle Kingdoms for the first time in her life, was a cruel postscript.

As for the world outside the Kingdoms: it was larger than she imagined, and significantly *weirder* than she thought possible.

Battine's highborn education taught her fluency in Endish (the closest thing the outside world had to a common tongue) along with all she *thought* she needed to know about the countries where that language might be useful. But: still images of the great cities and their massive structures—the Tether of Velon, the Hall of Records in Fendo, the ancient stone temples of Dunn—turned out to be an inadequate substitute for *seeing* them. Images gave no sense of scale, not really, because the only thing to compare, say, the Hall of Records to, was the buildings around it, and there was nothing to compare *those* buildings to, other than people, which were *not* represented in the images in her study texts.

There were not—and she had to *leave* to fully appreciate this —a lot of *people* in the Middle Kingdoms. Not in comparison with virtually every other corner of the planet. In the cities of the world, she saw people living in hovels and vast mansions, in elevated structures that looked dangerously unstable, on water, in traveling caravans, and on the street. They were *all* crowded in together, everywhere, only some of the time even speaking the same language.

And the *smells*. No dry recitation of the grounding economic principles that drove world economies, or essay on the day-to-day life of the average fisher, or novel about the hardscrabble existence of a Punkoahn farmer, could have prepared Battine for the massive assault of alien odors that greeted her nose every time they left whatever temporary safety they'd managed to hole up in.

Some of the smells were wonderful—street foods she'd never tried before usually smelled fantastic, especially when she was hungry—but most were some unfortunate variant of body odor that she was evidently the only one to detect.

They began their flight to freedom by flying directly south in the late Kenson Alcon's royal aero-car, over and above the kingdoms of South Eloni and into Mursk. After taking the car down to street level, they drove to the capital city of Fendo, where they holed up in an apartment that belonged to one of Damid's family members.

Fendo was clean, loud and frantic, the apartment was smaller than her bedroom in the Delphina, and she'd never been so far from the ground before, including in airships. She had to stay away from the windows for the first two days, as it felt as if she was standing at the edge of a cliff.

Battine was just starting to get used to the city, when they learned the Middle Kingdoms had decided to make their alleged crimes public. Then they had to lean on some more friends of Damid's to smuggle them out of Fendo, and away from anyone related to him by blood.

Everything after that was a confusing blur. First, a commercial air flight to an island in the Midpoint Ocean, then a boat to Kindon and a hike on foot over the Deterrent Mountains. This was followed by a boat ride down the Moilen River into Velon, where they met up with someone Damid *thought* would be able to help them but—as was the case with every other stop along the way—could only provide short-term shelter. They fled the city almost immediately, traveling north to hide in the village surrounding Callim University. There, they met up with a professor of mathematics (who was also, quite obviously, an ex-lover) who let them stay in her guest bedroom long enough for them to book passage on a cross-current ship to Wrimmad City, on the island of Botzis.

As internationally known fugitives, it shouldn't have been possible for them to have made it nearly this far, or so Battine thought. In the Kingdoms, the fastest method of communication was *bells*, which were terrible at transmitting detailed information. Next was carrier pigeon, and the next after that was the fastest horse in the stable. In short, it was possible to stay ahead of word-of-mouth in the Kingdoms for a *while*.

But the rest of the planet had voicers, and the Stream, and *everyone* (seemingly) was plugged into it. There was no staying ahead of anything.

And yet, they'd still managed to evade capture.

She and Damid continued to wear the Septal robes whenever they went out in public, but it seemed ridiculous that these would work as a disguise anywhere outside of Temple Island. (They were even *marked* as robes belonging to adherents from Temple Island, which really should have caught somebody's eye.) The robes worked, it seemed, only because the House was in some way *more* intrinsic to the society outside of the Kingdoms than the one within.

Damid had secured Battine a voicer; when she wasn't suffering from periodic bouts of panic at the sheer business of everything around her, she'd found time to acquaint herself with the virtual world. She already knew, then, that their faces were all over the Stream. All it would take was for the wrong person to look closely at one of them. Septal hood or not, they couldn't keep hiding forever.

"**I**t's good to see you too," Damid said, taking down his hood. The old man in the white robe, whose office they invaded some six hours prior, shook his head and closed the door firmly behind him. He was a religious leader, but of a faith that made no real sense to Battine. His title was Staffer, which meant he was the one in possession of the staff of Pal.

She assumed this to be metaphorical; to her understanding of the faith of the Five, the staff of Pal was a *symbol*, not a real, physical object. Yet this man had, in his hand, a large metallic staff.

She would have found this more amusing had she not been

raised among people who thought themselves literal incarnations of the gods. But none of the sovereigns of Choruscam—Pal incarnates—walked around with a staff of their own. Nor did the kings of Paulus and Extum fight over who was in possession the *true* sword of Honus.

"Just this morning, the parliament agreed to honor the warrant for your arrest," Staffer Calidon said. "You are about to make me into a liar. You look tired."

"It's been a long couple of months," Damid said.

"I'm sure it has." Calidon walked over to Battine, who had not moved from the window.

There were two things she liked about the Septal robes. The first was that they hid identities well. The second was that they hid swords well.

She'd already pulled her arm from one of the sleeves. Should things go poorly in the next few minutes—should this old man cry out for help, and send guards running into the room—she would be ready, either to silence him or take on the guards, whichever it came to.

"You would be Battine Alconnot, yes?" the Staffer asked. "It's all right, you can take down your hood. I well know how uncomfortable those can be."

"It's Princess Alconnot, Lady Delphina," she said, taking off the hood with her free hand. "And yes."

"It's an honor to make your acquaintance," he said, bowing as deeply as his back allowed. "I imagine this has been a... *tremendous* culture shock for you."

She nodded back to the window. "This city of yours is not so terrible," she said. "Had we come here first I might have found it tolerable. There is scarcely any evidence of forbidden technology."

This was one of the things she found most interesting about the world at large: the technological gadgetry she'd been raised to hate (and to envy, although that wasn't *taught*, just learned,) was as miraculous as anticipated, but was also unevenly distributed in ways that made little sense. Economic disparity was a partial explanation, but setting that aside, there were places—like Kindon, and now Botzis—where the people were not, as a whole, *poorer* than inhabitants of other countries, who made an active choice to do without the technology nonetheless.

"We *do* enjoy our hardscrabble existence," Polister Calidon said. "Now I must apologize, princess. I'm about to be a terrible host."

He turned back to Damid. "You can't stay."

"Polister..."

"I've already told you: the parliamentary council has agreed to honor the warrant. If you *stay*, I'll be forced to hand you over to the board of legates for extradition."

"We'll be executed," Battine said.

"I know," Polister said, "which is why you should go before it comes to that."

"You're not a *member* of the parliament," Damid said.

"*I* am not, but Wrimmad City *is*," Polister said. "And that is where you're standing."

"No, I'm standing in a Unital Chamber," Damid said, "petitioning the Holy Staffer for sanctuary."

"Don't do that."

"Do I have to make it a *formal* petition?" Damid asked. "Should I get on one knee? I'm not sure how it's supposed to work."

"Damid..."

"We've run out of *options*, Polister. You're our last port in this storm."

"I understand, and I'm sorry," Polister said. "But I can't offer sanctuary. All I can give you is a head start."

Damid turned to Battine and said, in Falshen, "*Show him.*"

"*Are you sure?*" she asked.

"*It's the only thing that will make a difference.*"

Nodding, she took her hand off the sword hilt and pulled something else from beneath her robes: the key.

"I found what I was looking for, Polister," Damid said, switching back to Endish. "It's on Temple Island: pre-Collapse *cloning* technology. It's real. And they can't run their machine without this key. Do you understand? *This* is all they care about. As long as we have it... You see the stakes now? It's not just our lives; it's the life and *future* of everyone being exploited in the Kingdoms."

"Great Pal," Polister muttered.

"The gradual change we were hoping for isn't gradual any longer," Damid said. "But if you hand us over? They'll never stop."

Polister Calidon's eyes flitted between Damid Magly and the key in Battine's hand. He looked horrified. "You could have tossed that indestructible key of yours into the ocean," he said, addressing Battine. "Why keep it with you?"

"It's a gift from the gods," she said. "The bottom of the ocean is no home for it."

"We also don't know what else it opens," Damid added.

"Staffer Calidon," Battine said. "Why do you say it's indestructible?"

"Because, my dear, it's not the first such key I've laid eyes on," Polister said. "You both look hungry. Let's get some food, and then we'll talk some more."

Polister set them up (only for the night, he told himself,) in the guest quarters attached to his private demesne, and gave his service staff the same cover story they'd told to Dwerik: these were family friends of Polister's, hailing from the Septal House in Dinton. Given Dinton was located in a remote corner of northern Inimata, the chance that anyone in Botzis possessed the requisite information to credibly challenge such a claim was small.

After settling in, the three of them reconvened for dinner. Damid and the princess kept their hoods on for the meal, not because Polister didn't trust his people to keep a secret, but because he'd prefer not to implicate them in what could be a crime.

On that point, he wasn't entirely sure of the law.

Damid was correct: an asylum claim would override a legal warrant in most countries. The problem was that Wrimmad City wasn't technically a country. There was a widening groundswell of interest in having the entirety of the Botzis coastal settlements *declared* a country, but they were a very long way away from that happening. Meanwhile, most of the laws governing Wrimmad City were draped off property rights boilerplate and scribbled on napkins. The best outcome Polister could imagine, should he officially grant the fugitives Damid Magly and Battine Alconnot asylum, was that doing so would trigger the creation of a new law.

New laws took time to add to the record, and there was no guarantee the asylum-seekers triggering it would remain safe in the time it took to hammer one out. Given how desperate the Middle Kingdoms were to recover Damid and the princess—and their stolen artifact—the more likely outcome was that they'd be taken into custody, and the laws would be changed after the fact so that didn't happen again.

That was only one complication with extending asylum. The story they told was another.

"So I understand," Polister said, rubbing his temple, "you did *not* commit the murder for which you've been charged, but you *did* murder someone else?"

"We didn't kill Kenson Alcon," Damid confirmed.

"The other eight sovereigns did," Battine added. "It was a sanctioned execution. We have proof."

"Although it's in Eglinat," Damid said. "Don't suppose you can *read* that?"

"I can, actually," Polister said.

"Good," Battine said. "We will show it to you, and then perhaps you can tell us what they decided his crimes were."

"But—and I'm sorry, but I need for this to be perfectly clear—princess, you personally *slew* the High Hat of Temple Island," Polister said. "And if I'm understanding the familial relations correctly, this act was witnessed by your sister, the widow queen—is that what she's called now? The widow queen of Totus?"

"Porra was there. Yes."

"That isn't the important part of the story, Polister," Damid said.

"Murder's not *un*important, professor," Polister said. "I'm just wondering why the warrant is for the murder of a sovereign and the theft of an artifact, and *not* for the murder of a High Hat."

"I don't think they want to admit anything is wrong in the Great Temple," Damid said.

"They can't very well pretend she's not dead."

"They mean to reclaim their key first," Battine said. "If the sovereigns *truly* understand the consequences of its theft, it would only make sense to coordinate things in that way. Imagine, a new High Hat is named at the same time the royal lines stop producing blessed children."

"I think how it *looks* would be the least of their problems," Polister said.

"That's because you don't know my family. How it looks is *all* that matters."

"Very well," Polister said. "And now we've reached to part of your story that is by far the most preposterous."

"The cloning," Damid said.

"Yes. The cloning."

"Before I left," Damid said, "I had three possible explanations for the royal families in the Kingdoms. One: despite having some of the most backward medical practices on the planet, with access to no modern technologies, they figured out how to create perfect clones, by themselves, *thousands* of years ago. Considering we can't do this with *modern* technology, that just never made sense. Two: what they believed was happening actually *was* happening, and the gods were responsible. I'm not personally a man of great faith, but I like to think if I *were,* I would still consider this an unreasonable conclusion."

"It wasn't unreasonable," Battine Alconnot said, "for those of us raised on that belief."

"Understood," Damid allowed. "Three: it's all a lie. The royals aren't at all identical, and either the Middle Kingdoms are, as a whole, lying to the rest of the world about it, or—by ignoring the obvious differences—they're lying to themselves. Or makeup and wigs, I guess."

This elicited a laugh from Battine. "Really," she said.

"Check the Stream," Damid said. "I'm not the first to suggest it." He turned back to Polister. "What I didn't expect, was that all three were right. It *is* cloning, using—I *guess*—a machine built by the gods, to perpetuate a lie that all royals are just *born* that way."

"You guess?" Battine asked. "Who else do you imagine was responsible for the machine?"

"Just because don't know the answer to that," he said, "doesn't mean the gods *are* the answer."

"Princess, you have perhaps not yet learned that your companion is a noted atheist," Polister said.

"That's an oversimplification," Damid snapped. To Battine, he said, "I think the House's virtual monopoly on higher education has skewed our understanding of the world, in an unnecessarily religious direction. That's all. We can't be happy with 'the gods did it', but sometimes, that's what we settle for. My detractors have classified that as proof that I don't believe in *any* gods, which is not what I'm saying at all."

"Some might say, it's atheism by another name," Polister said.

"And you're a heretic, last I heard," Damid said.

"Gentlemen," Battine said, annoyed. "If you could set aside

the debate long enough to tell me if I have to find another place to sleep, come morning, I would appreciate it."

"I'm not prepared to offer long-term shelter, princess," Polister said. "Not until I know what you plan to *do* with that time."

"We have to get the story out," Damid said. "People need to know what's been going on under the Great Temple all these centuries. The truth is our only protection."

"Yes, I was afraid you would propose this," Polister said. "It brings us back to the agreed-upon observation that the entire thing is utterly preposterous. You have no *proof*, Damid."

"I have geotagged images, captured from beneath the temple," Damid said.

"Not enough. Not *close* to enough."

"It's enough to stall our extradition."

"Did the other places you sought refuge believe that?" Polister asked dryly.

"*They* would have been committing a crime by providing us with shelter," Damid said. "*You* are the head of a religious order, offering sanctuary."

"Please," Battine said quietly. "We need a week or two. *I* need a week or two. Just to find my balance."

Grumbling. Polister got to his feet, for a nice, long, ponderous stare out the window. He could see the harbor. It was not quite as good a view as that from the banquet room, but wasn't bad. The fishers were still coming in for the night, the lights on the top of their mainmasts creating the illusion of stars floating atop a dark sea.

I wonder if we're missing any more boats, he thought. As if that was his biggest concern in the moment. He turned back to face them.

"I can absolutely hide the two of you," he admitted. "Safely, possibly for as long as you *need*, provided you don't do something foolish on the Stream that tips your location to the authorities. *Morally*...? I don't know if I should."

"Once more, we will be *executed* if you turn us over," Battine said.

"That's not the moral quandary I'm grappling with, princess," Polister said. "That key of yours is the problem. I'm certain my grasp of internecine political machinations in the Middle Kingdoms isn't a match for yours, but my understanding is that the blessed birth, as a concept, is foundational to the authority of the royal houses. If you take that away...?"

"There will be rioting," Damid said. "Not immediately. Possibly not for a generation. But eventually."

"You're talking about destabilizing an entire region, Damid," Polister said. "With intent. This is *nine* countries. How many people die?"

"You would rather have a direct hand in the continued exploitation..."

"I didn't say that," Polister interrupted. "But there are ways to promote change gradually. That's what you and Kenson Alcon were attempting, was it not?"

"And they killed him for it," Damid said.

"The question is whether having a direct hand in what will be a violent upheaval is *more* immoral than supporting a morally wrong political system that will take four times as long to correct peacefully. I don't know the answer."

"Except it isn't your decision," Battine said. "It's mine. Mine and Porra's. We made it, a month ago, underneath the temple. *We're* going to see that it all comes down. Not you, and not Damid. If you cannot accept the choice we made, then I will take the key and move on. Alone, if I have to. Understand that I will turn myself over to them if they want my head; they'll not get back this key. I *will* throw it in the ocean if it comes to that."

To show how serious she was, she extracted an actual *sword* from underneath her robe.

Perhaps it was that she was royalty, or that she was—current demeanor notwithstanding—really very charming. Or perhaps it was that she accompanied Damid Magly, someone he trusted to carry the Calidon family seal. Whatever the reason, Polister had completely forgotten that a few minutes ago, she'd confessed to murder, and showed no evident regret for it.

Of *course* she had a sword.

"Well," Polister said, with a laugh that sounded more nervous than he wished. "Let's leave aside questions of relative morality for now. Damid, I leave in the morning for a bread-breaking with the Botzos in the midlands; canceling now would raise too many questions. I'll be gone for two weeks. You can both stay for at least that long. I suggest you remain in my chambers for the duration. Once I've returned, we can discuss what comes next."

"I'm going to need some electronics," Damid said.

"I can lend you a voicer."

"More than that. Polister, I don't want to impose for any longer than I have to, but my plan depends on my reaching out to friends, undetected. A simple voicer won't do it. Is there someplace in town where I can pick up the necessary components? We can pay."

Polister resisted the urge to ask *what* components, never mind what master plan Damid had concocted; he likely wouldn't know what to do with the former, and wouldn't necessarily approve of the latter.

"Make a list," Polister said. "Give it to Vendar. She's head of the household. If it's sold in Wrimmad City, she can find it."

"**D**id you mean that?" Damid asked Battine. This was later, after Polister walked them back to the guest rooms, and excused himself for the evening. The question came as soon as they were alone in the common room.

Or, presumed to be alone; Damid had switched to Falshen, either because it was a language Battine was more comfortable with, or because he was concerned about an unsanctioned set of ears.

"Did I mean what?" she asked.

"That you'd sooner throw the key into the ocean than let them have it back."

"I am surprised you have to ask," she said, taking off the Septal robe and stepping into one of the bedrooms. (There were two; Damid, thankfully, had not assumed he would be sharing her bed.) Beneath the robe was a light cotton outfit—she'd swapped out the riding leathers back in Mursk—with her sword and a heavy belt to hang it on.

"There are a couple of things you should know about that key," Damid said, leaning on the doorway, as she tossed the robe onto the bed and continued to get undressed. This place had a bath, with proper hot water, and she was going to make full use of it. "I probably should have told you before."

"Such as?"

"That it's one of only five in the world. One of the reasons for my visit was to figure out which of the kingdoms had a key, if any."

"To steal it?" she asked. "You lead a charmed existence, professor, that fate put you in a position to do just that."

"Not to *steal* it, no. Do you remember the friend I mentioned, the one who was killed? He had this theory, about stopping the end of the world."

Battine laughed. "Nothing serious."

"I know, it sounds off. Thing is, I sort of believed him. He needed all five keys, but couldn't be sure where they were. He thought it was *possible* there was one in the Middle Kingdoms, and knew I was planning a trip, so he asked me to look into it. That's all."

"And now you have that key."

"*We* have that key," he said.

"But your friend is dead," she said.

"That doesn't mean what he set in motion is dead. Orno Linus was a man of unique conviction. I know for a fact that I wasn't the only one convinced. There will be others, I'm saying, who'll want that key."

"Well, they can't have it," she said.

"Not even if it would mean stopping the end of the world?" he asked.

She'd spent *entirely* too much time with Damid Magly by then. More time than she ever wanted to spend with anyone, including her closest family. She knew how to tell when he was lying, when he was exaggerating, when he was saying something that *sounded* deadly serious, but which was not. Which was how she could tell that about *this*, in particular, he was absolutely, earnestly serious... despite the self-evidently absurd premise.

"You mean to stop the end of the world with a key," she said. "How?"

"*Five* keys, and I don't know," he said. "Look, what I'm saying is I *agree* with you; we can't let it go back to Temple Island. But we also can't throw it in the ocean. And I know this sounds *insane*, but it's possible that keeping it safe is critical for the future of all life on the planet."

"So, don't throw it into the occan."

"Please."

"All right."

"Thank you," he said, turning to leave before she was completely disrobed.

"Damid," she said. "What others?"

"Hm?"

"Who will come asking for the key?"

"I don't know," he said. "But I'm sure they're out there. Probably looking for us, just like everyone else."

Chapter Four

Trips to the midlands were for the young. Or, at the very least, the younger than Polister.

It had become a twice-annual ritual. This was his ninth trip, and—as was true every other time—he didn't enjoy it in the slightest. The problem was, he couldn't figure out how to get out of going without risking offense. So he went, and would probably continue to do so, until he was no longer able. But he didn't have to like it.

They traveled via horse, rather than using one of the more modern means available—a car, say—because the point of the trip was a peaceful sit-down, and the Botzos tribes tended to react poorly to advanced technology.

Why? Nobody knew for sure. The Botzos and the coastal settlers didn't share a common language, and remained insufficiently immersed in one another's cultures to permit full fluency on either side. This was a frustration for Polister in particular, as he prided himself on his familiarity with many tongues. But there was no way to learn Botzo without *living* with them for a period —there were no books to study, or language vids to stream—and he didn't have the time to commit to that.

Considering *where* the tribes lived, Polister probably wouldn't survive long enough to become fluent anyway.

What Polister had, instead of personal fluency, was a government linguist named Hio-ai, who was a member of Representative Dravian's staff. Hio-ai was a Ghon-Dikan who had been studying the Botzo tongue for well over a decade. This, somehow, did not translate into him being fluent; just a slightly better guesser.

Officially—according to maps the tribes likely had no say in—they crossed into Botzo tribal territory as soon as they reached the flatlands beyond Mount Vesay. It took a day and a half just to get that far. Then, it was another five days across largely undifferentiated desert, before they made it to the grassy plain called the midlands.

From an ambassadorial standpoint, the trip had only two entirely necessary members—Myala and Polister—plus the one semi-necessary translator. Everyone else was there solely to get them to the midlands and back without anybody dying from a lack of food, water or shelter. This year, that meant twelve additional people, plus all the horses.

If Wrimmad City had a military, they would probably serve as escort. Since they did not, Polister and Myala had to rely on volunteers from the constable's office, able-bodied private citizens who (for some reason) enjoyed hiking through the desert in their spare time, and a stable hand whose sole job was to make sure the horses, taken from the city's extremely limited local supply, all came back alive.

It was, to say the least, a hodgepodge collection of persons.

But, they made it to the midlands in good time, and good health. And, apparently, early.

～

"How long do we wait?" Myala Dravian asked, at the end of their first day of camp. They'd built a fire, which was no doubt visible for a dozen kalomaders in every direction. She and Polister were both sitting at it, keeping warm.

The desert got cold at night. It was something Polister knew to expect, but which nonetheless was always a surprise on the first night. This was the sixth; he was used to it now.

"We have an extra two days of provisions," he said. "any additional time beyond that, and we risk running out of water before reaching the city."

"One more day, then," she said. "To be safe. I'm relatively new to these sojourns, Polister. Is this as unusual as it feels?"

"They're typically waiting for *us*; yes, it's unusual."

The idea for the biannual summits had been his. It struck him during a conversation, some nine years past, with a city planner named Drolth. Drolth was discussing plans—distant future plans—to expand the footprint of Wrimmad City into something more than just a coastal settlement; a *country*, say, one that encompassed most if not all of Botzis. Drolth's concern, regarding obstacles to such an expansion, focused entirely on the other coastal settlements.

"What about the Botzo tribes?" Polister asked him. "They might want a word."

"The primitives?" Drolth replied, laughing. "Do they even *have* words? Why waste our time?"

In hindsight, Drolth's attitude toward the Botzos seemed terrifically narrow; racist, even. But that was how nearly everyone on the coast viewed them: primitive, savage, animalistic. Also, despite the Botzos very much sticking to the desert, to the extent that nobody Polister knew back then had even *seen* one, they were considered beings to be feared and defended against, not communicated with.

While he hardly had the time to spare—this was during the

construction of the Holy Chamber—Polister decided to find out what he could about the Botzos.

Unfortunately, it seemed nobody in Wrimmad City knew anything about them that wasn't couched in legend or mythology, so he didn't get far, at first. Then he was introduced to Martus and Palla Stromin, an Inimatan couple from Dongy.

The Stromins had managed to combine their two favorite pastimes—extreme hiking, and trade in exotic merchandise—into an exclusive "friendship" with one of the Botzo tribes. They gave the tribe dried meat and fish, and the tribe gave them intricately woven crafts. (In the latter case, the weaving was strictly function over form: a shirt; a saddle; a belt. The value for the Stromins was in the intricacy of the design, sure, but mostly it was about the provenance.)

Martus and Palla agreed to take Polister north with them on one of their extreme hikes, which was just a bad idea for everyone involved. He *survived*, but it would be a lie to say that he enjoyed any aspect of it. But, he did meet the hunting party the Stromins were doing business with, and was therefore able to confirm with his own eyes that these were not animal-like primitives unworthy of anything but disdain and/or fear.

The Botzos and the Stromins didn't communicate verbally at all—their trade agreements were conducted via gesture—but somehow, the fact that Polister Calidon was a religious leader of some import managed to be successfully conveyed.

Dop, the leader of the Botzo hunting party, eagerly communicated his wish that Polister return another time, to that very same spot, for reasons the language barrier prevented him from elaborating on with any success. The *time* was coordinated non-verbally as well. (It was this element of the exchange that convinced Polister, more than anything, that he was dealing with a complex, intelligent people.) Dop buried a stick in the ground, gestured to the suns and then to the twin shadows being cast. Then he knelt down, "pushed" the two shadows together, and made a mark in the sand close to the stick.

Polister didn't understand what he was being told, but the Stromins did. "He's asking you to return to this spot," Palla had explained, "when Dyhine and Hadrine cast a uniform shadow, and when that shadow's length at midday reaches the line he's drawn."

The Stromins helped him work out roughly when that would be —it happened twice a year—and brought him back to the spot at the appointed time. For this second trip, Polister took a small retinue, some tents, and horses, because he had no intention of traveling on foot and sleeping under the stars a second time. He also—because he felt certain this was going to end up being an important meeting— didn't want to look and feel his absolute worst once they arrived.

He was right, because it was on the return visit that he first met Elder Ko.

Polister returned to the same spot twice yearly since, bringing with him a range of dignitaries eager to meet with the leader of the Botzos. They were typically disappointed to discover that there was almost never anything new to "discuss." Polister had learned about a hundred Botzo words, and Ko perhaps a hundred in the common tongue, so between them and without a translator, they could exchange pleasantries for roughly ninety seconds.

What, then, was the point? Polister had been asked, on a number of occasions. The point was, as long as Polister and Ko met, smiled, shook hands, and talked about the weather, the coastal villages and the inland tribes were at peace.

Which was why one party *not* showing up at the meeting place was a subject of concern.

"Should we be worried?" Myala asked, after a while.

"I don't know," Polister admitted. "Possibly."

Polister and Myala eventually retired to their respective tents for the night, with Polister instructing one of the constables —asking, really, since he had no formal authority over him—to keep the fire going through the night, as a beacon for their Botzo friends. The constable, no doubt imagining the potential horror of being the only one awake when the party was beset upon by a tribe of "savages" took this request about as well as he could, and then asked three others to stay up with him.

It was the same constable who woke Polister at sunrise.

"They're here," he said.

Polister rose and stumbled out of the tent, thankful, in that moment, that he traveled everywhere with the staff of Pal, as it made for an excellent walking stick. This was especially useful when one's left leg didn't feel like responding as quickly as one's right leg, first thing in the morning.

Elder Ko and his small band of Botzo tribespersons were standing at the edge of the camp, looking as if they'd always been there, just waiting for someone to acknowledge them.

The Botzos wore loosely woven robes and tunics, were always barefoot despite the heat of the sand, and carried sharp sticks. They wore their hair short and tied back, and scarred their faces intentionally with thin lines beneath the eyes. (There was a symbolism to the scarring at play, but Polister couldn't figure it out, and hadn't worked out the best way to ask politely.) He'd never met a Botzo who was too young, too old, or too sick to travel, and could only infer their existence. The ones he *had* met were all of the same basic body type: terribly thin but muscular, unnervingly still, and entirely unbothered by the heat (or cold) of the desert, or the harsh light from the suns.

On this day, there were seven of them—four men and three women—plus Ko. Of the seven, Polister thought three looked familiar, but as he'd never been officially introduced to any of them, he couldn't say for sure.

Ko stood out as different from the rest in a number of ways. He was dressed much the same, but was obviously older. His hair was white, grown long and tied up and away from his neck in an elaborate knot. The robe he wore was more ornate, with sewn-in whorls of brown and yellow and a touch of blue, like cresting waves. As with Polister, Ko was the only member of his party carrying a staff. His was made of twisted wood, with an elegantly carved head whose precise shape—it looked like an uneven mountaintop with jagged runnels—clearly represented something important to the Botzos. Polister didn't know what.

"Staffer Calidon," Ko greeted, bowing deeply.

Polister shuffled to the edge of the campground and returned the bow. "Elder Ko," he said.

What usually followed was an exchange of foodstuff. Back at their first meeting together, Polister brought dried fish for trade, just as the Stromins had done. Elder Ko, clearly not expecting a barter, responded in kind by offering some dried meat he happened to have on hand. (It was goat, and it was terrible.) They continued to adhere to this ritual in honor of that initial encounter, even though there was no larger meaning to it.

In his rush to get outside, Polister had left the tent without his dried fish. Ko's hands were also empty, but ritual was ritual; they made the gestures they usually made—dramatically lowering their prize to the desert floor—only empty-handed, before proceeding.

"Are you well?" Polister asked. He pointed at the suns and the shadows. "You are late."

"We are late," Ko agreed. "We are sorry."

Myala, who had no doubt been stirred from her tent shortly after Polister, came up behind him to quietly ask, "Did I miss anything? Did you exchange the food?"

"It's fine," Polister said. "We're fine."

"Where's Hio-ai?" she asked, looking around. She turned to the nearest constable. "Get Hio-ai here."

Ko stepped forward and held out his hand for Polister to take, which he did. "Staffer Calidon, time is now," he said, gripping Polister's hand tightly. "Very danger."

"Time is now?" Polister repeated. "Time is now for what, Elder Ko?"

"Is now time," Ko said. "Black waters rise."

"Very danger?"

Ko nodded, and let go of Polister's hand. Then he pointed in the direction of the coast and said, "Danger." Then he pointed toward the plains from which he had come, and said, "Safe."

"You don't like the ocean," Polister said. "The water. I know this."

It was a long-established truth and an impenetrable mystery: the Botzos lived on an island, yet refused to go near the shore. Whenever anyone asked *why*, if they got an answer at all, that answer was: water unsafe; desert safe. Nobody had ever gotten a Botzo to elaborate.

"Black waters rise" was something new.

It seemed Polister was missing something, as Ko had begun shaking his head. "Danger," he repeated. "Danger for Ko. Danger for Calidon. Time is now."

Hio-ai, still belting his trousers, arrived at the meeting. "What have I missed?" he asked Myala.

To Ko, Polister repeated, "Danger for Calidon. You think *I'm* in danger."

"All," Ko said, waving his staff in the air. It could mean *all of you here*, or *everyone on the coast*.

"Is he threatening us?" one of the constables asked.

"Don't be an idiot," Myala hissed. "Hio-ai, ask Elder Ko what he means."

Hio-ai stepped forward. Ko changed his stance somewhat; he and Hio-ai had met before, and while it was likely the young translator didn't know Ko well enough to recognize this, Polister could tell the Elder had little patience for him.

70

Hio-ai said something in the Botzo tongue. Ko listened, wearing an expression between confused and amused. The tribespeople behind him looked perplexed. One seemed about to laugh.

After Hio-ai finished, Ko responded. The sounds seemed essentially the same to Polister; he couldn't tell what Hio-ai was getting wrong that the others found so amusing.

"He's saying you're in danger," Hio-ai said.

"I think we already got that," Polister said.

"And... and there's more. Hang on."

Hio-ai repeated something to Ko, for clarification.

"What *kind* of danger, Hio-ai?" Myala asked. She sounded nervous.

"He wants Staffer Calidon to come with him," Hio-ai said. "Because of the danger."

"*Just* me?" Polister asked.

"What is this danger?" Myala repeated. "What does he think is wrong?"

"'Black waters rise,'" Polister said.

Ko nodded. "Black waters rise," he repeated.

"Well that's simply not helpful," Myala said. "I know they don't like the ocean, but... and *why* only you?"

Elder Ko, frustrated, stepped forward and delivered a lengthy soliloquy that nobody on the coastal side of the conference understood. He gestured grandly, pointed with his staff, stomped the ground, and carved symbols in the sand. He spoke faster, and with greater agitation than Polister had ever seen before from him. After he was finished, all he'd managed to make clear, really, was that he considered the matter to be urgent.

Polister picked up only four words out of the monologue: ocean, time, old, and now.

"Did you get all that?" Myala asked.

"I got some of it," Hio-ai said. He'd captured everything Ko said in a function on his voicer, and was now playing it back. "Many years back was a... um. Word I don't know. Large animal?

Or shadow. Could be shadow." He stopped and restarted the audio. "Shadow, sky, desert safe, water unsafe... hang on. Yes, that's the word for..."

He stopped the audio and asked Ko another question. Ko nodded.

"Whatever he's talking about happened a long time ago," Hio-ai said. "I don't know why he's bringing it up now."

"Ko," Polister said. Then he switched to the Botzo tongue, and said, "*time, now?*"

Very excited to be understood, Ko nodded vigorously, and repeated the words, in the common tongue. "Now is time."

"I think what he's saying is that whatever happened a long time ago is happening again," Polister said.

"Polister," Myala said, "they don't have books. Or a written language. I'm not sure they even conceive of *time* the same way we do. How could they possibly know this?"

"I'll ask," Hio-ai said. He switched to Botzo. Ko listened carefully, nodded, and replied.

"I'm sure I have this wrong," Hio-ai said, "but I *think* he said 'the wisdom of sand.'"

"Come, Polister Calidon," Elder Ko said, gesturing at Polister to go with him. "Time now."

Polister turned away from Ko to speak privately with Myala. "The only chance I have of understanding what he's trying to convey, is by going with him," he said.

"You're not thinking of *doing* it, are you?" she asked.

"I trust him."

"That isn't the issue. It's... yes, it's part of the issue; *I* wouldn't trust any of them to keep me safe, but I don't know them like you do. The issue is that you don't have nearly enough of what you need to stay alive in the desert for more than five days. They don't even ride *horses*, Polister."

"It would be a wonderful opportunity, though, you have to admit," he said. "Nobody from the coast has ever been invited to see how they live. Not even the Stromins. I don't know why he's fixated on saving only *me*, but I would love to understand why he believes he needs to, and I don't think I'll be in any danger. We may never get another invitation."

"Polister, you can't," she said. "You *know* you can't. Not right now."

He was sure she was wrong; his duties as head of the Unital faith could be handled by administrators until his return, he had other oath-bound under-Staffers who could care for the weekend services—they already did the bulk of it—and the parliament would be fine if he missed one or two meetings. (They *were* professional diplomats, after all.) As long as Myala returned safely to convey his wishes, it would be fine.

But then, there was his houseguests. He couldn't pass *them* off to anyone.

This is another one you will owe me, Damid, he thought.

"You're right, Myala," he said, grudgingly. "Not today." He turned back to Elder Ko. "Ko, I will go with you. But not today. Later."

"Today," Ko said.

"*Not* today."

Hio-ai said something that was probably "not today, but later," in Botzo. He evidently did this well enough to be understood without getting laughed at.

"Later," Ko repeated. "Not today." He looked very disappointed.

"I will go back," Polister said. "Make plan. *Next* time, I will go with you."

Hio-ai translated. Ko was shaking his head before the translation was complete. "Next time, not right," Ko said. "Next time, not..." flummoxed, he said the rest of it in his own language.

"Next time will be too late," Hio-ai translated.

"Too late," Ko agreed. "Wrong time. Right time now."

Then, the most peculiar thing happened: the tribespeople

behind Ko raised their sharpened sticks in an intentionally threatening manner. It seemed Ko was going to insist.

The team responsible for safeguarding Polister and Myala reacted in kind, drawing their projectile guns.

"Wait!" Polister said, to his own side. "Everyone, calm down."

He stepped forward, to meet Ko in the middle of what was about to become a battlefield. (More likely, a slaughter, unless there was something about Botzo combat acumen of which Polister was unaware.) "Ko," he said. "How do you know this?"

Ko repeated the phrase he'd used earlier, the one Hio-ai translated as "wisdom of sand."

"A prophesy, then," Polister offered. Ko didn't know what that meant. Hio-ai—who was keeping his distance, but listening—said something in Botzo that was hopefully close. Ko nodded cautiously.

"Your god, god of Botzos, says I must go with you?" Polister asked.

"Yes, yes," Ko said. "Polister Calidon *will* come with us. It is said."

"It is true, if I go with you now or if I go with you later. Your god says."

"Yes."

"I will go later. *Not* now. I will come back here. Later. To go with you."

"Later," Ko said. He was getting it. "God says you will, and you will. Before next time."

"If it is to be, it will be," Polister said.

"Yes."

Ko turned around and said something to the rest of the tribespeople. They lowered their sharpened sticks and stepped back. Polister exhaled.

Elder Ko turned back around. "We will wait," he said.

"Uh, wait here?" *Here* was, again, in the middle of a grassy plain, with no shelter. They had no food or water, and all evidence indicated they'd walked there.

"One will be here. For when Staffer Calidon is here."

"I understand."

"Do not be long." Ko extended a hand, and he and Polister shook on it. Then they parted, and returned to their separate sides.

"Polister," Myala said, as soon as they were out of earshot. "Did you just agree to go home and *pack*?"

"I think I may have," he said. "It's okay; as long as I come back here before the next scheduled trip, I'm within the terms."

She looked back over her shoulder at the Botzos, and their sharpened sticks. "You're sure about that?"

Chapter Five

Battine could only handle the safe seclusion of Staffer Calidon's private wing for so long.

At first, the sudden lack of haste in her life—no more absconding from one provisionally safe remove to another every few days—meant she could catch up on sorely needed sleep, and to do all the crying she'd been putting off since the day of Kenson's murder.

Well-rested and all cried out, she then haunted Polister Calidon's library, leafing through obscure Eglinat texts she could only sometimes read. At the end of the day, she ate large portions of passably good meals dominated by seafood, which was a new experience. (There was very little seafood to be had in Totus.)

It wasn't a terrible existence. Nor was it terribly uncomfortable; her hood could stay down as long as she was alone, or with Damid, which was most of the time.

No, not terrible at all. Just very, very boring.

Something she was only now learning about herself, was that she was unaccustomed to not being around *people* semi-regularly. Growing up, it seemed as if she was *often* alone, but that was only true if one didn't count the servants. Yes, she might go hours without seeing a fellow royal, but perhaps no more than minutes without a maid, manservant, cook, or castle guard nearby.

Since then, she had often found herself legitimately alone, but up until they reached Wrimmad City, she'd been too busy experiencing some combination of anxiety, sadness and fury to meditate on the impact of the isolation to her psyche.

Now that she *had* that time for self-reflection—now that there was no *next step* to be preoccupied with—she realized that she *hated* being alone, quite a lot.

And so, a mere nine days after they settled into Calidon's guest rooms, Battine was wandering the streets of another strange city, in her stolen Septal robes.

This was entirely against the advice of Damid Magly.

"You're exposing yourself unnecessarily," he said. "And by doing that, you're also exposing *me*."

He promised, again, that he was working on a solution to their fugitive problem. It was a promise he'd been making since they first escaped the Middle Kingdoms. His explanation of *how* he'd be doing this remained lacking.

There was a list of electronics that Damid claimed to need, and which Staffer Calidon's household head was working to obtain. Vendar seemed deeply conflicted about this, asking on multiple occasions whether any of the components were illegal, and not entirely satisfied by Damid's reassurances. (It probably didn't help that he instructed her not to buy all of them from the same shop.)

Once he'd gotten everything, Damid would be able to communicate safely with various like-minded cohorts, without directly leveraging the Stream. Or so he claimed.

What was *lacking*, was how this communication was going to help. Every time she asked for details on this part of his plan, he averred, until she gave up asking.

"I will be careful not to expose us both," she insisted. "I just can't stay here all day, every day. The hood will stay up."

"What about the sword?" he asked. "It's not as unobvious as you think. And the key?"

"I need the sword to defend myself from anyone seeking the key," she said.

He laughed. "If you're willing to go out with *neither*, I'll withdraw my objection."

"Very well," she said.

"Really? You'll part with the key?"

"You're right; it will be safer if it stays here, and the sword *will* draw attention. I'm sure I will be safe enough in this city unarmed."

Damid looked like he was anticipating her *handing over* the key and the sword, which wasn't going to happen. Instead, Battine went into her room and made a show of putting them inside one the cabinets, and locking it.

She *did* put the sword in there, but the *key* she hid in the mattress bedsprings, a last-minute decision borne of the discovery that she was no longer certain she could trust Damid Magly.

Thus began the next phase in Battine Alconnot's life.

Hardly anybody in the Middle Kingdoms made their living on the water. They were a self-sustaining agrarian culture, with limited trade agreements to their north (Punkoah) and south (Mursk and Wivvol.) If they wanted fish—and the royal houses often *did* want fish, specifically because it was *not* commonplace— they traded for it.

It was Battine's understanding that their coastal waters—the Norton to the west and the Midpoint to the east—were unkind to fishing boats, but she didn't know if that was *true*, or just a nice way of saying that people who grew up farming were bad at building boats and catching fish.

All of which was to say that, in her interest in exploring something *new*, she was naturally drawn to the harbor. The entirety of Wrimmad City was built off of the fishing economy—she could go to virtually any part of town to witness something new—but the harbor was the center of it all.

Every morning since that first day, Battine would rise early to eat whatever there was to eat (Unitals were not ascetics; the food was good, and plentiful,) put on her Septal robe, and wander down the hill to the harbor, to see what new boats were coming in and going out.

Sometimes, it was just one or two. Sometimes, it was seven or eight. Very occasionally, *no* boats came through at all. But, irrespective of the traffic on the water, on the docks it was *always* busy.

There were men (and some women, but mostly men) whose job it was to walk along the pier and shout, all day long: *this* boat should get a move on, *that* one needs to get their mooring lines sorted before the godsdamn suns set, and *you*, over there, what make you think you can unload *there*, no, no, no, you need to carry that shit up the pier and unload it *there*, and no I don't *care* who you work for.

The shouters were in the employ of the harbormaster—dock barkers, was what everyone called them—but they carried no mark of office; the entire weight of their authority rested in having a loud, booming voice, and a talent for clever profanity. And it worked. Everyone *argued* with them, but eventually did what they were told, with only occasional breakouts of violence.

Battine found them endlessly fascinating.

Then there was the mayhem of the fish market. Roughly one third of the boats leaving the harbor were going out with holds full of fish—salted, on ice, or a combination of both—bound for overseas ports in Geo, Unak, North or South Eloni. (She wondered if the port of Orch, in the Kingdoms, was one of the destinations, but knew better than to ask.) Most of the time, the fish going *out* was bought at the market on the same day it was brought in by one of the fishing boats... which at first seemed like a terrible waste of time: why not have the fishing boats fills their holds and just keep sailing until they reached whatever distant land was running low on seafood?

This was naïve, only it took her time to appreciate that. (She blamed her upbringing for her lack of familiarity with merchant capitalism.) The fish merchants had clients demanding specific fish, whereas the fishers came back with whatever they happened to have caught. It was no more possible to fish to a list than it was to hunt to one.

The Wrimmad fish market—where those merchants filled their list—was structured chaos. It was an open-air marketplace, with raised wooden troughs filled with ice. The fish would come off the ships, go into the ice, and get bought by whomever happened by. The haggling was constant, the noise—despite a lack of a roof and walls—oppressive, and the meaningful gesticulation captivating. (There was a merchant-specific sign language, for when buyers and sellers wanted to negotiate but couldn't be heard over the din. She'd spent days just watching this, trying to learn some of it, but so far it remained inscrutable.)

The last land-based component of the dockside ecosystem was the oceanside pubs. Once the fishing boats were moored and the holds emptied, the crew was discharged, free to wander about on land until their next engagement. The fishers—male, female, and non-binary—were all shapes, sizes and ages, but smelled approximately the same, which was: bad. Some had been at sea for only a day or two, many a week or longer. None had bathed, and all had spent the bulk of their time near fish in various stages of death.

Every vessel, on arrival, disgorged a miniature invasion of thirsty, hungry, overtired, malodorous, recently-paid fishers, looking to spend a decent share of their fresh coin in the first establishment that would have them. The pubs were there to answer that demand.

When Battine wasn't lingering at the edge of the docks, or the fish market, she was in the back of one of those pubs, watching and listening.

Everybody there had complaints, about which they were quite vocal, but what she found interesting was that none of them hated the *work*. The complaints had to do with the difference between the average fisher's ideal tour—perfect weather, massive haul, competent coworkers, graceful captain, and a good, sturdy, vessel—and how their latest trip failed to live up to that standard.

About half the stories she heard made her glad that she would never have to fish the ocean for a living. The other half left her wanting to know if she was up to it.

The idea was to stick to the shadows, watch and learn, and not engage. It was a fine plan, that worked perfectly well in every place she'd spent time in prior to Wrimmad City, because people tended to leave Septals well enough alone. But in all those prior instances, she wasn't spending so much time in the *same place*.

After a couple of weeks of lurking, the capacity of the locals to ignore her presence reached some sort of tipping point.

"You like to watch, don'tcha?"

By the time the dock worker named Frake took it upon himself to engage in a formal introduction, Battine had already created a new name for herself: Sister Orean.

Borrowing the name of the Totus castle serving girl who had saved Battine's life was not a fully intentional act on her part. What happened was, a young girl named Lenaia had approached her for advice and Battine, unwilling to act rudely, listened to the girl's story. After offering the girl solid, if anodyne advice, Lenaia asked for the "good sister's" name, and Orean was what came out.

Now, she was Sister Orean of the pier.

Lenaia wasn't the only one who came to Battine for advice.

She wasn't even the first; just the first to ask for a name other than "sister." It was all fairly awkward, because Batt didn't consider herself qualified to administer advice of any kind. She was not a House-trained scholar, nor had she lived a life that was remotely similar to anything the people of the dock could have related to, and she didn't think of herself as particularly wise.

She was, however, *educated* in a way few had been. She'd read the great philosophers, and the great poets, and (up to a point) the great scientists. There was a marvelous aggregation of *information* in her head, in short, and what she found was, parroting some of that information back as advice approximated true wisdom.

It had gotten to the point where she could expect a request for counsel three or four times a day. This was about three or four times too many, and if Batt were smart she'd stop going to the docks precisely *because* of it. But it was nice to draw interest for reasons unrelated to her title or her impending descent into the bosom of the Outcast. She didn't want to give that up.

"I suppose I do like to watch, yes," she said.

She was at a back table in a pub called the *Gray Gust*, sipping from a mug of ale and chewing on a bowl of salted, fried animal skins. (She didn't know which animal, and was afraid to ask.) Ten minutes earlier, she'd been in quiet conversation at the same table with an off-shift barmaid named Ulah-han, about Ulah-han's recalcitrant brother.

"And talk," the man added, sound vaguely accusatory. He was standing at the opposite end of the table; she couldn't ignore him, and there was no clean access to an exit. The only way out of the conversation was through it.

"And talk," she agreed. "Is there something I can help you with?"

Battine had seen him before, a few times; he worked the docks as one of the many scurrying everypersons, either employed by the harbormaster's office, or by one of the fishing fleet owners. He was too old and slight and soft of speech to be a dock barker, but was usually nearby to administrate a barker's commands. He walked with a limp and had only one eye, and now that he was standing in front of her, she noticed he was also missing two fingers on his right hand.

"Oh, yeah," he nodded, ignoring the question but having a seat nonetheless. "Up and down the pier, all morning, every day. You're a curious one. Thinking at first, you maybe were waiting on someone. Old friend, relative, lover, someone comin' off a boat, sure. But nah. Just curious, you are. You're not from here."

Battine had a working knowledge of the current state of the House temple in Wrimmad City. She knew they were underpopulated, and that local recruiting was an issue. But there *were* other Septals, *real* Septals, in the city. She saw two or three a day. She avoided them, because the last thing she could afford was to have one of them realize they'd never seen her in the temple. But they were around.

"How many locals do you know, who've taken the oath?" she asked.

"I've heard tell one or two," he said. "But I get your point. A lot of us hold the faith, sure, but not the lifestyle. You're *all* from elsewhere. But most hooded come around here to talk to us about this and that. Not you."

"My interests don't include proselytizing," she said.

"All the talking you've been doing, and you're not here to preach? You dress like a fundie. Are you a fundie?"

"Am I...?"

"A fundie. A fundamentalist sort. Most of the Seppies from the temple wear a hood, but go casual with the clothes."

"No," she said, smiling. "It's a...personal preference, to dress in the robes."

He nodded. "I'm glad. Met a few'a those Punkos from upshore, and... you ever spent time with someone what's convinced *you're* going to the Depths just for being not them? It's a weight."

She laughed. "Actually, yes. I know exactly what that's like."

He extended a two-fingered hand. "Name's Frake. And you're Orean, yeah?"

She shook his hand. "I am," she said. "And now I'm wondering if you already knew the answers to your questions."

"May be. Not much on the pier I don't already know, and *most* of what I don't is sittin' opposite me right now."

She was warming up to Frake. He was abrasive, and had an aggressive conversational style that was, perhaps, intended to keep her off-balance, but that only meant he was shrewd.

"You know my name is Sister Orean," she said, "and you know I'm not a fundamentalist. You *also* know I'm not preaching. All I *am* doing, is answering requests for guidance, when I can."

"And watching," he said.

"Yes. And watching. You know all of this; what's left?"

"I also know Sister Orean isn't boarding at the House temple. I *think* if I were to ask one of them that *do* live there, they'd say they don't know anyone named Orean."

Then again, there was such a thing as *too* shrewd. "I'm a guest of the Unital Court," she said.

"One who avoids the local Seppies as much as she can," he said. "I've seen. Why's that?"

"I'm afraid my reason for doing so is private, Frake. Allow me *some* secrets."

"I will. But only if you answer a *different* question, sister. What are you looking for?"

"Nothing particular," she admitted. "I'm following my curiosity."

"We're all *that* interesting to you?"

"Very much so," she said. "I'm fascinated by ways of living outside of that to which I've grown accustomed. My interest is...sociological."

"Where you're from, they don't have a pier?" he asked. Going fishing, appropriately enough, for more answers.

She smiled. "*Some* secrets, Mister Frake," she said.

"No 'mister.' Just Frake. Well, all right. Here's where I can be of service to you, because as it happens, I know my way 'round most of these specimens here. Unless you're looking to study *me*, in which case you'll lose your curiosity right off."

"You've already proven more interesting than most."

"Then you're terribly lost, sister. Now I *have* to help. I'll give you a taste: see the fella in the corner there, with the pelican tattoo? Name's Verigo, but we call him One-Ball. Would you care to know why we call him that?"

"Is it... does he only have..."

"One testicle, yes ma'am. Wasn't born that way, neither. Wanna hear the story of how he lost the other one?"

She smiled. "Why yes, I think I do."

Thanks to Frake, within only a couple of weeks, Battine was on a first name basis with seemingly the entire dockside community. Every time a new boat came in, Frake was there introducing her to someone new and interesting, and because he found *her* interesting, they did too.

It was all incredibly dangerous. Her initial impulse to seek out interesting people in interesting places, and to study them from a safe remove, wasn't a terrible one, provided she kept to the shadows. But now that she was almost entirely out in the open—the only thing she hadn't done was take her hood down—she was just *asking* to be discovered. All it would take would be for one of her new friends to connect Sister Orean to the fugitive Lady Delphina, and she (and Damid, and possibly Polister Calidon) would be in a fair amount of trouble.

On the other hand, it had been more than a month. Polister had long returned from his fourteen days in the desert—with fascinating stories of desert tribes—and had neither kicked them to the street nor announced their presence in a declaration of sanctuary. He and Damid *argued* about it often, but there seemed little risk of their host altering the dynamic meaningfully.

Battine felt as safe as she had in ages. Not safe enough to confess her identity to Frake or any of her other new friends, but maybe that day wasn't too far off.

Because maybe, just maybe, there wasn't anyone looking for her anymore.

Chapter Six

"I think it's coming back around again," Elicasta said, her tone betraying an elevated concern regarding this point.

"It's just a whale," Makk said.

He didn't know this for sure, because he'd never seen a whale up close. Neither had Elicasta, but since she had a world of knowledge attached to her *head*, she was far better informed.

"Whales don't do a lot of *circling*, Makk. That's there is predator behavior. That's stalking."

"Then it's a whale that's trying to mate with the ship," he said.

She made a hand gesture Makk was familiar with by now, a roll of her wrist that would be a head shake or an eye roll for someone who wasn't busy keeping a Streamer rig trained in one direction. *You're wrong*, the gesture meant, *and I'm disappointed in you in some way I'm not vocalizing right now.*

They were aboard the *Colusm*, a decently large steel-sided freighter, whose ultimate destination was a port in Lladn. The most direct route to Lladn was to cut across the north-to-south portion of the Great Current, past the southern end of Botzis, and along a northeastern route through the Norton Ocean.

The reason he and Elicasta were aboard, was that the *Colusm* had a planned stopover at the Botzis port of Dongy. Dongy was about thirty kalos from Wrimmad City, overland. The plan was for Makk and Elicasta to disembark there, and then find a way to reach their destination via some other means.

The last part was always, in his mind, the most difficult portion of this trip; he didn't know how easy it was to get from one Botzis city-state to another, but had a feeling they wouldn't be able to just hire a cab. There were, he was told, cars in some parts of Botzis, but not in the part they were going to. And aero-cars were entirely absent.

This was all based on information Elicasta provided, which was admittedly "spotty."

"The islanders don't Stream," she explained. "All I'm riding is third-hand UnVeeser vacay feeds."

Figuring out a quiet way from Dongy to Wrimmad City was no longer Makk's chief concern, though. *Now*, he was worried they wouldn't even reach Botzis.

The *Colusm* was their best option at the time. Yes, the freighter wasn't stopping *at* Wrimmad City, it didn't feature guest accommodations—they slept on bunks in the ship's hold— and the provided meals were of a quality that made Makk think fondly of his army diet. All good reasons not to go anywhere near the ship.

The problem was, hardly anyone *went* to Botzis. The only passenger ship that visited regularly (the one that *might* have taken Magly and Alconnot there) wouldn't be back at Oldhasken for another six weeks. That left the freighters, except most of *them* didn't go to the island either, because there just wasn't a lot of trade with Botzis, outside of fish and tourists. So when he and Elicasta saw the travel itinerary the *Colusm* filed with the harbor office—available to anyone in Oldhasken for a price—they knew they had to be aboard that ship.

They approached the captain first. Captain Selis was a thick-set woman with a northern Inimatan accent and leather for skin, who had zero interest in earning extra coin to take on a couple of passengers. When she proved immune to both reason and ever-larger quantities of C-Coin, they sought out the ship's owner.

He was perfectly happy to take their coin.

This made Selis deeply unhappy, which was an unfortunate byproduct, given how long they'd be spending a lot of time with her, but there wasn't much to be done. They *were* trying to save the world and all; may as well cut some corners and offend some people along the way.

There was another option, which Makk kept thinking back to as he stood at the rail of the *Colusm*, a good fifteen maders above the water. They could have dropped roughly the same amount of coin on a private charter. The problem there, was that the private boats-for-hire were really meant for travel along the coast, and not the open ocean. Sure, they could *do* it, but it wouldn't be a pleasant crossing. And, crucially, Makk would be about one mader from the water, rather than fifteen. That was too close for him, giant sea creature or not.

Given a second chance to make the decision that led him to this moment, he probably would have elected to accompany Viselle, Dorn and Xto to Pethis instead. *They* caught a passenger ship that left two days after the meeting in the *Nighdemon's Last*, and had already arrived in Pethis.

Sure, it would have been the wrong call: two days into their sea voyage aboard the *Colusm*, Makk received a direct from Viselle that read, *no Magly in Pethis*, followed by, *possible lead on another key, going silent for now*. But at least Makk would now be standing on dry land, instead of in the middle of the ocean, pondering the existence of sea monsters.

I t was difficult to get a decent idea of the shape and size of the thing in the water. At times, it seemed longer and wider than the ship itself. Other times, Makk got the impression that what he was looking at was mostly shadow, and the beast wasn't nearly as big.

Whatever it was, however *large* it was, it had been traveling near the *Colusm*—before it, behind it, beside it, beneath it—for more than an hour now. Even the crew looked nervous, which would surely not be the case if, as Makk wanted to believe, this really was just a whale in a mood.

He and Elicasta were standing at the prow of the ship, which was an optimal viewing position for when the creature got ahead of them, turned, and steered into a collision course. If it did the same thing again as it had the last two times, it would veer off at the last second, circle around behind the ship and come up on the other side. In case it *didn't* do this—if it decided *this* time it was going to *ram* the ship—Makk already knew where the nearest lifeboats and floatation vests were located. It seemed like relevant information.

"Maybe we shouldn't be standing *right here* for this," Makk suggested, for not the first time.

"Best angle," Elicasta said, tapping her rig.

"Can't you use a drone? Say, from the safety of the bridge?"

"Doesn't play the same. The lived up-close is the meat."

"Sure, until that thing decides *not* to turn away," he said.

"You want to shelter up, go," she said. "I'll be fine."

This was an obvious trap; he wasn't going to fall for it. Besides, by then it was too late to find a safer place to stand, as the creature was upon them.

Makk put both hands on the railing and braced for an impact that didn't happen: once more, the thing in the water shifted off-angle, and let the *Colusm* slide past.

Makk exhaled and wondered, again, if that was the end of it.

I'm not that lucky, he thought. *I'm* never *that lucky.*

His eyes drifted upward, to the freighter's elevated bridge. Captain Selis and her helmsperson were the only ones up there. Selis had binoculars trained on the stern.

"I think it's time we asked the captain what that thing is," he said. "Don't you? Besides, the view from there has to be pretty good."

"She hates us," Elicasta said.

"I'm a cop and a *Cholem*. I'm used to being hated. Point is, I don't know what it is, *you* don't know what it is, and the *Stream*—I'm guessing—doesn't know what it is. But *she* might. Don't you want to find out?"

'Casta sighed, like she did whenever forced to admit Makk was right about something. "I *could* stir a few down-angles," she said. "But when she kicks us off, I'm gonna told-you-so."

Getting to the ladder that led to the bridge took a lot of stagger-walking. All told, they'd been at sea for eleven days, and in that time, Makk had gone from nearly falling over every third step, and hardly eating for fear that he wouldn't be able to keep any of it down, to walking with almost no trouble and... well, he was still hardly eating, but that was because he didn't trust the food.

That was when the water was calm. The seas were much choppier now; every step meant first looking for the next railing, then lunging for it before the ocean rocked him onto his ass. Elicasta was having the same problem, which actually new for her; keeping steady in every conceivable environment was evidently a critical Veeser skill.

They reached the ladder, and climbed up to the bridge, where Captain Selis treated them to a three second look of disdain before returning to her binoculars.

"You two should get below," she said.

"Think it's any safer down there?" Makk asked.

"Yes, because down there, you're not in anybody's way." She turned to the helmsperson. "Ease back on the engine, Del; we're not gonna outrace it."

"I'm willing to give it a try," Del said.

"We're two days from any shore worth mention. Ease up."

"Aye."

Del throttled down the electric engine. When they did so, Makk caught a whiff of ozone, and added *being dead in the water because the engine's fried* to his list of concerns.

"So, uh, captain?" Makk said. "We know you're busy, but just what in the Depths *is* that out there?"

"The Depths is about right," she said. "I've never seen anything like it, detective."

"I was really hoping it was a whale."

"It's not a whale."

"I told you," Elicasta said.

The captain looked at Elicasta. "You Streaming?"

"I'm not live," she said. "It'll drop as a vid."

"Keep me out of it," the captain said. To the helmsperson, she said, "steady, Del. I think it's not done."

"Holding," Del said.

"You really don't know what that is?" Makk asked. "How many years have you been doing this?"

"Six," Selis said. "And I didn't say I don't know what it is; I said I never *seen* anything like it. Step aside."

The bridge was barely large enough to hold as many as three people, so it was basically impossible to be there without getting in someone's way. In this case, it was Elicasta, standing in front of the ship's audio dash. She stepped aside, so Selis could pick up the handheld.

"Cargo, this is the bridge. Tell me we're still secure."

"Wadz here," someone responded. "No shift. Still down tight."

"Keep track of drift, Wadz," the captain said.

"Understood."

Captain Selis returned the handheld to its cradle. "She's not great at absorbing a direct side impact," Selis said, to Makk and Elicasta. "Hard enough hit could dislodge something down there, and then we're looking at a cascade of problems. We list too far, we're swimming the rest of the way."

"Is that, um, *likely* to happen?" Makk asked.

"No. But we're in a mess of unlikelies right now, huh?"

"Yeah. Maybe not the best time to mention, but I can't swim."

"Not my problem."

Makk didn't know what was in the cargo hold, and not for lack of trying. The *Colusm* filed a manifest along with their itinerary, and on that manifest, they listed steel for Lladn, and spice for Dongy. The problem was, Makk slept in the hold, and while he could attest to the steel—long, flat sheets in heavy rolls, chained to flats—if the stuff sealed inside the massive, lead crates was some kind of *spice*, there was something very wrong with that spice.

He'd asked a couple of ship hands about it, but they either didn't know what was really in the crates, or *did* know and were above-average liars.

The captain stepped away from the dashboard to check out the stern again. "Yep, there it is," Selis said. "Coming 'round once more, Del. Brace for cross."

Del didn't move at all, which was evidently how one "braced for cross." The creature slid along the left side of the ship then and, as before, the wake buffeted them sideways. While Makk and Elicasta waited for the rocking to subside, Selis and Del adjusted course.

"So, what *is* it, captain?" Elicasta said, once the course correction had been settled on. "You never *saw* one before, but you *heard* of it, real?"

Selig took a look at 'Casta's blue light. "Not for that," she said.

"I'll loop you out. Promise."

Selis did not look content with this answer, but talked anyway.

Makk saw this a lot around Elicasta: someone would protest the rig; she'd say not to worry; they'd *continue* to look worried, but they'd *still* talk, as if they'd gotten their way.

"Fine," Selis said. "I'll sound crazy and lose my *job* for sounding crazy, but fine. I've no fucking idea what it is... but I've heard things. We all have, about giant beasts from the deep under. Every time a ship's late to port, the rumors start. Then they'd reach shore and it was like nobody even floated the notion.

"Used to be, it was only ever just that: rumors. Superstition. Every ocean-bound shipper, fisher and sailor's got a story about the thing they heard from the fella before them, who heard it from the one before *them*, who saw it for themselves. Never took 'em seriously. But I've been hearing a lot more of it since, and from people I trust."

"Same rumors as before, only now the ships *aren't* turning up eventually?" 'Casta asked. "Is that what we're talking about?"

"That's what I'm saying," Selis said.

"Hang on," Makk said. "There's no gray area here. Either ships are missing or they aren't."

"It's all second-hand is the problem, detective. Ship doesn't come in when it's supposed to, could be weather pushed the captain to seek a closer port, and they'll come in later. Could be the one doing the reporting is wrong about the missing ship's charter. I'm saying there's a big damn difference between a ship not being where someone thinks it's supposed to be, and a ship *sinking*. The fleet owners know, but they're sure as shit not announcing their vessels are unreliable. Insurance companies probably know too, and are jacking up premiums to account for it, but they won't talk about it either."

"The answer is yes, then," Makk said. "Ships *are* going missing. I'm asking, captain, because I'm a little concerned about *this* ship at the moment."

"We're all concerned," Selis said. "Don't I look concerned? Now get off my bridge."

Elicasta gasped. "It just broke apart," she said.

"What?" Selis asked, raising her binoculars. "I don't see that; how do you see that?"

"I have a drone at the prow," she said.

"I got it," Selis gasped. "Honus's sake. Did it *die?*"

Makk tried to see what they were seeing, but it just looked like all the water ahead of them had turned black. Like they'd steered into an oil slick.

"It wasn't just one creature," Elicasta said. "It was a swarm."

All of a sudden, there was a loud THWACK and a spark shot out of the side of Elicasta's rig. She screamed and fell to the ground. At the same time, every other system on the ship that relied on electricity—the engine, the audio dash, all the lights—shut down.

Makk reached Elicasta. Stunned but awake, her hair was charred and her eyes wild. Her blue light was off; the rig was out of commission.

"Did you do that?" Selis barked, grabbing the wheel to help Del keep them steady. *"Did she do that?"*

"What happened?" 'Casta asked Makk. "What... my optical..."

"No, she didn't do that," Makk said, to the captain. "That was an electrical pulse. It shorted everything, including her rig. I've seen weapons that can do that."

"You think there's a submersible nearby?" she asked.

"I'm saying, maybe whatever's in the water with us isn't an animal."

"Cap, I can't steer without power," Del said, straining to hold the wheel steady.

Selis looked to Makk. "And I can't call the engine room without power. I need you to get down there. We gotta restart her before your animal-or-not-an-animal pulls us under."

"You think the engine room doesn't know they should be restarting the engine?" he asked.

"I *think* I want someone down there I know for a fact isn't currently dead from electrocution, so go."

"I'm not leaving Elicasta."

"Go, Makk," 'Casta said. "I'll be fine."

In an effort to prove this, she took hold of the railing, pulled herself to her feet, and took off the rig. Assessing the damage to her equipment was more important than checking the damage to herself, which Makk took to mean she was probably going to be okay.

"What do you want me to do if they *are* all electrocuted?" Makk asked.

"You know what a circuit-breaker panel looks like?" Selis asked.

"More or less, sure."

"Big box with a bunch of steel pipes heading into and out of it, on the wall next to the engine. If it worked like it's supposed to, the engine's fine and the battery got fried by the surge. We *have* a backup battery in the pipe. All you gotta do is get to that panel and throw the circuits back open."

"Right," Makk said.

Just then, something large and oil-slick black *flew* out of the water to the left of the ship, directly over the bridge, and into the water on the right side of the ship.

"Whaaaaat the fuck was that?" Del asked.

"Sea monster," Elicasta said, not even looking up from the burnt-out rig.

Selis looked Makk in the eye. "Fast as you can, detective."

M akk slid down the ladder from the bridge and landed on the deck, with an impact his bad knee very much did not appreciate. Then he staggered to the railing, and pull-walked his way toward the rear. The engine room was down a set of stairs at the stern, under a trap that was currently closed.

Annoyingly, there wasn't anybody else on the main deck; if there had been, Makk would grab them, communicate the captain's orders, and not have to go down into the Sub-level of Probable Electrocution himself. But the *Colusm* only had a total of six crew: two were on the bridge and at least one was in the hold. The rest were either in the below-deck bunks or the engine room.

As he made his way to the back, it took a lot of concentration to not stop and look over the side; the ocean waters teemed with life, to such an extent it looked like it was boiling over. There was a part of him that very much wanted to understand just what in the name of Nita was going on down there.

Then another creature burst from the water and hit him in the side of the head, knocking him over. The large black what-ever-it-was hovered in the air above Makk's head for a few seconds—it made clicking noises like a large insect, which made sense because it was *flying*—before it dove back into the water again.

"Okay. Not curious anymore."

With the deck pitching all over the place, Makk decided that *crawling* the last few maders to the hatch made more sense than trying to walk. This proved a wise decision, because the *Colusm* was rocking ever more dramatically, and he was pretty sure he heard at least one more insectoid sea monster fly overhead.

When he reached the hatch to the engine room, he pulled it open from his knees, and looked down. It was pitch black down below.

"Hello?" he shouted.

No answer.

"The captain sent me," he said, really hoping he wasn't going to have to go down there. "She said..."

He didn't finish the sentence, because at that moment something in the water *roared*: a deep, low note that resonated with the pit of Makk's stomach and the hairs on the back of his neck.

Nighdemons, he thought.

A half-dozen of them burst from the water, over the railing and coming right for Makk. He sought shelter in the only place he could, by diving head-first down the stairs to the engine room. The trap fell shut as soon as he was through, plunging him into near-total darkness.

Something heavy impacted the trap door from the outside. Then came several more such impacts—*thump-thump-thump*. It sounded like the whole top deck was loading up with the night-mares of his youth.

"Hello?" someone called from the bottom of the stairs. It was a man's voice; Makk didn't recognize it, but he could count the number of conversations he'd had with the crew on one hand.

"I'm here," Makk said. There *was* a faint illumination on the stairs; some kind of luminescent paint at the lip of each step.

"Is that you, Kalwin?"

"No, it's, I'm one of the passengers. Makk."

He tried to get to his feet, just as the *Calusm* was rocked by a side impact. Makk's bad knee gave out, and then he was tumbling the rest of the way down.

"Ow," he said. He was now lying in a shallow pool of water at what he hoped was the bottom of the stairs.

"Are you all right?" the man asked.

"Great," Makk said. "The floor broke my fall. Where's this water coming from? Are we sinking?"

"Water gets down here, it's normal. Where are you? I can't see you."

Makk sat up and took a look around; the luminescent paint ran along the walls, but didn't do him much good, as far as working out the nature of the machinery was concerned. He did see a void in the paint near the floor in the far corner, and figured that was caused by whoever he was talking to.

"I can see you," Makk said. He waved his hand. "Do you see me?"

"No."

"Hang on, this is stupid," Makk said, getting to his feet. He felt around until he found his voicer, which had a torch function. But the voicer was as dead as Elicasta's rig.

The ship rocked again. He stumbled, but caught his balance with the help of a wall. The sound of multiple smaller impacts on the deck came off like a hailstorm.

"We need light, friend," Makk said. "Do you have anything down here that can give us some?"

"Yeah," he said. "Yeah, of course, yeah." The figure in the corner got to his feet and started feeling around the wall. "There's a hand-crank lantern to the right of the stairs. It's Izko."

"What's Izko?"

"My name. Here it is."

Izko turned the hand crank, and the lantern sprang to life. Dim life, but life.

"Oh, it's not working," he said.

"What are you talking about?" Makk said. "It's working fine."

Izko held the lantern up to his face. It did nothing to help him see any better, but did a lot to illuminate the larger problem, which was that Izko was missing part of his head.

"I... I think I'm blind, Makk," he said.

Makk took the lantern, and helped Izko sit down on the stairs. "It's okay," he said. "This is just what I was looking for. Sit tight; I'm still going to need your help."

Makk walked to the middle of the room. Lying face down in the ankle-deep water, next to the engine, was the body of another engineer. Makk didn't know her name, and felt strangely terrible about this.

The light reached the circuit breaker he was told to find. There was charring on the wall on both sides of it.

"What happened here, Izko?" he asked.

"A surge, I think. I can't... it was so bright. Oh. Oh, gods. Kalwin was here. She..."

"Don't worry about her right now, Izko," Makk said. "I have to restart the engine. Captain Selis said there's a secondary battery. Do I need to do anything to hook it up?"

"What is that noise?" Izko asked, his head tilted upward.

"Ah, terrifying monsters are coming out of the water and ripping apart the ship," Makk said. "That's why we need the engine."

"That sounds... oh. Makk, I think I'm bleeding. I..."

"Stay *with* me, Izko. Tell me what to do."

Silence. Makk tilted the lantern in the direction of the steps. Izko's one intact, but blind, eye, stared back at him.

The man was dead.

"Super," Makk said.

Just then, the ship was rocked by another heavy side impact, this time followed by the sound of metal *tearing*. Makk had heard that noise before; it wasn't the sort of thing one forgot.

Maybe there is *a submersible*, he thought, *and it just hit us with a torpedo.*

It was an oddly comforting notion.

He stepped up to the breaker box. There were three switches in closed position.

"She said the backup is already in place," he told himself. "Just have to throw the switches."

He looked down at Kalwin's body.

"Throw the *electrical* switches to the *electric* engine while standing in *water*," he added. "Yeah, I don't like this at all."

Then the water around his ankles started collecting at the other end of the room. The *Colusm* was tipping. Terrible news, except now he was no longer standing in water, so in that context it was fantastic.

He took a deep breath and threw the switches open. The first two went fine. The third one sparked, but in a delightfully non-lethal way, and the engine hummed to life.

"Can't believe that actually worked," he said.

The overhead lights blinked on, and Makk was thrown toward the back of the engine room as the entire ship lurched forward. They were still listing, but hopefully now heading *away* from whatever was trying to sink them.

Makk stumbled to the audio dash and opened a channel to the bridge. "Captain Selis, this is Makk. We have power. I'm heading back up."

No response.

"Bridge?" he asked.

The audio channel from the bridge opened from the other end. He heard a shriek of wind, followed by a shriek of something that was definitely *not* wind. Then the line went dead.

Elicasta, he thought. *What's happening up there?*

He got to the base of the stairs, preparing to storm back up and do something heroic and/or foolish, when the thought struck that he might be in the safest part of the ship, what with all those creatures outside. But then the ship pitched again, and shook, and he came to an entirely different realization.

"I'm going to drown if I stay here."

Makk spotted a floatation vest drifting in the pooled water at the other end of the room. He grabbed it, and was putting it on, while also unsteadily climbing the stairs to the trap, when something catastrophic happened to the *Colusm*.

It felt like standing in the middle of a building as it was being demolished: the steps disappeared under his feet, and he was thrown sidewise and up. He remained airborne for an alarmingly long time, before the side of the ship came up to meet him.

He screamed in pain, as the impact dislocated his left shoulder and rebroke a couple of ribs that were still trying to heal from his last beatdown. His legs still worked, but when he got a chance to use them again, he discovered the ship was at a 45 degree angle.

This was still level enough to walk on, so he reoriented, and charged ahead. He pushed the trap open with his good shoulder, and stumbled directly into the end of the world.

He couldn't see the sky, much less the bridge where he'd left Elicasta; the entire *ship* was being swarmed by these oversized, aquatic locusts. And when they weren't flying, they were scurrying around the deck on which Makk was trying to stand.

I should never have left you, 'Casta, he thought.

He got his first good look at one of the Nighdemons—which was what he decided these were going to be to him, from now on. The creature had six legs, two arms, giant eyes, a round, squishy black body, *wings,* and—which he discovered as soon as it identified Makk as a threat—a truly *massive* jaw, with three rows of teeth.

It was the Outcast. Multiplied by ten thousand.

The one who'd bared its teeth launched at him. Makk fell back a few steps, drew his gun, and fired once at the creature's head.

The face burst open satisfyingly; they could be *killed,* which was terrific. But there were a *lot* more of them than he had bullets.

Two came at him from the right. He hit one, missed the second, and then a third and a fourth slammed into him from behind. He lost his footing on the steeply angled deck, and began sliding toward the water.

I hope I drown, he thought, *before I'm eaten.*

The last thing to occur to him, before he went under, was that Viselle had been right all along. It would have been better if he'd let her have the key.

PART II
HERETICS

Chapter Seven

"Sister! Sister Orean! Come quick!"

The young girl named Lenaia shouted Battine's adopted name as she ran along the pier, her face red with exertion.

Battine was busy watching a ship called the *Phaespin* unload its cargo—tuna, if she was understanding her fish correctly. She stood in the shadow of an off-the-pier building, which should have made her difficult to spot, except that she'd already greeted ten people who'd done precisely that and then, having spotted her, came over to chat.

Lenaia was someone's daughter; Battine couldn't recall who. Feisty but adorable, she reminded Battine of Porra, as a child.

"I'm here," Battine said. "What's the matter?"

Lenaia reached her, stopped, and knelt down to catch her breath. "There's a death," she said. "I mean, there's to be a death. Someone... the girl will die soon, they said. She's a, she needs a hooded one."

"Lenaia, you aren't making sense," Battine said.

"Frake said, he sent me, he said you would know the words."

"The *words*," she repeated. "The *final* words? You mean the blessing of the Five?"

"Yes," she said. "That's it. I think that's it."

"I... can't," Battine said. What she *wanted* to say, was that she couldn't deliver the final blessing of the Five, because she wasn't an oath-bound Septal. But that wouldn't float; she'd already committed to the lie.

"You have to!" Lenaia said.

"I mean that there must be other Septals for such an honor, Lenaia. More qualified."

The girl blinked at her, confused. "But, you're the sister of the pier. There isn't anyone else."

"All right," Battine said. "Of course. Take me to this dying person."

They ran at Lenaia's pace, which was fine, as Battine couldn't figure out how to run any faster in the Septal garment anyway. She was wearing a simple cotton outfit underneath, with slip-on shoes that were never intended for running. If she had her riding boots, it might have been a different matter. (She would have also been more *comfortable*, walking around the pier all day, as the slip-on shoes were not really meant for walking in either, so much as they were for keeping her feet from touching the floor while traveling between places in which to sit.)

The girl brought her to a pier with a recently-moored fishing boat, the *Kalin-Ha*. All the usual signs of an orderly debarking were absent: nobody was unloading the hold and the boat hadn't been fully secured, and all the people who were supposed to be taking care of these things were instead huddled around a small figure lying on her back.

Frake, standing at the edge of the scene, saw Battine and waved her in. "Hurry," he said. "We're losing her."

"I don't understand," Battine said. "Tell me what's happened. Was there an accident?"

"Shipwreck, we think," he said. "Or an overboard, 'cept she

was clinging to a piece of what looked to be a mainmast when they found her. Said she come off the *Bekohai*, a fishing boat out of Djuk-Djuk."

The crowd parted for Battine as she approached. She walked forward slowly, which likely looked solemn and weighted, but was actually because she was trying to remember the words for the final blessing of the Five.

She'd heard them often enough. It was a frequent duty of royals—blessed or not—to bear witness to the final passing of an "important" subject. As a consequence, Battine spent more time at the bedside of dying persons than a young woman really ought to.

Getting it perfect *now* wouldn't be entirely necessary, because she only knew it in Eglinat, which she was confident nobody spoke. None would be the wiser if she got some of it wrong.

But: the *gods* would know.

The young woman lying on the dock looked twice-drowned. She was ashen, and skeletal, her too-wide eyes darting around in a panic. She was muttering something that sounded to Battine's ears like gibberish. A fisher from off the *Kalin-Ha* had her by the hand, and was applying a cold cloth to her forehead, for what good that might do.

She knew the fisher: his name was Easo, and he was married to a Kindonese man named Abogano, who worked in the fish market. They were interested in raising a child, looking into adoption versus surrogacy, and under the impression an oath-bound Septal might help them decide.

"What is her name?" Battine asked, as she knelt beside the half-drowned woman.

"Kaketora," the vessel's captain said. She knew nothing about him aside from his name, which was Jiqas. He was lingering at the edge of the scene along with the rest of his crew.

"Kaketora," Battine said, "can you hear me?"

The girl's eyes stopped darting about to settle on Battine's hooded visage. She said something Battine couldn't understand, but was definitely not gibberish.

"It's Kindonese," Easo said. "She's asked for forgiveness."

Battine took Kaketora's free hand. It was bony, and warm. The girl wasn't half-drowned at all; a fever was cooking her from the inside. On contact, Kaketora's grip tightened. She tilted her head, pulled Battine closer, and hissed, "*Dwanni. Dwanni! Hampa Dwanni.*"

"It's—it's all right, Kaketora," Battine said. "It's all right. Try to stay calm."

Once Battine initiated the final blessing, Kaketora *did* calm down, relaxing her grip and laying back, if her entire body exhaled.

The blessing of the Five was mercifully short. The rough translation was, *May the Five guide you to your place in the Haven. Sever from your burdens.* The names of people and things the dying was to sever from were supposed to follow, a process that could extend the blessing considerably, depending on how many were being left behind. But the important part was the first sentence, and the suggestion that one who was passing on to the Haven first had to let go of this world.

Once all the severing was done with, the final passage—again, roughly—was: *may the Outcast take no notice of your passing.*

Not knowing any family or worldly possessions to call out, Battine went from the initial phrase directly to the final passage. When she got to *Outcast*—the word in Eglinat was *avicto*—Kaketora sprang back to life.

"*Dwanni!*" she said again, with all the energy she had left. "*Avicto. Dwanni!*"

"What are you saying?" Battine asked, looking at Easo for help. "I don't understand."

"*Dwanni...*" Kaketora hissed once more. Then she sagged back against the dock, took one huge, staggering breath, and died.

After a solemn beat, Battine gave the final words of the

blessing—*so have they passed*, approximately—placed the girl's hands over her heart, and closed her eyes.

Then she looked at Jiqas and Easo.

"Please tell me what happened to this poor woman," she said. "And what, by the Five, does *Dwanni* mean?"

I t would be two hours before Battine got any answers. First, Kaketora's body had to be carried to the harbormaster's cabin: a large, square building that sat at the edge of the harbor, atop wooden risers. From there, someone would be reaching out to Wrimmad City's local law enforcement and/or government, and they would—Battine assumed—contact their opposite number in Djuk-Djuk.

She wondered if the Kindonese even knew the *Bekohai* was missing.

After that, the *Kalin-Ha* still had to be unloaded. *Then*, finally, the crew—the *Kalin-Ha* had a contingent of nine—Battine, and Frake convened in the back of a pub called *Scurvy's*.

"To Kaketora," Captain Jiqas declared, holding up a mug of beer. "May her net never empty."

The crew drank solemnly. It was as if they'd lost one of their own which, in a way, perhaps they had. But for the grace of the gods, it could have been one of them, floating out there in the middle of the ocean.

After a respectable silence, Battine asked, "Could one of you explain what happened to her?"

Captain Jiqas nodded. "We come across her three days past. Our hold was already full; we were on our way back. Slowed up for some flotsam."

"Thought sure it was another boat gone down," Easo said.

"On that, we were right," Jiqas said.

"*Another* boat?" Battine asked. "You've crossed the wreckage of more than one?"

"Not us, no," Jiwas said. "But we've heard the tales. The ocean's been cruel, of late."

"That's just muttering," Frake said. To Battine, he said, "there's *always* rumors on the sea, about ships going missing, pieced together from naught more than a scrap of wood afloat. It's what you get when so many vessels set out from so many harbors. I've been hearing the same whispers since boyhood."

"Ahh, you're a half-blind old man," Jiqas said.

"Been *years* since a Wrimmad fisher boat went down, and you know it, Jiqas," Frake said.

"Excuse me, please," Battine said, before Jiqas could offer a rejoinder, "but didn't the *Bekohai* sink? Is that not verified?"

"That's no Wrimmad ship," Frake said.

"I appreciate that, but it seems beside the point. *A* boat sank, and before now none of you were aware of it. *How* did it sink?" She turned to Easo. "She gave you her name. What else did she tell you, besides this? Did she say what happened?"

Jiqas and Easo shared a look. At the same time, the other seven crew members stepped away from the table, as if they wanted no part of this conversation.

"As I said, we pulled her from the drink three days back," Jiqas said. "Couldn't say how long she'd been afloat already by then, but two, three days at least. She was half-dead, and would'a been *all* dead, but that she tied her arm to the driftwood. We got her aboard, warmed her as well as we could. Tried to feed her, but she couldn't keep nothing down. Water, that was all."

"We headed ashore as fast as we were able," Easo said. "But with a full hold and unfavorable winds, that wasn't fast."

"I'm sure you did all you could," Battine said, realizing the captain and crew of the *Kalin-Ha* were seeking some sort of absolution. From *her*. Which was insane.

Only the gods administer absolution, she thought. *I'm just a woman in a hood, oath-bound or not.*

"Thank you for saying," Jiqas said.

"Of course," she said. "Please continue."

Jiqas shifted uncomfortably in his chair.

"She *did* speak of what happened," he said. "Only some."

"On the first day, just her name," Easo said. "After that... she said a great deal; not much of it made sense. I speak fluent Kindonese, and I could barely understand."

"Was *Dwanni* one of the words?" Battine asked.

Everyone in earshot reacted as if she'd just spoken a curse. A half-dozen fishers made the sign of the Five, and behind the bar the tender stepped forward with a heavy stick, ready to intervene in the event someone did something so foolish as to say it again.

"Gods," Frake said, "keep your voice down, sister."

"I will, if someone tells me what it means."

"Demon," Frake said. "A creature risen from the Depths to shatter boats, and drag its crew down with it. Every oceangoing culture has its own word. The one you just spoke is the Kindonese version."

"And *hampa?*"

Frake looked confused. "I don't know that word. Did she say this?"

"She did," Batt said. "Along with... the other one, she said *hampa*. I take it this is not a cursed word?"

"Many," Easo said. "It means many."

"*Many* demons."

She looked around the room. None of the fishers seemed interested in meeting her gaze.

"Friends, these were her dying words," she said. "They meant something to her, and I'd like to know why. Did she say this before? While still aboard?"

"She did," Jiqas said.

"Think she knew she was dying," Easo said. "Kept telling her to rest, keep her strength, try holding onto food, all that. Promising she'd have a doctor as soon as we docked. All she cared about was making sure we knew what happened to the *Bekohai*. But she was... as I said, I'm fluent. But Kaketora, she was all over. I couldn't get what she was saying; not the way *she* wanted me to get it. Then, after some ten hours of her rambling, in and out of sleep, she asks for something to write with."

"All we had was a coal pencil for the map," Jiqas said. "And all we had for *paper* was the map. Figured she was writing a note to loved ones or what-have-you, so we let her use the back of it."

Jiqas took a folded paper from the inside pocket of his jacket and slid it across the table.

"Honestly, thought we were just looking at a scribble at first," he said.

Battine unfolded the map, and laid it out on the table. It didn't look like anything. Then she turned it ninety degrees, and saw what it was that Kaketora wanted the fishers of the *Kalin-Ha* to know. It chilled her to the bone.

I have seen this before, she thought.

"I need for you to tell me every last thing she said, Easo," Battine said.

~

Polister Calidon didn't look impressed.

"Tell me again what it is I'm supposed to be looking at."

"You have it upside-down," Battine said.

Polister rotated it. "This does not help," he said.

"I last saw an image like this in the throne room of Totus castle," she said. "There's a massive fresco running along the upper border of the room's walls; a graphic description of the Tribulations. In the sequence depicting the final battle with the Outcast, *this* is what the Five have to face."

"So, it's a drawing of the Outcast," Damid said. He was also unimpressed.

In fairness, both of them were still trying to digest the news that Battine's daily trips into the city involved somewhat more *direct* interaction with the locals than either were comfortable with. Their repressed consternation was no doubt coloring their opinions.

"This girl, Kaketora, was aboard a fishing boat called the *Bekohai*," Battine said. "Out of Djuk-Djuk. She claimed the boat was *attacked* by a veritable army of creatures that looked just like that."

"She told you this?" Polister asked.

"She told a member of the *Kalin-Ha*, and he told me. They *caught* one; this appears to have been the instigation for the attack. She also described a much larger beast, traveling below the surface."

"You mean, a whale," Damid said.

He was not taking this seriously, which was working over her last nerve.

This was how most of their interactions went, of late. He continued to insist he was working on a solution, but still refused to explain what that solution was. He'd set up in a private room, with a collection of electronics nobody understood, so he could do something nobody understood.

Well, that was probably not entirely true. Battine certainly did not understand what he was doing, but her technical skill was essentially nonexistent. She got the sense that Polister also did not know, but his technical prowess could well be as underdeveloped as hers. There was an expectation on both of their parts that whenever he was done with...whatever he was doing, he'd *tell* them. Meanwhile, they were left with his infuriatingly vague responses to direct questions.

That he was visibly unhappy to learn that Battine had secrets of her own, only angered her more.

"Whales don't jump up on the decks of fishing boats," Battine growled. "They don't have claws or pincers. Or *legs*, for Honus's sake."

"No, but the thing in the water…"

"Damid, stop being an idiot."

"I'm only saying, there could be a benign explanation," he said. "It's a story told by a frightened girl, half-dead and half-delirious, and you're getting it second-hand from someone who had to translate it from Kindonese."

"I trust the word of the men who relayed this."

"Yes, of course. Your friends. I don't think I have to tell you how dangerous what you're doing is, for both of us, but I'm going to anyway. You shouldn't go back there."

"I'm not your *pet*, Damid. Or your prize. You have no command over me…"

"Please," Polister said, cutting her short. He held up the drawing. "Tell me what you think this means, princess."

"I think you know," she said.

"I do, but I want to hear you say it."

"I think Kaketora's last wish was to make it known that the Outcast has risen from the Depths. The *literal* ocean depths."

"That's…a stretch," Damid said.

"It's what your dead Septal friend told us to *expect*, Damid," she snapped. "How do you not see that?"

Damid stared at her for a beat. "This is not what he predicted," he said. "And I've still not heard anything that sounds plausible. This girl was of the faith. She drew what would have been an obvious nightmare character for someone with her background."

"Gods help us from the musings of lay professors," Polister said. "There's no widely accepted description of the Outcast in Septal teaching, Damid."

He put the paper down and rubbed his eyes.

"I happen to know, a number of vessels *have* gone missing of late. It came up in the parliamentary meeting. I'm not about to conclude that the Outcast is at sea, swallowing fishing boats. But *something* is going on."

He flipped the drawing over, to the map side. "Do you happen to know where the *Kalin-Ha* was when they found the wreckage?"

"No," she said. "But I can ask."

"That would be appreciated," he said. "I'll call on Myala Dravian of the council. She'll need to notify her Djuk-Djuk counterpart of the fate of the *Bekohai*; *where* it went down could go a long way in helping us understand what's actually going on out there."

Chapter Eight

Myala Dravian's office was on the top floor of Charter House, which was the closest thing Wrimmad City had to an official government building. It was the tallest structure in the upper city, and where the most important responsibility of the local government—license issuance—took place. This was the most Murskian of facts, as surely no other Botzis diaspora considered insurance and licensure of such paramount concern. Whereas in Wrimmad, they built the Charter House first, then planned the city around it.

The city's constabulary was on the ground floor. They were not what anyone would call a strong police force, concerning themselves mainly with keeping the peace in every part of the city that wasn't otherwise policed by the harbormaster. (D'magut Slan, the current harbormaster, was perhaps the second most powerful man in the city. He was corrupt, but to an acceptable degree.)

The constables saw a murder here and there, but mostly handled property disputes and domestic disturbances. If there were ever enough cars in Wrimmad City to constitute more than an oddity, they'd probably have to handle traffic too. But not yet.

Polister had to walk past the Wrimmad constable's desk on his way up the stairs. He'd been to Myala's office only a few times, but often enough to know what *normal* looked like for the constables; today, they looked busy, which was *not* normal.

Four flights—and several private complaints about the lack of an elevator—later, Polister reached her office.

He was shown directly inside, which was curious, as he had no appointment.

He was there to let Myala know—if she didn't already—that a Djuk-Djuk fishing boat had been sunk by what its sole survivor described as a swarm of nightmare creatures well outside zoological norm. That was clearly not what *she* wanted to talk about.

"I take it you've heard," Myala said, as soon as the door was closed.

"Heard what?" he asked.

"Don't play coy, Holy Staffer," she said. "We've known one another too long."

"I'm sorry, Myala. I don't know what we're talking about."

"Professor Magly. He's here. In Wrimmad."

"He *is?*" Polister said, hopefully registering the proper balance of shock and surprise at the news, but probably failing. He was not an accomplished liar, which made him an excellent religious leader, but a bad conspirator. "How do you know?"

"Someone from the board of legates reached out to Chief Ohn last night, said they managed to geotag the professor to the city. I don't know *how* they did that, but I don't understand these things."

Polister sat down slowly, trying to work through the implications of Damid and Battine possibly being geolocated to his *living room*, but not quite getting there. In truth, it was something he should have been pondering this entire time, but after the few weeks in which they went undiscovered, he had allowed himself to think things were going to just go on like that.

"Are they sure?" he asked.

"Sure enough to send a team to Botzis to collect him. They

should be here in about a week. They're expecting us to have Magly in custody by then."

"And if we *don't?*"

"I don't know. The whole thing is a political boondoggle. I'd wager the League of Countries will accuse us of harboring, and use it as another excuse to not formally recognize the parliament, but I don't think I'll find anyone to take that bet."

"And the other one?" he asked. "They were looking for two."

"He was the only fugitive mentioned by name," she said. "Probably only had proof of *him* being here. But I would assume wherever Magly is, the princess will be as well."

"I see," he said. "Out of curiosity, how... *exact* is this geotag?"

Myala smiled grimly. "As I said, I don't know how these things work. Do you have something to tell me, Polister?"

He thought he could probably trust Myala. They had known one another for over ten years, and had navigated a close friendship through the odd power dynamic of her outranking him in matters of politics, and him outranking her in matters of faith. He spoke the wedding bond when she and her partner were joined, and again when their first child was born. If he admitted to harboring Damid and Battine, and asked that she keep it to herself, she'd likely agree.

But: he would be implicating her in something that may very well be a crime and which would, at minimum, put her career in jeopardy.

He opted for tact.

"Certainly not," he said. "I was just wondering which part of the city the constabulary would be focusing on."

She stared at him for a beat too long, and then pressed a button on the intercom.

"Juth," she said, still staring at Polister, "I need you to pull the antecedent records on religious asylum."

"Wrimmad City, or do you want the Mursk records too?" Juth asked.

"Global," Myala said. "Go back two hundred years. And loop in Piasta. She's good with precedents."

"It'll take a while," Juth said. "Anything I should know?"

Myala took her finger off the audio button. "Anything she should know, Polister?" she asked.

He shook his head. She re-engaged the intercom. "Not right now, Juth, thanks." To Polister, she said, "never play cards."

"I don't know what you mean," he said.

She sighed. "Let's pretend that's true. Let's also pretend I don't know you've had two guests for well over a month, one of whom has been walking around town dressed like a Septal. High Hat Porl is already making inquiries; you weren't going to be able to keep them secret for much longer. You should have come to me from the start."

"I don't need to clear my hosting calendar with you," he said, and in this he wasn't sure if he was clinging to the lie or not. If he *really* wanted to grant them asylum, he didn't need to run that past the local political apparatus first. As Damid stressed, Polister Calidon was the head of an entire religion.

"Polister..." she began, shaking her head, "it's been too long since you've thought like a Murskite, my friend. Your lack of shrewdness in this matter is alarming. Let's imagine your friend Professor Magly showed up at a House temple instead. Not *here*: someplace central. Velon, say. Imagine that happening, and then imagine the Hat decided to *publicly* offer asylum. What do you think would happen?"

"I don't think they *would*," Polister said.

"That's why we're using our imaginations. Game it out. Go on."

"All right," he said.

He got up and paced, because he thought better that way. He also needed the time to bring down his heart rate.

I expected Damid to force the asylum question, he thought. *Not you, Myala.*

"It *would* have to be a place like Velon," he decided, after a few steadying breaths he hoped she didn't notice. "Because of the House's decentralization. Within the order itself, High Hat Plaint of Velon has no more power than High Hat Porl of Wrimmad, but *outside* the order, he's as important as a president, or a king. If *he* decided to shelter them, it would mean the entire *House* agreed to do so. And, because of the politics involved, the nation of Inimata would likely fall into step behind him. As the House goes, so goes the planet. But that would never happen, because Plaint would never do that."

"Stop, stop, stop," Myala said. "Don't qualify it. *He* wouldn't; that's not the point. The point is, the House's authority is *supposedly* due to its prominence as the largest and oldest established religion in the history of Dib. You happen to be the eastern seat of the *second* largest. Why should *your* extension of asylum be treated any differently? Especially since Unitism is *not* decentralized."

"Staffer Louban would disagree."

"No, she wouldn't. The final word in Unitism rests in the east, not the west, on top of which, her seat only exists because your predecessor thought it wise to emulate the House. Meanwhile, you sit in Arigo Span's chair, and hold the staff of Pal. This should mean you're at *least* as important as a Duqo Plaint."

"I suspect, outside of this room, you won't find anyone to agree with that," he said.

"Not *now*," she said. "Not yet. Polister, approach this more like a Calidon and less like a Spanner."

Polister laughed. "Perhaps if I *had* Damid Magly and Battine Alconnot, I would," he said. "Myala, just a moment ago you were framing this as a manifest threat; now, you act like it's an opportunity."

"Existential threats can also be opportunities. The League of Countries may not be so quick to denounce us, if doing so would give the appearance of religious persecution. Wrimmad City failing to hand over Magly and Alconnot is a political problem; you *refusing* to hand over Magly and Alconnot is a different kind of problem entirely."

"A useful one?" Polister asked.

"Potentially. Played right, we may come out ahead in both arenas at the same time."

"Well," he said, "I'll keep it in mind. Not that this is anything other than, as you said, an exercise in imagination."

"Do that," she said. "Now tell me why you *are* here, if not for this conversation?"

"I'm here about the missing boats," he said. "Have you heard mention of a Djuk-Djuk vessel called the *Bekohai*?"

"I *have*, yes," she said. "Qotid is already accusing Ghon-Dik. Tell me she didn't reach out to *you* as well?"

"She didn't. But you can tell her it wasn't pirates."

"What *was* it, then?"

"I'm not sure I can answer that without sounding insane," he said.

It was midday, on a slow day for new fishing boats in the harbor. Battine only saw three, before the suns reached the high point of the sky. It was about half the usual total. This *could* mean it was simply that: a slow day. But two of the merchants— she knew most of the fleet owners on sight by now—were pacing, agitatedly, along the pier, checking their timepieces, and barking into voicers. One had gone up to the harbormaster's cabin twice already, perhaps to lodge a complaint with a city official who could do nothing about a ship not in port.

It'd been three days since the Kindonese fisher named Kaketora died holding Battine's hand; nothing had changed in that time. Although, she had to admit, she wouldn't know what *change* would look like. Was there any single government entity with the authority to *call back* all of the ships hailing from Wrimmad City harbor? Did the technology to make that call even exist? Each merchant fleet had their own form of communication, and not all of it was electrical in nature. Some, she was told, communicated with gongs and lights from the city's highest point.

But the absence of boats that should perhaps not have been absent was only the first peculiar thing to note about this slow day. She had also seen, from a distance, an unusually large representation of city constables. Easy to identify, even from afar, they all wore the same uniform: pressed, olive-green cotton, with a black metal helmet that looked like a cannonball cut in two, and a projectile gun in a black leather holster, displayed prominently on their hip.

It was unusual to see Wrimmad City's police force this close to the water. She wondered if they were worried about the missing boats too, and considered approaching one to ask.

She spotted one constable questioning a friend of hers, a boatswain named Ovix. Ovix claimed to have once caught a waterwoman—which he described, crudely, as "half fish, half tits" —and seen a waterspout carry a school of dolphins over a coral reef. He was preposterous, but had lovely stories, especially after a few drinks.

Ovix taught her some of the sign language the merchants used to communicate when bartering in the fish market. It turned out, after all the work she'd put in to decipher it, that there wasn't much involved: yes-no, this-that, up-down, numbers—which were, oddly, the most complicated element of the signing—and deal-no deal. Once she had all that down, she was effectively fluent.

It was a fun thing to learn. She never expected to need it.

While talking to the constable, Ovix caught Battine out of the corner of his eye, lowered his right hand, and made the symbol for "no," followed by "no deal." Then he reengaged in his conversation with the officer.

He was telling Battine to get away from him.

Battine had only a few seconds to puzzle over why this could be, before someone grabbed her arm and dragged her into an alley between two warehouses. Instinctively, she spun an elbow around, meaning to break the nose of whatever stranger had the audacity to put their hands on her royal person, and managed to strike Frake, albeit in the forearm—he parried the blow—rather than the nose.

"*Gods*, sister," he said, stumbling backwards. The force knocked him into the wall, but with nothing broken, which was a fortuitous outcome. "It's me. Is hand combat a lesson taught to Septals? I thought you were all scholars."

"I'm sorry," she said. "I don't respond well to surprise."

"That's well understood."

"Why did you grab me?"

"To get you off the main," he said. "They're looking for you."

"*Who* is looking for me?" she asked.

"The constabulary. And I'll skip ahead, because we don't have time to play at this: they're not asking for Sister Orean."

"I don't..."

"We know who you are, princess," he said.

Hearing the word "princess" from Frake was jarring; two of her worlds were colliding in the most peculiar of settings.

"I don't know who you mean," she said. "I'm a Septal, not a princess."

He laughed. "You can relax. Nobody is going to turn over the sister of the pier to the ballheads."

"How...?" she began, but her brain was failing to deliver words in a comprehensive manner, so she didn't continue.

"How long, or how many?" he asked.

"How many."

"Not sure. It's not a *secret*, but it's also not something we talk about. If you're worrying, know that the reward on your head's enough for any one of us to live comfortably, for good, despite which nobody turned you in."

"This is a peculiar assertion given the constables are presently looking for me."

"Sure, but again, they're not looking for Sister Orean, are they? They're looking for Princess Alconnot of Totus. *Someone* else spilled, sure; not one of us."

"All right," she said. "All right, then I'm not as good at hiding in plain sight as I thought I was. How *long*? When did you know?"

"Not long after we first spoke. It was the accent tipped me off. You don't speak the common like an Inimatan."

"Frake..." she began. She was rubbing her temples, as the implications were threatening to burst open her forehead. "When you sent Lenaia for me, to speak over Kaketora in her final moments: you *knew* this already?"

"Sure."

"You *knew* I'd taken no oath, and still allowed that I administer the final words to that poor girl. A girl who I may now have condemned to the Depths for this very act. You *knew*?"

"Oh, well. I'm not up on my Septal rules and regulations, princess. The girl needed the comfort of someone wearing a hood in her last moments, and you were the nearest. Plus, you could actually recite the whole thing, which was a real bonus; didn't expect that."

"Frake..."

"Sister, you gave her peace. If the gods you believe in think there's something wrong with that, you maybe should look into finding some different gods. Now can we get off the street before one of the ballheads stumbles down here?"

∼

F rake brought Battine to a back room at *Scurvy's* by way of a side door. Lenaia, who was evidently his go-to when needing people fetched, was there waiting. He whispered a list of names to her, and off she went.

"What is happening?" Battine asked.

"For you? Nothing. Sit down, I'll have Bnaka bring us drinks. We're short on information, sister; Lenaia is out collecting it."

"Lenaia is a child."

"Which means nobody looks twice at her," he said. "Relax, you're in the safest place in Wrimmad City right now."

Battine thought that for everyone's sake, the safest place for *her* was the Unital chamber, rather than cornered in the back of a dockside alehouse. She trusted Frake as much as anyone, and thought it true that many of the friends she made were equally genuine; they wouldn't turn her in. But as long as she stayed where she was, *they* were in danger. She'd already been through a version of this, in her escape from Totus castle, and it remained a minor miracle that the servant girl who helped—the *real* Orean—hadn't been summarily executed for her role in that escape.

"I should just go," Battine said.

"Go where?"

"Elsewhere. You are all at risk."

"Sister, you've reached the end of the world. There *is* nowhere else to go. Now sit tight, okay? I don't know what it was like where you came from, but here, we take care of our own."

This is what concerns me, she thought.

It was a half an hour of pacing before Ovix came in, through the same side door. Ten minutes after that, it was Jiqas, the captain of the still-in-port *Kalin-Ha*. Then came a fisher named Uleen, memorable for being the only woman to ever outdrink Batt; a merchant everyone called Squint (it was surely not his given name) who once spent an entire morning teaching Battine how to haggle; and a sex girl named Moaita, to whom Battine had been providing reading lessons.

After a lifetime spent around literal incarnations of gods, this was the kind of company Battine now kept. That she felt significantly more comfortable among *this* crowd was a fact she expected to spend some time interrogating, once this was over.

Lenaia returned shortly thereafter, to report that they would not be joined by any others. There were *more* co-conspirators on Frake's list—half the harbor, seemingly—but none who could get away without drawing attention.

That was fine; the group Frake assembled had already, collectively, amassed a formidable amount of information.

To begin with, the search wasn't exclusively taking place at the harbor; it was citywide. Also, the constables were mostly asking after Damid Magly, not Battine, even though it was clear—to everyone in the room, at least—that Princess Alconnot was the bigger prize of the two.

The constables were acting on a tip, but that tip didn't originate locally, meaning Frake was likely correct: nobody on the docks was responsible. *Damid* must have done something to tip off the authorities, was the consensus.

"I think the best place for you right now, sister," Ovix said, "is anywhere that guy isn't at." He stared at her with a look of bemusement. "Hey, do we still have to call you 'sister'?"

"I think that would be for the best," Battine said.

"Let's not get in the habit of using her highness's other names," Frake said. "Easy to slip, in front of the wrong set of ears."

"Perhaps also don't call me *highness*," Battine added. "That's a title for a queen, which I will never be."

"Not even if…"

"I can never be queen, Frake. To explain why that's so would take more time than we have at present. Can we move on?"

"Could we see…" Moaita began. "I mean to say, your high…

um... sister... how about if you took the hood down? Just for us. I'd like to tell someone someday that I looked in the eyes of a real princess."

"All right," Battine said. She was taken aback by the request. "If it's important to you."

She took the hood down.

The reaction was startling. Everyone seemed... *awed*, for some reason. In her entire life, Batt couldn't once think of a time when any aspect of her person inspired awe.

"What are you, ah, what are you all looking at?" Battine asked.

"Sorry, princess," Moaita said. "I mean, sister."

"You're very lovely," Jiqas said.

"Thank you. I'm... I'm going to put the hood back on now," she said, thinking now she had *two* things to spend her free time unpacking, once this was over.

"Stay away from Damid, then," she said, to Ovix, as she pulled the hood back up. "That's your advice."

"It's where I'd start," Ovix said. "Since they seem to care more about him."

"*Can* you stay away?" Frake asked. "I mean, d'you know where he is, so as to avoid him?"

"I do. It is, unfortunately, the same place I retire to each night."

"The Spanner compound," Uleen said, nodding. "That scans."

"Well, you can't go back *there*, then," Frake said. "That's just asking for more trouble, which you've got enough of right here."

"I'm not so sure," Battine said. "If I'm there, I have the full protection of Staffer Calidon and his entire religious order. My *leaving* is what has compromised my safety."

"No, no," Uleen said. "*That* place? The one building in Wrimmad what looks like a gods-damned castle? That's the first door I'd knock on if I were looking for royalty in hiding."

"I agree," Frake said. "Sister, where you need to be, is the *last* place anyone would look for a princess. Right *now*, that's the back room of a shitty dockside bar."

"I can't stay here, Frake," Batt said.

"We can hide you," Moaita said. "Yes? Move you around."

Battine shook her head. "Meeting me here is one thing," she said. "Sheltering me in your homes is a different matter. I can't endanger all of you like that."

"You're not staying *here*, you can't go back to the Unital chamber, and like I said, you're already on the last stop at the edge of the world," Frake said. "Outside of surrendering, I don't see how you've got any other choices. Unless I'm missing something."

"Actually," Battine said, an idea forming, "you just might be." She turned to Jiqas. "Has the *Kalin-Ha* been grounded?"

"Grounded? Nah. We leave in the morning. Why?"

"Could you use another deckhand?" she asked.

It took a beat before Jiqas figured out what she was actually suggesting. Then he started to laugh. "You know anything about working a fish boat, sister?" he asked.

"I could learn," she said.

"It's not a terrible idea," Ovix said, to Jiqas. "She's fit, and not stupid. I've taken on worse."

"Hiding at sea," Frake said. "Could be, we just keep tacking you onto different crew until the search is over. Come ashore, hop a new boat, head back out again."

"We'd have to ugly you up first, sister," Uleen said, with a laugh. "A hood aboard a fishing boat'll draw more attention than you want."

"We'll get her clothes," Frake said.

"Isn't..." Moaita said, "the ocean doesn't sound *safe* right now. What that drowned girl said, I heard..."

"It's a big ocean," Jiqas said. "And a small city. She'll be safer out there."

"Could you take on *two* inexperienced hands?" Battine asked

Jiqas. "I don't expect him to agree, but I should offer Damid the same opportunity."

"Didn't we just say your best place to be is where he ain't?" Frake said.

"We did," Batt said. "I should still give him the option. He *did* get me this far."

"Sister, I don't think you should leave this room before sunrise, and then only to climb aboard the *Kalin-Ha*," Ovix said. "Going back to the compound for him is not a hot idea."

"I would ordinarily agree with you, Ovix," she said. "But I have to return to the Unital chamber one last time either way. There's something I need to retrieve."

"What is it?" Frake asked. "We can probably find a replacement in town."

"I guarantee, you cannot," she said.

"Taking on one pair of dry hands is gonna be a tough sell as is, sister," Jiqas said. "Not sure I can swing two."

"Tell you what," Frake said. "You bring him here, and we'll find a boat that can take him on. I'll just tell 'em the sister of the pier insisted. Now get going, and hurry back. We're gonna need all night to get you looking like a common dockhand; sooner we start, the better."

Chapter Nine

❦

There was a half-dozen ways out of the Unital compound. For the first month, Battine, who usually left at sunrise, used a different one each day. This was the best way, she thought, to keep anyone from connecting her—dressed as a Septal—to the compound of another faith.

One morning, Polister rose early enough to witness her departure. (He was on his way out himself, to spend time with the statue in the center of the compound. He promised to one day explain why it was such an important piece of art, but had not yet done so.)

"No, no, no," he said. "Turn around."

He excused himself from his assistant Dwerik, and walked her back inside. She thought he was about to lecture her on the risk of leaving, and possibly insisting she not. But that wasn't it at all.

"Come with me," he said.

He led her through the ground level of the residential wing, and down a staircase she didn't know existed, into a basement she also didn't know existed.

"You have a *dungeon?*" she exclaimed.

He laughed. "Tunnels," he said. "That's all. Nominally secret, but only because they're unused. We're beneath the dome now. I don't know if you noticed, but the center dome, the administrative wing, and my residence are effectively the same building. We're just walking through the footprint."

"And why are we doing this?" she asked.

He stopped at a left-turning corridor. "This is why. Down there is a gate to a tunnel that's *not* a part of the footprint. It'll drop you off a half kalomader away, well outside the compound walls."

"Why is this even here?"

"We modeled some of what we built on Septal architecture," he said. "That's what I tell people. But the truth is, I helped design this building, and I *wanted* it, because what could be more fun than secret tunnels? I only wish they'd let me put some in the walls."

Since that day, Battine came and went by way of the secret tunnel. She mostly took it because she agreed with Polister—why not have a secret tunnel? And in having one, why not use it?—but now she was *very* thankful that it existed. Surely, the constables would be reaching the compound shortly; better she not be seen setting foot in it.

Battine reached her private quarters unimpeded. Polister had a staff of four to attend to his—and his guests'—personal needs, but he wasn't there, and neither was anyone else. They were probably busy in the kitchen.

Once in the room, she shed the Septal robes and the cotton clothes underneath, and changed back into the riding leathers she'd left Totus in. She doubted very much that she'd be wearing this particular outfit while at sea, but also didn't want to leave it behind. It was one of the few things in Polister's living space that unquestionably belonged to Battine Alconnot; better to give her host deniability if she could.

It felt good, putting the leathers back on. Like rediscovering an aspect of herself she'd been forced to ignore for a long time. Especially the boots.

Once changed, she retrieved the other objects that could be definitively tied to her: the sword—still locked in the cabinet— and the key. (She didn't know if Damid searched her room for it or not, but it never moved from the bedsprings; she checked each night.) Then she put the robes back on and went looking for Damid.

He was in Polister's office, looking over one of the ancient texts. Anything *interesting* in the library was written in Eglinat (likely in archaic Eglinat, which was a considerably greater challenge compared to the contemporary style) so, unless he'd recently learned to read it, she figured he was looking at one of the uninteresting modern texts instead.

"There you are," she said.

"Here I am," he agreed, not looking up. "Did you know the Septal texts include cookbooks?"

"I... didn't, no."

"I can only read a couple of the words, but I think this is a recipe for venison."

"Damid, we have to go," she said.

He looked up enough to note that she had her boots on. "Do we?" he asked. "Why? I don't hear anyone kicking down the door."

Damid got to his feet. He was no longer the healthy, smiling professor she'd found appealing not-so-long ago in not-so-distant Totus castle. Pale and gaunt, he looked like he hadn't slept or eaten in a while.

Unlike Battine, Damid hadn't left Polister's quarters since the beginning of their unofficial asylum. What he *had* done, he said, was work on a solution, with his room full of electronics. All of that was moot now; the time for solutions had passed.

"The idea is to be gone *before* any doors are kicked down," she said. "The constables know we're in the city; they were questioning locals on the docks all day. I've already made arrangements."

"*You've* made arrangements," he repeated. He walked around the desk, leaned against it and smiled, in no evident hurry. "You look livelier than I've seen in a while."

"That's because you haven't seen me in a while, Damid," she said. "You've been locked in your room."

"Where are you going to go?"

"Where are *we* going to go, you mean? I have friends in the town who will help us hide," she said. She wasn't going to tell him exactly what the plan was before they were back at the pier; he might not take well to the news that he'd been volunteered for a fishing boat.

"I told you, *I* have a plan," he said. "You're perfectly safe where you are."

"You're not hearing me, Damid," she said. "That plan, whatever it was, is over. Someone tipped off the constables. It's only a matter of..."

"I'm the one who tipped them off."

"You... what?"

"It was me," he said.

"Your solution to the threat of us being captured, tried and executed is to have us captured, tried and executed?"

He laughed. "It won't come to that. I have Veesers lined up and all the gear I need to dump the whole thing on the Stream, live. The world will be watching."

She stared at him, aghast. "The *world* will be watching us arrested and carried off, then. How is this good for us, Damid?"

"Again, it won't come to that. The *truth* is our way out, Battine. I've been telling you, *both* of you, since we got here. The *truth* is that the culture you grew up in is a lie, set up to exploit the peasant class, in order to enrich the royalty, and we can prove it."

"We could prove it three months ago," she said. "What makes right now any different?"

"Now we can control the narrative. We don't have to worry that our voice isn't going to be heard. The Veesers I've talked to are highly respected; they won't be ignored."

"Then what's to stop you from Streaming your proof *now*? Or a month ago? Why do you need... oh, I see. You *want* them kicking down the door. You mean to make us martyrs for your cause."

"Our cause."

"No, Damid, this has only ever been your cause."

"*You're* the one who took the key," he said. "That wasn't me."

"Yes," she said. "Yes, I took the key, and I murdered Alva, but I did both of those things out of spite, and vengeance, not to further a political cause. I'm not going to justify my actions after the fact by pretending it was some grand, noble gesture."

"If that's how you feel, why don't you give it back?" he asked.

"I'm also not going to do that."

He grinned. "Then give it to me," he said.

"I'm not doing that either."

"I didn't think so. Because you know that as long as you have it and *they* don't, the kings will fall. It's the only way to exact revenge on those responsible for Kenson's death. What did you say before? You'll throw yourself *and* the key into the ocean, before seeing it returned to them?"

"Something to that effect, yes."

"How is what you're doing and what *I'm* doing any different? We both want the same thing."

It wasn't the same thing. They'd gone back and forth on this already, and when *they* weren't going back and forth, Damid and Polister were having a version of the same argument. It was one of the reasons she and Damid had stopped talking almost entirely.

The problem was, until now it was an argument of hypotheticals, the crux of which was this: if the people of the Middle Kingdoms wanted to rise up and overthrow the royalty, they should go ahead and do that. It would be bloody, and terrible, but it would be a choice made *by* the Middle Kingdoms. They would still control their fate in some way.

That was how she saw it. Crucially, it meant all Battine had to do, going forward, was exactly nothing. She'd already lit the fuse; the bomb just hadn't gone off yet.

Damid wanted to blow it all up *now*, by spurring outsiders to *force* change, which would only encourage the people living there to double down on their beliefs and stand together, to reject the outsiders attempting to alter their way of life. This way might alter how the Middle Kingdoms are run, but it wouldn't change *minds* at all.

There was an important component of Damid's preferred approach that she hadn't appreciated until just now: his way, he comes out a hero. That, perhaps, was what *actually* appealed to him.

"Damid, I'm not going to go through this with you again," she said. "I'm also not staying."

"You have to," he said. "This only works if we're both here."

She sighed. "Does Polister know you've alerted the authorities? Or was his ignorance another aspect of your master plan?"

"Polister is being stupid. I've handed him an opportunity he'll likely never see again. All he has to do is formally extend asylum. It would have global implications; he and his faith can only come out better for it on the other side."

"Perhaps he's as disinterested in being forced into martyrdom as I am."

"To answer your question, I didn't tell him, but he does know. He sent a runner four hours ago, to warn us. If he's half the man I think he is, he'll be here before the constables reach the door. And stop calling it martyrdom. The only plan where someone dies is the one where you throw yourself into the ocean. Trust me."

"Sorry, I have my own way out," she said. "But I wish you luck with yours."

Damid nodded slowly, and then drew a blaster from his pocket and pointed it at her.

"Like I said, you *can't* go," he said.

She stared down the barrel for a couple of beats. She wasn't terribly concerned that he was going to actually shoot her, but she couldn't entirely ignore the threat, because the truth was, Damid hadn't been himself for a while.

"Are you going to tie me *up?*" she asked. "I promise, the story you want to tell on the Stream won't look the same if I'm bound and gagged."

"I don't have to do that," he said. "I just need you to hand over the key. As long as it's here, you won't leave."

"I see."

"If you're not sure about my resolve, Battine, I can probably work out a way to prove it to you that doesn't end with your death. This blaster has some pretty unpleasant non-lethal settings."

Battine took a step closer. She was still well out of range, if she wanted to grab the gun, so he didn't register any particular concern. "It's always been about the key, hasn't it?" she said. "It didn't matter if I came with you or not."

"Not true. You're an important witness. Look, Batt, you were half-catatonic for a month. I took *care* of you. I figured when the time came, you'd return the trust."

"I *am* returning it," she said. "That's why I came here to offer you a way out."

"It's just a new place to run," he said, "not a way out. Are you going to surrender the key, or not?"

"I'm not," she said.

Possibly, Damid had forgotten about her sword by now. Or maybe he just didn't appreciate how much it extended her reach. Or how fast she was with it. Whatever the reason, he was unprepared for what happened next, which was that she drew the sword, and slapped the gun out of his hand with the tip's flat side.

It skittered across the stone floor. He yelped in surprise and, instinctively, lunged forward to retrieve it. Then he realized the same blade that had disarmed him was now pressed up against his throat, and he froze.

"You won't do that," he said. He didn't sound at all certain.

"Damid, I murdered an unarmed High Hat in front of you, and I'd known that woman my entire life. What makes you think I'd hesitate for *you*? Now step back."

He straightened up and backed away. She crossed the room to the blaster, picked it up, and slipped it into a sleeve in her robe. "I'll keep this," she said, "in case you feel like using it on anyone else on your path to martyrdom."

"It's *not...*" he began, exasperated. "It's a solid plan, Battine. You don't understand how the world outside of the Kingdoms works. Not like I do."

"Does Polister?" she asked. "If you told him *everything*, would he agree with you? Or with me?"

"He's... he lacks vision."

She laughed. "I hope it works out, Damid. But I'm leaving."

"Batt," he said, urgently, when she was halfway to the door. "The key. None of it works without the threat of the key."

"It's safer in my hands," she said. "Tell them you still have it; I won't be here to contradict you."

"I'm just trying to get the truth out," he said, softly. "I thought you would get that."

"Truth is whatever power says it is, Damid. I've known this since I was a child. Tell Polister I'm sorry for leaving without saying goodbye. I'm sure he'll understand."

With that, she left. They would be expecting her at the docks; she would not be disappointing them.

Chapter Ten

It was ocean in every direction.

Elicasta had been at sea before, but until this trip, never so far that she couldn't see the land. Intellectually, she grasped that there had to be such places on Dib where it was nothing but water each way; the planet *was* two-thirds water, so that scanned. Emotionally? She was unprepared to deal.

They were in a lifeboat, which thoroughly did not help. At least on the deck of the *Colusm*, there was some vertical distance between her and the horrific endlessness of the Norton. Now, her eyes were more or less *at* sea level; she could see and feel each swell as the boat rolled through.

Every few minutes, they were hit with something steep enough that for a blink, she thought they were going to capsize. It hadn't happened yet, and according to Del it wasn't *going* to happen in anything less than an extreme weather punch, but their reassurance didn't land with Elicasta.

Del was at the back of the lifeboat, fiddling with the beacon, something they did with regularity. The former helmsperson and only apparent survivor of the original *Colusm* crew was under the impression that the beacon was glitching; all they had to do was fix it, and they would be rescued. This absolutely didn't gibe with reality, obviously, since the ocean was as vessel-free in all directions as it was shore-free.

I can see five days out each way, Elicasta thought. It probably wasn't true, but it sure felt true.

'Casta was sitting at the front of the boat, tweaking her own gear. (She knew there were other words for these parts of the lifeboat, but "front" and "back" were perfectly good words, and she didn't care to ask for different ones.) The rig had been shorted by something the sea bugs did, which was super unpleasant when it happened. She hadn't put it back on since, in part because the side of her head was still raw, and in part because the rig refused to spin up. It hadn't suffered a full meltdown—for the coin she fronted, it *better* ride an electrical surge intact—but she couldn't get it to full-on pair with the Stream. Which meant she couldn't use it the way Del thought their low signal fuzz-burst beacon was supposed to work. She couldn't call for help.

The good: all 'Casta's data was still solid. So was Ba-Ugna Kev's chip. She could even tap the Stream, off and on, but only one way. But the rig wasn't sending, and so far, nothing she'd tried had changed that.

Makk groaned again. He was lying on his back in the middle of the boat, twitching fitfully, which was how they knew he wasn't dead. He was having another nightmare, which was probably a byproduct of the fever.

"Hang on, babe," Elicasta muttered. "We'll get out of this."

She wanted to believe that, but—much like the lack of shoreline, or other boats—she couldn't see it.

E licasta wasn't a hundred percent sure how she even made it to the lifeboat. One minute, she was standing beside Selis and Del, and the next minute, all three of them were running and ducking and screaming. 'Casta was already not entirely in her own head, as she'd just had that head zapped by the feedback short, which not only *hurt*, it killed her rig which, for her, was like losing sight in one eye.

Someone lifted her up, carried her to the boat and threw her in. She thought it might have been Selis. Del was in the boat next, and then the boat was plummeting straight down to the water.

Maybe the captain had to stay behind to release the lifeboat. Maybe she was supposed to be joining them, but lost a fight with a sea bug before she had a chance. Maybe Selis never even made it as far as the deck, and Elicasta was misremembering her being there.

Del probably knew. But, except for when they were telling Elicasta not to drink so much or eat so much, Del hardly talked, and 'Casta didn't want to push it by asking for details.

They hit the water hard enough to nearly bounce right out of the boat. But they held on, Del reached the oars, and somehow, the little wooden boat wasn't destroyed by the army of sea bugs.

(She was calling them "sea bugs" because she didn't know what else to call them. If she had access to the Stream, she could run a descrip up against a couple of zoologicals to see if a better name shook out. But something about how Selis and Del reacted left the imprint that these were *new* creatures, that *nobody* had seen before. Or, nobody had survived long enough to tell.)

Del got the lifeboat clear of the *Colusm* before it went down outright. 'Casta very much wished her rig had been active for this, because apart from being utterly terrifying, the sea bugs ripping apart a metal-hulled ship was extraordinary. She didn't altogether get *how* they did it—she rubbed up against several of them on her way off the ship, and the only word that seemed on point was "gooey"—but if she had a vid to review, she'd probably be able to work it out on the rewatch.

Then they disappeared, leaving Del and Elicasta alone in a debris field.

Del spent the rest of the day rowing in a circle, looking for any survivors. 'Casta didn't expect to find any, but when they did —some six hours after the boat went down—she was shocked that it was *Makk*. The last 'Casta knew, he was in the engine room, which was now at the bottom of the ocean.

But there he was, in a float vest, clinging to a fragment of wood crate. His left shoulder was dislocated, he was barely conscious and not at *all* cogent, but he was alive.

The world's luckiest Cholem, she thought. *That's what I'll call you, when I stream this.* Then she laughed, loud enough for Del to shoot a look.

She was never going to get to stream this. It had been three days since the *Colusm* went down. They were running out of food and fresh water. Nobody was coming.

Del had a pretty good idea of where the *Colusm* went down: just on the other side of the Great Current. They were closer, geographically, to the northeastern tip of Inimata, but if they rowed in that direction, the current would carry them south and away from Geo, and Unak, and—if they didn't get back out of it again—into the South Cap, where they would freeze to death well before the current turned north and swung past South Eloni.

(This was academic. They would die of starvation and/or dehydration well before reaching the Cap.)

So they couldn't go back the way they came. There was only forward, which meant rowing in a north-north-easterly direction, toward Botzis.

Provided Del—who was the only one rowing, and Elicasta *did* offer—didn't get confused on the right direction to head (Elicasta had her doubts about this) they'd reach the island in roughly fifty days.

Which, again, was academic; they'd never make the coast.

Their only real hope was to run into one of the fishing boats coming south from Botzis or east from Ghon-Dik, or for a merchant ship in the area to respond to the emergency beacon that possibly wasn't working.

Frustrated at being able to do nothing, aside from watch Del grunt their way through another day of rowing, listen to Makk mutter gibberish with a seasoning of legit words—"nighdemon" came up a lot, which she hadn't heard since she was small—and stare at the provisions she couldn't eat, Elicasta slipped her rig on over the raw skin on the side of her head, and tried to access the Stream through the optical.

"Same, same, same," she muttered, as she skimmed the vids. 'Casta followed a handful of Veesers whose work she respected and whose genres vibed with her own. Since she herself wasn't dropping new vids—she had a churn of preset evergreens and best-of's going, to keep out of archive—the best way to get the pulse was to spin up on what she *would* be chewing if her life hadn't been turned upside-down.

"What's that?" Del asked. They were in the middle of a break, taking a sip of water. Del and Elicasta only got a sip every two hours, according to some metric Del made up.

"I tapped the Stream," Elicasta said. "Skimmed my faves."

Del shook their head. "I don't know what anything you just said means."

The former pilot of the *Colusm* was a person of simple tastes. Del and 'Casta hadn't reached the stage where they traded life stories, but would no doubt be arriving there shortly. What she *did* know was that Del's parents raised them in northern Inimata, but weren't *from* northern Inimata; their father was from Dunn and their mother from Ghon-Dik, the latter explaining Del's slightly darker complexion.

Del had spent most of their life at sea, starting as a deck hand on cargo freighters. This meant they had spent virtually zero time interacting with the Stream, which was the one part of their existence Elicasta was still trying to get her head around.

"I mean, I went looking for news," Elicasta said, "by checking Veesers I know on the Stream. You know what a Veeser is?"

"I've heard the word."

"It's what I do. I'm a Veeser. When I'm not shipwrecked. It's my job title. It means Verified Streamer."

Del nodded. Del had a large chest, huge arms, big (bald) head and no neck; it had taken Elicasta more than a day to figure out how to detect the nod, which was their preferred method of small talk. "Is that an important job?" they asked.

"You know what? It *isn't*, most of the time. I thought it was; I thought the vids I dropped on the reg were prime, but now I'm skimming my kind and... I don't know. None of this content *matters*."

They shrugged, which was another gesture that, in most, would be an easily identifiable physical act, but for Del was effectively a micro-expression. "Never mattered to me."

"I know. You've said as much."

"Didn't mean it that way. Mean that there's never been anything on the Stream that's directly impacted *my* life. That's what makes it unimportant to me."

"How would you know?" Elicasta asked.

Del looked off in the distance—westward, if 'Casta had her compass points down—and said, "Anything on the Stream about giant fucking underwater mutant jellyfish with wings?"

"Not yet," 'Casta said. *Because I can't stream,* she thought.

"*That* would have been useful," Del said.

"Jellyfish? They looked like bugs to me."

"No bones. I punched one."

"They had teeth," Elicasta said.

"Cartilage." Del pulled something out of their pocket and tossed it to 'Casta. "Here," they said. It was a tooth. "Feel it."

If it were possible for something to be both sharp and rubbery, the tooth was it.

"That's the meat," Elicasta said.

"No, it's—"

"It's an expression. I mean, *this* is the story."

"Keep it, then," Del said. "I'm holding out for a whole carcass of one of those fucks."

~

Makk wasn't waking up anymore. He'd also stopped muttering in his sleep, if "unconscious and with a fever" could be called sleep. He was still *breathing*, but Elicasta thought that might be the next thing to go.

He'd been in the water for well over six hours by the time they'd gotten him out. The water was cold, and they had nothing warm or dry to change him into. They did have two emergency blankets, both of which were wrapped around him, but they weren't doing the trick. Even midday, when the suns were high in the sky and it was legit *hot*, he shivered under those blankets.

He was going to die. And she couldn't do anything about it.

The fact that the water was cold at all was something she needed explaining. Were they not heading to Botzis? In the images she'd pulled down from the Stream, Botzis looked like either an island paradise or a desert wasteland, depending on who was in the foreground of the image. (Suntanned fisher in the former, Botzo tribesman in the latter.) Both of those were *hot* destination spots; surely the offshore water would be temperate enough to not kill someone who spent too much time in it.

According to Del, the Great Current was the answer. The Current went north from the South Cap, past the eastern coast of Wivvol, and between North Eloni and the Canos-Holo island chain before rubbing up against the North Cap and heading south again, past Dorabon, Botzis and Geo. The

Colusm went down just beyond the southerly half of the Current, when the waters within it were still cold from its trip along the North Cap. Assuming they were going in the correct direction—away from the Current and toward Botzis—the waters would continue to warm, until they were eventually at a temperature where a six hour exposure wasn't a death sentence.

This was all interesting information. It didn't help Makk's current circumstances whatsoever, but it was interesting.

At first, when the alert came up on Elicasta's rig, she didn't know what she was looking at. She forgot she'd set up a listmatch skim off some of the names on Kev's list of potential coconspirators.

The alert was a dull flash in the corner of her optical, that she didn't see until a few hours after it began flashing; she had been busy doing other things, like staring off into the endless ocean, panicking about the next wave, and convincing herself the shadow she just saw beneath the surface wasn't a sea bug, wasn't anything, wasn't a shadow at all.

She had a lot going on.

"Open alert," she said. The rig, which was still not working correctly, ignored her, so she said it again louder. Del raised an eyebrow at this, but didn't speak.

It opened.

The alert was for Damid Magly. She skipped into the deets, and got exactly enough news to annoy her.

"Follow hard, Chiglins!" Dowanna Chiggle declared breathlessly.

Dowanna was a hard news Veeser in Elicasta's vein, more or less. Dowanna was younger and had bigger breasts, two reasons she'd been scraping Elicasta's vid subs since before 'Casta's world flipped and she went dark. Veeser Elicasta kind of hated her, but Elicasta the real liked her just fine.

The important thing to know about Dowanna, in this context, was that the girl's stat sheet was legit; if Dowanna said she had the meat, she had the meat. You could trust her not to shade it.

"He's hot, he's wanted, and we've got him. Hop this stream tomorrow for a *live* up-close with the professor with the goods, Damid Magly. Real, Chiglins, he's got a *lot* to say, and it's gonna *blow down your castle*. High ten, be here."

Half of being a good Veeser is knowing how to listen to Stream-speak, especially from the competition, *especially* especially if they're jumping a red hot over you. In this case, the two things missing from Dowanna's tease were: *face-to*, and *exclusive*.

Dowanna wouldn't be in the same room with Magly; they'd be talking through the Stream. And she wouldn't be the only Veeser on the feed.

Elicasta pulled back for a wide skim, and found three other Veesers—one whose work she respected, one whose slant she didn't care for, and one asshole whose Stream was 50/50 glory-riding. (Glory-riding was breakneck quick-churning someone else's exclusive, then pretending to co-launch.) It was a decently wide net, sub-wise.

She wondered if there was an invite to the co-stream waiting in one of her boxes, but since she hadn't been able to jump the rig to her private drops, she couldn't do more than wonder.

What she *could* do, was skip through all five teasers for clues. This, she did three times, but didn't get much of anything beyond Dowanna's weird use of the word "castle." Magly was on a heater for theft and murder, with both crimes committed in and against the Middle Kingdoms. Which had castles. Could be Dowanna was just tying the professor to the crime scene. Or, Magly had more to say than just who he killed and what he stole.

Elicasta did a deep skim on Magly when his name first came up; she knew he had a connect to a Free the Kingdoms group, but didn't think there was anything to it at the time, because Magly's professorship was in Kingdoms history. *Not* being one or two steps removed from a radical anti-Kingdoms organization would be a story. But arranging a live vid with this kind of Veeser topic spread wasn't something anyone did. Not even someone trying to prove they didn't do what they were accused of doing.

It *was* something that radicals with a short window on the pulse of the Stream would do, if they had something to say.

Elicasta set an alarm to buzz when it hit ten, Velon local time. Assuming the rig was still working, and she wasn't dead, she'd be watching.

It was on the morning of the fifth day that Elicasta spotted something on the horizon, to their west. It was a horizontal line if it was anything, which didn't usually denote a watercraft of some sort. Land, or a deep sea platform.

Or, a hallucination.

"Do you see that?" she asked Del, pointing toward the object that probably wasn't there.

"Do I see what?" Del asked.

"Um. I don't know what. That. I saw a... a that."

Del squinted. "I don't see anything but water."

"Could be land," Elicasta said.

"There's no land in that direction. Not unless you're counting the North Cap."

"Must be a shadow. Or my eyes are going."

"You should sleep," Del said.

"I can't sleep anymore. Keep thinking I won't wake up again."

Del shrugged. "How bad would that be?"

Elicasta was starving, thirsty, sunburned, exhausted, and pre-grieving the loss of Makk Stidgeon. But she wasn't ready to say that death would be a better option. Not yet.

"Probably me," she said.

An hour later, the line across the western horizon had grown. Now it looked a lot more like a deep sea platform.

"Del, I'm serious, I think there's something out there," she said.

Del stopped rowing to fix on the horizon again. "Is it getting bigger?" they asked.

"You don't see it?"

"My distance vision is for shit," Del admitted.

This seemed like a bad thing for the pilot of a cargo ship, but Elicasta didn't think this was a terrific time to say so. "Well, it's there, and I think it's real, and I think it's getting closer."

"What's it look like?"

"I don't know. Like a dock. Or a sea platform. Are there any sea platforms out here?"

"No," Del said. "And a platform wouldn't be getting closer, would it?"

"It would if we're the ones getting closer to *it*."

"It's a boat, or it's your eyes," Del said. Then they kept rowing, as if the matter was settled.

Another hour passed before Elicasta could definitively rule out faulty eyes as the culprit.

"There. There, look, you see it now, don't you?"

Again, Del stopped rowing, and squinted. What they should have seen was a long flat line just above the water with a vertical *something* in the middle: a mast, a forecastle, something. It wasn't a whale, or a sea bug, or any kind of *vessel* Elicasta was familiar with, but it was *there*, and it was coming towards them.

Del's face went pale. "Oh, fuck," they said. "Oh, fuck, fuck, no, fuck."

"What is it?" she asked.

Del dove for the back of the boat, to the beacon they promised had been working this whole time. They whacked the side of it and checked the display. "It's dead," they said.

"So?"

"We need them to know we're here, and the best way for that to happen is for them to pick up the beacon, which is dead."

"Who are we talking about right now, Del?" Elicasta asked.

"It's that fucking rich prick's floating city. Asealand."

"Asealand?? You're kidding!" She knew what it was, but she thought it was confined to the Midpoint Ocean, and that it didn't move.

"Not kidding."

"Then... then we're saved!" Elicasta said.

Del laughed. "That thing is the scourge of the ocean. They don't follow maritime law, they go too fast for something that size, their ship steers like a brick, and the reason it looks like a sea platform is because that's what it *is*. They're using null-gravity tech to stay above the water."

"So, we're *not* saved."

"If we can't get them to stop, or turn, and we can't get out of their way...? Do you have any idea what happens if you're caught in the middle of a null-gravity field?"

"I don't, actually."

"I don't either, but I know they won't be passing over us harmlessly," Del said. "There've been collisions in the past, and it was always the boat on the water that lost."

Elicasta wished she could get her optical to zoom, or wake up the drone function. She wasn't used to being stuck with what her own eyes had to report. That said, the still-very-distant vessel called Asealand didn't look much like a threat.

"What do you mean when you say it's going too fast?" she asked. "It looks from here like it's barely moving. It's gotten bigger on the horizon, but not *that* much bigger."

"Too fast for something that size," Del said, "because something that size shouldn't be moving at all; once it gets going, it needs a huge stretch of ocean to slow to a stop. And it basically can't steer. You'll see what I mean when it gets closer."

"But we have *time* to get them to notice us."

"Sure," Del said. "If anyone's even looking, which I doubt. I got a flare; if this is our one shot at rescue, gods help us, but we can use it to signal when it gets closer. Can that thing on your head help?"

"I can skim; I can't drop."

"Say that in normal."

"The Stream can talk to me, but I can't talk back."

"Right," Del said. "That ship will be on us before the suns set; I'm gonna spend that time rowing and hope I'm heading the right way to get out of its path. You have until then to figure something out. Worst-case, we'll use our flare, but we don't get to take it back. You understand?"

"I'll try to fix my rig," Elicasta said.

Not, she didn't add, like she hadn't been trying to do that for the past five days.

In all the excitement, Elicasta had forgotten about the passive alarm she'd set for Dowanna Chiggle's vid drop. It didn't help that she and Del weren't currently floating in the same time zone as Velon local; ten for Dowanna was thirteen for Elicasta, according to her rig.

She had been busy looking for *some* avenue of two-way communication in the tangle of computer-driven interactions that was her micro drive. It was this, or crack open the processor with no tools or antistatic gloves. When the alarm flashed in the corner of her vision, she at first thought a comm line had opened, which would have been terrific.

"Dump live vid," she commanded the rig. "Save off, set new remind."

Del, rowing hard as promised, looked at Elicasta quizzically.

"A vid that may be important is dropping now," she explained. "I'll want to skim it."

"You just *talk* to that thing to get it to do stuff?"

"For simple commands, yes," she said. "I have a remote interface to swing the complex."

Del did not looked impressed. They put their head down and kept rowing.

Makk groaned. Elicasta knelt down next to him, wet a finger with water from their one fresh-water bottle, and dripped some into his mouth. His breathing, through chapped lips, was jagged, but he'd stopped shivering so much; it was possible his fever was going down. It was also possible he was on the throes of death. Hard to say.

"We're not out of time yet, Makk," she muttered. "Hang in there."

Then she had an idea.

Time.

Her *rig* knew what the local time was. That meant its geotag wasn't fritzed, which *had* to mean one of the global sats was talking to it and it was *talking back.*

Great, she thought. *How do I use that?*

She wasn't going to get anywhere with the satellite itself. The rig sent a ping to the sat and the sat pinged back with the sender's geolocation, and that was the entire interaction. Figuring out how to go from that function to a different part of the satellite and then communicate *from* it somehow... if that was possible at all, she had neither the knowledge nor the means.

Could she direct the geo ping *elsewhere?* She didn't know how to do that either, but wondered if someone else on the Stream did. Probably, someone in the less savory parts.

It would have to be a freevid; she didn't have access to her C-Coins, and had no way to communicate the hack she was looking to buy anyway.

The odds of a freevid with the exact hack she was looking for

—and that actually *worked,* and didn't inadvertently fry her rig—seemed unlikely. Worse, about fifty percent of the freevids out there had grievously miscategorized title/content matchups. But there were no better ideas lining up; she may as well try.

Please, she thought, as she queued up the query, *not* too *many penises this time.*

"Yep, guessed wrong," Del said, startling Elicasta.

"What?" she asked. Del had stopped rowing.

"Oh, you're back."

"I was... researching something. You stopped rowing."

"No point," Del said, nodding in the direction of the approaching ship.

It had gotten a *lot* closer, close enough for Elicasta to begin to understand the nature of their situation better than when all she had to go on was Del's word that they were screwed.

Asealand was, indeed, huge, and not at all shaped like a boat. Which, perhaps, it didn't have to be, given it was hovering above the water. The ship was designed to maximize deck space without worrying about silly things like buoyancy or hydrodynamics. It was, in short, a massive square, with the "front" of it—the part heading straight for their little lifeboat—being one of the sides of the square. It was like watching a ten story building approach.

"Do you have anything?" Del asked. "Because in about an hour, nothing on Dib will stop that ship from running us over."

What Elicasta had was nausea. She didn't know exactly how long she'd been deep in the Stream, but most of that time had been wasted on mislabeled freevids. (Yes, a *lot* of penises.) But it hadn't been an entire waste of time.

"I might have," she said. "It's risky."

"Risky compared to what?"

What she'd found was a hack of the geo ping that would turn

her rig into a short range pulse override; any nearby electronics would either auto-pingback, short out, or explode. That was provided Bazbro Fech—the freevidder who streamed it—was telling the truth. Given Fech had a *terrorism* tag on his vid files, she had her doubts. On the one hand, this could mean it absolutely *would* work—that tag only went on bombmaking vids and the like, and the hack was effectively about turning a Veeser rig into a weapon—but it could also mean it was a self-sab tweak. It could blow *her* up; it could also be that blowing her up was Fech's intended outcome.

Intrinsic in the hack was a manual override of the rig's surge gate, which was there to prevent a deadly feedback loop. The surge gate was one of the first things she learned not to mess with. Now a rando pseudo with a terror tag was telling her to do just that.

"Uh, pretty risky," Elicasta said. "We might explode and die. It'll definitely fry my rig."

"You can replace a rig."

"Maybe you didn't hear the 'explode and die' part. What about the flare?"

"Flares only work if someone's looking for them," Del said. "You think you can guarantee anyone on that floating city is looking at the water?"

"What if they picked up your beacon, and are looking for us right now?"

"The beacon died two days ago."

"Again, it could explode and we could die," Elicasta said.

"I understand," Del said. "We *will* die, otherwise. When can you start, and what can I do?"

Elicasta sighed. "I need a piece of dry fabric, a waterproof bag, some wire, and a screwdriver. And a moment of silence for this rig."

～

An hour later, Asealand was officially too close to come to a complete stop before running them down, which was bad, but was also now within range of the pulse override Elicasta was about to inflict upon it, which was good.

She removed all the chips—including Ba-Ugna Kev's one-of-a-kind program chip—and the main hard drive, each of which was wrapped in the dry cloth and stuffed in the waterproof bag. (The bag had previously held something dreadful called hardtack, which they'd finished eating a day earlier.) What was left of the rig was the hardcoded functionality, which included the geotag cycle.

Thanks to the screwdriver, which was part of a universal tool Del carried with them, 'Casta pried open the casing, pulled the sat echo board and disabled the surge gate. She now had one end of the wire (yanked from the guts of the disabled beacon) connected to the main power source: a battery with enough juice to vaporize all three of them.

"That little thing?" Del asked, when told this.

"It could power an aero-car, in flight, for about ten minutes," Elicasta said. "So, yes."

"Huh."

The last step was to connect the other end of the wire to the geo ping.

What was supposed to happen then was, every ten seconds the pulse that was supposed ping a satellite in low orbit would instead be sent in all directions—because the sat echo board was missing—and the signal would be boosted iteratively, more powerful with each pulse thanks to the missing surge gate. This would continue until the rig shorted, melted, or exploded. Or, until Elicasta cut the feedback loop by disconnecting the wire.

What was *not* supposed to happen—but still definitely could —was that it exploded immediately and killed all of them.

She figured the odds were about even.

Elicasta held the wire above the pulse circuit, took a deep

breath, and asked, "are you ready?"

Del nodded. "Do it."

She exhaled and lowered the wire.

Electricity arced between the wire and the circuit before they even made contact. Startled, Elicasta dropped the whole thing. The rig landed safely on Makk's blanketed legs and not—thankfully—in the water.

"Ow," she said, not because of her hands—which were fine—but her eyes. She tried to blink them clear. "Did not expect brightness. Don't suppose we have anything rubber I can put over my hand before I try that again? For some reason, I hadn't factored my getting electrocuted into the odds."

It took another minute of scrounging before Elicasta had what she needed: a strip of rubber, peeled from an oar handle.

Pinching the wire with the rubber strip, she lowered it again, this time closing her eyes before contact.

She heard a spark, and felt the rig tremble in her free hand. She opened her eyes. There was definitely electricity surging through the system—she could feel it—but there wasn't anything visibly or audibly transpiring.

"Is it working?" Del asked.

"I think so."

"I was expecting more."

"Me too," Elicasta admitted. "Like, I expected to *hear* the pulse, even though it's not a sound wave, strictly speaking."

"Oh, here we go," Del said, looking at Asealand.

It was possible to make out some of the structures on the ship's deck now. Elicasta had already spotted a couple of stand-alone buildings (they weren't buildings, but that was what they looked like) jutting out over the sides, with a clutch of similarly-shaped structures rimming the edge. They were all conical—like huts, or silos—with dome ceilings. They probably had windows, but she wasn't close enough yet to see those.

There was now a couple dozen lights ringing the domes.

Those hadn't been there before.

The lights flared up and then went out. About ten seconds later, they flared up again, brighter this time, before going out again.

"The electrical system's networked!" Elicasta said.

More lights, not in time with the ones on the domes, came up now. These were moving, like someone was holding a personal torch.

The main lights flared up again after the ten seconds, this time shining so brightly that half of them exploded.

"Oops," Del said, with a laugh. Del appeared to be enjoying this a lot.

The rig was heating up in Elicasta's hands, which was alarming given she wasn't directly touching any of the current points. She wouldn't be able to do this for much longer.

The next pulse popped a couple more of the rooftop lights, and then a set of spotlights mounted on the front of the floating city sprang to life—lights evidently *not* networked—and started roaming the sea foam.

"Do you think someone's on the other side of those lights, looking for us?" 'Casta asked.

Del studied the movement of the lights for a beat. In the meantime, another pulse went off. She didn't need to see its effects to know it happened, because this time the rig trembled.

"Looks random," Del said. "Could be."

"Good, I have to stop."

"Not yet," Del said. They turned and opened the storage bin they were sitting on, and pulled out the flare gun. Then three things happened at about the same time: the next pulse went out; the rig's metal casing popped open and burst into flames; and Del fired the flare.

In response to the rig catching fire, Elicasta yelped in surprise (although, it shouldn't have been that big a surprise) and tossed the entire thing away...directly into the ocean.

She and Del watched it disappear in a puff of steam.

"Well," Del said. "Guess that's that."

"Yeah," Elicasta said. "That was a topline rig. Gonna miss it."

A few seconds later, one of the spotlights landed on them.

"It died saving us," Del suggested, waving to whoever had the light on them. "Worth the sacrifice, I'd say."

"Now what?" Elicasta asked, as the second spotlight found its way to them.

"Now we see if they feel like saving us," Del said.

"Don't they *have* to? Isn't that some sort of maritime regulation?"

"Sure, but they ignore every *other* regulation."

"They *wouldn't*," Elicasta said.

"Probably not. But I'd feel a lot more comfortable if that was a fishing boat or a Wivvolian freighter."

After a few minutes of being spotlit, Elicasta heard a familiar buzzing.

Drone in the air, she thought.

It was an old model, the kind that without a Stream uplink in the command chain. That meant it didn't have a lot of the functions mostly taken for granted in later models, but it *also* meant it wasn't going to get taken down by a rogue pulse.

The drone got good and close, hovering just above their heads. If they wanted, Del could have taken it out with one of the oars.

"Hey, what...?" Del exclaimed, as the drone's optical looked Del in the eye.

"The optical on that model doesn't autofocus," Elicasta said. "Sit still and let it get a look at you."

"Sure, okay. I hate this."

"I think they just want to know who launched an attack on them."

"If they think we're a threat," Del said, "they can just keep going."

The drone looked at Elicasta much longer than it looked at Del. Elicasta was trying hard not to interpret anything out of it, other than perhaps that the owner was working out where they'd seen her before. (Facematch wasn't possible without a Stream hook.)

It was sometimes possible to read the equivalent of body language from an active-operator drone; she got the distinct impression that this one was *angry* with her for some reason.

When it finally broke off, it was to examine the third person in the boat: Makk, who was barely visible, bundled as he was in the blanket. It dropped low and narrowed in on his face, and *shook*.

Then—and this just proved how old this model was—the drone spoke.

"I don't fucking believe it," it said.

The words were spoken in the inflection-free digital tone of old computing; there was no way to tell who was talking on the other end. Despite that, Elicasta felt as if she should know who it was.

"Excuse me?" Del asked.

The drone turned to them, as if having forgotten Del was also in the boat.

"We could use a rescue," Elicasta said. It spun back on her. "Sorry if we damaged anything on your ship," she added. "We're a little desperate."

It went back to her, then to Makk, then to her. "Is the device disabled?" it asked.

"It's... yes. It blew up. We threw it in the water."

There was a long pause. Then the drone committed to a lengthy examination of the entire lifeboat from end to end.

"We can't send another pulse," Elicasta said. "I promise."

"Stand by for helo rescue," it said. "Assuming the helo's not fucking broken too."

Chapter Eleven

Polister Calidon always thought of himself as a pragmatist. Pragmatism was one of the three governing characteristics—the other two were frugality, and a willingness to compromise—drilled into him and his three siblings at a very young age. In fairness, these were qualities favored by *everyone* in Mursk, but seemed doubly so for the children of Dueay and Madda Calidon, who—in theory—ran the family's insurance empire by following these guiding principles.

It seemed Polister ended up with all the pragmatism, while his older brother Hawnat—the current head of Tandem Insurance—was entirely dedicated to the frugality of the company bottom line. Appropriately enough, then, the middle siblings (Lot and Farrlan,) as Tandem Insurance middle-management, got stuck with all the compromise.

Polister was supposed to be the family's religious branch, more or less literally. Despite being one of the few families in Mursk considered important in their own right—rather than as adjuncts to more important government or corporate hubs—the Calidons had virtually no pull with the House. Since the House was Dib's most significant single entity—politically and economically, but also in matters of religion and education—this would not do. And so, as young as two, Polister was told that he would be oath-bound one day.

Not that their ambitions for him stopped at the oath. Polister recalled, quite clearly, a drunken Madda Calidon telling him that he would be a High Hat someday, and that he would be getting the entire family into the Haven thanks to his connections with the Five.

(Mother knew a great deal about insurance, fine jewelry, and alcohol—not in that order—but very little about Septalism.)

Although he did little self-evaluation at the time, he later decided that it was the second mandate (getting the family into the Haven) rather than the first (representing the Calidon family in the House) that most directly contributed to his eventual renunciation of Septalism, and embrace of Unitism. After all, he couldn't very well put in a good word for his family with the Haven's gatekeeper if he didn't first embrace Pal, the one true god.

It didn't *really* happen that way; he wasn't thinking of his family at *all* when he renounced. But it made a better story, especially when in conversation with Murskites who knew his lineage. More importantly, that explanation was a good example of *pragmatism*, which was, again, what he considered his governing principle.

It was very much the case that Polister, in his capacity as Holy Staffer Calidon, ran the Unital faith pragmatically. Under his guidance, in matters spiritual, Unitism existed in the gaps between the Septal brethren and the common folk. This could have resulted in *conflict* with the House, but, whenever possible, Polister steered the faith away from direct confrontation.

Yes, he would tell the occasional headstrong adherent, *we believe in different things than they do, and we believe we are right and they are wrong. However, their power and influence in this sphere is worth respecting, and besides, they're almost right; let's not push the point.*

The idea, for this generation, was to usher Unitism away from "heresy" and toward respectability. Let the *next* Holy Staffer challenge the House; maybe by that time there would be enough adherents to make for a fair fight.

That was how this was supposed to go. Unfortunately, and entirely out of his control, the revolution to *come* had already arrived. And he was, quite frustratingly, still alive for it.

～

Polister was sitting at his desk, as his erstwhile friend, a man Polister once thought so highly of that he gifted him a Calidon seal, sought to explain why he was still there.

"Damid," Polister said, rubbing his temples, "I don't think you've thought this through. You need to leave, right now. Both of you."

"You're not seeing it," Damid said. "This is your *time*, Polister. This is *our* time, to make a stand."

"Believe it or not, you're the second person to tell me that today. When did you all get so confrontational?"

"All you have to do..."

"I know. Give you asylum. Stand at the door and *dare* the constables to violate centuries-old settled law on the granting of sanctuary, thereby formally demanding Unitism stand on equal terms with the House. I've already heard *that* today too. In fact, you'll be happy to hear that Representative Dravian is looking for sanctuary precedents in non-settled territories as we speak. None of that matters, both because I have *not* granted sanctuary, to either of you, and because what you think is going to happen is not what's going to happen. If anything, you—and Myala as well, Pal help her—are going to set this faith back a hundred years. That's if we're very fortunate."

"Battine's not here," Damid said.

"*That's* the part you would correct me on? She comes in late, we both know this."

"I mean she's gone. She got word that the constables were looking for us and decided to run. For all I know, they've already picked her up."

"Did she say *where* she was going?" Polister asked.

"No. She did offer to take me with her, and I declined. She also apologized for leaving without saying goodbye."

"Well that's lovely, Damid. Why *didn't* you go with her?"

He laughed. "What sense would that make? I've already arranged to be caught *here*."

In most of the classic depictions of Pal, the god was seen using their staff—the same one resting against Polister's desk—as a walking stick, but there were also a number of artistic renderings in which it was brandished as a weapon. For some reason, it was the second usage that sprang to mind in this moment.

"You... arranged," Polister repeated, while internally reminding himself he was not a man of violence.

"It's the only way to bring attention to what's been happening in the Kingdoms," Damid said. "A siege, a religious conflict, and evidence that Septalism *itself* is rotten, all in one package; it will be *huge* on the Stream. You and I are about to accomplish so much."

"Again," Polister said, "what you think is about to happen is not what is about to happen. In the eyes of the House, Unitism is a breakaway cult, *not* a separate religious faith. Up until now, that's been an unimportant distinction, because up until now we've been *harmless*. If we *cease* being harmless, they will return to calling us heretics and drive us back underground. There may come a time when we're strong enough to present a real threat, but this is not that time."

There was a knock on the door to the study. Polister looked expectantly at Damid, who was unhooded. After a brief, silent argument, Damid covered himself, and sat in a chair in the corner.

"Enter," Polister said. Vendar, the head of the household staff stepped into the room.

"Apologies," she said, "it sounded urgent."

She stepped aside, allowing Dwerik to enter. One look at the boy's face, and it was clear that Damid—and Polister, by extension—had already run out of time.

Polister signaled to Vendar, who stepped out and closed the door.

"I'm sorry for the intrusion," Dwerik said. He was addressing Polister, but staring at the Septal in the corner. "Ah. The, ah, the chief constable is downstairs. He has asked to conduct a search."

"A search of...?"

"The facility, Holy Staffer. He has... there's a team of constables with him. They're in the courtyard now."

Damid rose silently, and went to the window to see for himself.

"He's saying we're suspected of harboring international fugitives, Staffer," Dwerik added, holding up a piece of paper. "He has a warrant."

"Well," Polister said, "at least he's kind enough to *ask* before entering."

"Looks like the whole force out there," Damid said. "That's for your sake, Polister. It's a bluff."

"You think they *won't* search?" Polister asked.

"I think they want to save you and the city the embarrassment of a search."

"I'm sorry, Staffer," Dwerik said, "who is your guest? If I can ask."

"It's exactly who you think it is, Dwerik; his name is on that paper in your hands. I expect the professor is exactly right. Chief Constable Hellin's show of force is to convince me to hand over the fugitives voluntarily."

"Should we, ah, will we be doing that?" Dwerik asked.

"Not today." Polister looked at Damid. "Shall I assume you mean to remain here?"

"You shall," Damid said.

"Very well." Polister stood. "Dwerik, tell the constable I'll be downstairs momentarily. First—and you can tell him this as well, if you like—I'll be placing a direct to Myala Dravian."

"That... that may not stay their hand, Holy Staffer," Dwerik stammered. "If they try to come in..."

"If Kolm Hellin seems impatient," Polister said with a heavy sigh, "tell him this: sanctuary. And Pal help us all."

Myala was considerably more excited by the prospect of a neighborhood international crisis than Polister would ever be.

"Do *not* let them in," she insisted, over the voicer. "I've already reached out to Waint Felling. We'll be there in an hour."

Waint Felling was the Wrimmad City high court representative. Much in the way the island's parliamentary system was occupied by members from each of the major coastal settlements, so too was the high court. Felling couldn't make laws, but he could adjudicate on their enforcement, something he was evidently willing to do on the fly.

After disconnecting with Myala, Polister made one last plea with Damid, to flee before the situation escalated.

"It's too late," Damid said. "We're surrounded."

"There's an underground exit," Polister said. "I can get you out if we leave right now."

"Is there really? That's incredible. Didn't *you* supervise this project?"

"*Why* it exists is unimportant right now, Damid," Polister said. "Know that it's there, and we are *not* surrounded. I can take you to it; will you go?"

"No."

Grumbling, Polister left to go confront the chief constable.

On the way through his private quarters, for a half a second, he considered taking the underground exit himself. The constables conducting a search when the Staffer was out of office would play very differently, politically, than doing so while he was there.

If only you'd thought of that ten minutes ago, he thought. *Before you sent Dwerik off with the word "sanctuary" on his lips.*

Maybe Myala was right and he *had* lost touch with his inner Murskite.

Polister continued through the dome, to the administrative building, and down to the front door.

Dwerik stood at the entrance, in front of a decently large contingent of city constables, including Chief Hellin.

"There you are," Hellin said, on seeing Polister. He seemed angry. Polister knew very little about Kolm Hellin, other than that he was strict, and competent, and an adherent of Septalism. This was not to say he was *biased* in any way; only that Polister's influence didn't extend very far.

"As I was telling your assistant," Hellim said, "I have a warrant to search this entire building, and I mean to do so."

"I've been told. May I see the warrant?"

Hellin raised an eyebrow at Dwerik, who handed over the warrant. Polister opened it up, fumbling with reading glasses he didn't entirely need, but which made for a useful stall, and then took his time reading it through.

He got all he needed on the initial glance, in which he noted that the warrant had been signed by Judge Azy, from the city court. With Judge Felling on the way, they were about to add the question of judicial provenance to this burgeoning legal crisis.

"Ah," he said, reading the warrant slowly. "Battine Alconnot, you say? *And* Damid Magly?"

"Staffer Calidon, the sooner we get inside, the sooner we can clear this up," Hellin said. "We know they're here."

"Yes," Polister agreed, pocketing the reading glasses and the warrant. "They are. But I'm afraid you can't come in. They have asked for sanctuary, and I've granted it. I believe the *right* to sanctuary negates your warrant. I will also not be sending them *out*, which I'm sure you'd prefer."

Hellin looked at Dwerik—who had no doubt already told him this—and back at Polister. "You don't *have* the right of sanctuary, Staffer Calidon," he said. "You're not—"

"I would think very carefully about what you say next, Kolm," Polister interrupted. "You wouldn't want anyone to confuse your personal opinion with the official position of your office."

That stopped him short. "No," he agreed. "We wouldn't want that."

"Don't worry," Polister said. "Legal advice is on the way. Meanwhile, are your people thirsty? Dwerik, let's get them some water, shall we? And coffee? It's going to be a long night."

Chief Constable Hellin agreed to not storm the premises until Judge Felling and Myala arrived, which happened forty minutes later.

The judge vacated the search warrant on the spot, and sent a direct to Judge Azy asserting the right to vacate. Azy showed up half an hour later, and suddenly the courtyard was an impromptu courtroom.

Did Polister Calidon, in his role as Holy Staffer, have the right to extend sanctuary to Battine Alconnot and Damid Magly, or did the international warrant—which everyone agreed stood on firmer legal grounds—overrule the claim? Was the chief constable of Wrimmad City answerable to international law or local law? Was there even a local law that covered this sort of thing? Did the high court outrank the city court, or was a jurisdictional line being crossed?

Myala's office had already identified precedents for the sanctuary claim, but the most recent example was over three hundred years old, and only *barely* qualified, in that the sanctuary had been granted to a pig who had wandered off a farm and onto a Septal campus, where it had become a pet of the local sisters. This didn't stop her from asserting it as a valid precedent, but everyone else was dubious so now, she was waiting on her office staff to look into sustained legal assertions of farm animal personhood. Meanwhile, clerks in the offices of Judge Azy and Judge Felling were sprinting through reams of bylaws for documentation that supported each judge's assertion, while Polister had his people digging up the original land grant to determine if the property on which the Unital compound sat could be legally classified as an international consulate.

It was the sort of mess only a Murskite or a lawyer would love, and since the courtyard was full of both, everyone involved expected it to last several days, spawn a dozen new laws, a dozen more letters of understanding, and perhaps a criminal charge or two.

Polister—not a lawyer, but a Murskite—was not enjoying it all. There continued to be enough constables in his courtyard to lead one to wonder if there was anyone policing the rest of the city. Every time one of them walked near Cole's statue of Pal, he had to restrain himself from shouting that they step *back* before they damage it with their boots and helmeted heads and projectile guns.

The whole thing *looked* like a siege. At times, it even *felt* like a siege, especially whenever he stepped into the courtyard for any reason; doing so meant getting eyed suspiciously by any number of the constables, who clearly thought he was directly to blame for all of this, and perhaps were wondering if they could resolve it by simply taking him into custody on the spot.

By sunrise, the only thing anyone could agree on was that the constables couldn't go inside yet. There *was* positive momentum in the direction of everybody going home, and regrouping in a courtroom at a later date, which seemed the only course of action with no irreversibility in consequence. They could not, for instance, *un*arrest Magly and Alconnot once they'd been arrested. Better to leave them where they were and wait for the law to settle everything.

They'd probably have the whole matter settled by the end of the month.

Then the House arrived, and it all went wrong.

The security force dispatched by the board of legates for the purpose of collecting Magly and Alconnot wasn't supposed to arrive for another four days and yet, a little after dawn, the now exhausted parties in the courtyard were treated to the entirely uncommon sight of a massive null-grav aero ship overhead.

Polister was on the front steps at the time, a few paces from the door to the administrative building. He was dumbfounded by the sight, as he'd never seen a vehicle quite like the one now blotting out a portion of the sky.

Myala, evidently, *had* seen something like it before. "Polister!" she shouted, from half a courtyard away. "Get your people inside and lock the doors."

"I don't understand. Who is that? Is that legate security?"

"That's a military drop ship."

"Military? *What* military?" he asked.

"Just get inside." She looked at the chief constable. "Kolm?"

Polister got everyone associated with the Holy Chamber in, closed the door, and went to the nearest window. By then, Kolm Hellin had given his constables a drastically new set of orders: they formed a line in front of the three main entrances to the building, and were facing out.

Ropes dropped from the sky, and a team of heavily armed brethren in tactical hoods slid down.

Sentries, Polister realized with a gasp.

He knew, of course, about the Sentries. One didn't get as far up the career ladder in the Septal faith as he had, without running into one from time to time. He always thought of them as high-end security for the important Hats, not as a proper military force. What he was witnessing now was an aspect of the House he didn't know existed, outside of the paranoid fringe of the Stream.

As soon as their boots hit the ground, the Sentries drew impressive-looking heavy blasters from their backs and pointed them at the line of constables, while the drop ship lifted up and over the courtyard walls, landing in a clearing on the other side.

The lead Sentry stepped forward.

"We're here to collect the fugitives and their stolen artifact," he said. "Stand aside."

"You can't have them," Myala Dravin said. She was the only one who didn't look intimidated. Even Kolm Hellin, a combat veteran, seemed shaken. "They've been granted sanctuary by the Holy Staffer of this chamber. You don't have the authority."

The lead Sentry seemed to find this amusing. He looked up and down his line of heavily armed soldiers, in a somewhat exaggerated fashion, as if to say, *you see what I've got on my side, right?*

"We have the authority, ma'am," he said. "Let's not make this a thing."

"I'm not a 'ma'am,' sir," she said. "I'm the parliamentary representative of Wrimmad City, which makes me the highest civil authority in a hundred kalomaders. Judge Felling is Wrimmad's high court representative, making him the highest *judicial* authority in a hundred kalomaders. Over there is chief constable..."

"Yes, yes," the Sentry said. "All very impressive. We have a warrant issued by the League of Countries, while *you* have two fugitives from justice, and stolen House property. I promise, if this goes poorly, we will be found in the right. Now stand aside."

"We will not."

The Sentry sighed and raised his weapon.

"Hold, Brother Caiwel," someone said, from well behind the line of Sentries. A tall, stocky Septal in a hood and a suit strode into the middle of the courtyard. Behind him were three other Septals dressed just as formally, plus two Sentries whose job, evidently, was to guard the tall one in the lead.

"Who is *that*?" gasped Dwerik.

"That would be Mavis Spack," Polister said. "The High Hat of Agon."

"I am sure that we can settle this quickly and amicably," Spack said, gesturing for the Sentries to lower their weapons. He pointed to Myala. "You: I would speak to Polister Calidon. Get him for me."

"Who are you?" she asked. "Do you have authority over these Septals?"

"As much as it can be said that anyone does, I do, yes."

"They've drawn weapons in a sovereign territory and threatened local law enforcement with violence," she said. "I mean to have them arrested and charged. And you as well, if they're acting on your orders."

He muttered something about Murskites to the nearest Septal, then said, "Dravian, right? If you're *looking* for an international incident, we can provide. But when I say that isn't what you really *want*...? I strongly urge you to take me at my word. Now: Polister Calidon. Where is he?"

"I'm here," Polister said, through the window. "It's all right, Myala. Let him pass."

❧

They met in the dome. Customarily, important meetings with visiting dignitaries would take place in Polister's study, but that was in his private rooms, which was where Damid was holed up.

High Hat Spack entered without guards or retinue. After taking a moment to appreciate the dome—it looked best on mornings such as this, when the sunlight lit up the place through the high windows—he took a seat in the first row. Polister sat behind the offering table, on the altar.

"This place is nice," Spack said. "You did good work with the design. I'm impressed."

"Thank you."

"I mean it; if you're going to build a dome on a hill, why *not* take advantage of the suns? This is where the House falls short, in my opinion; we hardly *ever* build anything new, and when we *do*, it's the same tired architectural beats. But this...?"

"We can talk about the Chamber all morning if you'd like," Polister said, "but that isn't why you're here."

"No, it is not," he agreed, leaning forward.

For such a large man, Mavis Spack had a leonine quality to his movements. Even relaxed, he seemed capable of leaping into an attack at any moment. Or perhaps Polister was still unnerved by the team of Sentries in his courtyard.

"We've met before, haven't we?" Spack asked. "At that thing, the charity event, in Fendo. You were still wearing the hood."

"I was. And you were still working your way up. Please accept my overdue congratulations on your ascent. Youngest Hat in Dunn's history, if I recall. Caused quite a stir."

"As did your embrace of the heretical, Staffer Calidon. You know what I *heard*; I heard I have you to thank for my title. Seems you were the one in line for it."

"I've heard that too."

"Ironic, given our current circumstance." Spack stood again, to pace in the small area between the first row and the altar. The time for small talk was over. "I'm hoping you can help us with our problem, Polister."

"'Us.' Are you speaking for the House now?"

"I am. You know what's a shame? It's a shame you didn't stick it out a *little* longer, before renouncing. I don't pretend to know what... modes of thinking sent you down this path..."

"The true nature of our god was revealed to me, Mavis," Polister said. "That is what happened."

"You had a *personal* revelation?"

"I did."

"Well. I'm jealous. None of the gods have deigned to show themselves to me. My point, had you ascended to High Hat, you would have been exposed to more *concrete* revelations. Information with, let's say, real-world implications. But you weren't, so now, in order to avoid what's frankly going to be a *massacre,* not to mention a public relations nightmare, I'm going to tell you a few things I'm not supposed to be telling you. After which, I sincerely hope you do the right thing."

"If the *right thing* is to hand over Magly and Alconnot so that they can be *executed*...? You must appreciate the moral quandary."

Spack laughed. "I sincerely do not care about them. I'll let them go if that's what it takes. I mean it."

"You can't expect me to believe that," Polister said. "Not when they're wanted for the murder of a sovereign and a High Hat."

"I sincerely don't." He smiled. "Given we didn't let what befell Vilto Alva get out, I appreciate the confirmation that you have, in fact, spoken with the fugitives. Did they also tell you about the *key?*"

"Yes," Polister acknowledged. "They claimed the key started up a cloning machine, of all things."

"'Cloning machine,' yes, I guess that's close. It's what they were *using* it for, certainly."

"I didn't know how seriously to take any of it," Polister said, more than a little surprised that Mavis was *confirming* Damid's tall tale of ancient machinery.

"You need to take it *very* seriously. We need that key back, Polister. And not so the Kingdoms can go back to their royal birthing nonsense. That whole blessed/unblessed business is an affront to the *actual* gods, in my estimation. No, I don't think we'll be returning it to their care."

"Not sure how happy they'll be about that."

"In a few years, it won't matter," Spack said. "In fact, in a few years very nearly *nothing* will matter, except that the House lives on. Not the Kingdoms, not this lovely building, not your heretical beliefs, none of it. What *will* matter, and I'm speaking now on an existential level, is five irreplaceable keys that were given to us by the five gods. *One* of those keys was taken by Alconnot and Magly, and when I say there is nothing I won't do right now in order to get it back, I need you to believe me."

"I heard that exact thing before, from a professor named Orno Linus. He said he couldn't convince anyone in the House. Now here you are..."

"Brother Linus," Spack said, nodding. "Yes, he's caused immeasurable harm, even in death. Orno was right about the importance of the keys, but not in the way he thought. That was a misinterpretation of the archival texts on his part. The keys can't prevent what's to come, but they're critical for what happens after. Unfortunately, he was also a *passionate* man, and deeply persuasive, to a degree that caught us *all* by surprise."

Spack pulled a parchment from his jacket and unfolded it on the offering table. It was a world map, an old one, with location names hand-lettered in Eglinat. "The one stolen by your fugitives came from here," he said, pointing to the location of the Great Temple, between North and South Eloni. The map was old enough to still have the land bridge on which the temple was built.

"The other keys are *supposed* to be found in House temples in

Velon, Chnta, the Dunn temple of Agon, and—you'll appreciate this—Flain, in Ghon-Dik."

The reason Mavis paused to underline the last location was that when Arigo Span founded Unitism, he did so as the High Hat of Flain.

"Now, pick whatever reason you'd prefer," Spack said. "The decentralized nature of the House power structure is my choice, but laziness, overconfidence, or simply underestimating Orno Linus... those are all valid. The fact of the matter is, as of three days ago, we couldn't put our hands on *four* of these keys. Linus himself stole the key from the vault in Velon."

He looked up from the map, hesitating. "You knew Orno well, didn't you?" he asked.

"We were associates," Polister said.

"Mm. We'll circle back on that. There's a vid I don't know if you've seen. The star of the vid is a woman named Viselle Daska. In it, she claimed to be working off a plan hatched by Orno to steal *something* from the Septal vaults. She wouldn't say what, but she did say she wasn't working alone. She also claimed not to have what was stolen, and that the culprit was likely whoever murdered Orno. As it happens, he was murdered by his brother, Calcut Linus. Are you following?"

"I don't know what any of this has to do with why you're here today, so no."

"Patience, Staffer. Ms. Daska, in the same vid, claimed her father, Ba-Ugna Kev, was responsible for a series of crimes she likely committed herself. Then, *Kev* was murdered by Calcut Linus. So. We think either Calcut Linus or Viselle Daska have the key now, and are likely working together to obtain more."

He went back to the map, and put his finger on the Eloni land bridge.

"You already know what happened to the key from Temple Island," he said, "but perhaps you don't know—although I think you probably do—that one of the thieves also had connections to

Orno. It's our considered opinion that Damid Magly is acting in concert with Daska and Linus."

He shifted to Wivvol. "In Chnta, which barely has a Septal House at all, the High Hat claims to have willingly smuggled his key out of the country more than *two years ago*, and that he did so at the behest of brother Linus. He has since gone silent, and the key's current whereabouts are unknown."

Spack put his finger on Ghon-Dik. "The fourth should be in the vaults beneath Flain, but we have not yet been able to locate it. Perhaps, Staffer Calidon, you can help us there."

"Honestly, no," he said. "When I abandoned the temple, I kept some of the vault's lesser tomes, true, but the older ones went back to the House, as did *all* the artifacts. Any key would have been moved along with all the others."

Spack grinned toothlessly. "And yet, it was not," he said. He stabbed his finger on the Dunn half of Unak. "Now, if you want to know why I am *here* today, instead of allowing the local constabulary to do the job for me, it's because I no longer have faith in anyone other than the House to resolve this problem. Whatever Linus, and Daska, and Magly, and whoever else is conspiring with them actually plans to *do* with the keys, we have to stop them. That begins here, today, with Damid Magly and Battine Alconnot, and the immediate recovery of that key."

Polister's eyes were fixed on Spack's finger, pushing a hole through the map at the spot of the Agon temple. "You couldn't put your hands on four keys as of three days ago," Polister said. "What happened three days ago?"

"Three days ago," Spack hissed, barely containing his rage, "*somebody* broke into my vault, killed a half dozen brethren, and stole the fifth key. So I am asking you, religious leader to religious leader, to hand over Magly so that I can extract from him the information I need."

"I thought you didn't care about Magly."

"I said I didn't care if he lived or died; I didn't say I didn't want to *talk* to him first."

"I see," Polister said, leaning back. "Why won't it matter in a few years?"

"Why won't *what* matter?" Spack asked.

"Earlier, you said nothing will matter in a few years. What do you mean?"

He smiled, genuinely. "You're playing coy with me, Polister. The Cull is coming. Linus knew it, and *you* should too, either through your interactions with him or from your time as a Septal."

"The *Cull?*" Polister said, in disbelief. "The House has never treated the Outcast as a literal figure, any more than the Unitals have. It's that very conviction that separated me from Orno, and why I'm no secret *anything* as far as any of this key nonsense goes."

"Oh, we *teach* that the Outcast is a metaphorical concern, as an embodiment of evil. On this, we agree. We also infer that the *gods* are metaphorical embodiments of good. The House has to straddle the world of science and proof, and the world of faith and belief, much in the way Professor Linus had to find consilience in his two main areas of expertise. So, yes: out of one side of our mouths we praise the gods and denounce the Outcast, while out of the other we say they're archetypes and non-literal manifestations of our selves. But Polister, the gods were *real*, the Outcast *is* real, and you should already know this."

"What I *know* is that there is one god, and their name is Pal," Polister said. "I rejected the rest of it when I rejected Septalism."

Mavis stared at him for a beat, perhaps to see if he was serious.

"That's a shame," he said. "I was really hoping you'd be reasonable. Also..." he laughed, "between the missing key from Flain and the one in your houseguests' possession, you can't expect me to *believe* you're not a coconspirator."

"I don't know what to tell you, Mavis," Polister said. "I didn't take Orno's concerns seriously, and if you can't locate the Ghon-Dik temple key...? As I said, I handed over all the artifacts that belonged to the House. If you can't find it now, that's not my problem. As for the Temple Island key, you're welcome to discuss that with Professor Magly. I'm sure he'd be interested in everything you just said. I expect you can reach him via direct, without taking another step into my Holy Chamber. I will not be rescinding the sanctuary."

Spack sighed, and shook his head, the way one might when one's pet misbehaved. "Sanctuary is not an option. I *could* say you have no authority; not only are you not a High Hat, as far as the House is concerned, this lovely dome of yours is *our* property. I could point out that we've allowed Unitism to exist only because up until this very moment, it has proven to be mostly harmless; *harmful* heresies get stamped out, violently. Instead, let me make this perfectly clear: the five keys are *everything*. When I say I will kill everyone here and take this building to the ground in order to get just *one* of them back, believe me. Please."

"Do you really think the League of Countries would stand for that?" Polister asked. "Listen to yourself. The House can't just commit a massacre without any consequence. You're powerful, but not *that* powerful."

"We do not *care* what it will look like, because *none of it will matter*. The House must endure; if you want to talk moral duty, *that is ours*. We're willing to set the rest of the world on fire if we have to. Now, we're coming in here one way or another. *How* that happens is up to you. Last chance."

Staring at Mavis Spack's hooded face, Polister wished he knew the man a little better, if only so he could get a decent read on him. On the one hand, Spack seemed fully committed; he looked and sounded entirely capable of overseeing a mass murder, which wasn't something that could be said about most people. On the other hand, the idea of the House—never anything less than politically astute—would, as an entity, sign off on such an act, seemed like pure madness. The House didn't control the Stream; the news would get out, and that news would (as Spack said) set the world on fire.

This was the kind of thing that started wars. They wouldn't go that far. Not the House *he* knew.

"I'm sorry I can't be of more help," Polister said.

Mavis Spack hung his head. "All right," he said. "We'll do it the other way."

He marched out of the chamber.

Ten minutes later, the Sentries opened fire.

PART III
SAND AND WATER

Chapter Twelve

✦

The biggest surprise for Makk, on waking up in a hospital bed, was that he was alive at all.

It was not the first thought to come to him. The first thought arrived in the hazy midpoint between awake and not, in which Makk assumed his current location to be the Depths—because that was where *Cholem* went when they died. This was followed by the observation that the Depths were not as bad as he'd been told to expect. He was not, for instance, actively on fire, or constantly drowning, or stuck in a loop, reliving the worst moments of his life.

(These were all, it should be noted, entertainment vid depictions of the Depths; Septal canon didn't really get into it in detail. "We don't want to tell you exactly, but it'll suck and you should avoid it," was the general thesis.)

But no: he was quite comfortably horizontal, on something soft, which wasn't at all unpleasant. He wondered if maybe he was in the Haven instead, which, if so, was surely due to a clerical error.

Then he tried to move, and the pain of that experience sent him back into thoughts of the Depths.

He decided it was time to wake up enough to figure out what was going on; that was when he realized he was still alive, and lying in a hospital bed.

But that couldn't be right either. His last memory was of going into the water, surrounded by inky black monsters with scary teeth and a profound dislike for the ship he'd been aboard. He had a vague recollection of being elsewhere after that, perhaps, possibly, and of hearing Elicasta's voice, perhaps, possibly, but it didn't seem solid enough to have been based on a real-world event.

He tried to move again, which sucked. The pain came from all over, but was worst in his ribcage, left shoulder, right arm, head and neck. The latter two were because he hadn't moved either in so long, the muscles going up the neck and to the back of his skull were stiff. The right arm hurt because he had just, in attempting to move, put stress on the intravenous drip attached to that arm. The other two problems were (if his memory could be trusted) from injuries incurred while going down with that ship.

With a little work, and a lot of breaks, he managed to sit up and have a proper look around.

It *wasn't* a hospital. He was in a room full of medical equipment, sure, but the windows were round and the one doorway was curved on the edges and didn't reach all the way to the floor.

He was aboard a ship.

Terrific, he thought. *And my last time on a ship went* so *well, too.*

Except, he'd learned what it felt like to have the deck of a ship under him, and the hospital room didn't have that kind of feel. There was no rocking, however gentle that might be, from the moods of the ocean.

He reached up with his left hand (the arm moved okay as long as he didn't bother the shoulder too much) and felt his face. There was, he guessed, between a week's and ten days' worth of growth. That was assuming nobody had been shaving him while he was unconscious.

In addition to the IV drip, he was also attached to a machine intended to monitor his vital signs. (According to the readouts, he was indeed alive.) Beneath that, on the table, was a button.

He hit the button. Two minutes later, a woman he did not know, who was dressed like a naval officer, came rushing into the room.

"Welcome back!" she said. She was not a naval officer, or if she was, it was for a country Makk had never heard of before; the insignia on her arm didn't belong to any of the ones he knew about. "How do you feel?"

"Not great!" he said. "Where the fuck am I?"

A Dr. Whallip came in a few minutes later, wearing the same nonsensical uniform, plus a white lab coat and a stethoscope. She gave him a series of cognitive tests—did he remember his name, can he identify the animal in the picture, and so on— checked his sight and hearing, made sure he had sensation in his extremities, and took his vitals.

"It looks like you're on track to make a full recovery, detective," the doctor said, once the exam was complete. He had a dislocated shoulder, there was a hairline fracture in his left shoulder blade, and his ribs were still broken, but all of that was healing okay; as long as he didn't do anything stupid for a while, he'd be fine.

"That's great," Makk said.

"It's remarkable, is what it is."

"Ah, I've had my share of fractures."

"I don't mean the physical damage," the doctor said. "Between nearly drowning, and the hypothermia, a significant diminishment of cognition was a likely outcome. But you appear to have come through just fine."

"Super," he said. He didn't specifically remember either nearly drowning or suffering through hypothermia, but didn't want her to backtrack on the cognitive test, so he didn't say so. "Now can you tell me where I am, and how I got here?"

The doctor looked at the nurse—her name was Poyp, according to her name tag—who shrugged, and back at him. "Sorry, I thought you were told. Welcome to the sovereign nation of Asealand."

"Asealand," he repeated.

"I assume you've heard of us."

"I've heard of Asealand, yes," he confirmed. "It's a floating raft off the southern tip of Kindon. I may not know a ton about navigating the open seas, but I'm not bad with geography; the ship I was on didn't go down south of Kindon. And I don't know what this *nation* you're talking about is."

Dr. Whallip laughed. "We did used to have a fixed position in the southern seas, but that was well before my time. The admiral steers us to wherever we can find a friendly harbor, these days."

Pretty much everything Makk had heard about Asealand was negative. It was where the rich who weren't rich enough to buy on Lys lived instead. It was for shut-ins who liked to travel. It was so wealthy people could still have access to scurvy.

And it was full of delusional people who thought that by living in international waters, they weren't subject to the laws of *actual* nations. He once heard it called the "murder barge" for this reason, although while *some* laws did not apply, the laws against murder definitely still did.

It wasn't supposed to be this nice. Granted, Makk had only seen one room so far, but in his mind, Asealand was supposed to look like a proper naval vessel—only wider—and full of rich people who didn't know how boats worked. Naval vessels weren't designed with comfort in mind.

"And the uniforms?" he asked. "You guys salute each other, or what?"

"Yes," Nurse Poyp said, entirely serious. "Why wouldn't we?"

"Uh, sure," Makk said, deciding not to say a whole bunch of unkind things about being in the pretend military. "How did I get here?"

Right then, the door opened and Elicasta came rushing in.

"You're awake!" she said, half-hugging him, half-jumping on top of him.

"Ow," he said, then, "ow, ow, ow," for emphasis.

"Sorry!" she said, pulling back. "Are you..." she turned to the doctor, "is he going to be okay?"

"We think so," she said. "We'll leave you two to catch up. Hit the button if you need anything. And don't stay long, Ms. Sangristy; he still needs plenty of rest."

"I thought you were *dead*, 'Casta," Makk said, as soon as they were alone. "I thought you went down with the *Colusm*. How did you not go down with the *Colusm*?"

"Del got us to a lifeboat," she said. She perhaps assumed he remembered who Del was. He did not.

"Speaking of *dead*," she said, "How about *you*? We thought you died five times, real."

"*You* fished me from the water," he said, remembering now. Then he remembered something else. "The key? Did I lose the key?"

"I have it," she said. For proof, she reached around behind her back and pulled it out. "Snagged it when they stripped you out of the wet clothes; they didn't even ask what it was. I'll give it back when you're wearing pants again."

"You can hang onto it."

"No thank you," she said. "Lots of people dying for keys lately. You're sturdier than I am."

"I don't know about that; how many times have *you* been presumed dead by now?"

"Fair."

"You got me out of the water," he said, getting back to the point. "How did we end up in the lap of luxury?"

"Good luck that almost skipped bad. Nearly got run down before we got their attention, which was a whole thing."

"Hey! You're not wearing your rig!" he said. It had been bugging him since she walked in, why she looked so different. The only time he ever saw her without it was when they were intimate, which hadn't been often of late. "I can see your whole face and everything."

"It's slag," she said. "But I still have the chips. I've got something slapped up from spares; it's low bar unVee quality, but it'll get it done when the time comes. Listen, there's something you need to know about this place."

"I know. Floating city. Rich people. Scurvy."

"It's nice, actually. You'll see, when you're up and about. They're decent here. Little weird, but decent. And there's no weapons allowed."

"I lost mine when I went overboard."

"I know," she said, taking a breath to steel herself for something like bad news, which seemed weird. They were alive; how bad could any news be, right now? "I want you to understand before I say the next part that *nobody* has guns here. As stupid as it sounds to call Coigo Staipa an *admiral*, he runs a tight ship. He keeps all these rich people in line. You're not in danger, I'm saying."

"Why would I think I *was* in danger here, Elicasta?" he asked. Because nothing says *you're in danger* like someone telling him he's not in any danger.

"Because he's here," she said. "That's why. We were tracking him, but... this is where he was."

"He *who?*" Makk asked, although he had a terrible suspicion he knew precisely who they were talking about.

Then the door opened again, and Calcut Linus stormed in.

"Finally, this asshole's awake," he said. "Get up, Stidgeon. We have business to finish."

Makk's heart was still working just fine, self-evidently, because as soon as Calcut appeared in his hospital room, the machine responsible for audibly tracking his heart rate went nuts.

Makk's first instinct was to reach for the gun that had already been established as absent.

"You're under arrest," Makk said, which was a really funny thing to say, given he didn't know if the Velon police department still considered him a cop.

"Fuck you too, Stidgeon," Linus said.

"Cut it *out*, Calcut," Elicasta scolded, and well, that was a surprise. She was there when Calcut murdered Ba-Ugna Kev, and *tried* to murder both of *them*. If anything, she should have been at *least* as terrified to be encountering him, in a situation in which Makk couldn't defend her or himself. Linus could, if he wanted, strangle Elicasta with his bare hands right there, and Makk wouldn't have been able to do much about it.

That Linus wasn't launching himself at either of them was weird, but not impossibly so. He was known to have a violent temper—which was very much what got all three of them into this mess in the first place—but he was also known to prefer having someone else commit the violence for him whenever possible. Were his goons outside, waiting for the order?

What was going on here?

"Fine, fine," Calcut said, hands up, stepping back. He sounded chastened, which, again, was super weird. "I'm not gonna kill you right now, Stidgeon. Wouldn't be, ah, what's the word I want? Sporting."

"Since when did you care about sporting?" Makk asked.

Calcut lunged forward again. This time, Elicasta stepped between them.

"I'll *explain* it," Elicasta said. "All right? Give him time."

"Give *me* time?" Makk repeated.

What the fuck is happening?

Pacing at the foot of the bed like a caged tiger, Calcut said, "I don't want any of his bullshit, or the deal's off."

"Nothing's changed, Calcut," she said.

Fuming, he went back to the door. "I'm glad you're not a fucking vegetable, Stidgeon," he said. "That's all I came here to say."

He left before Makk could come up with a decent comeback.

Makk turned to Elicasta. "'Deal?' What deal? Are we in league with an international criminal now?"

"I know that must've sounded insane from your perspective, babe, but a *lot* has happened."

"I'm getting that."

"And he saved our lives."

"Really. How did he do that?"

"It was his null-grav auto helo that pulled us off the lifeboat," she said. "And he did it already knowing it was us."

"Sure. He'd want to kill us himself," Makk said. "Look at what happened with Kev; you think Linus didn't have it in him to slip a bomb on that exo? He didn't do it, because he wanted to watch. Only reason he's happy that I'm alive is he wants to make sure I'm healthy enough to endure a good long torture. He'll probably make a vid and drop it on the dark once it's over."

"That may have been it at first," she said. "But he can't do that to us *here*. This is what I've been saying; he doesn't have any authority in Asealand, and neither do you. If he tried to do *anything* to either of us, he'd be exiled, and he doesn't have anywhere else to go right now."

"That'd be small comfort after you and I are both dead. *Restraint* has not been his strength. He killed his own brother, for Honus's sake."

"I know. Believe me, Makk, I know. I almost asked to be put

back in the lifeboat when I saw who was on the other end of the auto helo. But things have changed."

"You keep saying that," Makk said. "It can't have changed *that* much. He's still a psychopath, and we still can't trust him. I thought you, more than anyone, wouldn't need convincing."

She nodded, sat on the edge of the bed, and took his right hand. "Which should mean that when I say we *have* to trust him, you'll believe me."

"It should," he agreed. "And it doesn't. I'm gonna need a lot more."

Makk wasn't going to get his answers right away, because the doctor wouldn't let him. Which was fair; he'd only just woken up after being almost dead for a decently long time, and he was tired. Given he'd woken up in a strange new world that he didn't think he much cared for, he was happy to close his eyes for a few hours, on the off-chance that he'd erroneously been shuffled to the wrong reality. The universe would no doubt self-correct if given the chance.

This did not happen. When he woke up again, it was to a light meal of bland food, and Elicasta setting up a vid screen.

"I think you're probably right about Calcut," she was saying, as she worked. "He probably had a different motive when he pulled us out. But that was before."

"Before everything changed," he said. "I remember."

"Yeah."

She explained how she'd used her rig to signal the ship, at the same time blowing up half of Asealand's networked electronic devices.

"'Unintentionally,' I told them," she said, "even though I knew it was gonna do exactly what it did."

That left the crew of Asealand with the certainty that there was someone in the water, but with no means to find out any more than that. They reached out to the closest thing they had to a tech genius for a solution. That happened to be Calcut Linus.

Makk had only ever known Calcut as a rich criminal, but if it weren't for him, C-Coins might not even exist, the Black Market would definitely not exist, and the Stream itself would be fundamentally different. He was an asshole with serious anger management issues and zero respect for the law, but he wasn't a *stupid* asshole.

Like a lot of tech savvy semi-geniuses, Linus preferred non-networked equipment when it was feasible. (This was according to Elicasta. Makk didn't ask her *why* this was so, but took her word for it that it was.) He was thus the only person who could not only explain what had happened, but had the tools to effect a rescue.

As for what Calcut was doing aboard Asealand in the first place... it turned out the ship was a better place for wealthy people to wait out an international arrest warrant than even Lys. To this point, Elicasta added, cryptically, "especially now."

When Makk asked what *that* meant, she said, "because now, the House is after him too."

She didn't say why.

"Okay, ready," she said, once the screen was set up and wired to something that looked only a little like Elicasta's previous optical rig.

Makk didn't know much about the technological requirements of life as a Veeser, but he inferred that the type of equipment they used was Very Important, and the one Elicasta used to have was Very Expensive. In contrast, the one she had now looked like it had been made in someone's basement. This was evidently close to correct; she said she'd put it together from spare parts. It gave her access to the Stream again, and her accounts, and it had slots for her memory chips, but it had almost no onboard memory. "I parked my vids in an off-drop," she explained, when he asked. This didn't explain anything, but he appreciated the effort.

She could post new vids to her account with this rig, supposedly. She had not done so, but emphasized that it was possible. He didn't know why he needed to know this; he never cared all that much about her Veeser work. Were she to retire, he doubted his life would be much different, except that it would probably make conversations with her easier.

"Great," he said. "What are we watching?"

"So, the day before our rescue, I caught news of a vid drop from a Veeser I follow. Do you know Dowanna Chiggle?"

"Sounds familiar."

"She probably ran up against you a couple. We jogged the same gigs, mostly."

"Crime," he said, translating. "Real news."

"Real-ish, yeah. She's legit, I'm saying; she says it's the deal, you can expect her to come right. The vid she teased was a face-to with Damid Magly."

Makk had almost forgotten the reason for their ill-advised trip across the ocean. "Magly surfaced."

"You could say that," she said. "In all the rescuing, and the panicking with Calcut in my orbit and my *own* recoup, I didn't catch up on the vid stream until two days later. By then, everything was... yeah, I'm getting ahead. You should take this in episode order. Here's the face-to."

She flipped on the vid screen, and the frozen face of Dowanna Chiggle—who *did* look familiar—filled up the screen. Elicasta hit *go*.

"...this morning with none other than *the* most wanted man on the *planet*, Chiglins! Thaaaaat's right, Damid Magly him*self,* in the *flesh*, on a secret vid locale! He's on the *move* with a princess, and he has a *lot* to say! He promises, the Middle Kingdoms will *shake*, and the House will *fall down* with what he's got. Let's get it *up!*"

The screen blacked out for a three-count, and then lit up with a split screen. The left side had four faces in a grid: Dowanna, and three other Veesers. This was not, evidently, an entirely exclusive interview.

The right half was taken up by Damid Magly.

Magly looked a lot thinner than the last image Makk had of him. There was a haunted look behind his eyes that Makk had seen before. This was a man weighed down either by secrets, or a vitamin deficiency.

"Professor," one of the other Veesers said, "the whole Stream's watching, real. Hit us with the goods."

"Thank you for agreeing to do this," he said. He had a deep voice that probably got him pretty far in life. "To begin, I want to explain why the Middle Kingdoms want us captured, and killed. It's not for the reasons you've been told."

He then went on to tell an *insane* story about underground machinery and cloning. There was a whole corner of Stream fic vids dedicated to paranoid fantasies regarding the House; what he was saying would have fit right in. He also mentioned…

"A key," Makk said.

"Yes," Elicasta said. "It's like we thought. They found a key, and they took it."

"Do they still have it?"

"I don't know. They did when this streamed."

Magly drifted into what seemed like a tangent then, about the Kingdoms being "a crisis of exploitation" and how the rest of the world had to step up to save the peasantry from their embrace of "warped and misshapen Septalism."

It did not, probably, go off as well as he thought it would. Makk's impression was that the professor was accustomed to carrying a room via charisma and physical appeal. (And that voice.) But he was tired, didn't look that appealing in the moment, and his charisma wasn't translating as well over the Stream as it probably did in person.

He seemed to be expecting to set the Stream on fire with this revelation. The Veesers on the other end didn't feel exactly the same way, given the questions they asked.

Question, really. The same one, phrased differently, over and over: "When can we speak to Battine Alconnot?"

He kept putting them off by saying the princess would be on later, but that was clearly a lie. Makk wondered if he landed the Veesers by explicitly promising a chance to see and speak to Alconnot, or if he just let them convince themselves.

Is she even there? he wondered. If she wasn't, did that mean they'd separated sometime in the past two months?

Which one of them has the key?

"Where is he, here?" Makk asked, as the interview got bogged down in the details of his escape across continents. "It looks like an office, or a library."

"He never says," Elicasta said, "but it's Wrimmad City. You'll find that out soon enough."

It was around then that the interview started to drift off-script.

"Can you guys hold tight for one minute?" he asked. Then he stepped away from the optical, leaving the four Veesers to speak to one another for several seconds. They thought maybe he was *finally* dragging Alconnot into the vid, which would be a good reason to stick around.

He didn't return with anyone.

"They're here," he said breathlessly, sliding back into the picture. He looked excited, but also scared.

"Who?" one of the Veesers asked. (Makk thought their name was "Slam" but couldn't be sure, and didn't care enough to find out.) "Who is there?"

"They've found me," he said. He shot a furtive glance off-optical, then said, "hang on. You need to see."

He left again. Dowanna complained that they should not have conducted this live, and the others agreed.

"Where in Wrimmad is he?" Makk asked, while they were waiting.

"The Unital Holy Chamber," Elicasta said. "The consensus is, he's in Staffer Calidon's private rooms."

"Consensus."

"Just watch."

The portion of the vid dedicated to Magly split in half, with a second, fuzzy image filling up the blacked-out quadrant. It gradually came into focus, to a wide-angle view of a large compound, filled with a bunch of people.

"Can you see?" Magly asked, off-vid.

"We can see," the Veeser named Happabap (possibly?) said.

"Javilon's balls," Makk said, leaning forward. "Those are Sentries."

They'd dropped down from a military-quality airship that was supposed to be the kind of thing only actual governments with actual armies had at their disposal. As soon as their boots hit, they drew long-rod blasters from their backs.

Makk remembered a more rudimentary version of the same kind of gun from his time in the military. The generals called them road-clearers; the foot soldiers called them suicide guns, because they could only fire once before needing forty seconds to recharge. Sure, that one blast could take out a small car, but forty seconds was a long time to find out not every hostile in the vicinity was *in* that car. Makk had to think the newer model didn't have the same weakness.

Needless to say, these guns also didn't belong in the hands of an ostensibly religious, non-governmental organization.

"It's the House," Magly said, "they've found me."

Then his end of the vid cut out.

"What?" Makk asked. "What happened to him?"

"Stream-theory, the airship dropped a blocker as soon as they landed."

"That's the end of it?"

"Magly was able to make a vid from there, and either got it out after the block came down, or someone else did."

Elicasta engaged her end of the vid output, the screen changed, and now they were looking at a frozen image captured by a voicer. "He dropped this in the box of all four Veesers from the face-to. They vetted and dumped it on the Stream at around the same time. Two hours later, they had their Verifieds yanked."

Elicasta said this in the same tone one uses to announce a death. From her perspective, that's probably exactly what it was.

"That's crazy," Makk said. "I don't know a *lot* about the Stream, but that kind of thing doesn't just happen, does it? Nobody has the power to do that unilaterally."

"There's a whole appeals process before the flag is changed," she said. "So no, that doesn't *just* happen. It's also what Kev threatened me with, up on Lys. If he had a rail to it, figure he's not alone."

"You're saying the *House* pushed a button, and discredited four established Veesers. I can't imagine anyone would stand for that."

"Makk, if this was the worst thing they did that day, pretty sure yeah, that's all anyone'd want to talk about. But it wasn't close."

Before he could ask what *that* meant, she hit *go* on the vid.

The image jumped to life; it was, as before, a down-angle view of a courtyard. Sentries stood at one side. It was hard to see who they were facing off against, because the view from the pinpoint optical on the voicer wasn't terrific. Every now and then, someone would wander into view, either wearing the kind of clothing Makk associated with the civilian population, or a uniform-wearing person, wearing a metal hat. Local law enforcement, or local military. The audio was tweaked high enough to pick up the wind; if anyone in the courtyard was talking, it would come through.

What are they waiting for? Makk wondered.

When Magly spoke—not visible, he must have been holding the voicer out of the window—Makk jumped.

"A few minutes ago, their leader demanded an audience with Polister Calidon," he whispered. "Staffer Calidon has already told them he's providing us with sanctuary; they're discussing the legalities of it now."

The voicer moved, and there was some rustling on the audio as Magly changed positions. He was trying to get a full view of the courtyard, but he was doing it half-blind—he couldn't see what the optical was capturing without sticking his head out the window, which was something he probably didn't want to do. Makk saw at least two dozen locals this time, all standing between the line of Sentries and the doors to the building.

"I don't know who the leader is," Magly said. "Very tall, deep voice. Hooded, of course. Dressed in a suit. I think he's probably a High Hat. Wait. Something's happening."

They could hear, but not see, the door open. Out strode the man Magly described.

"Might be a Hat," Makk said. "But it's not one I know."

"That's High Hat Spack of Agon," Elicasta said.

Spack walked across the empty middle of the courtyard, with a woman trailing behind.

"Well?" the woman asked. She seemed confused, and kept looking back at the door from which he'd left.

"The Stream identified her as Myala Dravian," Elicasta said. "Local politician."

When Spack didn't respond, Dravian turned back to the door.

"What's the answer?" she asked. The question was directed to someone out of view. "Sanctuary?"

"I'm afraid not," Spack said, without turning. He was now on the other side of the line of Sentries.

"Oh, shit," Makk muttered.

Spack looked at a Sentry, and gave a subtle nod. Then they opened fire.

Only about three seconds of it was captured by Magly's voicer, because he screamed and pulled it back inside, and then the image froze again.

When it came back, the timestamp had jumped ahead three minutes; Magly was throwing things in a bag, out of breath, in a panic.

"I know," he was saying, "that this isn't going out. They're blocking all signals."

He got the bag closed, picked up the voicer, and stared into the optical. Already undernourished and haunted-looking, he now looked terrified.

"They're killing everyone. They just..." he let out a sob. "Gods, I'm sorry. I'm so sorry. I never thought they'd..." He stopped to compose himself, then continued packing. "I think the building's on fire."

There were gunshots in the distance, and the familiar *whoosh* of blaster fire, followed by an explosion.

"I'm going to do everything I can to get this message out," Magly said.

Then he was running. It was hard to pick up on any of it, because he had the voicer in his hand, and the hand was bouncing around. There were glimpses of a door, and a hallway, and the sound his footsteps, and of distant gunshots.

"I want whoever gets this message to know," Magly said, "that it was the *House* that did this. All to protect..."

He ran into someone; an older man. "Come with me!" the man said, grabbing Magly by the arm.

They both ran, through doors and down halls, and then, for maybe a second, the optical picked up the ceiling of a vast room, seen through a cloud of thick smoke. The building was indeed on fire.

"Polister!" Magly shouted. "Take..."

There was a bright flash, a scream, and the voicer fell to the floor. The image froze again.

After an appropriate moment of silence, Elicasta said, "that's it. That's everything Magly got out."

"But *he* got out," Makk said. "He must have, or we wouldn't have been able to see that."

"The vids didn't make it past the sig jam for nearly twenty hours," she said. "This could mean the House brought it down and the voicer auto-transmitted. That's what most of the Stream thinks happened. We don't agree."

"*We.*"

"Makk, here's the sit. Between the first drop and the second, something like a third of the Stream became *very* interested in what happened in Wrimmad City that morning. Interested enough to jump-task sats in orbit over Botzis and snag some images. What they caught was, the Unital Holy Chamber is straight *gone*. I mean, it's smoking rubble. There were also fires in three other parts of the city, and like five more of those drop ships. Then the *satellites* went dark. *Then* Magly's voicer vids dropped, with proof that the House was straight killing people, just in case not *everybody'd* figured it out already. The House has turned against us, and I mean *all* of us. When I say *we*, you're on the right vibe because, yeah, I'm talking about me and Calcut Linus. He's an asshole, and a killer, and he terrifies the fuck out of me. But about two hours before they took down the Unitals, that same kill squad pushed a search pulse for Calcut Linus on their own network. When the *House* is the enemy, even Calcut recognizes that everyone else is a friend."

Makk nodded, took a deep breath, and tried to take all of this in.

Definitely woke up in the wrong universe, he thought.

"Okay," he said. "All right let's... let me walk my way through this. Start with why you two don't think that was an auto-transmission from a discarded voicer."

"We *have* access to tech the rest of the Stream doesn't," she said. "Partly because Calcut's... Makk, he's got a whole second network running under the Stream. It's all kinds of illegal, but I mean, right now? It's useful."

"What *kind* of all kinds of illegal?"

"C-Coin movement tracking, comm data mapping, stuff that's supposed to be impossible. Not your gig, not murder police illegal, but the cyber team would probably love to know about it. He's also got tasked sats the House can't touch, because unlike the rest of us, Calcut has gone out of his way to cut out or modify House tech on this second network of his. I'd call him paranoid, but..."

"But he was right," Makk said. "And now it's useful, as you said."

"Between his network and Kev's program, and with every other satellite covering Botzis fritzed, we're the only people on the planet, I'm pretty sure, who could geolocate Magly's voicer at the moment it sent that vid."

Makk was ready to ask *how* they did that in greater detail, because if he understood the steps taken in the handling of the vid in question, it wasn't sent to the Stream directly, but to the boxes of the Veesers who released it. *That* timestamp would be on record in their drop files, and nowhere else. Either Elicasta reached out to one of them for that information, or Calcut looked it up on his "second network." Makk didn't ask which it was. Instead, he said, "So where was that?"

"*Not* in the middle of the Unital compound," she said. "Which is where we saw it fall. The ping was about thirty kalomaders north, at the base of Mount Vesay. Whoever has it, they're fleeing the city."

"It could be Magly," Makk said. "That last bit looked pretty bad, but he may have survived."

"Possibly, except he didn't add anything to the vid he'd already set down."

"Because he didn't want them to know he was still alive."

"Enh. He likes being face-forward a little too much for that to fly," she said. "Just a theory, but I know the type well enough. After going off so hard about the Kingdom, he'd take the risk just to let the House know they missed."

"Yeah, I think you're right," he said. "Then someone else."

"Someone else," she agreed. "Someone who maybe didn't know the voicer they were carrying was rigged to boost a vid upstream on auto. Someone who didn't know their way around one so well, I mean."

"Battine Alconnot."

"It makes sense, doesn't it?"

"We never once saw her," Makk said. "Yes, I agree, it makes *some* sense, but we *did* see Polister Calidon. Why not him?"

"Also possible. Or both of them. Whoever it is, we think they may have the key."

Makk nodded. "The attack on the rest of the city," he said.

"They took the Chamber down to the ground and didn't find what they were looking for, so now they're dismantling the rest of the place. But you get what I'm saying, right?"

"I think you're saying Battine Alconnot still has the key, *and* she's survived the House's declaration of war on Unitism, *and* you, me, and Calcut Linus, the most corrupt and venal man on the planet, are the only ones who know this. I assume since the two of you are now fast friends, you've let him in on what his brother had been planning, before Calcut brained him with a rolling pin."

She made a face. "I might have," she said. "We *need* him, Makk. If anything Orno told us…"

"Viselle, not Orno," Makk interrupted. "We're working with information from *another* murderer who also happened to have tried to kill us. Tell me the provenance isn't sketchy."

"You piss me off sometimes, Makk Stidgeon," she said. "You saying you want to give the House back their keys?"

"No," he said. "But given what they're willing to do to find just one, I'm now *very* curious about what the House needs the keys for. It has to be something more than just turning on a magic cloning machine."

Makk thought back to the Orno Linus murder case, and how interested the House was in recovering their stolen artifact. At the time, Makk thought they were talking about the book that went from his hands, to Leemie's, to (he assumed) Dorn Jimbal's... but it was the *key* they were after. It was important enough that the Sentries were willing to literally step over the murdered body of Professor Linus to look for it.

At the time, Makk was appalled that they would prioritize the artifact's recovery over the death of a colleague. Now? What was happening in Wrimmad City made their handling of Orno's death look like a minor error.

"It could be just that," Elicasta said. "Or it could be for a different device. This isn't the first time we've heard a story about a machine from the gods hidden underground, real? Magly said he took images down there, as proof, but he never got a chance to share them with anyone."

"They'd be on his voicer too," Makk said.

"Another reason to catch up with whoever's carrying it."

"Yes, fine, but back up and talk through this with me," Makk said. "Orno Linus's whole plan was to collect the five keys, find the secret machine with the Outcast-killing death ray or whatever, turn it on and save the world. We already know the House rejected this idea academically, and we also know *their* plan is to hide underground for however long it takes until the surface world is habitable again. So, again, what do *they* need the keys for?"

"And, do they need all five?" Elicasta asked.

"That's a good question. It can't be just about *stopping* what we're trying to do, although... I can't even imagine why they'd care; if it doesn't work, it doesn't work. But they only have to keep their hands on one of the five keys to do it. Let's hypothesize that the House needs all five, though, just as badly as Orno did, but for some entirely different purpose. What are they willing to do to get their hands on our key, or the one Viselle has? Burn down another city? Blow up a giant ship? I'm guessing the only reason there's no international warrant for our heads is that they don't know we have one."

He had a terrible thought. "Does Calcut know about the keys?" he asked.

"I told him some of his brother's plan, but I didn't mention who *has* the keys. He's probably figured it out."

"That's not great." He sighed. "This is fucking annoying."

"Calcut?"

"No, not that; he's going to sell us to the highest bidder, or kill us, when our backs are turned, and I'm okay with that because it would mean he's acting predictably. The *House* is acting out of character, and that bothers me a *lot*. Say what you will about the Septals, but the reason they've always had their fingers in everything is because it was always *okay*, because they don't *do* things like this. Every Septal in the world didn't just... turn evil overnight; there has to be an angle we're not seeing."

Elicasta rolled the vid screen away from the bed and shut down her optical. "Maybe so," she said. "But that *angle* is currently at war with a small fishing village, and nobody's doing anything about it except act about as surprised as you are right now."

She sat on the bed in silence for a couple of beats. "I've been living with this for a little longer than you, Makk, and here's what I think: I think they know the Outcast is coming, and it's going to kill most of the life on this planet, and Orno's plan *would* work, but they don't *want* it to. I think there's a splinter group of Septals out there, and this is their way of cleansing the planet of non-adherents and starting over. That's what I think. And as soon as I can get a clean stream out of this rig, I'm going to tell the world that."

She leaned over and kissed him on the cheek. "But enough. I

know this was a lot at once. Get some rest, think of some more things to argue about, and we'll take this up again later."

He hated being babied, but she wasn't wrong. "Fine," he said. "In the meantime, don't turn your back on Calcut."

She laughed and headed to the door. "Did they say when you're expected to be up and about?" she asked. "The admiral wants to meet you."

"I don't know," he said. "Do I have to call him admiral?"

"Actually yes. It's a condition of being allowed to stay."

"I'll work on that," he said. "Don't suppose you told him *how* we ended up shipwrecked."

"The sea bugs? He knows. Del and I both told him, but I'm not sure he believed us. Even if he did, I think he thinks Asealand is indestructible."

Makk sighed. "Speaking as a professional bad luck charm, that's not a good sign."

Chapter Thirteen

Makk was walking under his own power a day later, and got to eat real food a day after that. This was the only good news to be had, possibly worldwide.

Wrimmad City was an ongoing crisis, but hardly anybody on the Stream could get their hands on verifiable evidence of it, because the House—and it appeared nobody knew this beforehand—had built censorship functionality into the network. Every new release of information was quickly blocked, and a lot of Veesers, many considered the most reliable source of real news internationally for years, were losing their Verified flags.

Officially, nobody from the House had any comment. Some leaned on the decentralized nature of Septalism to argue that *if* something bad was happening somewhere, it wasn't in *their* control. Others simply denied anything was wrong at all.

Meanwhile, the counterfactual story that it was all just a hoax was gaining momentum on the Stream. It was an easy fit for the mentalities of a significant portion of the world, because nobody wanted to confront the potential consequences of a House gone bad. Better to embrace a version where hoaxers on the Stream invented a story about the House destroying a distant place that hardly anyone knew anything about anyway. Wrimmad City—and, really, most of Botzis—was so routinely off the Stream, there was hardly anyone available to push back and say, no, this is happening; I am experiencing it personally.

But the "hoax" spin was only going to hold for so long. Multiple news sources—straight news Veesers and high profile UnVeesers, but also a generous number of Corpers and Exters— were reporting what very much looked like military buildups taking place on House campuses in various parts of the world. Most notably in Dunn—where the army-like contingent tearing apart Wrimmad came from—Velon, and Fendo.

Makk, who secretly preferred Exter and Corper news to Veeser news, thought Corpers picking up the story was especially notable; if the corporate-bought newsfeeds were disseminating stories that made the *House* look bad—an act which would undeniably have a negative impact on their profit margin—the Septals could be in trouble.

That was, provided the Septals even *cared*. If the House decided to ignore the rights of nations to self-govern and just take over Dibble...? It would be bloody, but they could absolutely do it.

Hopefully, that wasn't where this was all headed. Elicasta, despite being suddenly and stridently anti-Septal (Veesers getting summarily unverified was the trigger) seemed to believe, sincerely, that this was evidence of an internal House problem that, once called out, would get peacefully resolved. In other words, someone *within* the House had gone astray—High Hat Spack being the most likely candidate—but could be corralled from within by purer of spirit chapter heads like Duqo Plaint, or Elaran Mai.

Makk hoped she was right. But from everything he'd seen and read so far, it was looking a lot more like a paradigm shift. If that was true, they were all in a lot of trouble.

Then again, the world would be ending shortly, so how much did it really matter?

~

E licasta came to collect Makk one afternoon. It wasn't entirely without warning; he had been working his way up to a trip outside for a while, with the ultimate intention being a sit-down with Coigo Staipa, who for some reason felt it imperative that he speak to Makk as soon as he was healthy enough to make "the journey" to see the admiral.

There were a couple of things about this that bugged Makk. One was that Staipa could very easily come visit Makk if it was a matter of urgency. Another was the word "journey," which was how Elicasta kept framing it.

Anyway, he knew it was going to be happening, and he knew roughly *when* it was going to be happening, but for some reason he was still surprised when it happened.

"You can make it, right?" was the first thing she asked. 'Casta was back to wearing a rig everywhere. It was the homemade one, and it wasn't lit, which either meant the optical wasn't active, or the light was broken. Probably, she was using it to passively monitor the Stream, something she used to do all the time. It made for a more distracted version of his girlfriend. He was used to her being like this, and didn't much care for it, but knew saying that would create a problem, so he didn't. Being distracted likely meant not noticing how uncomfortable Makk looked when bending down to put his pants on.

But yes, he could make it.

"I'll be fine," he said.

"He'll feed you," she pointed out, adding, "better food than what you've been getting."

"The army had better food than what I've been getting. It's not a big hurdle."

He had been under the mistaken impression that the wardroom he had been recuperating in was below deck somewhere. Yes, he had a window, but that window only saw ocean, and the corridor where he practiced walking was fully enclosed. It was wider than he might have expected aboard a ship, though, which was a good indication that he hadn't gotten his head straight yet as regards to Asealand.

Then there was the lack of a sense of movement. He knew, from inside his room, that the ship was moving, but only because the water out the window was moving; as had been the case when he first woke up, he couldn't *feel* the motion.

This was for two reasons. One, they were traveling at an almost constant rate of speed, with acceleration and deceleration so gentle, you had to know it was happening beforehand to have a chance of detecting it. Two, they weren't floating on water, but hovering above it.

The ocean, he was told, occasionally produced a wave that reached the bottom or sides of the ship, but the distance between the deck and sea level was so vast that the only time water made it up there was when it rained.

This jibed with the view, as it very much felt like he was in a building, looking down at the water from the tenth floor.

But again, he was underestimating the vastness of the ship. In his mind, it was still just a kind of boat, albeit a stupidly tall one.

Then he got his first look outside.

To begin with, Asealand was a giant fucking square that had no business traveling in any particular direction. It remained, in other words, the *raft* Makk remembered it being, only now it was —for some inexplicable reason—ambulatory. The structure they exited from was part of a larger building on what he decided to call the right side of the deck, which he was basing on its position in respect to the direction they were traveling.

There was no prow or stern. Were the ship to suddenly head right by ninety degrees, he saw no reason for it to *turn* first; it would just be that the right side had become the front. The propulsion system probably didn't work that way, but it *could have* because, again, structurally, there was no difference between one squared side and another.

They emerged onto a balcony that provided a view of the back half of the ship; a three-dimensional nightmare that made Kindontown look like a well-designed urban landscape. There were towers and stairs, corridors and ramps, turrets, sloped rooftops, and more than a few swimming pools. There were hardly any straight lines. It was as if the designers had modeled their approach on fungal growth.

"Holy shit," he said. It was about all he *could* say; his position at the railing suddenly felt perilous, as if gravity could shift at any moment and send him tumbling into this maze of ordered chaos.

"That was my first reaction too," Elicasta said. "I'd say you get used to it, but I'm not there yet so I don't know if that's legit."

"It's hard to believe something this big is moving."

"It is, but not real fast. Even at this speed, the admiral says it takes about five hours to come to a stop. I think they can probably do it faster if they *have* to, and the five is to make sure nobody spills a drink. But even stomping on the brake, it's gotta take a while. Del told me Asealand's taken out cargo ships."

"I don't find that surprising at all," Makk said.

A woman from the next building over (they weren't buildings, but he couldn't think of what else to call them) stepped out of her living quarters onto a sun deck, stretched, and took a seat in a lounge chair, on a plot of artificial grass. She looked about retirement age, and just familiar enough for Makk to think he should probably know her name. A man on his porch atop a spire a hundred maders away from her waved, she waved back, and then he went about watering his plants. Roughly the same age, the man and also had the kind of face that made Makk think he was somebody.

"It's a *retirement* community," Makk realized. "That's what this is; a floating retirement home."

"It's a mix," Elicasta said. "Yeah, median age is high, just on sight, but if you're not crew, you've gotta be decently rich to afford the space. Figure that's your well-off retirees first. Come on, Coigo's waiting."

Makk wanted to go back to bed.

"Where are we going, from here?" he asked, not quite believing 'Casta figured out how to navigate this maze.

She nodded to the front half of the ship. "The castle. Can't see it from here."

"There's a... castle?"

"That's what everyone calls it," she said, grabbing him by the elbow and leading him down the nearest flight of stairs.

Although it didn't seem obvious on first blush, it was actually a lot easier to walk around aboard Asealand than it had been on the *Colusm*. There wasn't nearly as much unanticipated rocking and swaying. However, his bad knee remained furious with him for trying to walk, his fractured ribs didn't appreciate any kind of movement, and the collarbone fracture was letting him know what a bad idea it was to use his left arm. So, it was still a challenge.

At the bottom of the stairs, they moved through a wide corridor between structures on the actual deck. There were signs everywhere, pointing this way and that and calling out things that didn't make sense on a ship, like a vid theater, a concert hall, a grocer. The wide corridors also had their own *street* names. (They were on Oak Street, which was hilarious inasmuch as trees were a distant memory here.)

They went about twenty paces down Oak Street and hung a right at a four way intersection, and then they were on Main, and nearly getting run over by someone on a bicycle.

Main cut directly through the building with the hospital wing.

"Everything behind us and half of what's in front of us is private residences," 'Casta explained. "Like, legit private; these people *own* the, ah, not land, but you get me."

"The footprint," Makk suggested.

"That. The building we're passing through here is more like a public admin building. Hospital, crew quarters, permit offices. I think there's some kind of courtroom too."

"Permit," Makk laughed. "For what?"

"To build," she said, entirely serious.

They emerged from the tunnel. In the middle of the front half of the ship was a large structure with a triangular base, a glass-enclosed room at the top surrounded by an open deck, and an extremely tall pole jutting out of the peak. The pole—it was a *mast*, because it was on a ship, but there wasn't a sail attached, nor did it look like there had ever been one, so it was a pole—was by far the tallest thing on Asealand.

"That's the castle," Elicasta said.

"Doesn't look like a castle," Makk said. Then, the part of his brain that stored random trivia about boats woke up, and he said, "*fore*castle."

"Sure. Nobody calls it that, but sure."

The front half of the ship was just as stacked with random assortments of private residences as the back, and the comparison he'd made to the design and fungal growth was looking pretty apt: everyone bought a part of the deck and built whatever they wanted on top of it, limited only by available material, the permit office, and the laws of physics.

They came upon a modest shopping area next, with stores for clothing and various sundries, and the occasional *street vendor*, which was just insane. Makk tried to imagine what it would be like to live on an exclusive, private yacht the size of a small city, and still have to hawk wares all day long. He couldn't do it.

Main led straight to the castle. They were most of the way there, when Elicasta hesitated at a side street (Poplar—they were really fond of tree names on this thing) and pointed to one of the private residences. "That's Calcut's," she said.

Makk stopped to look, grateful for the break.

Calcut's place didn't look any different than the others; just a main spire with lots of windows. Kind of a lighthouse design, which seemed popular. Linus's Norg Hill estate was styled after House architecture, but there was no trace of that here.

"We're not going *there* too, are we?" he asked.

"No, we're not going there," she said. "Not right now."

She started to move again, but Makk needed another minute. "Are you okay?" she asked.

"You said, 'journey' and I didn't get it," he said. "Now I do; this is a lot more walking than I was expecting."

"I know, but we're almost there," she said. "There's a little forced perspective going on; the castle's closer than it looks."

Makk nodded, said a quiet prayer to Ho (who was, among other things, the god of pain relief) and got moving again.

"Where are *you* staying?" he asked.

"One of the admiral's guest rooms, in the castle. He has a room for you too, once the doctor gives the all-clear. You just have to make nice first."

"Make nice?"

"Yeah, the admiral is a ride," she said.

"*Admiral*," Makk repeated under his breath.

She stopped him with a hand on his shoulder. "That is *exactly* the kind of slap-back I mean. No sarcasm, Makk. I get that's a reach."

"'Casta... I don't know very much about Coigo Staipa, but what I *do* know is that he never served."

"Real, if you don't play, he'll put you off at the nearest port, which is somewhere on Botzis. You want to visit Botzis right now?"

"You mean, would I rather be on *land* right now? The answer is yes. Besides, isn't that where we're *both* going?"

She made that exasperated sound she reserved just for him, then said, "we can talk about the next steps later," which sounded like a no. "We're safe here for now, and based on what I'm getting out of the Stream, safe places are at a premium. They're rioting in Velon, did you know?"

"No, how could I possibly?"

"They are. I get that *nice* isn't your deal, Makk. I do. But do you know how many self-important Pollies I've had to blink and coo for to get my in? A *lot*. Sometimes, this is the gig, and you gotta roll. I *know* you know how to do that. I've seen it. Just... pretend he's a suspect and you're the nice detective who wants him to think he's *not* a suspect. Or, I don't care; whatever frame works for you. Just play."

"Fine, I'll play."

"Thank you."

"Just tell me one thing. Am I one of the self-important Pollies you're talking about?"

She shook her head and stormed off. Which wasn't the answer he was hoping for.

Makk wasn't telling the entire truth when he said he didn't know much about Coigo Staipa; he knew a *lot*, because the Staipa clan was one of those families everyone who grew up in Inimata knew at least something about, whether or not they wanted to.

The Staipas were a minor political empire unto themselves. The scion of the family—Coigo's great-great-grandfather, Phel Staipa—made their fortune on real estate and timber, officially, and unofficially by cornering the market on wood-grain alcohol. Phel at one time was the largest private landowner in all of Geo, although 1/3 of that was Kindonese forest land, purchased during the final stages of the Mokhi dynasty.

(The devaluation of the local currency in Emperor Vassama the Fifth's government was one of the factors that led to the Kindonese war nearly three generations later. It also led to the end of true dynastic rule in Kindon. Perversely, this made Vassama Five one of the most accomplished of his line; he just didn't accomplish anything *good*.)

Great-great-grandfather Staipa leveraged his wealth and influence into political appointments for his children in various governments worldwide. By the time of his passing, there was at least one Staipa in every national governing body outside of Wivvol. Even the Middle Kingdoms employed one—Phel's grand-niece, Harbit—as an ambassador, who was there for close to ten years.

With family hands on so many levers of power, the Staipas faced many, many opportunities to benefit financially, but what was sort of interesting was that if they *did*, it wasn't obvious; they seemed to enjoy public service, and more often than not actually cared about doing the job well. If anything, the fact that none of them *needed* the coin made them *more* trustworthy, if only because taking bribes was off the table. Yes, there were manifold conflicts of interest, but the smarter members of the Staipa clan, the ones who *lasted* in their appointed and/or elected positions, went out of their way to put a neutral party between themselves and any potential conflicts or, if that was impossible, recuse themselves.

Then came Coigo Staipa.

It wouldn't be fair to say that Coigo was missing the same instinct toward duty and public service as the rest of his family; he just executed this charitibility in a novel way.

The first office he tried to run for was president of the moon. This was problematic for a whole variety of reasons, foremost being that there was no such title. There were people living on Dibble's moon, sure, but it was nothing more than a skeleton crew, conducting scientific research under the flags of the five nations that had funded the project. The moon base wasn't an independent sovereignty, which meant it had no government and no voters.

Coigo was undeterred. His argument was: there *should* be a

thriving community up there. Because there wasn't, his first act as president would be to finance the expansion of the moon base, and his second would be to get people up there. What they were going to eat, drink and breathe was a detail he promised to work out later.

"A moon to call our own," was his campaign motto. (He had a campaign team, and a campaign, even though he was running unopposed to get votes that didn't exist for a title he couldn't have.)

It was probably the case that the majority of people, on being confronted by the obvious absurdity of this plan, assumed he was just deeply committed to a complicated, expensive, joke. But if he *was* joking, he never came out and said so.

He eventually suspended the campaign. This was after his parents, Torge and Nitalia, stepped in with a public statement that, A: the Staipa family did *not* support Coigo's presidential campaign, and B: no family money would be going toward a hypothetical moon colony buildout. This was interpreted as a threat to cut him off if he didn't stop with this nonsense.

Coigo disappeared for a while after that, but clearly never gave up on the dream of his own moon colony; when he resurfaced, it was to announce the development of Asealand, which he initially pitched—to investors and early buyers—as moon base 1.0.

"Just as no one nation has a claim on the moon, so too does no one nation have claim on the ocean," he said, in the press conference announcing his plans. "I will *prove* the government-first approach can work, with the right man in charge."

Moving people to a barge just on the other side of the international waters border was a *lot* easier than putting them on the moon, it turned out. Absolutely nothing Coigo promised worked out precisely as he said it would, but that didn't mean it was a terrible idea given what it *did* turn out to be.

(The most obvious difference was that Asealand was very

much private property, with residents renting, leasing or buying lots. These were not citizens living in a separate nation-state.)

He had discovered a niche market: a vacation home for everyone who was either not wealthy enough to afford Lys or just didn't like the idea of leaving the planet, with the latter being the exact *opposite* of Coigo's ideal moon base property buyer.

Why this was so appealing was something Makk couldn't entirely get his mind around. Surely, sharing *less* space than one could otherwise afford, while living on a barge in the middle of the ocean where (he assumed) scarcity of goods was a real issue, was a worse way to spend one's time than... well, than anything. Skiing. Visiting a Canos-Holo resort. Hiking in the Deterrents. Getting your teeth cleaned.

Now that he was seeing it for himself, he sort of understood: everyone on board was either resident or staff, and that was the extent of it. There were not, in short, any poor people.

Oh, and it also made for a pretty good place to hide from the law. He wondered, if he started knocking on doors, how many outstanding warrants he'd be able to close.

E licasta was taking him to the bridge, which was the glassed-in top of the castle at the peak of the triangle. Getting there looked like it was going to take more than Makk had in him, especially once Main Street terminated at a left-right ramp. They followed the left side of it, and ended up at a *ladder* going up the side of the structure.

"How about if he comes down, and he and I chat right here?" Makk asked.

"The bridge is awesome. You'll love it."

"Send me an image."

"It's okay, we don't have to do any climbing," she said with a laugh. She then proceeded to climb up the ladder.

"Do you call what you're doing right now something different in Stream-speak?" he asked. "Because that's what I call climbing."

"I'm just getting out of your way. Hop on."

With tremendous reluctance, he stepped onto the ladder beneath her.

"Golden," she said, looking down at him. "Now hold tight. Both hands."

She pushed a button embedded on the inside left of the ladder, and the whole thing started moving.

"Oh," he said. "Uh."

"You have the same button to your left," she said. "Up-arrow for going up, down-arrow for going down, middle button for stop."

"This is cute, but wouldn't an elevator have been more practical?"

"There's one inside," she said. "There's a hatch around the front of the base that leads to a lobby. It'll take you to the admiral's quarters, or straight up to the bridge."

"You have access to the admiral's quarters," Makk said. They had already cleared the height of most of the other buildings and were getting hit by the wind off the ocean, which was not insubstantial. "So, we didn't we take the elevator?"

"Because this way's more fun."

A stray thought from the unkind part of Makk's brain—about wishing upon Elicasta broken ribs and a fractured collarbone and a bum knee so she could experience this *fun* exactly the same way he was—nearly made it out of his mouth.

"Right," he said.

The view *was* pretty impressive. The Dancers were heading west, the waters were calm, and there were hardly any clouds in the sky. He could make out a land mass north-north-west, which he thought was probably Botzis.

They went past a dozen windows in the side of the castle,

which reminded Makk he could have seen all of this without the concern of death-by-falling.

"Watch your head," Elicasta said. He looked up in time to see her disappear through an opening in the floor of the deck that surrounded the bridge. She hopped off.

When it was his turn, rather than do the same, he pushed the STOP button, and then calmly stepped off.

"Hey, that sucked, let's not do that again," he said.

"Ah, I like it. If I thought the admiral would let me, I'd drop a whole vid on this place, starting with that ladder. Come on."

She knocked on glass a few steps from the ladder, waved to someone inside—the glass was tinted; Makk couldn't see in, but they could surely see out—and a door slid open.

Admiral Coigo Staipa was waiting for them inside.

"Ms. Sangristy!" he exclaimed. Nearly everyone in the Staipa clan was blessed by the gods with a resonant, booming voice, Coigo included. "Felicitations, on this glorious of days!"

Staipa was wearing the neatly pressed dress whites of a naval admiral on his way to the funeral of somebody important. The suit didn't *fit* all that well, but that was the fault of the man and not the suit; he either needed a tailor, or a new workout regimen. The cap that went with the suit fit poorly as well, but in this case, it was too large, not because his head had shrunk but because it had been sized at a time when he had hair.

Rounding out the *just a guy wearing a costume* look to it all, Coigo had a heavy beard, which was gray and white and a little yellow, the latter being a remnant of whatever he'd had for lunch. (Makk couldn't think of a single military that was okay with uniformed officers sporting long facial hair.) The Staipa family visage was still there—in the eyes, and the nose—but mostly hidden beneath the beard.

"Felicitations!" Elicasta said, with equivalent enthusiasm. She bowed with a flourish.

Should I bow? Makk wondered. *I'm not bowing. I'm not...*

"And Detective Stidgeon!" Staipa said, taking Makk's hand and shaking it vigorously. "Welcome, welcome, welcome!"

"Thanks," Makk said. "Thank you for saving my life. Admiral."

Makk checked Elicasta out of the corner of his eye, for a reaction. He was pretty bad at modulating sarcasm, and frankly didn't know for sure if he'd just used it or not. She seemed pleased, so he figured he was doing okay.

Deadly serious, Staipa looked Makk in the eye and said, "it is our solemn *duty*, as stewards of the ocean! To help those in need, no *matter* the cost!"

"Uh, yes. Sure."

"Come, let me give you a tour! And when we're finished, I have some questions for you! Ensign, bring our guests coffee! Double-time!"

To go along with being overdressed, Admiral Staipa tended over-emote during the course of what should be a perfectly normal conversation. He also criminally overused superlatives to an alarming degree. It was like spending time with someone who was 100% committed to a comically exaggerated impression of one of his brothers—Mol, say, who was the Velon League of Countries representative, or President Kask Staipa of Honegin— except he was doing a terrible job of it. Makk kept waiting for him to cut it out and talk normal, but that wasn't happening.

All that said, whoever Coigo engaged to design and support the technology that was keeping Asealand going was pretty competent.

The bridge was two levels deep. On the top level, Coigo had his own chair, with a wheel more at home on a vessel like the *Colusm*. Neither appeared to be necessary to the ship's operation, but they made for a nice image: the admiral, at the helm of his vessel, looking out on the ocean vista.

Makk wondered if the wheel even worked.

The top level ended—prematurely, as it was just a half-floor—with a railing, and stairs on both sides, leading to the control center that was actually responsible for piloting Asealand. Like the top floor, the lower level was surrounded on all sides by windows, but that was probably just so nobody working there got too depressed about spending their whole day at *sea*, but staring at a vid screen.

"Here is where it all happens!" Staipa said, as he brought Makk and Elicasta down the stairs. He gestured grandly, as if he'd personally installed the equipment. There were six people there, all dressed in the same pseudo-naval white dress uniforms, in various states of busy. None of them looked up at their guests; either they just didn't care, or having guests was a common thing. What was clear, from watching their interactions, was that the admiral's presence was entirely optional.

About half of what was on the vid screens looked like the sort of thing one would expect to see on an ocean-going vessel: water, from multiple angles. There was also a windspeed tracker, a live map, and a satellite weather feed.

The other half of the screen readouts looked more like the dash of Viselle's aero-car in flight, only a *lot* larger. These measured things like altitude and attitude, energy output and speed, plus a focus on potential airborne collision concerns. Makk already knew Asealand was using null-grav to travel across the ocean, but this was the first time he considered that it was actually a massive aero-car, rather than a massive boat.

"As you can see, it takes a team to keep us afloat," Staipa said.

"I do see that," Makk said. "Although *afloat* is an interesting choice of words."

Elicasta, who was standing behind Staipa and out of his line of sight, shook her head aggressively: *Don't say that.*

"Wellll," Staipa said, "we are, of *course*, a seagoing vessel, detective! We make certain accommodations for our guests, but the null gravity function is only there to *stabilize* us when the ocean fails to produce as smooth a ride as we would all prefer. I *assure* you, we're very much a ship at sea."

Makk caught one of the crew shaking her head at this little speech, and going back to her vid screens. One of her readouts had a dot that showed where the surface of the water was in relation to bottom of Asealand. The measure of the gap was variable, but self-evidently not zero.

"Of course," Makk said, adding, "admiral."

It was possible that this time, Makk failed to temper his sarcasm, because Coigo Staipa paused for a three-count before continuing with the tour.

What followed was about fifteen minutes of patter that the admiral had clearly been delivering for years. It got to the point where Makk went from thinking this was a special honor, to realizing that everyone got the same treatment when they came aboard. What was a little frustrating was that, despite not being capable with computers, boats, or aero-cars, Makk could figure out what each station did without the speech or the presentation. Yet every time Makk looked like he was anything other than actively interested in Coigo's overlong explanations—if, for instance, he visibly showed exhaustion (he was exhausted) or pain (he was very uncomfortable)—Elicasta would elbow him in the side.

She was acting like Staipa's wrath was something to be concerned about, which was pretty funny from someone who'd been palling around with Calcut Linus. But placating important people wasn't really Makk's style. He was *trying*, though.

It wasn't until they got to the geolocation screen that Makk stopped feigning interest and became *actually* interested.

"So where are we?" he asked. "Right now."

"Hasok," Staipa said, patting the navigation technician at the screen on the shoulder, "tell our guest where we are right now."

"Coming up on Botzis, admiral," Hasok said. "Another two days."

"What part of Botzis?" Makk asked. "Wrimmad?"

"Further east," Staipa said. "Dongy. We prefer Dongy to the other ports; it's just *lovely*, and the shops...! You must come ashore with us, if you can."

Makk wanted to say that he could think of nothing better than to stand on solid ground again, but didn't want to risk another elbow from his girlfriend. "I definitely will," he said. "And, where on this chart did you pick us up?"

"Hasok, where did we recover our friends?"

Hasok, who didn't seem to mind having direct questions channeled through Staipa, put his finger on a featureless spot in the ocean to the west and south of their current position. "Here, just about."

"Where did we go down?" Makk asked Elicasta.

"That would be here," Hasok said, before 'Casta took a guess. He didn't point this time; he hit a button and a dot popped up on the screen.

"That's... very precise," Makk noted.

"Because we..." Hasok began, before Staipa cut him off.

"An unsavory topic!" the admiral said. His hand was on Hasok's shoulder still, only now he was squeezing it. "We will discuss the *Colusm* later, detective! I promise!"

"I just want to make sure we've put plenty of distance between us and those... uh." Makk said. He didn't finish, because Elicasta elbowed him in the ribs. "Just, some distance."

Coigo fixed him with a disquieting stare, and held it for a five-count. This was the version of him that Elicasta was trying to avoid, evidently, because she was holding her breath.

And then he was back, and 'Casta exhaled. "Ms. Sangristy, thank you *so* much for escorting our friend here. Detective, I would be honored if you joined me for a private meal!"

Makk looked at Elicasta. "You're not coming?"

"No, but I'll see you later," she said. She gave him a quick kiss on the cheek, squeezed his arm and whispered, "he insisted. Remember to play nice."

Then she let Staipa kiss her hand, and left Makk to have dinner alone with the admiral.

That it went the way it did shouldn't have come as a surprise to anybody.

There was a banquet table set up on the top floor of Coigo Staipa's private quarters, which seemed like a peculiar place to put one, except that the view—from roughly the midpoint of the castle—was better. Makk, who had had his fill of ocean views by now, was still pretty impressed by the vista.

More impressive, though, was how comfortable the chairs were. He probably would have given high marks to *any* chair by then, but the one he got to sit in, hopefully for hours, while his knee stopped throbbing and his *ribs* stopped throbbing and his collarbone stopped throbbing and his lungs stopped acting like he'd smoked a whole box of 'bacco sticks, was just a terrific chair.

The table sat a dozen, in a room large enough to accommodate two more such tables, which it no doubt did, at great frequency; Coigo seemed like the kind of guy who enjoyed hosting banquets, and there were plenty of people aboard in need of impressing.

They spent an hour drinking Lladn wine and eating a range of seafood-centric delicacies Makk couldn't identify with great accuracy. (None of it, thankfully, was in the Kindonese tradition of, "food that looks alive enough to bite you back.")

Coigo talked nearly non-stop the entire time. This, too, was patter, but of a more concentrated sort. He had a story about how Asealand had come to be, and he wanted to tell it. The story was a wild divergence from anything Makk had ever heard before about the place, which would have been more fascinating—in an abstract, scholarly sense—if Makk wasn't currently suffering under the charitable rule of the admiral who appeared to *believe* what he was saying.

Among other things, according to Staipa, Asealand was an internationally recognized free nation-state, which was simply not true. It was his "life's work," which *may* end up being true depending on how much longer he lived, but omitted the awkward-but-amusing moon president campaign. Its residents, and the lives they enjoyed aboard the vessel, were the envy of the world, and its economic and political structure would be the model for all future governance, which… okay? Makk wasn't a political scientist, an economist, or a historian, but it sure looked like the only reason any of this worked was because everyone was very rich and mostly harmless.

But it made for a nice story.

They finally went off-script when the subject of the *Colusm* came up.

"Now then!" Coigo said expansively. (He said almost everything expansively.) "On the matter of your *unfortunate* shipwreck! I have already discussed it in some detail, with both Ms. Sangristy and the other survivor. Del?"

"Del is right," Makk said. "They were the pilot of the *Colusm* when we went down. Are they still aboard? I wanted to thank them for their help rescuing me."

"Yes, yes. Del's working below," he said, waving his hand in the air dismissively. Makk didn't know what "working below" entailed, but it didn't sound like they were being treated as a guest, the way Elicasta was. Makk wondered if Del had failed to play nice.

"They, both of them, separately and together, told the *most* preposterous story I think I have ever heard! I mean…" he laughed. "Sea monsters! All black! Rising from the very *Depths* to claim their ship!"

"Hah!" Makk said. "Imagine that."

"Indeed! I'm glad you think so too!" Staipa laughed again. It was impossible to tell, with him, which of his laughs were fake and which were real, so Makk decided to assume they were all fake.

"I *understand,* of course," Staipa said. "*Days* alone at sea, baking in the sun, not knowing if the next day, the next *hour*, will be your last. The mind plays tricks! Of course it does! Memories... they can be tricky!"

"Sure, sure," Makk said.

"As I understand it, you were unconscious for most of the time, is that so?"

"Yes, that's right."

"But you were there *when the ship went down!* And *because* of that, you... well. I don't want to say you suffered *less*, but an unconscious mind has less opportunity to, to..."

"I think the word you're looking for is collude," Makk said.

Staipa laughed. "A word for criminals! You are a detective through and through, Makk! May I call you Makk?"

"Sure," Makk said. *Can I call you Coigo?* died on his lips.

"Calcut said as much," Staipa added. "Pure detective, he said. I don't think he meant it as a compliment, but that's Calcut! But no, I don't mean *collude* I mean...to, to arrive at a mutual comprehension of what transpired. Which of *course* is nobody's fault! Please! I'm not saying this to denigrate Ms. Sangristy at *all!*"

"Or Del."

"Or them!"

"I understand what you're getting at," Makk said. "There's a Kindonese phrase for it. I don't remember the exact words, but the translation is something like, 'the madness of two.' It comes up surprisingly often in criminal investigations."

Staipa practically lunged across the table at him, he was so happy. "Yes! *You* understand!"

"Perfectly."

"*Wonderful.* Well! That little *story* of theirs has put us in quite a *conundrum*, if you can believe it!"

"How so?"

"Technically, we were the first to transmit the news of the *Colusm*'s demise, despite it being many days after the fact. It's what one does, as a steward of the sea!"

Makk thought *steward of the sea* was a bit over the top, but nodded affirmatively anyway.

"*As* first responders," Staipa continued, "we have to submit a formal report to the appropriate authorities. This report included our best guess on last-known-location, and *proximate cause*. You see now where the problem begins?"

"I'm not sure I do," Makk admitted. He did, but he wanted to hear the admiral say it.

"What we *said*, was 'cataclysmic engine failure,' which in the parlance of the *sea* has very little meaning these days. It's a designation relating to the old fission/fusion models, for which accidents could *easily* take down a ship, but the *Colusm* had an electric engine, and those simply don't explode."

"Then why did you say that was the cause?" Makk asked.

"It's what we check off when what we really mean is, 'we have no idea'. And usually! Usually that's sufficient! A ship went down, and we don't know why, but that's where it happened, and now we've done our part!"

Makk refilled his glass of Lladn wine. This was going to be a longer afternoon than he was prepared to tolerate, clearly. "I take it," he said, "that this wasn't sufficient for the respective authorities."

"Insurance companies!" Staipa said, as if this was itself an expletive. "There is no peace when insurers are involved! The rote explanation has been deemed inadequate, which I am certain means that the ship was insured for *some* fatal outcomes and not others. It has been rightly pointed out that, as I said, electric engines don't simply explode! Seeing as we *have* survivors, they are looking for a better answer! But the answer we've *gotten...?*"

"It's problematic?"

"It's an *enormous problem!* So please, detective, for my edification and theirs, what *did* cause the *Colusm* to sink? Something in the cargo, perhaps? What *were* they shipping? I haven't been able to get a straight answer on that point. But, but here I am, speculating! When you're right here! I shall let you speak. What did it? To *your* understanding?"

"Yeah, okay," Makk said, leaning forward. The gesture was interpreted by his host as something approaching either the conspiratorial or the dramatic, as Coigo leaned forward in response.

"All right, here's the truth," Makk said. "What I remember was... how did you put it? Sea monsters? All black, rising from the very *Depths* to claim our mighty ship? I think that covers it."

There was a lengthy silence, as Makk watched Staipa's expression go from magnanimous to furious.

"I *see*," he said. "Then you're all in this together."

"It's what happened. I don't know what you want me to say."

"The *truth*, detective! I want you to say the truth! Was it an accident? Something the captain did? Who are you three protecting? Because whoever it is, I am *not amused!*"

"Hey, great," Makk said. "I'm not doing it to be amusing. Wasn't any fun when it happened, either."

"I can't...!" Staipa began. "I can't tell the International Maritime Commission that *sea monsters* took down a mid-sized freighter!"

He was literally trembling with rage.

"I don't understand the issue," Makk said. "You're not the one telling them that; *we* are."

"No, no, no, no." Staipa got up from the table. For a heartbeat, Makk thought the admiral was about to physically assault him, which wouldn't have been a fantastic idea. Sure, Staipa was bigger, and Makk was injured, but Makk was pretty sure he could take him.

He didn't come at Makk, though; standing, angrily, he pushed his chair away, angrily, and marched (angrily) to the window.

"This is to make me look foolish," Staipa said. "That's what this is. The *minute* I repeat that insane story... Consider the *source*, they'll say. I know. I know."

He went to muttering to himself. Makk poured another drink and wondered if his life was in danger. Given the past few months, that didn't seem like such a big deal.

"Admiral," Makk said, once it became clear his host was spiraling, and may not come out on his own. "Let's just *pretend* the things we described are real."

"Don't test me, detective!" Staipa said.

"Use your imagination. So, poof, argument's sake, now they're real. How many people are aboard this ship?"

The admiral moved from the window and back to the table, the better to glower at Makk. "You *imply* that by not embracing this absurdity, I'm putting everyone in *danger*, is that right?"

Oh, whatever, Makk thought. *May as well.*

"It occurs to me," Makk said, "as safe as Asealand *feels*, I'd very much prefer not being on the water for about the rest of my life. And that anyone who went through what I did might feel the same. It *also* occurs to me that anyone who'd been told of the risk, and ignored it would be, charitably, making an error in judgement."

"'An error in judgement,'" he repeated.

"A fucking mistake," Makk clarified. "The kind that ends with everybody dead."

Fuming, Staipa took his seat at the table again. "Let me ask you something, detective. How did you feel when you first learned Mr. Linus was a guest aboard my ship?"

"I wasn't happy."

"I'm sure! I am of course aware of Calcut's violent tendencies, the crimes for which he's been charged, which *you* charged him with, if I'm correct."

"Yeah, the one where he bashed in his brother's head."

"And yet, he walks around here freely, unconcerned," Staipa said. "Do you know why?"

"I don't know, maybe you've got an excellent masseuse aboard. I haven't had a chance to ask."

Staipa smiled, not even trying to make it look genuine. "He's unconcerned, because while Asealand is indeed an internationally recognized city-state, that recognition has yet to be formalized by the League of Countries."

"You don't say," Makk said, wondering what kind of international recognition Staipa could possibly be talking about, if it didn't come from the League.

"Which means, at present, the only laws governing this ship are maritime," Staipa said, "which hold that the highest ranking officer on the ship is the final arbiter of the law *aboard* that ship. Calcut, for all his faults, is no fool; he knows there will be consequences to stepping out of line."

Makk was beginning to understand where this was going. "I take it the highest ranking officer also has final say in the definition of, 'stepping out of line?'"

"It has a surprisingly wide range of applications."

"I'm sure," Makk said. "Is Del *really* working below, admiral?"

On the one hand, it didn't seem possible that Asealand had a policy of throwing people they didn't like overboard. Makk also imagined, if that had been Del's fate, Elicasta would have said something. On the other hand, the admiral sure didn't sound like he was issuing a hollow threat.

"Yes," Staipa said, after an uncomfortable pause. "Yes, of course they are. Del... *forcefully* disagreed, which I cannot have. But I would never punish someone who was obviously suffering from some sort of trauma!"

"You just stuck her in a dungeon."

"It's not so bad below deck," Staipa said. "I'll arrange a tour, if you like."

"Some other time. So I understand: you want me to lie about what happened, and if I *don't*, you'll either throw me overboard or lock me in the basement."

"Not *lie!* I want the truth, but without sea monsters."

Makk laughed. "Sure, easy."

"I would also appreciate it if you didn't speak of those obviously *imaginary* things as long as you're aboard my ship; you'll frighten my guests."

"They *should* be frightened," Makk said. "You should be too."

Exasperated, Staipa said, "all right, detective, *using* my imagination, let's all pretend they *are* real. What do you expect me to *do?* There isn't a port in the world large enough to accommodate us."

"How high can you fly?"

Staipa shook his head. "That's out of the question. Makk, do what I ask, and never speak of sea monsters again, and you can stay as long as you like. Otherwise, I will have to assess my options."

"I'll think about it," Makk said.

"The updated report is due in twenty-six hours."

"Then I'll think about it for twenty-five."

Staipa was about to offer a rejoinder, when a speaker on the wall crackled to life.

"Admiral, sorry to interrupt," someone said. Staipa engaged a button next to the speaker. "It's all right, Bybrid, we're done here. What's the matter?"

"We have a vessel alongside," Bybrid said. "We've opened communications; you should come up."

"You can handle a trade on your *own*, Bybrid. You don't need my help with that." Staipa looked at Makk as if to say, *do you see what I have to deal with here?*

"It's not that, admiral. It's someone requesting asylum."

"Out *here?*" Staipa said. "Who *is* it?"

"I don't think you'd believe me."

Chapter Fourteen

B attine loved fishing.

She had no idea if she would. Her previous experiences on water all involved being a passenger, where the interesting part of the journey was what was at the end of it, not the in-between.

Aboard the *Kalin-Ha,* it was nothing *but* the in-between. Their destination was wherever the fish were, and their trip was however long it took to fill the hold.

She didn't know how to *do* anything, and since nobody aside from Jiqas knew her by either of her names (Princess Alconnot, or Sister Orean,) this led to some initial frustration among the more experienced hands. This was especially true once she discovered there were certain *rituals* normally applied to any "dry fisher" on the ship. Said rituals mainly involved doing the worst jobs, while being subjected to intermittent volleys of profanity, which was supposed to last until he, she or they collapsed from exhaustion, broke down crying, or tossed themselves overboard.

It sounded charming.

However, not only was Jiqas the *one* crewmate who knew her; he was also the captain. If he said nobody was allowed to ritually abuse Henaia (this was the name they made up for her) then nobody would be ritually abusing Henaia.

At first, when Batt learned there were aspects of this experience that she was missing out on, she was mad at Jiqas, and expressed—in privacy, as much as that was possible—her dissatisfaction.

"I'll curse at you more if you want," he said. "Beyond that, I don't think it wise."

"Are you worried I'm not up to the task?"

"No, princess. I saw your sword. It's them I'm worried for. You're not the like to take it."

She was dressed in baggy clothing that carried a persistent whiff of body odor and fish. Frake had provided the clothes, promising the whole time that they had just been cleaned. This was probably true, and the only way to really get rid of the odor was to set the clothes on fire, so she lived with it. Nobody aside from her seemed to notice, which likely meant she smelled like everyone else., and by the second day, she didn't notice it either.

The clothes she'd worn to the docks on the night she left included the Septal robes and her riding leathers, with the key hidden in the small of her back, and the sword on her belt.

When Jiqas saw the sword, he tried to convince her to leave it behind. "It'll be here when you get back," he said.

"This sword was handcrafted in the Kingdoms," she said. "Anyone finding it would know I'd been there, which is why I took it from the Unital chamber, and why I'm not leaving it behind now."

So the sword made it to the fishing boat, tucked in with two changes of clothing and stuffed beneath her cot.

The first couple of days was nothing but tossing out the nets, pulling them back in, getting regularly doused by sea spray, and falling over a lot. The ocean was always rocking the *Kalin-Ha* one way or another, which didn't seem to bother anyone else, but which routinely knocked her down. Depending on what was going on at the time, her crewmates found this either infuriating or hilarious.

She was just glad she wasn't prone to seasickness. That would surely not go over well.

It wasn't until the third day that anyone other than Jiqas said something to her that wasn't a barked command, or generic hiss of disappointment. It was at night, while she was trying to sleep.

"I recognize you," one of the men said, from the next cot over. His name was Ma-On, and that was all she knew about him. "Don't I? Somewhere or other." He was talking to the ceiling, but it was directed at her.

"I don't know," she said. "Do you?"

"Somewhere," he said. "Not sure."

"You related to old Paiswick?" Alaising said, from her bunk at the other end of the room. They worked the deck in shifts; there were only five of them below for this conversation.

"Oh, yeah," Ma-On said, turning to look at Battine. "Is that it? Must be."

"Sorry," Battine said. "I don't know Paiswick."

"No," Alaising said. "Guess not. No, you're too pretty."

Ma-On stared at her for a long beat. "Yah," he said. "Something though. I'll get it."

"Don't hurt yourself," Battine said. "I'm nobody."

News of what was happening in Wrimmad City didn't reach them until the fourth day.

They *had* an audio device aboard, which was something that was only true of a small portion of the fishing boats out of Wrimmad. It was all right for nearby ship-to-ship conversation, but could only reach the shore when it had direct line-of-sight, or under certain atmospheric conditions. Those conditions involved low clouds, of which they'd had none. Thus, the news came via ship-to-ship.

It was just before midday, when Jiqas shouted for her.

"Henaia, you bitch, get in here!" he roared from the doorway of the forecastle. (He made a point of insulting her graphically whenever given the opportunity, which was much appreciated.)

She was at the back of the boat, helping pull a net.

"Know that tone," Alaising muttered.

Another fisher, named Saitok, laughed and said, "she's in the shit now."

"Mind your own rope," Battine said, dropping her portion of the net.

Up the center steps to the forecastle, she passed Eok, the helmsperson. The look on his face made it clear something was terribly wrong.

Another ship's gone down, she thought.

Despite the consistently lovely weather, mind-numbingly hard work, and indifferent-but-tolerable company, Battine had been unable to shake the memory of what happened to the *Bekohai*. Every time they pulled up a net, she worried that this time, surely, there would be a pitch-black monster inside, presaging imminent doom for the entire vessel.

Jiqas saw her enter. He looked about as upset as Eok.

"Close the door," he said.

She did so. Whether this afforded them any meaningful privacy was debatable; the door and walls were sufficient to keep rain off the pilot and the equipment, but didn't do much to prevent sound from coming through.

"Is it the sea creatures?" she asked. "Do we need to head back?"

"It isn't," he said quietly. He was sitting next to the electronics dash, which was situated to the left of the wheel. A few of the vessels out of Wrimmad were of the old style, operated by purists who used sails and oars to travel. (The portion of sailboats was higher out of different ports, she'd been told.) The rest—including the *Kalin-Ha*—used an electric engine.

"We will not be going back to Wrimmad City," Jiqas added. "Not for now. Not for a while. If I had the provisions to reach Ghon-Dik, I would."

"Why do you say this?"

"On the audio... The *Lightel* reached out. She's our sister ship, same..." he trailed off, staring into the middle distance.

"Jiqas, what *is* it?"

"The city is under siege," he said. "Agents of the House, tearing Wrimmad apart."

"Looking for me," she said quietly. "That's what you're saying, isn't it? They found Damid, and now they're tossing the city for me. We thought this might happen."

"We thought *something* might happen," he agreed. "Not this. Not this. Understand when I say they're tearing Wrimmad apart, I'm speaking literal. There are fires. People are... They're executing people in the streets, princess."

"That's absurd. The House doesn't—"

"I know, I know, the House doesn't *kill*, only now they do. 'Deliver Battine Alconnot.' This is all the Septals are saying, to a one."

"We have to go back," she said. "I'll turn myself in, before it gets worse."

Jiqas nodded slowly, stood, and looked her in the eyes. "Tell me something. What is it you did to them that was so terrible, that *this* would be the price?"

"I..."

"My *home!*" he roared. "All our homes, our families...! For what? Tell me this much!"

It was about the key. It had to be. The Septals hunted down Damid, just like he wanted them to, only he failed to appreciate what they would do to recover their precious key. They didn't care about *her*, which meant they also wouldn't be satisfied if she simply turned herself over and—as she'd threatened to do in Polister's study—threw the key into the ocean.

Why is this key worth so many lives? she wondered. Then she wondered what had become of Polister; did Damid bring *him* down as well?

"It isn't me they want," she said. "It's what I took from them."

"And what is that? Is it aboard my ship?"

"No," she lied.

"What did you take?"

"Jiqas, if I said you would be better off not knowing, would you believe me?"

He studied her. "You didn't expect this?"

"I would never knowingly jeopardize your lives, and the lives of your families. This plan of ours, to have me at sea, we made it to keep *everyone* safe. You were there; you remember."

"I do."

"Bring me back, and this will end," she said.

"Aye," he said. "Except I swore to keep you safe."

"I absolve you of that promise, Jiqas."

"Mm. Thank you for the absolution. But I keep my word. In this kingdom of yours, you were brought up as a Septal, yes? You wore the hood of the sister so well, I can't imagine otherwise."

"It was Septalism, yes," she said. "But not of the sort practiced by the House. Why?"

"I was raised to *distrust* the House," he said. "It was the only faith my family held to."

She smiled gently. "Our upbringing was not so different, then."

"Anything *this* important to the Seppies is worth keeping away from them," he said. "We'll find us another solution."

"We haven't the provisions to make it to Ghon-Dik, as you said. If you mean to come ashore at another port on Botzis, I worry you'll only be inviting an expansion of the violence, especially if anyone in Wrimmad connects me to the *Kalin-Ha*. Short of handing me over or tossing me overboard, I see no good options, Jiqas."

He was looking at a sea chart. "I may have a third option."

He took some measurements and performed a few calculations. "They should be about here..." he muttered, marking a spot on the map. "We're *here*... Yep, that'll do." He looked up at her. "Two days out of our way. All goes well, we can off-board you and make it back to shore before anyone considers us late."

She looked at the spot he'd marked, which was very much in the middle of the ocean. "You mean to drown me at an oddly specific location."

He laughed. "They'll take you. I'm sure of it. We just have to stave off a mutiny for the next forty hours."

"Is that a serious concern?"

He didn't answer. Instead, he stepped out of the cabin and loudly announced, "Take in the nets! Double-fast, you bastards, we have time to make up!"

The threat of mutiny manifested quickly.

The pilot, Eok, who had been with Jiqas when they received word of the siege, had already told the entire crew before Jiqas ordered the nets taken in. The effort to do so as quickly as possible was conducted sincerely, by sailors expecting to then make haste for Wrimmad City. None knew what they might do once getting there—take up arms with the resistance (they assumed there was one) or find their loved ones and hide—but all agreed they had to *be* there.

And obviously, Captain Jiqas agreed. Otherwise, why would he order the nets pulled?

But then he set a south-south-east heading. Wrimmad was to the north.

When asked—first by Eok, then by fishers whose experience,

they felt, gave them the authority to challenge the captain—he told them to stuff their questions and start swimming if they didn't like the ship's heading.

This held the crew at bay for about twelve hours. Then, as they retired to their bunks, Ma-On remembered where he'd seen Batt before.

"It's *her*," he declared loudly, extending an accusatory arm toward the dry fisher they all knew as Henaia. "I'm a fucking idiot; *you're* the princess. You're the one they're tearin' up Wrimmad for."

"You're right about the first part," Battine said. "You *are* a fucking idiot. I'm not anybody. Leave me be."

Alaising jumped in.

"Oh, yeah!" she said. "That explains it!"

She hopped down from her bunk and crossed the narrow middle aisle, as the other fishers on relief (all but those needed to keep the ship moving, as the nets were in) sat up to get a closer look at Battine.

"Sure, sure," Alaising said. "We're running from Wrimmad on account of they're looking for *you*. Princess Battine Al-something-or-other. Hiding out on a fishboat. I *knew* she smelled off."

Three more fishers, whose names Batt hadn't had a chance to learn, hopped to their feet to flank Alaising, Ma-On stood looming over Battine, and Saitok barred the exit. They had her surrounded.

"Very well," Battine said, trying to keep her voice calm. "Before I was Henaia, I was Sister Orean of the pier, and before that I was Battine Alconnot. None of that should matter to any of you."

"Sure, 'cept if we turn you in we get a nice reward," Alaising said, "and stop the violence to boot."

"Have'ta force Jiqas to turn about first," Saitok said.

"I say we break her neck and toss her to the sharks," Ma-On

said. "Captain'll have no excuse to make for the Eloni coast after that. Damn the reward."

I'm done with this, she thought, drawing her sword from beneath the bunk. One wild-looking, but controlled, swing cleared plenty of space in the middle of the room.

"That's more than enough from all of you," she said, backing to the wall. "Saitok, let me pass."

"You gonna run us all through with that blade, princess?" Alaising asked. "Don't think you're fast enough."

"Only half, I'd wager," Battine said. "Which half would you like to be a part of? And don't be such fools as to think I've never *used* this; they want me for murder for a reason."

This was all the convincing Saitok needed to step aside. When the others objected, he said, "where is she going to run?"

Which was a very good point.

She got outside, slammed the door behind her and looked for a means to bar it, but there was none readily available. Not that it mattered; nobody was eager to race out and launch themselves at the madwoman with the sword. What they'd do, if they were smart, was wait until her back was turned, or her guard was down, or—as would inevitably happen—she fell asleep.

It was the middle of the night. The deck was lit by lanterns and moonlight; quite the peaceful contrast to the trouble she'd just left behind. All was quiet, save for the splash from the ocean as the *Kalin-Ha* cut through, and the high-pitched revving of an engine at full.

She climbed the center stair to the foredeck. Jiqas was alone at the wheel.

"We have a problem," she said.

He saw the sword. "I see that," he said. "Didn't take long. You bloody anyone?"

"Not yet."

"Good, that'll make this easier."

He stepped past her, to the railing that overlooked the back two thirds of the boat. Her accusers filed onto the deck, looking more like a mob than a crew.

"Nita's tits, I told you dogs to lay out for the night!" he roared. Jiqas had a commanding voice that seemed to get deeper and stronger the louder it got. "Fuck if you can't even do *that* much right!"

"You know what this is about, captain!" Alaising, self-appointed mob leader, shouted back. "Turn us about so we can offer that one's head in exchange for our city."

"I thought you the smart one, Alaising," he said. "See I was wrong."

"There's a reward!" Ma-On added. This was, based on the hooting and hollering that followed, of greater import to the crew of the *Kalin-Ha* than possibly ending the violence on the shore.

"You I *did* expect that from, Ma-On. You're dumb as a trout. Think through what you're saying, you dogs. Really believe after a week of bloodshed, the Seppies are handing you a *reward?* We're the assholes that gave her a spot to hide."

"That was just *you*, captain," Alaising said. She looked past him and Battine. "Go on, grab her, Eok."

Eok ,the pilot, came up behind Battine and tried to grab her, thinking maybe that princesses are easy to subdue. As soon as he had his arms around her, she ducked down and forward, rolled her shoulders, and threw him over the railing. He landed hard on his back, but didn't break his neck.

"Thank you for the warning," Battine said, spinning around to see if there was anyone else lurking. There was: two young fishers whose names she didn't know, but who didn't look like they had any interest in testing her sword-fighting skills.

"That's enough!" Jiqas said. "All 'a you, use your brains once in your idiot lives. You *really* think the Seppies will *care* who done what? We come to port with her on board, we're as dead as if the sea took us."

"Then toss her over and be done with it," Saitok suggested. "It's a kinder fate than awaits her on the shore."

"I vowed to keep her safe, and keep her safe I will," he said. "Not that it's any of you dogs' fucking business, but I'm making hard for Asealand. Let that fool admiral take her in. *Then* we turn about and make for Wrimmad, and we swear on every one of your fucking graves that you don't know a gods-damned thing about a gods-damned princess. Is that *all right* with you?"

He paused, waiting for an objection.

"Aye," Alaising said, after a beat. "It's a good play."

"Thank you for your approval. Until we reach Asealand, you leave her be. Or, you can deal with the limb she'll take on your own. And for Ho's sake, someone make sure Eok is okay."

Slowly, the group dispersed. Eok got up, holding his neck but looking otherwise okay.

"I'd say that went better than I expected," Jiqas said to Battine.

"Could have been worse," she agreed. "But tell me: what in the name of the Outcast is *Asealand?*"

Makk was alone in Coigo Staipa's banquet hall for roughly ten seconds, before a tall, young, muscular, pleasant-looking guy wearing one of Asealand's naval outfits, stepped into the room. He had to be one of the ship's security people, whose existence was until now only inferred.

"Detective Stidgeon," he said, "I'm Rayno. I'm here to escort you out."

"Hello, Rayno," Makk said, standing. He took a measure of his new friend, quickly determining that, in a fight, Makk would definitely lose. "Yeah, thanks, I have no idea how to get out of here."

"Understood. It's this way," he said, stepping aside and holding open the door. "I take it you'd like to return to the hospital?"

"I would very much like to go back to the hospital room, take some pain medication, lie down in the bed, and sleep for the next twenty," Makk said. "But I need to have a conversation first. Can you point me in the direction of Elicasta Sangristy?"

"Certainly. But you shouldn't. Have pain meds, I mean. You've been drinking."

Makk laughed, as he limped to the door—his knee was giving him a time—and said, "kid, at a certain age none of that shit matters. Besides, wine barely counts."

Rayno took him from the banquet back to the elevator, then down to the ground floor lobby, with doors leading to the main deck. Makk was a little surprised to not be taken to whatever room 'Casta was staying in, but the surprise only lasted until they took a turn that put them on the path to Calcut Linus's place.

"I'm told you and Mr. Linus have a history," Rayno said breezily.

"I guess you could call it that," Makk said. "He had some guys beat the shit out of me, I arrested him for murder, he kidnapped and tried to murder me... You know. Normal stuff."

Rayno laughed. "You don't have to worry about any of that here," he said.

"So I've been told."

The front of the Linus estate looked a lot like every other property on the deck. Lots of painted white metal and shiny glass, with an external spiral staircase and doors along the side of a turret-shaped structure. It was a little like a lighthouse, and a little like a penis.

Rayno brought him up to the deck-level double doors, standing outside of which was another large employee dressed the same way and possessed of the same "too pleasant to be a part of the same reality as the rest of us" demeanor as Rayno.

"D'val, this is Detective Stidgeon," Rayno said.

"Sure!" D'val said, with frankly unwarranted enthusiasm. "I think Mr. Linus is expecting you, come on in!"

He pulled open the door. Makk resisted a very strong urge to throat-punch the two of them, and followed Rayno inside.

"Calcut gets his own private guard?" Makk asked, as Rayno took him down a hallway that curled around the center of the building. Everything in this place seemed to have a circular blueprint, which was pretty funny on a giant, square ship. "Does he have a lot of threats aboard? All I've seen outside of staff is the elderly rich."

Rayno laughed. "That isn't why D'val is there," he said.

They reached a door. Like every other door on the ship, it was actually a hatch. If what Staipa claimed about Asealand was true, there was no reason at all to worry about having to seal bulkheads due to a loss of integrity, or water on the deck or whatever. Which either meant the doors were because people wanted to pretend otherwise, or Staipa was exaggerating his own boat's integrity.

Rayno opened the door and led Makk in. Calcut was on the other side, at a desk with two screens and a laptop. Sitting in the corner nearby, was another ship employee dressed like Rayno and D'val, with a similar physique. (*Was there a sale?* Makk wondered.) The guy started to get up when they entered, saw Rayno, and relaxed.

Elicasta was there too, at the other end of the room, at a much larger computer console, with a dozen screens. She had on her rig and looked fully engaged in the Stream.

"What do *you* want?" Calcut asked.

"Her," Makk said, pointing across the room.

"She's busy. Don't interrupt."

Ordinarily, Makk would respond poorly to being told, by the closest thing he had to a mortal enemy, how to interact with his own girlfriend. But Calcut was making a good point, because interrupting Elicasta when she was deep in the Stream—even if it had been ten hours, and she hadn't had any food or water, and there was a fire—was a bad idea.

"Yeah, fair," he said. "I'll wait."

Makk sat down opposite Calcut's desk. Rayno took a seat next to the other guard in the room, in the corner, while Calcut made an effort to ignore Makk. This lasted about three seconds.

"All right, let's do this," Linus said, closing his laptop.

"Happy to," Makk said, although he wasn't entirely positive he knew what they were talking about. Were they about to fight? Arm-wrestle?

"You're a fucking asshole, you know that?" Linus said.

"I got about fifteen fratricide jokes loaded and ready, Calcut. Let's talk about the asshole who did *that*."

"Hey, fuck you!" Linus jumped to his feet. Makk thought he was surely about to lunge across the desk, but then—weirdly—he looked over at Rayno and the other one, still in the corner. In a not-dissimilar setting not so long ago, the two men in the back of the room would have been Calcut's goons, and they would be beating the living Depths out of Makk right now. But that wasn't who they were or why they were there. Calcut sat back down.

Makk realized then that these security people in Calcut's house weren't there to protect him; they were there to protect everyone else. *Then* he realized that was also why Rayno was there —to keep *Makk* under control.

"Okay, Calcut," Makk said. "Tell me why I'm a fucking asshole."

"Because you don't get it. You don't see the whole picture. *She* does. She sees it. But you, you're like some little fucking... I don't know, some animal stuck in a yard, who thinks that yard is the whole world. But it's not."

"You're very bad at analogies."

"Sure, what the fuck, charge me for that too."

"What are you talking about, Calcut?" Makk asked. "Is there a part of the world where *murder* isn't a crime?"

"You tell me. Look at Wrimmad and tell me."

"No, no, no, this isn't a moral equivalence thing. You don't get to say killing the two people we *know* you killed personally wasn't *all that bad* because sometimes other people die in larger numbers."

"I'm saying the House has ripped off the fucking mask and now everybody knows, and the only thing standing between them and the rest of us is what *I've built*, and it don't matter what it took to build it; what matters is, it's there, because *I* fought for it."

"Oh," Makk said, laughing. "You're a freedom fighter now?"

"You didn't see!" Calcut said. "You don't know! *I* do! They can't shut down *my* network, because they don't got a hand in it."

"What do you mean, shut down?"

"I mean if those Septal fuckers want, they can bring down the *entire* thing. The Stream, *all* the gods-damn governments, the cars, the trains, the wingplanes, the aeros. The House is in everything. But not *my* shit."

"Amazing," Makk said. "You want me to believe you built a criminal empire for the good of the planet? I can't even tell if you think this because it makes you feel better about yourself, or so you'll think *I'll* feel better about you, like maybe if I think hard enough I won't arrest you the first chance I get. You built the Black Market so people could commit crimes, and you built C-Coins so they could pay for it, and if it's *true* that there's no House tech in the important parts, that's only because you didn't want any of those crimes to get traced back to you. Now if it just so happens that *because* of your venality, the House can't shut you down, what we're talking about there is an unintended consequence."

"You're gonna arrest me," Calcut said. "You? See, this is why you're a fucking asshole. No family, no friends, you don't care about money and I don't think you even care if you live or die. I can't bribe you, or threaten you, or hold a hostage, none of that, because all you *do* care about is the law. The law doesn't care about *you*, Stidgeon. Not one fucking bit."

"An unhealthy obsession with catching murderers isn't the insult you think it is."

"You turned on your badge lately?"

"No, why?" Makk asked.

"Good," Calcut said. "Don't." Linus turned one of his screens around so Makk could see. It was an international warrant for Makk's arrest."Just came out."

"That doesn't... who issued that?"

"That's the funny part, huh? The tracking numbers don't match up. This didn't go down the chain from city to national to international; it jumped the line. You wanna know who can do that?"

"The House."

"There you go. I got one too."

"Right, but that was for killing Ba-Ugna Kev," Makk said.

"This is a second one," Calcut said. "I could shake the other one, but when the House puts a marker on you, you're fucked." He looked over at the guards in the corner. "If the admiral was smart, he'd kick me off his yacht. He doesn't want this kind of trouble."

"Staipa seems to think he doesn't have to abide by the laws of nations," Makk said, "as long as those nations refuse to recognize him as one of them."

"Yeah, you know who else doesn't abide by the laws of nations?"

"Every time the answer is 'the House' you sound a little more paranoid, Calcut. What's my warrant for?"

"Possession of a stolen House artifact of high import," Calcut said. "Mine is too, because for whatever reason they think I'm involved in your bullshit. Elicasta's got a warrant of her own, for the same. They think you two took something, and I helped. Ironic, seeing how, thanks to them, I'm now in it with you."

"No, it's ironic because you tried to kill us at the same time you killed Kev."

"I thought you were in with him, and he had it coming."

"That isn't why," Makk said.

"No, it isn't," Linus admitted. "It was because of the other thing."

"Exposing you as Orno's killer," Makk said. "*That* other thing."

Calcut stared off to the side, because any other reaction could have been interpreted as a confession, and the one thing he refused to do was admit to having killed his brother.

"Why did Kev have it coming?" Makk asked.

"The tech he was working on, it would'a given the House a back door into my network," Calcut said. "I couldn't have that. This is what I keep telling you, Stidgeon. Big picture: I do what I have to do, to protect what's mine, from *anyone*, any way I can. If that means roughing up a cop, or bribing a mayor, or killing some Dunnite who's too smart for his own good, then that's what I gotta do."

"Even if you're murdering people."

Calcut shrugged, which just set Makk off. They weren't talking about broken eggs here.

Makk shot a glance at Rayno, who was only pretending not to pay attention. It wasn't that Makk would actually *do* this, but he considered, briefly, whether he could reach Calcut before Rayno could stop him. Probably not.

"Even if it's family," Makk added. Because talking about Orno got Calcut's blood pressure up, which was positive outcome under the circumstances.

"Stop poking the bear," Elicasta said, from across the room.

"Thought you were busy," Makk said. "How long have you been listening?"

"A little while."

"Hey, which one of us is the bear?" Calcut asked.

She unhooked the rig from the main console, stood and stretched. "You both are." She looked past them to the guards in the corner. "Micho, any coffee left?"

The second guard—Micho—stood. "I can check." He looked at Rayno, who gave him a gentle nod. *I won't let them kill each other,* Rayno was saying. Micho left the room.

"The fighting's stopped in Wrimmad," she said. "Not sure why. Stream hum is, pressure from the other Hats did it, but I'm not sunny on that." To Calcut, she asked, "What's the buzz on the Seppie channel?"

"I'm sorry, the what?" Makk asked.

"Calcut's got an ear on their private," 'Casta said.

"Lotta noise," Calcut said. "Everyone's pissed at everyone else. This is what you get when you don't put anybody in charge. Nobody can agree on a good time to overthrow the world governments. It's pitiful."

"Maybe hop on Spack's local," she suggested. "He called it off, be good to know why. Did they find her, or did they decide they're not going to?"

"I'll mine it," Calcut said, opening his laptop.

Elicasta looked at Makk as if she'd just noticed he was still in the room. "How'd the meeting with the admiral go? You play nice?"

"He wants me to lie about how the *Colusm* went down," Makk said. "You could have warned me."

She frowned. "Real? I had no vibe on that. He said he didn't want me or Del to talk about it with anybody else, which I get; no need for a panic."

"He seemed to think you were either confused or lying, and had it in his head that I'd be able to set the record straight. Pretty sure if I don't agree to submit an official statement that blames the wreck on the captain or the cargo, he's going to throw me overboard."

"I doubt it," she said. "But you should do it anyway. We're going to need him on our side. Asealand might be the only safe place for us on Dib right now."

"You're serious."

"What would it hurt?"

"I think everyone *else* on a ship in the Norton Ocean might want to know there's a flotilla of sea monsters out there," he said. "You have proof. Or have you given up being a Veeser?"

"I'll drop the vid when the time's right," she said. "Real, nothing I do is going to stop commerce on the water. Maybe if we knew why they attacked *us* and, like, nobody else..."

"We don't know that they haven't attacked anyone else," Makk said. "We don't know if they're going to attack *us*, right now. Maybe it's because I nearly drowned, but I feel like everyone here is underestimating how fucked we would be if they came back."

"Holy shit," Calcut said. His attention had gone from his laptop to one of his screens.

"What is it?" Elicasta asked.

"I've got an open back door on Asealand's drones," he said.

"Of course you do," Makk said.

"Shut up, Makk," 'Casta said. To Calcut, she said, "and?"

"Spack's army didn't find the princess."

"How do you know?" Elicasta asked.

Calcut tweaked the pirated optical feed to fill out the whole screen, and tilted it so they could both get a look. Staring back at them, in ill-fitting fisher's clothes, shorn hair and a dirty face, and holding a *sword,* was none other than Princess Battine Alconnot of Totus.

"I know because right now, she's a hundred maders that way," Calcut said, pointing at one of the walls, "and Staipa's about to welcome her on board."

Chapter Fifteen

Polister's horse died on the third day.

She was an old mare, well past the age when it would have been okay to take her on a journey into the desert, and expect both rider and mount to come back out again. Her name had been Winnat, and up until three days ago, she was living peacefully enough on a small farm near the foot of Mount Vesay.

Polister came upon the farm, and its farmer—a stout Wivvolian expat named Bnxt—while in flight from the utter destruction of the Unital compound at the hands of the House Sentries, acting on the order of High Hat Spack.

It had not been Polister's intention to flee. He meant to remain in the chamber, protect whatever members of his flock needed his protection, and probably die a martyr's death. And it wasn't as if he lacked the courage or conviction to do precisely that. But in the midst of the massacre, watching *everyone* fall (Dwerik! Myala!) some while protecting *him*, he realized three things.

First, for all his obvious, critical faults, Damid had been right in one important way: people had to know what happened.

(These were his last words, spoken while shoving a voicer into Polister's hands.) Second, Polister actually *did* have something Mavis Spack wanted—whether or not Spack even knew it—and a duty to keep it from him. Third, Polister was in a unique position to escape, because unlike essentially everyone else, he knew about the secret exit underneath the dome.

The entire building was on fire when he made it out of the tunnel, which dropped him on the other side of the compound's rear wall. The way was unguarded, which came as a shock; Polister fully expected to find a contingent of Sentries waiting for him there.

A decent portion of the coastal side of the Vesay range was still untamed wilderness; legitimate forest land not yet cleared for settlement. Mount Vesay, and the pass that led to the desert, was on the other side.

He ran for the tree line, and didn't stop until he'd reached the edge of Bnxt's farm.

There were a couple dozen friendly households between the Unital compound and Bnxt's farm that he *could* have stopped at. He didn't, and couldn't explain why. Maybe he had just seen enough people he knew and loved die already, and wanted no part in endangering more by his simple presence. Maybe he was just running blindly, absent any thought at all.

Bnxt wasn't a Unital or a Septal, and knew almost nothing about local or national politics. He just farmed the land, sold vegetables in the city now and again, and kept to himself. He was aware of some sort of violence in Wrimmad City, because he could hear the explosions and see the glow from the fires on the night sky, and inferred that Polister was a fugitive from said violence. That was all the farmer needed to know.

Bnxt provided food, water, and a place for Polister to rest, calm down, and think: about where he was, why he'd gone there, and what he was going to do next.

After some time, Polister decided that non-rational, not-thinking-straight version of himself, the one who'd blindly fled the city, had made a good decision.

It was his duty to protect his people; in that regard, he should have stayed. But he also had a duty to Unitism as a whole. That meant living long enough to entrust the Staff of Pal to another.

The docks weren't safe, surely, and fleeing to another of the city-states would only endanger more lives. No, the best recourse was to seek shelter in the one part of Botzis known to have no shelter.

He would head to the midlands. He would seek out Elder Ko.

And so Bnxt, who self-evidently thought Polister unwell for even considering such a thing, gifted him with Winnat, plus as much dried food and water as he could spare.

Polister fully intended to repay Bnxt for his kindness, eventually. But when the midday heat claimed Winnat's life—Polister hadn't even been riding her that hard—he realized how foolish it was to imagine such a thing.

He would be dying too, alone, in the Botzis desert, and the Staff of Pal would be lost to the sands.

The midland was not without landmarks. There were hills, valleys, and rocky outcrops with shapes that had come to look familiar to Polister over time. Which was to say that he *thought* he was heading in the correct direction. But by the end of the fourth day—all on foot—he realized nothing around him looked familiar anymore. He was lost.

He looked back at his own footprints; as far as he could see, he'd been going in a straight line.

"How do you get lost, going in a straight line?" he asked.

He kept walking.

The walking stopped when the suns set. Polister didn't have enough clothing for the cold nights and too much for the hot days. He had no tent for shelter from the wind, and no wood for a fire. So, he chewed some dried meat, sipped his dwindling supply of water, and hoped that this time, when he slept, he wouldn't be awakened by uncontrollable shivering.

"Stupid idea," he muttered. "Stupid, stupid. Only know how to get halfway as it is."

This was the part he should have put more thought into. No southerner had ever been allowed into the Botzo village. Nobody outside of the tribes even knew where to find it. Or if there was more than one. He knew how to reach the meeting point, which they always assumed was roughly halfway between Vesay and the village, but not only did Polister not know if that was even *true*, he had no clue which direction he should be heading after he reached the meeting spot.

"You're not making it that far anyway, old man," he said, curling up in a ball. The staff, as always, he kept resting beneath the palm of his hand. It usually gave him comfort, having it there. Not this time.

"Pal," he whispered. "I am, as always, your servant. I ask for your deliverance from this wasteland."

He slept. And when the morning came, he did not wake up.

"Y ou were long, Polister Calidon."

The voice was familiar.

"Ko?" Polister tried to say. His lips were chapped and his throat was dry. He was afraid to open his eyes or move, but the situation called for at least one of those, so he opened his eyes, blinked the fuzziness away, and looked around.

He was in a tent, laid out on some cushions on the ground. Elder Ko was on a stool nearby.

"Not awake," Ko said. "A long time."

Polister tried to sit up, but that was out of the question. "Too much weak," Ko said. "Stay."

The elder knelt down and retrieved a bowl of water, which he pressed up to Polister's lips. "Slow," he said.

Polister sipped. It was so wonderful, he leaned his head forward to get more of it, but Ko pulled it away. "Slow," he repeated. "Polister has been dead. Drink slow."

"I understand," Polister said. He looked down at the bowl again. "You have *water* here."

"Yes."

"I thought you didn't like the water."

"All die without water," Ko said.

"Where does it come from?"

Ko smiled, and didn't answer. Polister tried a new question. "Can you say how I got here? I don't remember."

"Polister found by one who waited," Ko said. He got to his feet. "You rest, we talk. Much about."

"All right," he said, putting his head back. "Oh! My staff!"

Ko tapped the side of the cushions with the tip of his own staff. There was a muted *clunk*. Polister reached over the side until he felt its cool metal.

"Staffer Calidon must have staff," Ko said.

It became obvious how close to death Polister had gotten when he tried to do anything other than sit up, so he stopped trying to do anything for a while.

He was visited frequently by a woman who looked to be roughly as old as Ko, who was their equivalent of a medical expert. How old Ko, the medical woman, or any of the others actually *were,* was something destined to remain unknown. Life in the desert suns was unkind to the skin, and they didn't share the same calendar as the rest of the planet, so questions about their age delivered nonsensical answers.

The woman—she called herself Deen, but Polister didn't know if that was her name or her title—didn't speak any of the common tongue, so whatever communication they accomplished was done via gestures, and the words Polister knew in her language. That was okay, because there wasn't anything too terribly complicated to talk about; Deen needed him to drink and eat only what she gave him, and only in the quantities provided (although he couldn't ask for more because he didn't know how.) Perhaps unsurprisingly, she had plenty of experience in treating severe dehydration.

After about a week of recuperation, he and Deen arrived at a joint agreement that Polister was strong enough, and Ko returned.

"Come," Ko said, taking Polister by the hand, and helping him to his feet. "See." Polister was a little shaky, but he had the staff to help keep him from falling over. Ko walked him to the edge of the tent, and pushed open the flap.

And then, Polister Calidon became the first outsider in recent history to see how the Botzos actually lived.

The tent in which he'd been recovering was at the edge of a compound surrounded on three sides by rocky hills: a valley, with caves dotting the inner walls. There was ample shade, and a light breeze. Polister spotted about a dozen tribespeople. There were more—a lot more, he thought, as he felt keenly aware that he was being studied. He just couldn't see them.

"You live in caves," he muttered. When Ko made it clear he didn't understand, Polister pointed to the caves with his staff. This act caused a murmur to cascade through the valley. Ko put his hand on the Staff of Pal and gently pushed it down.

"No," he said. "Scare."

"Sorry," Polister said.

Who or what do these people think I am? he thought.

There was something about the middle of the three rocky hill-sides that was both novel and familiar. He stopped to stare at it, contrary to Ko's urging that they continue.

God, he thought. *That can't be correct.*

He scrambled past Ko, to a slight rise at the limit of the village, Ko saying something in his own language and the cliffs chattering, all of which Polister ignored.

When he got to where he thought he'd have the right angle for a proper perspective, he turned again to look at the hill.

Jutting out of the very top of what in all other respects looked like a natural rock formation was nine decidedly artificial-looking columns. They were made of stone as well, these columns, crumbling in spots, and with jagged tips, but there was no mistaking what he was looking at: the same nine Fingers that graced the roof of every Septal temple on the planet.

"Ko," he gasped, "what am I looking at?"

Elder Ko came up beside Polister, a calming hand on his arm. He gestured with his root wood staff at the scene that had made his guest breathless. "Home," he said. "This home. Come. This is not see."

Ko guided Polister down into the middle of the village, a flat circular space no tents occupied. Several Botzos were milling about in the middle. Two of them had stiff brooms they were using to whisk the sand out of the circle. There was a large wooden stick jutting out of a hole in the center, like a pin jabbed into a map.

Ko led him in the direction of the stick. As he did so, more of the villagers started to make themselves visible, either by stepping out of a tent or away from the dark shadows of cave openings.

The ground on which they were walking transitioned from sand to stone. Only, it wasn't just *any* stone. There was something carved into it; concentric rings with symbols, and regularly space holes intended for the tip of a stick not unlike the one in the center.

Polister shrugged off Ko's guiding hand and knelt down for a closer look. He brushed away sand from the nearest set of symbols. They were numbers and letters, and the only reason he knew that was because the carvings were in some variant of Eglinat; something *older*, perhaps, than what the House called "archaic."

"Ko," he said. "What is this?"

Ko answered, in his own tongue, a phrase Polister hadn't learned. Then the elder thought about it for a moment, and tried again. "Spoken before," he said. "Botzo speaker say, 'wisdom of sand.'"

Polister remembered the conversation. "The wisdom of sand is how you know it is time," he said. "Time for me to come with you, to this place."

"It is time," Ko agreed.

"How does this tell you?"

Ko gestured at the circle, as though the answer was self-evident.

Polister got to his feet and, rather than walking straight toward the middle, followed one of the circle rings in a counter-clockwise direction. It wasn't long before he realized his initial assumption—that these were concentric rings—was erroneous. It was a spiral.

He was standing on a calendar.

Ko, who by then had made it to the stick in the middle of the spiral, gestured him over.

This is a calendar, and it's counting down, Polister thought.

High Hat Spack had argued that the Outcast would be arriving soon, *so* soon that all manner of terrible things was justified if it meant rejoining the House with their precious missing keys. Polister took it to be the holier-than-thou justifications of a man with too much power. But now? *What else could something like this be counting down to?*

Polister reached Ko, and the embedded stick, which was *not* in the very center of the calendar; it was one hole away.

"How soon?" Polister asked. When Ko didn't understand, Polister tapped the base of the stick with his staff, and then pointed to the final hole.

"How soon?" he repeated.

"Ah," Ko said. "Shadows together. Point here." He pointed at the tallest of the Fingers. Then he took ten paces directly toward the Fingers, and stopped. "Reach here. Is time then."

"But, when will that be?" Polister asked.

"It will be when it is."

"Right."

"See, Polister," Ko said, pointing at Polister's feet. "See."

Ko was directing him to look at the carvings near the center of the spiral. They weren't letters or numbers this time. They were pictures: crude depictions of the Five, holding their symbolic weapons.

In the lead, and positioned above the hole in which the stick had been inserted, was Pal, holding the staff.

"Wisdom of sand say it is time for Polister Calidon to be here," Ko said. "Here is Polister Calidon."

"This isn't me," Polister said, standing. "This is... this is my god, Elder Ko. This is Pal." He held off on saying this was *the* god, because after all these years he still didn't know if the Botzos had a god of their own. So far, this calendar was the only thing he'd seen them treat as sacred.

"Here is Staffer Polister Calidon," Ko said. "Wisdom of sand knows."

"Then I thank you," Polister said. "For bringing me here. Now I must..."

"No," Ko interrupted. "You ask, how do I know. This is how I know. This is not why."

"You've already got a calendar carved in bedrock predicting the end of the world; what else can there possibly be?"

Ko, who definitely didn't get any of that, just smiled and nodded. "Come," he said. He pointed to a large opening at the foot of the nine Fingers rock face.

~

The cavern was large, cool, and not as dry as one might expect for the middle of the desert. Polister didn't see any water, but his desert-dry skin was absorbing the unexpected moisture from the air with great alacrity.

The way was lit by torches embedded in wall sconces that looked like a part of the natural rock formations, but could not possibly have been; not unless nature itself had conspired to form this chamber. It didn't seem at all possible that the Botzos did it, which left him with the question of who that left.

Elder Ko, who had a torch of his own, led Polister along a modest downslope. When the route took a hard righthand curl—they lost sight of the entrance for the first time—Ko stopped and held the torch up to the wall.

"See," he said, gesturing with the flame.

There was artwork on the wall, ancient drawings that were both new to Polister's eyes, and unsettlingly familiar.

A great body of water dominated the scene, above which were two opposing forces. On one side, there were the triangular boats of an armada, foregrounded by people brandishing weapons: bows and arrows, swords, and staffs. On the other? No boats; just multi-legged, dark-shaded, winged creatures with wide open mouths full of teeth.

Their resemblance to Kaketora's crude drawing could not be denied. These were the same things that had taken down the *Bekohai*.

"Black waters rise," Polister said, recalling Ko's words from their last meeting. "This is why you don't go near the ocean, isn't it?"

"You understand."

"Do you know what these are?" he asked, pointing to one of the creatures.

"In my words, they are *lymokk*. In yours... word means, one who was... sent away. With anger. Is there a word for this?"

"Exiled," Polister said. "Or cast out. An outcast."

"Outcast," Ko repeated, nodding.

"One of these was seen," Polister said. "A boat sank. This was recent."

"'Recent' is 'now?'"

"Yes."

Ko nodded again. "Black waters rise, Staffer Calidon comes. Now is time. You see."

"I do see," he said. "But I don't understand."

They continued down the passage, stopping periodically to examine other wall drawings. None had quite the spectacular impact, prediction-wise, as the set with the *lymokk*, but they were fascinating from a sociological perspective. Polister knew of more than one historian who argued the Botzo tribes could well predate the Collapse, but until he saw these drawings—which were, in part, a pictorial history of the tribes—he didn't consider the hypothesis well-founded.

They turned another corner, and nearly ran into a woman carrying a jug of water on her head. She had no torch of her own, and the wall sconces were only one every thirty paces—and the light didn't carry that far—but she clearly knew where she was going. This was a well-traveled route.

It would have to be; it led to water.

"You have an underground water source," he said.

"Water ahead," Ko said with a nod. "Safe water."

"I would like to see that."

"You can. Not now."

They switched to a path that diverged from the one that led to the water, the latter sloping further downward, and then took sharp left turn.

Ko stopped again, at something that should not have existed within a natural rock formation: a metal door.

At least, that was Polister's first impression. It was definitely metallic, rectangular, and the right height and width to be one. But there were no visible hinges, and no doorknob.

"Here," Ko said. "Here is why Polister Calidon has come."

"Uh, all right. Is this a door, Ko?"

"Door," Ko agreed.

"Have you ever opened it?"

"I cannot open. None can, but you, when it is time."

"And time is now," Polister said.

Ko nodded.

"How do you imagine I might do that?"

Ko brought the torch up to the wall beside the door. At eye-level was another depiction of the Five, only now in a circle, with Pal and their staff the bottommost member. Directly underneath Pal was a metal panel. Ko brushed the side of the panel to remove a layer of dust and reveal a *hole* in the middle of it.

Polister leaned in for a closer look.

By the grace of Pal, he thought. *I think that's a keyhole.*

"Elder Ko," he said, "would you be offended if I asked for you to leave?"

Ko's brow wrinkled. "You alone?" he asked, for clarification.

"Yes."

"This is understood." He looked neither surprised nor offended by the request. If anything, he expected it.

"Thank you," Polister said. "I will need light."

Ko found a vacant wall sconce and stuffed his torch into it. "Find when done," he said. "Way out is way in."

"I'll figure it out," Polister said.

Elder Ko bowed deeply. "We wait."

Then he left.

Polister had a mental image of hundreds of Botzos standing outside the mouth of the cavern, waiting on Polister to emerge. It would mirror the final step in the Tribulations of the Five: their return to the surface, after the fall of the Outcast.

"Getting a little full of yourself, Polister," he said. "You're no god."

Although... he could be an *instrument* of god. After all, *someone* set him on this path. It could have been Pal. It could also have been the Outcast.

Only way to know was to open the door.

Once he was certain Elder Ko had put sufficient distance between them, Polister set to work doing something he'd only ever done once before, on the day he succeeded Lane Wycon as Holy Staffer.

He ran his finger along the side of the staff until coming to a barely-detectable seam, about a quarter of the way down. Putting his hands on both sides of the seam, he twisted the two parts in opposite directions until—reluctantly—the Staff of Pal screwed open.

Carefully, he pulled the staff apart. Hidden inside, in a sleeve cushioned to mask the partial hollowness, was a key.

Wycon didn't know what it was for. Nor did his predecessor. But they knew the *House* wanted it, and would one day come looking for it. "On that day," Wycon told him, "be prepared to bargain from a position of strength."

"On that, old friend," Polister muttered, "I have failed utterly." He pulled the key from its sleeve. "But perhaps I have figured out what it's *for*."

He slid the key into the keyhole. It took some fiddling to get it to engage with the lock—he had to keep pushing it in deeper until it found purchase—but then it turned easily.

With a loud clunk, the metal door dropped inward, about two

centimaders, and then—with a loud hiss and a tremendous rush of air—slid to the left.

There was a room on the other side of the door. It was cool and dark, and the air was stale, and Polister didn't want to go inside to find out anything more than that.

(It was, though, a promising sign when nothing came *out*.)

He pulled the key from the keyhole—the door didn't close again, which was good, as he didn't want to leave it behind—returned it to its sleeve, and restored the Staff of Pal. Then, taking the torch from its sconce, he crossed the threshold into... a *control* room.

The first thing to note about the place was that, remarkably, it had electric power. He discovered this as soon as he was two steps beyond the threshold, when the room's lights, triggered by his motion, rendered the torch unnecessary.

The floor and most of the walls were metal, and the embedded lights in the ceiling were devised out of some sort of luminescent fluid. At the other end of the room was a control panel, and beyond that, a pane of glass.

Stepping closer, he saw the writing on the panel, and recognized it as the same odd pre-archaic strain of Eglinat that was carved into the canyon floor.

When he waved his hand over the console, it must have activated something, because then the lights embedded in the panel came to life, as did the ceiling illumination for the room on the other side of the pane of glass.

"Pal, what am I looking at?" he asked.

The way his day was going, it wouldn't have been a surprise if Pal answered directly.

The second room was enormous. He had to look down to see most of it, but what he saw was a vast machine of some kind, with pipes traveling out in multiple directions through the rock walls, floor and ceiling.

The Botzos didn't make this, obviously; if Ko was to be

believed—and Polister did believe him—they didn't even know the machine existed. So, who did?

The gods, he thought. That's what the Septals, with their eminently practical deities, would say.

"'For with the Engine of the World, the Five did hang the stars and raise the continents, fill the seas and scatter the beasts,'" he said. It was a quote from one of the more interesting canonical Septal texts, the *Lidra Gantis.* Widely regarded as a purely allegorical entry in the canon, it provided (with great poetic license) a description of how the gods created Dib, the rest of the universe, the Haven, and the Depths.

Polister knew of no Septal who took it remotely literally, and as a Unital he not only *also* didn't consider it literal, he rejected outright the entire Septal canon, as a longstanding misinterpretation of the true face of the god Pal.

He had, in short, plenty of motivation to reject what his eyes were telling him: that he was currently *looking* at the Engine.

Unless...

There was a section of the control panel that didn't look very control panel-like: no buttons, of switches or meters. It was just a large circle with five slots, with a distinct symbol above each slot.

Quickly, he opened the Staff of Pal again, and extracted the key. It fit snugly into one of the slots, but wouldn't turn. And it wasn't a match for the other four.

"Five keyholes for five keys," he said, laughing. "Orno, my old friend? I think I've found what you were looking for."

Chapter Sixteen

Battine was unprepared to be treated like royalty, either aboard Asealand, or ever again in general. Yet the minute her feet went from the hovering drone device that took her off the deck of the *Kalin-Ha*, to the massive platform deck of Asealand, she had people bowing, and curtseying, and doing the things people who had never been around actual royalty thought they were supposed to do in front of royalty.

It was incredibly awkward, no less so for the fact that she couldn't have looked (or smelled) less like a princess. She would have liked nothing better than to have been spirited aboard by way of some midlevel entrance, shown to a small bunk room for a shower with perfumed soap, a clean set of clothes, and a decent night's sleep on something soft. Maybe *then* she could work on looking more like a princess.

She was met on the deck by the indelibly pompous "admiral" Coigo Staipa. She learned this about him—that he was pompous, and that he was not a real admiral—beforehand, when negotiating the conditions of her asylum.

As far as that went: there *were* no conditions, once he was satisfied she was who she said she was. She thought he would be reluctant, given everything happening to Wrimmad City. He was not. There *was* a hold-up in getting aboard, but only because prior to formally inviting her, Staipa wanted to be flattered. A lot. For roughly forty minutes. He would have made an excellent Alcon.

Accompanying Staipa was a small army of crew members—a virtual sea of white cotton—along with an untold number of residents, looking down from balconies.

This was when all the bowing, and curtseying (nobody who did it was wearing a dress, which just made it look even sillier) and *applause* happened. It was ridiculous, and stupid, and it was probably putting her, and everyone else on board, in tremendous danger.

She waved halfheartedly, hoped sincerely that nobody was expecting a speech, gathered her bags and hurried over to the Coigo Staipa.

"Admiral," she said, "the more who know I'm here..."

"Oh, don't worry about any of that!" he said. "I've already told them! You're under *my* protection! Besides..." he pulled her aside, conspiratorially, and muttered, "you are hardly the only fugitive aboard."

He put his arm around her shoulders. (This was *not* okay, but breaking her host's arm in front of a crowd would not be the most politically astute thing she had ever done. Not that she was known for her political astuteness.) Then he steered her to a woman in one of the white cotton pants suits. "This is Avanar," he said. "She will show you to your quarters!"

"Thank you," Battine said, separating herself from the admiral to shake Avanar's hand. The girl tried to kiss it, which Batt put a stop to right away. She pulled Avenar close. "Please get me out of here."

Staipa said, loudly, "A last round of applause for the princess!"

Everyone clapped. These people had lost their minds.

Avenar smiled. "Right away, princess," she said.

Keeping hold of Batt's hand, Avenar pushed through the

crowd. They were headed for the large triangle shape near the front half of the ship. "It's called the castle," Avenar said. "I'm sure you'll like that."

"I have had my fill of castles," Battine said.

Battine felt a thousand times better after a proper shower and a change into clothing that didn't look or smell as if it had last been worn by a large man with a trout fetish. She had been gifted with undergarments, a pair of slacks, and a blouse, from a resident who was a fair approximation of Batt's size. Rubber shoes were also a part of the donation, but she preferred her riding boots.

The room was a quarter the size of her bedroom at Castle Delphina, and half the size of the one in Polister's residence, but it was *twice* the size of the *Kalin-Ha* bunk room, so she could hardly complain.

More importantly, it was private. Now, if she could convince the admiral to let her take meals in her room, for however long she might be staying, that would be ideal. She'd had her fill of other people.

Naturally, just as she entertained that thought, there came a knock at the door.

Battine cracked it open; there was a woman in the hallway, dressed like a resident.

"Oh good, it looks like everything fit okay," the woman said.

"Are these your clothes?" Batt asked. "They are perfect, thank you."

She moved to close the door again, which was probably rude, but she really did not care.

"I'm Elicasta Sangristy," the woman in the hall blurted out. "It's nice to meet you."

"And you."

Gods, was this what it was going to be like, to be *known* as a princess outside of the Kingdoms? Strangers showing up at her door to introduce themselves awkwardly, because they just *had* to meet her?

"We have to talk," Elicasta said.

"I'm sure we will," Battine said. "But right now, I'm very tired, Ms. Sangristy."

"It's extremely important."

"Ms. Sangristy…"

"It's about the key," Elicasta said.

Battine really *should* have closed the door then. "What key?" she asked.

"The one I think you might still have. We thought at first you'd fled north with it, into the midlands, but now…"

"I'm sorry," Batt said, cutting her off. "I don't know what you're talking about."

"We also have one. And we know where to find a third key. I think Professor Magly would have told you what he knew? And… Orno Linus. We're working with him, just like the professor was. Look, I really shouldn't be talking about this where other people can hear."

Battine opened the door all the way. "Orno Linus is dead," she said.

"He is," Elicasta agreed. "Doesn't mean we're not working with him. He set this whole thing in motion. And he must've been onto something, because the House just burned down Wrimmad City looking for what you still have. Am I wrong?"

Batt stuck her head into the hallway, and looked both ways.

"No," she said. "You're not wrong. Get in here."

As soon as the door was closed, Battine had her sword out.

"Tell me how you know all of this," she said. "And then I'll decide if I should let you live."

"Whoa, whoa, we're all friends here," Elicasta said, not

looking terribly distressed about having a sword at her throat. She raised her hands, but only performatively.

"Who is 'we?'" Battine asked.

"Me, my friend Makk—he's a detective from Velon and he... yeah, long story—and Orno Linus's brother. We're working with three others, but they aren't aboard. Plus, hopefully, you."

"Damid warned me to expect something like this. You can't have my key. I went through too much to obtain it."

"I don't want it," Elicasta said. "I promise."

Battine lowered the sword. "Did Orno Linus's brother not *kill* him? I thought I read this."

Elicasta sighed. "Yeah, we have a *lot* to go over, princess."

"**W**ell, there goes the neighborhood," Calcut said, as they watched the princess disappear into a crowd.

Makk laughed. He still wanted to punch Calcut Linus in the face and handcuff him to something heavy, but aside from all that, he wasn't bad company.

Plus, Calcut had access to some excellent Murskan scotch, and a balcony with a pretty sweet view. It was a view of the *ocean*, which Makk had had quite enough of, but it was still pretty sweet.

"Look at these fucking people," Calcut said. Now he was talking about his neighbors. "Bunch'a wannabes."

"What do they want to be?" Makk asked.

"Rich."

Makk took a good look at the crowd of balcony-sitters, all in their own private mini-estates. The show over, they were heading back in. Meanwhile, on the deck, the fake navy—the ones who spent their whole time making life nice for the ones on the balcony—had already dispersed.

"They look pretty wealthy from here," he said.

"To *you*, my fucking body guy is rich. I mean, enough to live off-planet. Best they can do is twenty maders above the water."

"You're slumming, is what you're saying," Makk said. "Why didn't you just go to Lys?"

"Everyone knows I got a place up there. Hardly anyone knows I got one here too. *You* didn't know."

"That's true. This doesn't seem like your kind of place."

"I financed half this fucking thing," Calcut said.

"I thought Coigo paid for all of it," Makk said.

"He's not rich either. His *family* is. 'Course, I only threw in because he promised to put a casino onboard. Bad investment."

"Doesn't look so bad now."

"Yeah, we'll see," Calcut said.

Makk refilled his glass and shifted a quarter of the way around the balcony, for an unobstructed view of the suns setting in the west, and the *Kalin-Ha* in the distance.

I should be back in bed right now, he thought.

That was how this day was supposed to go. Step one, meet the admiral. Step two, go back to bed. There wasn't supposed to be a step three (confront his girlfriend about putting him into a situation where he'd have to lie on an official record to assuage the ego of their host,) or a step four (make plans to get close to the suddenly-about-to-arrive Princess Battine, so as to get her help in possibly saving the world from a possibly imaginary destroyer-god,) much less a step five (have drinks with fucking Calcut Linus.) He was exhausted, and sore, and nearly positive none of the food or drink he'd consumed or walking he'd done was physician-recommended.

Calcut got to his feet and stepped behind Makk.

"I could probably get you over this railing from here," Calcut said.

Makk turned slowly. The two men whose job it was to keep both Makk and Calcut from committing acts of violence, while aboard Asealand, were absent. This was because Makk and Calcut had agreed to play nice and because Calcut pulled out the bottle of scotch. This should not have been a convincing argument, although it was possible Coigo Staipa wouldn't mind if the two of them managed to kill one another as long as nobody else got hurt. The point was, there wasn't anyone around to stop Calcut, if he drifted into a homicidal mood.

"You think?" Makk asked.

"You don't look so tough. Bad ribs, bad knee."

"Don't forget the broken collarbone."

"I could tell everyone you got so drunk you tipped over before I could do anything," Calcut said.

"Nobody would believe that," Makk said.

"Wouldn't matter if they did or not. Like I said, I financed half this fucking thing. That's a lotta juice."

Makk sipped his scotch and turned back around. "You're not going to do that," he said.

Calcut sidled next to him on the railing. "Why not?"

"Because that's the kind of shit you do when you're angry," Makk said. "And you're not angry right now."

"Yeah, you're right," Calcut said. "Plus, your girlfriend'd kill me. I'm way more afraid of her than of you."

"You should be."

Elicasta wasn't there to prevent them from killing each other, because once they knew for sure that Staipa was going to allow Battine Alconnot to board, she ran back to the castle to prepare. It made a lot more sense to have just one of them reach out to the princess initially, and Elicasta was a much better option than Makk; she was capable of charm and he was mostly not.

Whatever they did next would largely depend on what the princess had to say and, more importantly, whether she still had that key. They also needed to hear from Viselle, Dorn and Xto, which could conceivably happen as soon as Makk turned his voicer back on.

Elicasta was supposed to message Calcut once she'd made contact. That hadn't happened yet.

"Hey," Calcut said. "Did you see that?"

Makk was busy looking at the sunset. "See what?"

Calcut pointed to a spot near the back of the ship. "Something jumped out of the water," he said.

No, no, no, Makk thought. "What *kind* of something?" he asked urgently.

Calcut squinted. "Ah. Nothing. Shadows from the sunset off the water. That's... oh, there, did you see *that?*"

Makk didn't. "You know what happened to us, right? How we ended up shipwrecked?"

"I'm not supposed to, but yeah," Calcut said.

"So you're just fucking with me right now."

"Bet it was a dolphin. That's what it was."

"You're an asshole," Makk said.

"Lots of things in the water, Stidgeon."

Just then, something flew out of the water right beneath them, reached the same height as Calcut's balcony, and dropped back down.

It was all black, it had wings, it had teeth. It was a sea bug. And if there was one, there would be more.

"Shit," Makk said.

"That, what the fuck was that?" Calcut asked.

Makk really wished it had just been that Calcut was screwing with him.

Two more breached the water. These curled over the side and landed on the deck. Somewhere below, somebody screamed.

"Dammit, I told him this was going to happen," Makk said. "Are there any guns aboard?"

"If there are, d'you think he'd let me have access to them?"

"I thought you half-owned this thing. Never mind, come on; we have to get to the admiral."

"You want me to what?" Staipa said, in that jolly tone of voice of his, the one that was at least ninety percent an act.

"Take us as high as you can," Makk said. "As soon as you can."

They were in Staipa's office, which was one level below the banquet room, in the admiral's rather large private quarters. Unlike the banquet floor, at least half of which was taken up by a kitchen, the office took up the entire level. There were windows on all four sides, with an elevator shaft—which may have also been a support column—down the middle. This was how Makk and Calcut entered the office, and also how Makk reached the banquet room earlier in the day. He wondered what the plans were in the event of a power failure.

"Gentlemen!" Staipa said. "We are a ship at sea! Not a wing-plane! I don't understand your request."

"Don't be an ass, Coigo," Calcut said. "Asealand is a hovercraft and always has been. No difference between being up five maders and a hundred, and you know it."

Staipa was behind an enormous desk that had been set up on a slight platform, which meant he could look down on anyone else in the room. The rest of the space was decorated in a style best described as Hyper Nautical: netting hanging from the ceiling; furniture carved from driftwood; a display of different types of knots; multiple barometers and compasses, and so on. Makk had eaten in a few seafood restaurants in Velon with the same decorative theme.

When they'd arrived, uninvited and unannounced, the admiral looked in the midst of a celebratory drink, as there was an open bottle of sherry in the middle of his desk. He seemed disappointed when the elevator doors opened to reveal Makk and Calcut instead of whoever he was expecting. Makk wondered which of Staipa's guests and/or crew *was* expected, and if the couch (decorated with sailing ships, of course) at the other end of the room opened out into a bed.

"*Why* would I do any such thing?" Staipa asked, with a withering stare.

"Because they're here," Makk said. "The *nighdemons*, or sea bugs, or whatever you want to call them. We're under attack."

Staipa laughed. "Your imaginary monsters are *here* now?" he asked. "Do they want to meet the princess? Is that it?"

"*I* saw one, you fucking idiot," Calcut said. "Flew right past my head. While I was on my *balcony*."

Makk had never experienced being the *more* tactful one in the room before. He decided he liked it.

"We aren't the only ones who saw them," Makk said. "A couple landed on the deck. Ask your people; they'll confirm it. It's not bad now, but it's going to get bad, and very soon. But Asealand can do something the *Colusm* never could: it can get *away* from the water. I'm willing to bet you can go higher than they can fly. And the *big* one, the one that punched a hole through the steel siding of the *Colusm*, I'm pretty sure can't fly at all. What we're suggesting isn't unreasonable, admiral."

Coigo Staipa looked at them for a beat: the detective he could probably surreptitiously toss overboard if he became too problematic, but the gangster he probably could *not* toss overboard. Then he picked up the audio box on his desk.

"Bridge," he said, "come in."

"This is the bridge."

"Sawma, put us in storm lockdown. Hurricane protocol."

"Admiral?" Sawma asked. "Please repeat."

"I said, put us in storm lockdown. *Now*, please."

"It's just that the night skies are clear, sir."

"Do not make me repeat myself."

"Yes, admiral," Sawma said. "Hurricane protocol, right away."

Staipa disconnected the audio, as a loud alarm sounded.

"I don't suppose hurricane protocol means hovering above a hurricane?" Makk asked.

"No such luck," Calcut said, crossing the room to a liquor cabinet shaped like a sperm whale. He looked disgusted.

"Asealand is unsinkable, detective," Staipa said. "When we lock down for a storm, all hatches are sealed and all windows shuttered. Everyone aboard is under orders to shelter in place, and not go out on the deck for any reason, until the notice is lifted."

"Get comfortable," Calcut said, extracting what was probably the most expensive bourbon in the cabinet, unsealing it, and taking a swig directly from the bottle. "We're gonna be guests of the admiral for a while."

"Unsinkable," Makk repeated. "That's what you think."

"We've experienced all manner of catastrophic weather conditions," Staipa said. "This will be no different."

On cue, something big struck one of the windows. It didn't hit with enough force to put a crack in the glass, but it made plenty of noise.

"It'll be a *little* different," Makk said.

Staipa hurried over to a wall panel, and flicked four switches. Shutters began to come down on the outside of the windows.

"Sure you don't want to wait a while?" Calcut asked. "Four or five more hits like that and you'll get a closeup of these things you keep sayin' can't exist. Huh? How about it, Coigo?"

There were three more impacts on the windows (from two sides) before the shutters made it all the way down.

"We will be just fine!" Staipa said, going back to his desk and refilling his sherry glass. It wasn't clear who he was trying to convince: them, or himself.

E licasta had made it most of the way through the story of Orno Linus and the five keys, when they were interrupted by a loud siren.

"Oh," Battine said, instinctively putting her hand on the hilt of the sword on her belt. (The belt in question was, like everything else the princess was wearing, Elicasta's; it was not designed to hold a sword, but was doing an okay job of it.) "What is that?"

"I don't know," Elicasta said. "Never heard it before."

'Casta moved to the window. The suns had just set; the only illumination out there was the artificial kind, from the strategically placed light stanchions. There wasn't much to see.

A member of the crew burst into the room. "Is everyone okay?" she asked.

"Avenar," Battine said, "what is happening? Is something wrong?"

"I don't know. I heard the siren, and..." She tilted her head. "Oh, that's the lockdown siren. But that doesn't make any sense."

"Lockdown for what?" Elicasta asked.

"Bad weather. Don't, don't go anywhere," Avenar said. "I'll check with upstairs. Maybe it's a drill?"

She stepped back out, closing the door behind her. What was a little interesting was that the "door" was actually a hatch, with a wheel in the middle that locked it in place, and when Avenar left, she spun it until it clicked.

Battine joined Elicasta at the window. There were a number of crew members out there, running around in their dress whites.

"Doesn't *look* like bad weather," 'Casta said.

"I do not like this," Battine said.

Something big and pitch-black flew past the window.

"Gods!" Batt exclaimed, jumping backwards. Elicasta felt the same way, but was suddenly without words.

It's them, she thought. *They've found us.*

There was a whirring noise, and then a steel shutter started to roll closed over the glass of the window. Which would be a great idea, if they were worried about a hailstorm or something.

"I know of these things," Battine was saying. She'd begun to pace. "I was told about them. They destroyed a fishing boat."

"A fishing boat? A wooden fishing boat? Like the one you came in on?"

The princess went pale. "The *Kalin-Ha*. Should we warn them?"

"I don't know how," Elicasta said.

"They had an audio device, we could..." she stopped, on seeing the look on Elicasta's face. "You know these creatures as well, don't you?"

'Casta hadn't gotten to the part in her story about the *Colusm* yet. "They destroyed the last vessel I was on," she explained. "A freighter. It wasn't made of wood."

"I spoke to the only survivor of the *Bekohai*," Battine said, frowning. "She said they caught one of these... *Dwanni* was her word for them. They caught one in a net and pulled it aboard. This was why the swarm took down the vessel, and why every other ship from Botzis was imperiled by this threat."

"We need to reach the *Kalin-Ha*," Elicasta said. "I get it."

"The *Kalin-Ha* have their nets up; that isn't what I'm saying. I'm asking why your freighter was a target."

"I don't know. Looks like catching one isn't the only way to piss off the *Dwanni*."

"I agree," Battine said. "But what are the other ways? And has *this* vessel committed a similar offense?"

"That's a good question."

Elicasta reached up to the left side of her head, which was where the rig optical trigger was supposed to be. But she wasn't wearing the rig—they didn't know how the princess would react to it—so she was just flicking the side of her head.

"Right," Elicasta muttered, pulling a voicer from her back

pocket. When Battine eyed her suspiciously, she explained, "this is called a voicer. It's—"

"I know what it is," Battine said. "I was wondering who you planned to direct, and if it was safe, as I'm told the device can be used to track the user. You did say there was a warrant for you?"

"Oh," 'Casta said. "Wow. You are *way* more tech savvy than I expected. This is tapping a loop circuit, pure local, no sat hit. Is that okay?"

"I don't understand anything you just said."

"It's, uh...? Yeah, don't worry, it's safe."

"Very well."

Elicasta double-checked to make sure the voicer was still slaved to the local—it'd be awkward if the princess ended up being right because the voicer had an auto repoint—and directed Calcut.

"What?" he said. He answered every direct like this.

"I need to talk to Makk, is he still with you?"

"We're both here. Come on up; I got a bet with the admiral that these shutters won't hold. Bring her highness. We can all watch him be wrong together."

"Up? Calcut, where are you?"

Chapter Seventeen

"**T**hey're not going away."

The observation seemed abundantly self-evident to Makk, but was greeted by a lot of head-shaking and general consternation from the bridge crew.

The problem appeared to be that their preferred method of resolving the situation—doing nothing—wasn't working, and they didn't like that.

Not long after Elicasta and Battine Alconnot arrived at Coigo's office, they decided to relocate to the already-over-crowded Asealand bridge. From there, they could get up-to-date reports on what was happening outside. It was a much better option than the alternative, which was to sit and listen to the deeply unnerving, arrhythmic drumbeat of giant sea bugs attacking the ship, with no view of the outside whatsoever.

Or so they thought. In truth, it was just as unnerving to be *fully* aware of what was happening as it was to imagine Asealand under assault from some aggressively large hailstones. The bridge leveraged dozens of angles from fixed opticals and aerial drones (although they kept losing those.) They also hadn't closed the window shutters for some reason—perhaps thinking they were too high to be at risk.

What was clear, from every perspective, was that they were being overrun.

The entire surface of the ship was crawling with black sea bugs. They walked, climbed, and flew, smashing into walls and looking for openings. They were trying to get inside, and nobody knew why.

"They have to go away eventually, detective," Admiral Staipa said, with a little quiver in his voice.

"Waiting them out can't be the only plan," Makk said.

"We have another breach," one of the crew shouted. "Aft 312. Shutter collapse."

"Who lives at 312?" the admiral asked. He was pacing in front of his chair.

"The Awsels. They're not aboard right now."

"Thank the gods for that." To Makk, he said, "they will give up."

Makk muttered a few choice curses under his breath, and drifted back to the middle of the room.

So far, no residents had been harmed. Every building had at least one room with no windows, that could be fully sealed, with an independent oxygen supply to keep everyone alive until the all-clear. So while the bridge had been fielding messages since the start of the attack—from terrified residents, screaming at whoever answered and demanding to speak to the admiral—things could have been much, much worse.

Staipa fielded a few directs initially, but soon gave up; he could no longer sell his go-to response—"Don't worry, we have every-thing under control and this will all be over soon"—and didn't know what to say instead, that sounded both plausible and soothing.

Makk wasn't worried about Staipa's public relations problems, so he mostly ignored that part of the bridge and concentrated on the section devoted to the continued seaworthiness of the vessel. In that regard, they were still doing okay; the *Dwanni* were causing plenty of damage, but none of it had changed the ship's effectiveness as a low-flying craft. (The word *Dwanni* came from Battine Alconnot. As something akin to a proper name, it was quickly adopted.)

Perhaps it was because nobody had been hurt, and the *Dwanni* weren't wreaking more havoc, that waiting out the attack made more sense than just heading skyward until the creatures couldn't reach the deck any longer. Makk thought this was a ridiculous attitude to take, but nobody was listening to him.

"Another drone down," someone from the other end of the bridge shouted. Elicasta and Calcut were at that end, trying to assist with the electronic surveillance. Calcut had his own fleet of drones he was trying to wake up. He wasn't trying that *hard*—he still had Staipa's expensive bottle of bourbon—but Elicasta was helping; she had her rig on and was using it to interact directly with the fleet.

Battine Alconnot, meanwhile, had taken up a position at one of the windows. Makk—with nothing else to do—sidled up next to her.

The deck and the skies were full of *Dwanni*; seeing it through a window had a visceral impact that a vid screen did not.

"We need to know what they want," she said.

"Aside from sinking the ship?" Makk asked.

She looked at him. "They are swarming us like bees in search of their queen. Until we know why, they won't go away."

"According to the admiral, they'll just get tired and go home."

"The admiral is an idiot. You are *not* an idiot, Makk Stidgeon. And you know I'm right."

He laughed. "I do," he said. "Just don't know what to do about it."

She was about to offer a suggestion, when the window to their right exploded, spraying glass across the room.

The *Dwanni* who'd broken the glass landed on the floor two maders from the admiral's chair.

"Get back!" Makk said, jumping between it and the admiral.

The creature shrieked, fluttered its wings, and lunged at Makk. It was intercepted, in midair, by Battine Alconnot's sword: a straight, up-down swing, that cut the *Dwanni* in two.

She spun around to face the breach.

"Close the bridge shutters!" Staipa shouted, as a second *Dwanni* flew in. Battine killed that one too, its blood—more purple than crimson—arcing across the room.

The steel shutters came down before a third one got through. But now that the bugs knew the bridge was *there*, they were going to keep trying. *Thump, thump, thump*, on all sides.

"You won't let me have a gun, but you let her keep a *sword?*" Makk asked Staipa.

"I'd say it's a good thing I did," he said. "Thank you, princess."

Wiping the blood off the sword blade with her sleeve, Battine said, "I would not have let you take it away." Then she knelt down to study the things she'd just killed. "I have never seen anything like this," she said to Makk. "Have you?"

"Aside from when they tried to drown me, no," he said.

She poked it with the tip of the sword. "Cartilage. No bones. Like a jellyfish with sharp bits."

The corpse *sparked* in response to her sword.

No, that wasn't right. It was doing that on its own, like it was powering up.

Oh shit, Makk thought. "Everyone, step away from the electronics. 'Casta, take off that rig."

Elicasta took one look at the sparking corpse on the floor, then fumbled to power down her optical rig and set it on a countertop.

"What's happening, detective?" the princess asked, backing away from the corpses.

Makk turned to the admiral. "Coigo, please tell me this fucking ship can float."

"What?"

There was a huge electrical surge then. It caused every console to glow twice as brightly as it should have, and the hairs on Makk's arms to stand up. There was a *thud* he felt more than heard, a bright, blinding spark from seemingly every direction, and everything went dead.

And they were falling.

It was like being back in the army again; Makk, stuck in that null-gravity troop transport with the faulty engine, plunged into sudden darkness with his entire squad, abruptly weightless and dropping, dropping, and then landing in a crush of screams, broken necks, crushed heads and broken limbs.

Asealand didn't drop that far—just a few maders. The weightlessness was much briefer, and the landing not as lethal. But it still sucked, both in terms of physical pain, and relived trauma.

Red-tinted emergency lights kicked in. They didn't help too much, but at least now it wasn't perfectly coffin-dark.

"Staipa!" Makk shouted. He was lying on his side, on top of one half of a *Dwanni* corpse, which was really gross. "Answer me! Can she float?"

"She will," someone from the other side of the room shouted. "Pontoons on the underside. We won't sink."

We won't sink yet, Makk thought. *Let's not get ahead of ourselves.*

Makk got to his feet and looked around. "'Casta?" he called out.

"I'm okay," she said, as the rest of the room stirred. He could hear, more than see, the other members of the bridge moving around.

"Anyone need medical?" somebody shouted.

"I think my arm is broken," someone else said.

"What the fuck was that?" Calcut asked. He sounded unharmed, which was a shame.

"It was the bugs," 'Casta said. "They did the same thing to the *Colusm*."

Makk found Battine, leaning against the wall. "Are you hurt, princess?"

"Stunned," she said, "but all right. I think that I have lost my appetite for this world's technological contrivances."

He held out a hand and helped her to her feet. "You and me both."

Together, they found Coigo Staipa on the floor in front of his chair. He was awake and apparently unhurt.

"Unsinkable," he muttered. "Unsinkable."

"Coigo," Makk said, "this ship could really use its admiral right now."

He looked past Makk to Battine. "Princess," he said. "I'm so sorry."

"Get up, you jackass," she said, "and explain why this nuclear boat of yours suddenly has no power."

He stared at her, in utter shock. It was possible nobody outside of his own family had ever spoken to Coigo Staipa like that. But while the Staipas were *treated* like royalty, Battine Alconnot actually *was* royalty, which it turned out meant she got to say all the things Makk wished *he* could say without consequence.

"Bybrid!" the admiral shouted, clambering to his feet. "Bybrid, why have we no power?"

"The surge blew all the relays," somebody—not Bybrid, but somebody—answered. "We're checking now."

"I want reports from every part of the ship!" Staipa said.

"We're deaf without power, Staipa," Calcut said. "Deaf and blind."

"What about your non-networked devices, Calcut?" Staipa asked.

"Nah, this isn't like what Sangristy did. My shit's as dead as yours."

There came a deep, booming—and unfortunately familiar—howl, that seemed to emanate from all directions, and then the ship was hit by something *large*. They all felt the impact, as the vibration traveled through the steel hull.

"Oh, that's not good," Makk said.

"A volunteer!" Staipa said. "I need word on the status of the reactor."

Battine pulled Makk aside. "Again: what do they want? If we can give it to them *before* they sink us..."

"Yeah, that would be good," Makk agreed. "But unless..."

He had a thought.

"Unless what?" Battine asked.

"This isn't *random*, is it?"

"That is what I have been saying."

"It was something in the hold," he said. "It had to be." He turned to Staipa. "Admiral, where is Del?"

Coigo looked confused. "Cargo, I think. Why does that matter?"

"I need to speak to them. Right now."

"Right *now*, I need someone to get power to my null-gravity field, detective," Coigo said. "If Del can help with that, then by the gods, go find them. Otherwise, you can wait until we've made it through this crisis."

"We volunteer," Battine said.

Staipa looked *more* confused. "Volunteer for what?"

"Your reactor is below deck, and this Del is below deck. We volunteer."

"Princess, some of that trip is in the open," Staipa said.

"Give Detective Stidgeon a weapon of his own," she said, "and we'll do it." She looked at Makk. "Yes?"

"Sure," Makk said, wondering if now would be a good time to tell Battine that he was a professional bad luck charm. "Sounds like fun."

"It's unsafe," Staipa said. "I should be the one to go."

"You're needed here, admiral," Makk said, although he probably wasn't. Best he seemed capable of doing was barking orders at people who were already doing what he was ordering them to do. But he'd be dead weight outside. "Besides, I think I'd rather have the princess with the sword, if it's all right by you."

They didn't have to climb down the ladder on the outside of the castle in order to reach the deck; there was one inside, an emergency exit tunnel that ran alongside the elevator shaft.

Phota, a member of the bridge crew, volunteered to take them down as far as the admiral's quarters, where they would find a locked weapons cabinet.

Before they left, Elicasta gave Makk a big hug. "Last time you volunteered to go below deck, you nearly drowned," she pointed out.

"Thanks for reminding me. If I don't make it back, do me a favor and shoot Calcut, would you?"

"Get fucked, Stidgeon," Calcut said.

The way down sucked, but it didn't last long; soon enough Phota had them at a hatch to the residential floor.

They ended up in an open entryway, with a nice carpet, and pictures hung on the wall. It looked a little macabre in the red emergency lighting, but was probably really nice under normal conditions.

"It's this way," Phota said, leading them through an open hatchway, down a hall, around a corner, and to a locked hatch. She pulled out a huge ring of keys and fiddled until she found the right one, stuck it in the keyhole in the middle of the door's wheel, and spun it open.

There was a decent-sized arsenal on the other side.

"Gods," Makk said. "You guys expecting pirates?"

"It's all confiscated weapons," Phota said. "Everyone comes aboard thinking they're the exception."

"You don't give them back when people leave?"

"We would, but hardly anybody leaves."

"I suspect that will change," Battine said. "Do you see what you need, detective?"

"Plenty," he said, stepping into the room and picking up a shotgun and a full box of shells. "You want a couple of guns, while we're here?"

Makk couldn't convince Battine to take a gun, but she did agree to carry a bag of ammunition. He'd have carried all of it himself, but he had to make room for the *grenades*.

These were actual, live Inimatan army surplus grenades, sitting in a glass case like they were collector's items. It was true that the army had a habit of reinventing the hand grenade every few years, and that the subtle design differences meant, in *theory*, that the outdated models could be considered collector's items. But one didn't customarily collect *live* ordnance; one collected disarmed *shells* of live ordnance. If the display was on a wall somewhere, Makk would have assumed the grenades were exactly that. But these were, A: in the secret gun storage locker, and B: in a case with a plaque that *said* they were real, live grenades.

Asealand had some pretty eccentric residents.

There were other charming surprises, including some expensive-looking blasters, which Makk ignored, because he didn't trust blasters, a couple of projectile handguns he *did* trust, and an unreasonable amount of archery equipment he had no use for.

Once they'd loaded up, Phota brought them back to the emergency exit shaft. "There's a hatch at the bottom that opens up to the deck lobby," she said. "You guys know where to go from there?"

"Forty maders straight," Battine said. "The bulkhead on the left."

"Will it be locked?" Makk asked. He wasn't relishing having to play with a set of keys under those circumstances.

"It'll definitely be *closed*, but none of the bulkhead doors lock," Phota said, hopping on the ladder. "Good luck, you two."

As thankful as Makk was for the steel shutters over the windows, it would have been nice to see what the exposed deck looked like *before* opening the lobby door. At least then, they'd have an idea of how dense the resistance was going to be.

"We should have more with us," Battine said, her hand on the wheel of the hatch door. "It looked as if Staipa had an army when I got here; where did they all go?"

"They're wherever they were when he ordered the lockdown," Makk said. "And they're unarmed, so it's probably for the best. By the way, thanks a bunch for volunteering me to do this."

She laughed. "You were going to volunteer yourself if I hadn't. I could see that."

"Fair. But why are *you* doing it?"

"If you knew what I'd been through this past year, you wouldn't have to ask," she said. "Let us say I have some aggression to work through. Are you ready?"

He had a double-barreled shotgun in his hands, a handgun in his pocket, and a second shotgun and rifle on his back. "I'm as ready as I can be. You lead, I'll watch the flank."

Nodding, she looked at his knee, which he'd been favoring the entire time down the ladder. "I will be moving quickly; try to keep up."

"Yes, your highness."

"I'm not a queen. That title is for queens."

"Just open the door."

She spun the wheel, opened the hatch, and jumped out.

The push for the sub-level hatch was honestly pretty cathartic for both of them, as evidently Makk had some aggression of his own to work through. The dozen or so *Dwanni* on the deck between them and their destination were surprised to encounter resistance where there had previously been none, which made them easy targets for either Battine's sword or Makk's guns. She'd swing at the nearest bug, leaving her flank exposed; he'd shoot the bug that came at her from the side, then she'd dispatch the bug that came at his back while he was firing, and on they went.

Halfway to the door, they actually ran out of things to kill. It was so surprising, they stopped for a beat to make sure they weren't missing something.

"Is that all?" Battine asked, spinning around. She was covered in bug blood and looking pretty happy about it.

"It's not," Makk said. "Listen."

The air above was humming.

"Oh," she said, "I forgot they can fly."

"Yeah, let's run."

They made it to the turn, and *saw* the door before the wave of reinforcements arrived; then they were in the shit.

The attacks came from all sides, with bugs lunging forward and back in something like a coordinated attack that quickly overwhelmed their position. Battine managed to clear a circle around herself, but remained exposed to an overhead attack, which Makk couldn't defend against because he had a dozen bugs of his own to contend with. Twice, the bugs came within centimaders of her head before she managed to duck and ward them off with a swipe at the air.

The *Dwanni* seemed to respect the guns more than the sword —they were perhaps more familiar with the concept of a sharp object than a projectile weapon—so he was getting a wider berth. And he was shooting in every direction that didn't have Battine in the line of fire. It was *working*, in that he wasn't dead yet, but he wasn't making any forward progress.

Then Makk ran out of shotgun shells; there were more, but in the bag on Battine's back, which he couldn't get to. He switched to the handgun and the rifle, which wasn't nearly as efficient—bullets only hit one target at a time—but held the *Dwanni* off anyway, because of the noise they made. The open question was whether they'd figure out the risk had changed before or after he ran out of bullets.

"Oh, fuck this," he said. He threw an empty shotgun into the face of the bug that stood between him and Battine, and started pulling out grenades with his free hand. He tossed one directly behind him, one to his left, one to his right, and then one over Batt's head, where it landed (hopefully—he couldn't see) in the space between her and the door. Then he ran at the princess.

"Get down!" he shouted.

She saw him running, turned around and dropped to her knees.

He landed on top of her, just as the grenades went off.

The explosions lit up the night: *bang, bang, bang,* in rapid succession, followed by the shrieks of the dying, as the *Dwanni* learned about another new kind of weapon.

The ones not harmed by the grenades fell away, fearful of a second volley. It was the opening they needed.

Makk got to his feet, pulled Battine up, and together they ran the rest of the way to the bulkhead hatch.

They fell inside, slammed the hatch behind them—it vibrated with the impact of a dive-bombing bug a second too late—and spun the lock.

Then they sat in the semi-dark of the emergency lighting for a while, just breathing.

"Well," Makk said. "That was a lot. Are you hurt?"

"Some cuts," she said. "Nothing deep. You?"

"I can't move my left arm," he admitted. "And there's a cut on the right that'll need stitches. But I think I'm okay."

"What did they do to your arm?"

"That was the shotgun," he said. "I think the hairline fracture in my collarbone isn't a hairline fracture anymore."

"Does it hurt?" she asked.

"Doesn't tickle." He got to his feet. "Come on, let's figure out where we are."

Where they were was, standing at the top of a down staircase, on a landing just large enough for the two of them. Despite the emergency lights on the walls, the bottom of the flight was obscured by darkness.

"I hear something," Battine muttered. She put herself in front of Makk and took the first step down.

He didn't hear anything, but trusted the princess on this. "Anyone down there?" he shouted.

"Hello?" someone at the bottom of the stairs shouted. "Who goes there?"

"It's us," Makk said. "The giant bugs. We can talk now."

"Is that you, detective?"

"Rayno?" Makk asked. "Where in the Depths have you been?"

If it could be said that the Asealand main deck was its own little city, then the sub-levels were that city's sewers.

The lighting, as with the rest of the ship, was red-tinted from the battery-powered emergency lights affixed to the ceiling at regular intervals. But unlike up above, one got the distinct sense that this was *normal conditions* for below deck. The corridors were narrow, with cutaways at regular intervals to other corridors and the occasional door. And pipes, pipes everywhere, conveying who knew what—water, sewage, energy—to various parts of the ship.

Rayno, who they tasked with showing them around, didn't

know who Del was, but he *could* lead them to the reactor, so they headed that way first.

It was near the back of the ship. On the way, they passed cargo bays (nobody there had heard of Del either,) freezer units and food pantries, the waste management room (which was larger than the cargo bays, freezer units and food pantries combined,) and some very depressing crew quarters.

Whether what was attacking the underside of the ship was a single, massive *Dwanni* or a swarm acting in concert, as Makk and Battine traveled, it became obvious that they were heading in the direction of the attack's epicenter. The creatures were targeting the power station.

It would be the exact right place to focus an assault, if the goal was to disable Asealand. If they were facing off against a submersible armed with missiles, this would make perfect sense. But this was a swarm of animals. It seemed unreasonable to assume they knew how ships worked.

Unless disabling the ship isn't the point, he thought.

Rayno brought Makk and Battine to the power station's control center, which was a small room overlooking a larger one. The control panels were dark, and the center empty.

"They must all be on the floor," Rayno said, opening a hatch that led to a ladder down.

That was self-evidently the case, although when they reached the power station main floor, they didn't *see* anyone. But they could hear them shouting back and forth—"try that," "how about now?" and so on—and the occasional flash of hand torches.

What they were running around, was a massive aggregation of machinery that took up half the length of Asealand.

"Dr. Albit?" Rayno shouted.

An older man poked a yellow-helmeted head up from behind a nearby machine component. "What?"

"These two came from the castle. The admiral sent them."

Albit turned his head and shouted, "Try again now!" then turned back to Rayno, Makk and Battine. "Are they engineers?"

"No," Makk said.

"Then what the fuck did he send you for?"

"No good!" someone at another piece of machinery, behind Makk somewhere, shouted in response.

"Balls," Albit grumbled. "Hang on!"

"He sent us to ask why his nuclear engine isn't working," Battine said.

"Oh, *did* he? Thanks to his advanced degree in nuclear physics?" He disappeared behind the machinery, rattling off a litany of curses largely pertaining to Coigo Staipa's intellect.

"This is perhaps not the best time to ask him about his engine," Battine said to Makk.

After some loud fiddling, they heard a *zzzap!* in time with a bright spark, and an "aha!" from Dr. Albit. He resurfaced, coming around the machine and past them, to a second machine with a control panel. He began throwing switches and pushing buttons, even though it didn't look like the panel had any power going through it.

"The admiral wants to know how an electrical surge shut down a nuclear reactor, is that it?" the doctor asked.

"That's the gist of it," Makk said.

"I think he just wants to know when the power will be back," Rayno offered.

"We'll have *power* in a minute," Albit said. "Battery power. Lights, heat, comms. We won't have the *reactor* back for a while."

They were hit from below by a massive blow that nearly knocked everyone over. "Or never," Dr. Albit added, "if that shit keeps up. Can either of you not-engineers tell me what in the gods is attacking us? I can't get a straight answer."

"Sea monsters," someone said, from in the darkness at the far end of the room. "I *told* you."

"Yes, that one thinks we're being pulled down by nightmare

creatures from the Depths," Albit said. "What is it *really?* A new weapon?"

Makk turned to the voice from the darkness. "Del?" he said. "Is that you?"

Del emerged, covered in grease and sweat. "Oh hey, detective. Thought you would've died by now."

"Not for lack of trying," he said. "You're just the person I wanted to talk to."

Del looked confused. "All right," they said.

"Everyone clear!" Albit shouted. "I think we've got it!"

He waited a five-count and then lowered a switch on his panel and locked it into place. The overhead lights blinked, and turned on.

A cheer sounded from seven different directions. Then they were hit again from below—this time accompanied by the unmistakable sound of metal bending—and the cheering stopped.

"Holath, check the reactor," Albit barked, at someone on the other side of the room. "Emrik, power up communications, keep everything else dark; we're not out of this yet, people." *Thump.* "Gods, sounds like it's coming through the floor." He disappeared behind another bank of machinery, shouting commands for a range of unseen people.

"Why were you looking for me?" Del asked.

"Right," Makk said. "Sorry. I'm trying to understand what's happening here."

"We have lights, but the engine isn't running," Battine said. "Or so it seems."

"Emergency battery," Del said, recognizing Battine. "Should I...? Should I be bowing or something?"

"I will give you a gold florin to *not* bow," Battine said.

"Can *you* explain how an electrical pulse shut down a fusion reactor?" Makk asked.

"Is that what you wanted to know?" Del asked. "Because I think Dr. Albit is your man for that."

"I was just curious, and he looks busy."

"I don't know either," Del admitted. "I got stuck down here when they figured out I knew my way around electrical circuits. That's after the admiral accused me of lying."

"I thought he might have thrown you overboard," Makk said.

"That was on the table."

Thump.

"I should get back," Del added. They looked nervous, no doubt for the same reason every impact triggered a sick feeling in Makk's stomach: they'd been through this before. "What do you want from *me*, detective?"

"Can you tell me what the *Colusm* was shipping?"

"Steel."

"What else?" Makk asked. "What was in the crates?"

They hesitated. "I don't actually know. The *captain* knew. But she'd rip us a new one if we asked, so we didn't ask. Orders were to not open them, not go *near* them, and don't worry about it."

"Where were these crates being delivered?" Battine asked.

"Lladn," Del said. "Now I really have to go. Glad you're not dead."

Del hurried off.

"That sounded... ominous," Battine said.

"Didn't it, though," Makk said. "What would you ship in big metal crates, that you didn't want even the *crew* to know about?"

"Something illegal."

"That almost goes without saying. But what?"

Battine shrugged. "This is more your expertise than mine, Makk Stidgeon."

"Large and illegal," he said. "Large and illegal and dangerous and secret."

What was it Staipa said? Makk thought. *Something about old fission reactors.*

"You have an idea, don't you?" Battine said.

"I might. Let's track down Dr. Albit. I need a quick lesson in nuclear energy."

Thump.

This impact was on the side of the ship, accompanied by something that sounded a lot like steel being torn open. Then came the clattering of pincer-sharp legs, a familiar buzz, and lots of screaming.

"They've broken in," Battine said.

"Give me the bag of ammo," Makk said.

Makk and Battine ran in the direction of the screaming to find a dozen people—Rayno included—fighting off the creatures with whatever they could swing: a steel rod, a wrench, a fist.

"Get back!" Makk shouted to anyone capable of both hearing him and moving. He stepped in front of Rayno and two others, lowered the shotgun—without a left arm, he had to brace the stock with his stomach—and fired one-handed.

It had the desired effect, but when he set up to fire again, one of the engineers he just saved grabbed the barrel, and shouted, "What are you doing? Don't shoot that down here!"

"Why not?" Makk asked, as Battine jumped between them and the *Dwanni* to eviscerate a couple more.

"Put a crack in one of those pipes and we're all dead!" the engineer said. He pointed to a set of pipes running along the ceiling, that were in the line of fire. (He could have pointed in any direction; there were pipes all around.)

"All right, all right," Makk said, "I'll try not to, but no promises."

A bug dive-bombed Makk, so he used the shotgun like a club to bat it back.

A few paces away, an engineer went down, when two bugs pounced and took out his legs.

Ahead, Battine screamed as one got past her and swiped a sharpened leg down her back. Meanwhile, Makk had lost sight of Rayno entirely, and everyone else had scattered.

Makk was really close to not caring about the pipes on the ceiling.

A loud horn sounded. Red lights flashed from the middle of the ship.

"They're dropping the partition!" somebody shouted. "Everybody move!"

If the "partition" was what Makk *thought* it was, he didn't want to end up on the wrong side of it. He dropped the shotgun, pulled out the handgun, helped Battine to her feet, and blew the head off the nearest *Dwanni* before it could reach them. "We're falling back," he said.

They ran toward the flashing lights, dodging bugs when they could, cutting or shooting them when they couldn't.

In the middle of the room, a heavy metal door was sliding down from the ceiling. It was nearly to the floor.

"Hurry!" Battine said, pulling on his useless left arm, which was very unpleasant. She got to the door first, slid underneath it, and held out a hand to him. He dove on his stomach, got halfway, and had to be pulled the rest of the way through. The door clicked into place a second later.

"Thanks," he said. "This is fun, isn't it?"

"I am no longer enjoying myself."

Some bugs made it through; there were about a dozen people doing their best to fight them off with steel pipes, and not doing so hot.

"This would be easier if more of you had swords," Battine said, getting to her feet. "You rest; I can take care of these stragglers."

"Can't rest," he said, forcing himself to his feet. "I need to find Albit, or we're never getting out of this."

"I don't think we *are* getting out of this."

She ran off, sword at the ready. Makk leaned against the steel partition, caught his breath, and reevaluated everything he thought he knew about princesses. Then he stumbled ahead.

~

An eternity later, Makk found Albit, fiddling with yet another control panel at the far end of the sealed chamber. He looked unharmed, and—all things considered—pretty calm.

"Albit!" Makk barked. He was in a lot of pain and had run out of tact. "I have questions."

Albit looked at him for a solid three-count. "You're the one firing guns in my engine room," he said.

"The guns are what got me this far. Maybe you noticed we're under attack."

"Yes. I apologize for not believing you, about the sea monsters, or whatever those are. I'll apologize to Del too, if they made it this far." He checked a meter. "You have until this reaches 100%. What are your questions?"

"That's not a regular bulkhead door we're on the other side of, is it?" Makk asked. "I've seen a half-dozen radiation warning symbols on the walls, and someone out there said if I popped a hole in a pipe I'd kill everyone. I don't know much about fusion reactors, but I know there's not a lot of radiation involved, so..."

"So what kind of reactor do we have?" Albit said, finishing the thought. "You're from Velon, aren't you?"

"I am."

"Seen a lot of aero-cars?"

"More than I ever wanted to," Makk said.

"Aeros use compact a fusion reactor with a non-radioactive byproduct. They'd have to, or nobody would let them fly around the city like that."

Makk wanted to say that nobody should let them do that anyway, but didn't. "Go on," he said.

"The energy generated from a micro-reactor is more than enough to keep something that small up, and to power the negative gravity field at the front of the car, which is how they move. But the technology doesn't scale."

"You're saying you don't use a fusion reactor?"

"I'm saying the technology is different. To create a fusion reaction *our* way requires an enormous amount of pressure; enough to push two atoms together, many times over. You can't get that kind of energy from a chemical reaction. For that, you need is a *fission* reactor, which *does* involve highly radioactive material. *That* is why we have a lead-lined partition, and plenty of warnings about not firing *projectiles* around the engine room floor."

"Is this a common setup?" Makk asked.

"I would say it's not *common*, but not uncommon either. Lys uses one, I'm quite sure. Zero-Ball fields as well. I expect there are other application I'm unaware of."

"Do fission reactors produce a radioactive byproduct? Say, something that has to be taken away in large metal crates?"

"The control rods, yes," Albit said.

"What are those?"

"They prevent the fission reaction from running away. This is why we lost the reactor when we lost power; the control rods drop automatically during a power failure. Your minute is up, but now I have to know: why are you asking these questions?"

"Because I think the things attacking the ship are interested in your radioactive core, doctor," Makk said. "And I think they're going to keep attacking the ship until we give it to them."

Chapter Eighteen

Everyone on the bridge cheered when the power came back.

"Excellent! Well done!" Staipa declared, as if anyone in the room had a hand in it. "Get us out of here, helm!"

But the engine hadn't been restored yet; all they had was power for the lights and the communications—they could reach the Stream again, for whatever good that would do them—and the alarm systems.

It seemed every single alarm on Asealand was going off at once.

"I have a breach alarm!" one of them shouted.

"I do too!"

"Got three over here! And a fire on Elm."

All anyone was doing was reporting the information on the suddenly-awake displays in front of their faces. They couldn't do anything about any of it.

Elicasta was sitting at an idle console at the edge of the room. Calcut was next to her, checking out things on a slightly less-idle console; he had an access level (either granted or hacked) to the ship's systems that she didn't have. He also had a half-empty bottle of bourbon. The fact that he was personally responsible for the missing half didn't impair him much.

"How bad?" she asked, beneath the din, as he scrolled through the same menus as the rest of the room.

"We're a little fucked," he said.

"Only a little?"

"More than ten holes in the hull, three fires on the deck—and the fire suppression system's not online yet, so that's not gonna change. Looks like they managed to tip over Donsa Banni's place. Never liked him."

"Are we sinking?" she asked.

"Nah. As long as they leave the pontoons alone we won't even take on water. But we're not moving, either, and they ain't leaving, so…"

"So it's only a matter of time before they figure out that they should be attacking the pontoons."

"Yeah."

Elicasta had a packet of vid streams in her vault and ready to push. They covered everything from the past year: Orno Linus and the five keys; Xto's life story, and the secret space station on the sunny side of an asteroid; the Outcast, and where in the night sky to look for it; the razing of Wrimmad City; the sea bugs sinking the *Colusm*; and the truth about the House's underground bunkers. Any one of these stories would be *the* most important vid to hit the Stream in a generation. If she wanted to max the subs, the smart thing would be to drop one every few months, giving each vid a runway for a full cycle.

These weren't ordinary times. With the House backdoor stripping Veesers, the only way each one of those vids hits the Stream as a Veeser product is if they're dropped at the same time.

That was one good reason to execute a full dump. Another was, there was a decent possibility she was about to die.

She needed Stream access to execute the drop. (She had a deadman's switch on the vault; if she didn't check in after a certain amount of time, it would auto-drop. But the lag was a year. The way the House was acting, who knew if there'd even be a Stream in a year?) She had that access *now*. Would it still be there in another hour?

"Admiral, got the engine room," the comms officer said.

"Finally!" Staipa said. "Put them on wide audio, Tolus."

There was a burst of static over the room audio, then, "Admiral, it's Nem Albit, can you hear me?"

"Dr. Albit! We need to get out of here. Where is my engine?"

"These things breached the main floor," Albit said. "We're locked in control. If they make it in *here*, you're not *getting* your reactor back."

"Well hurry up the work then!" Staipa said. "Double-quick!"

"Yes, I understand what 'hurry' means, Coigo. I didn't contact you for a stern talking-to about the speed of my team under adverse conditions. There's someone here who has an odd suggestion."

"Hi Admiral," Makk said.

"Fucking unbelievable," Calcut muttered. "Your boyfriend is the luckiest *Cholem* in history. Look at you; were you even worried?"

"I was a *little* worried," she said.

"Detective Stidgeon!" Staipa said. He sounded surprised; he either didn't think Makk would make it, or forgot he ever sent him. "Is the princess...?"

"She's here too," Makk said. "Look, I have an idea for how to get these things to go away. You're not gonna like it."

"I'm open to all suggestions!"

"We have to dump the fission reactor's core."

Staipa's entire demeanor changed. "This is no time for jokes!" he barked.

"I'm not joking," Makk said.

"Dumping the core is a contingency," Albit said. "If the control rods fail, we can dump the core in the ocean."

Staipa looked like he was having a stroke in slow motion. "Doctor, without the core, we have no fission reactor..."

"And without that we can't light the *fusion* reactor and fire up the null-gravity engine," Albit said. "I know what I'm saying."

"Which would mean we're effectively dead in the water, and unable to get away from these creatures."

"Only if I'm wrong," Makk said.

"Well!" Staipa said, with a laugh. "We're not doing *that!*"

"Admiral," Makk said. "I think they're attracted to the radiation. They were drawn to the *Colusm* because they were shipping spent control rods, and now they're attacking *us* because they can sense the radiation from the fission reactor. They won't stop until they get it."

"Attracted to radiation makes sense *how?*"

Battine spoke up over the audio. "I believe it's how they breed."

"Gods," Elicasta said, standing. "That makes sense. Admiral, that makes sense."

"What sense does that make? It's preposterous!"

"You don't have the whole story," Elicasta said. Mentally, she was already running lines on her next vid. "What if the reason we never saw these things before is that they only come to the surface to breed? And they need radiation for that?"

"Asealand has been traveling the ocean for *years* without incident. You expect me to believe that only *now*...?"

"*Now* is start of their breeding cycle," she said. "That's the rest of the story. In a few years, the entire surface of Dib is going to be bathed in gamma radiation. Battine, Makk, I think you're right."

Coigo Staipa looked like he wanted to ask five questions at once, and didn't know which one to start with or who to ask. And there was no time to explain any of it to him.

"Makk, you should do it," Elicasta said.

"I can't from here, or I already would have," he said.

"The core dump can only be done from the bridge," Dr. Albit

said. "As a precaution. In the event nobody down here is still alive. Which is very nearly the case right now. Coigo, as I said, they've taken the main floor. I don't think I can bring the reactor up from here at *all*, but if I can it won't be for several hours. We don't *have* several hours. I'm not even sure of the next ten minutes. I don't believe we'll be any worse off if this plan does *not* work. Although the marine life we irradiate may disagree."

"We would be adrift, Nem," Staipa said. "It would mean the end of Asealand. I can't countenance that."

"Or we could all be dead, Coigo," Calcut said. "Just eject the thing. You got insurance, for fuck's sake."

For whatever reason, Calcut's words had a galvanizing effect on the admiral. Only, not the right kind. "No," he said, taking a seat. "No, we'll ride it out. Dr. Albit, do whatever you have to do to get the reactor going." He laughed. "Gamma radiation. Honestly."

"Admiral..." Makk began.

"Message me when you have news, engine room," Staipa said. "Tolus, cut the audio."

"Dammit, Coigo..." Dr. Albit said, before he disappeared into static.

The admiral looked around the room, to see if there was anyone willing to challenge his orders. "Well, let's get moving. Work the problems, go, go."

There were seven of them, not counting Calcut and Elicasta. If they wanted to, they could easily overpower the admiral. None did; instead, they turned around and got back to work.

"Ahhh, shit," Calcut muttered.

"He'd rather die than live with embarrassment, is that it?" Elicasta asked.

"More or less. I should've known better when I funded this death barge." Calcut was undoing his belt, which was a peculiar thing to do under the circumstances. "Hey, do me a favor, huh? Make sure nobody pays attention to me for a minute."

"What are you doing?" she asked.

"I'm gonna take the bridge, honey," he said, bending down to untie his shoes. "Coigo wants a noble death; I'm gonna give him one."

~

Making sure nobody paid attention to Calcut wasn't actually that difficult, because everyone was too busy trying to accomplish the impossible, from the comparative safety of the bridge, to notice the man in the corner gradually removing articles of clothing. Elicasta drifted to the middle of the room, making sure she was keeping herself between the bridge crew and Calcut, pointing at screens and asking various questions about what they were looking at.

(She was also capturing the whole thing on local vid with the rig. The light on the rig wasn't working, which was a clear violation of Veeser etiquette, but they were so far on the other side of something like that mattering that she didn't think anyone would care.)

"Listen," Elicasta said quietly, having sidled up to the nearest crew member. Her name was Olina; she'd previously described herself as a fan, which 'Casta hoped to use as leverage. "You guys don't *have* to follow his orders. You know that, right? It's not a mutiny if you're not in an actual navy."

Olina side-eyed her. "I don't have anywhere else to go," she said.

"Okay, sure, but you wouldn't rather *die*, right?"

Olina didn't answer that, which was an answer in its own way.

"At least tell me where the button is," Elicasta said. "The one that flushes the core. Like, I don't suppose you can do that from here."

"I didn't know there *was* such a button," Olina said. "If it exists, it's command only."

Elicasta looked over at Staipa. He was sitting in his chair, watching everyone else work. He didn't have a control panel or vid screen of his own.

"There's a console in the arm," Olina said. "But I've only ever seen him use it for ship-wide audios."

"Thanks," Elicasta said.

"Sure." She stopped what she was doing—which was redirecting angles on the various opticals throughout the ship—long enough to look up at Elicasta. "What's this about the planet being bathed in radiation? You were making that up, right?"

Elicasta didn't end up having to answer that question, which was great because she didn't want to. It was one thing to tell the *world* that everyone was going to die, by dropping a vid with the proof. It was another to look someone in the eye and inform them that they personally weren't going to be alive as long as they were expecting.

The reason she didn't have to answer was that just then, Calcut shattered the bourbon bottle on a railing. This was to call attention to the fact that he was holding something that looked suspiciously like a gun (a small one) and also to give him something sharp for the other hand.

"Enough of this shit," Calcut said. He pointed the jagged end of the bottle at the crew, and the barrel of the gun at the admiral. "Coigo, do what Stidgeon said and flush the core, or I'll blow your fucking brains out and do it myself."

Initially, the admiral was as shocked as everyone else. Then he got a better look at what Calcut was aiming at him. "Oh, come on, Calcut," he said. "Is that a toy? Don't be ridiculous! We don't have the time for it!"

"You're right. We don't," Calcut agreed.

Elicasta was busy having flashbacks to the death of Ba-Ugna Kev, a trauma she *thought* she'd managed to get past. But the Calcut Linus with a gun in his hand was a very different individual than the Calcut Linus she'd spent the past couple of weeks around.

"Admiral, I think you should..." she began to say, before Calcut pulled the trigger.

It was, in fact, a real projectile gun that fired real bullets, one of which hit Coigo Staipa in the shoulder.

Staipa screamed, grabbing his shoulder and sliding out of the chair. "Calcut, what...?"

"Shut up, shut up!" Calcut said, stepping up next to the admiral's chair. A few of the bridge crew lunged forward instinctively. "Don't," Calcut said to them. "I see you, Bybrid. Fucking try me."

Bybrid, who was the second in command on the bridge at the moment, and who was also probably the most capable among them if it came down to disarming Calcut, said, "you can't have more than a couple of bullets in that thing, Mr. Linus."

"You think I *need* the gun, boy?" Calcut barked. Then he kicked the admiral in the head and, when this didn't bring the man all the way to the ground, kicked him again in the stomach and slashed his cheek with the sharp edge of the broken bottle. Then Calcut put his foot on Staipa's neck and pointed the gun at his temple. "Tell me how to dump the core *right now*, or I swear by all five of the fucking gods, I'll paint this floor with your brains."

Staipa, bleeding from his shoulder and cheek, unable to move except to take in the occasional ragged breath, took this moment to stare his would-be executioner in the face, and say, calmly, "I will not."

Calcut smiled. "You know, I'm actually glad you said that, Coigo. Goodbye."

"Calcut!" Elicasta shouted. Hands up, she stepped over to the admiral's chair.

"What is it, Sangristy," he growled. "I'm busy here."

She sat in the chair and flipped open the arm console. "It can't be that complicated, right?" she said. "Not if *he* could do it."

Calcut glared at her, as if preventing him from murdering Coigo Staipa was the worst offense she could have committed.

There it is, she thought. *That's the temper that got Orno killed.*

She glared back. "Just wait."

"Fine," he growled.

There was a tiny vid screen in the arm console, with a simple menu. She started scrolling through.

"Bybrid," Staipa said. "Stop her, Bybrid. She's not armed."

Calcut pressed the barrel up to Staipa's forehead.

"Found it!" Elicasta said. She looked at the rest of the bridge crew. "You guys, you can either try to get to me before I hit this button, or you can open a feed to the engine room so they're not surprised when the bottom drops out of the reactor. I'm pushing this either way."

Bybrid stared at her for a long count, in case she was bluffing. Seeing something like resolve staring back at him, he said, "Tolus? Let them know."

Things were not going well in the engine room. Shortly after the admiral unceremoniously disconnected the bridge audio feed, their safe area was breached.

The bugs didn't make it through the heavy, lead-lined partitions, (that would have been impressive, and also terrifying) although not without trying. Instead, they punched a hole in the *floor*.

After a short melee in which the most valuable person in the room was a princess with a sword, the survivors—Makk, Battine, Dr. Albit, Del, Rayno, and two engineers—got pinned down behind a water pump.

The only thing holding back the bugs was Makk, popping up every few seconds and firing at whatever was moving. Nobody appeared interested in voicing objections on the matter of bullets striking pipes.

After one of his barrages, Battine crouched down next to him. "I have decided on something, detective," she said. "I have decided that I would rather go out on my feet and facing forward, than huddling behind a machine in an inch of water."

"I don't know what you're saying," he said.

"I'm saying before your next volley, I mean to charge those monsters and kill as many as I can. But before I do that, I want you to have this." She pressed the Temple Island key into his hand. "Do whatever it is you and Elicasta think you have to do. I only ask that it never be returned to the Kingdoms while you live."

"Uh, sure," he said. "Problem is, I think my life expectancy is about the same as yours."

"I doubt that," she said. "I have only known you a short time, but I can tell you lead a charmed existence. Whether you realize it or not. If anyone comes out of this alive, it will be you. Now: I have some bugs to kill."

She climbed to her feet, and was about to disappear around the corner when the audio feed to the room kicked in.

"Engineering, this is the bridge. Uh, how's it going down there?"

"Terrific, bridge," Makk shouted. Battine ducked down again, pointed to their left and right, and clutched her hands together. Translation: the bugs were creeping in from two sides.

Makk stood and fired the rifle twice, in the directions Batt indicated, and then ducked back down again.

"They've breached the room," Dr. Albit said, to whoever was on the audio. "Tell the admiral he's not getting his engine."

"Makk, I'm dumping the core," Elicasta said. "In case you need to do anything to prepare."

"Do we?" Makk asked Albit.

Dr. Albit shrugged. "Let's hope not."

"Go ahead, 'Casta," Makk said.

"Here goes," she said.

Alarms sounded all over the place, in time with more red flashing lights. It was similar to the noise made when the blast door closed, only this time accompanied by a robotic announcement on repeat: "Core dump imminent."

The noise and lights made the bugs go crazy, and not in a good way; he could hear them screaming. Makk knew what an approaching *Dwanni* sounded like, and he heard a lot of that too.

He pushed the key back into Battine's hands, jumped to his feet, and started firing. This time, it wasn't having the same effect; they kept coming.

Abruptly, there was a loud clang, followed by a thump that they felt through the floor, a new siren, and something that sounded a whole lot like an explosion.

The *Dwanni* dropped back. If it could be said that a small army of giant black jellyfish-like bug things could collectively look *confused*, they looked confused.

"Uh," Makk said. "Was that the reactor *exploding?*"

"No," Dr. Albit said, climbing to his feet. "We were supposed to shut down and detach the coolant system before purging. Since we did not, that was probably a coolant tank. The water from the tank is highly radioactive, but those doors should protect us."

"I thought you said we were ready to drop the core."

"I didn't say precisely that."

"Look," Battine said. "Look at them."

The bugs had fallen back. They still looked really interested in ripping people apart, but they were being told—by whatever channel they used to communicate—to leave instead.

"I think it's working," Makk said.

As one, the *Dwanni* took flight, buzzed over their heads a couple of times, and dove through the hole in the floor.

And then they were alone.

"Well," Dr. Albit said, after a long, breathless silence. "It looks as if your plan worked, Detective Stidgeon. Perhaps once we've figured out how to get out of this room, you can explain *why* it worked."

~

The best kind of sunrise was the kind you didn't expect to be alive for. Makk learned that in the army, and had it reinforced at least five or six times since.

This sunrise was particularly nice, because it was at sea, and the suns coming up on the ocean was just a terrific view. Again, it was probably at least in part because he didn't expect to see another one that he felt that way. It could also be the pain meds.

Asealand didn't have enough medical staff to go around; there were plenty of injuries to people who were older, weaker, and richer than Makk, so he got pain meds, a sling for his left arm, and a promise to see him later.

Battine, they treated right away. But her injuries were more serious and besides, she was royalty.

So, he took his pills, claimed a deck chair—there was loose balcony furniture all over the place—plopped it down on the eastern-facing edge of the deck, and watched the suns come up.

Elicasta found him a few minutes later. "Hey," she said, pulling up her own chair. "You look a mess."

"Yeah, thanks," he said.

She sat down, pulled a can of beer from a pocket, opened it, and handed it to him. Now that was love.

He smiled, and drank half of it, while she took a second one out for herself.

"Nice view," she said.

"I could get used to it. Hey, good work talking Coigo into purging the core. How'd you do it?"

"Calcut did that," she said.

"Seriously? How?"

"Ah, he shot him a little. And cut him. And stomped on him, just a bit. Coigo's still with the doctors; I think he'll be fine."

"Calcut had a gun," Makk said.

"Turns out."

Makk sighed.

"I know, I know," she said. "He's still useful. Plus, he *kinda* saved all of us, in his own scary, ultraviolent way."

"Uh-huh."

She sipped her beer and didn't say anything for a little while. Probably, this was a sign that Makk wasn't going to like the next thing she had to say, but he was too tired and sore to care. (Also: pain meds.)

"At the end there, I wasn't sure we were gonna make it," she said.

"Same."

"No, but, I was worried I... well, okay. Makk, I did something. I thought you should be the first to know."

"Go on," he said.

"You know what a deadman's switch is?"

"In the context of a bomb vest? Sure. That's not what we're talking about, is it?"

"No," she said. "I made all this vid content, about what we learned, over the past year? I was worried if I died... So I dropped it. All of it. All at once."

Makk nodded slowly. "All right," he said. "Okay. Can't take *that* back."

"Nope."

"Was one of these vids about the Outcast?"

"It was," she said.

"Kinda wish you hadn't done that."

"I was going to do it eventually anyway," she said.

"There'll be riots," he said.

"Pretty much every one of those vids could trigger a riot

somewhere. But yeah. That one? That'll land hard. Look on the bright side."

"There's a bright side?"

"Now people know the truth," she said.

"That's not a very good bright side."

"All right. How about: we're adrift on a giant raft in the middle of the ocean, there's beer, and a nice view, and none of the riots are going to be happening *here*."

"That's a *little* better," he said.

"I thought so too," she said. "Oh, and there's another thing."

"More bad news?"

"No, just news. Viselle checked in. She has the fourth key."

"Great," Makk said. "Tell her to head on over and we'll go save the world together. After we finish the beer."

About the Author

Gene Doucette is the author of over twenty sci-fi/fantasy titles, including the Sorrow Falls series (*The Spaceship Next Door*, *The Frequency of Aliens,* and *Graffiti on the Wall of the Universe*), the Immortal series, *Fixer* and *Fixer Redux*, the *Tandemstar* books, and *The Apocalypse Seven*. Gene lives in Cambridge, MA.

For the latest on Gene Doucette, follow him online
genedoucette.me
genedoucette@me.com

www.ingramcontent.com/pod-product-compliance
Lightning Source LLC
Chambersburg PA
CBHW071208210726
48293CB00002B/335